Her hands found   around them. "Paul,   lifted her head for his

It was exactly as she had anticipated. His mouth was firm and hot, and those pleasant sensations began to warm her blood. When he wrapped his arms around her and jerked her hard against his full length, she gave a little start of surprise, but that warm, mobile mouth on hers insisted that she yield to him. She laughed softly when he kissed her throat, then she stopped breathing altogether when he bent her back and kissed her breasts, just above the lace on her bodice. He'd never gone that far before . . . she got out a shaken whisper, "I never knew it could be like this. You make me feel things I never knew existed, sensations I've never experienced before. You seem so different tonight."

And he did. His body was harder, his shoulders seemed broader, and she hadn't known he was so tall. As for his fragrance—

Then she knew, she *knew*. . . . "Trevenan!" she gasped, and fairly leaped out of his arms.

He made no move to stop her, but said in a laconic tone that grated on her ears, "What a pity. And just when things were beginning to turn interesting."

Also by Elizabeth Thornton

Dangerous to Hold
Dangerous to Kiss
Dangerous to Love

ELIZABETH THORNTON

THE
BRIDE'S BODYGUARD

BANTAM BOOKS
NEW YORK   TORONTO   LONDON   SYDNEY   AUCKLAND

THE BRIDE'S BODYGUARD
A Bantam Book / April 1997

ISBN 0-553-57425-6

Published simultaneously in the United States and Canada

Bantam Books are published by Bantam Books, a division of Bantam
Doubleday Dell Publishing Group, Inc. Its trademark, consisting of the
words "Bantam Books" and the portrayal of a rooster, is Registered in
U.S. Patent and Trademark Office and in other countries. Marca Reg-
istrada. Bantam Books, 1540 Broadway, New York, New York 10036.

PRINTED IN THE UNITED STATES OF AMERICA

OPM   0 9 8 7 6 5 4 3

for our granddaughter, Emma

Prologue

*I*t was one of those rare English summer afternoons when the sky was almost cloudless and there wasn't a breeze stirring. She stood at the stone balustrade of the small pavilion, a dark-haired, dark-eyed young woman in floating muslins, admiring the panorama before her—the graceful sweep of small hills and dales, the artfully laid out stands of mature plane trees and beeches, and the pretty man-made lake with its inevitable complement of swans. It had taken many generations to bring the park to this peak of perfection, a jewel of a setting for her husband's stately home. Everything looked so still, so familiar, she had the impression she had taken a step back in time.

A memory tried to intrude and she shivered. Resolutely pushing it to the back of her mind, she struck out along one of the many flagstone paths that led off from the pavilion. She'd been told to make herself scarce for an hour or two, and she wasn't going to run back to the house like some silly schoolgirl who couldn't amuse herself for a few minutes at a time.

There wasn't a footman or gardener in sight, and she knew why. Today was her birthday and her husband had planned something extraordinary to surprise her back at the house. Though she wasn't supposed to know it, a marquee was to be set up on the west lawn, and every able-bodied man on the estate had been ordered to lend a hand. She chuckled to herself. She would have had to be blind and deaf these last few weeks not to know that a horde of guests had been invited to help her celebrate her birthday.

Smiling a slow smile to herself, she touched a hand to her abdomen in a gentle caress. Her husband wasn't the only one who was keeping secrets. Tonight, she decided, she would tell him tonight, after the loving, when he held her in his strong arms and told her how much he loved her. It was something neither of them had anticipated, this bond that had formed between them. They hadn't married for love. She'd come up to London for the season, knowing that it was her duty to find a suitable husband. No one had expected her to capture the biggest matrimonial prize in the whole of England, a man who could have had his pick of any girl he wanted.

He'd told her that he'd been in much the same position as she, that it had been pressed home to him that it was his duty to marry. He'd chosen her because there wasn't an ounce of affectation in her. Not only was she beautiful, but she also had the sweetest disposition of any girl he knew. A month after the wedding, to their mutual delight, they discovered they were in love.

When she came out of the trees, the small lake was spread out before her like an immense looking glass that reflected the world back at itself. It was a shallow lake, no more than five or six feet deep at its widest point, but that knowledge did not prevent the involuntary chill that brought goose bumps out on her bare arms.

With slow but steady steps, she forced herself onto the narrow wooden bridge that separated the lake from a waterfall and pool on the other side. She'd watched some of the estate children throw makeshift boats into the lake, then run to the other side of the bridge to watch them tumble over the waterfall and pop up close to shore.

There was nothing to fear here. The lake was a shimmering work of art, a thing of beauty, a triumph of man's ingenuity. She stayed there for a long time, her arms stretched out on the wooden rail, her chin resting on her clasped hands, but she knew that she was trying to look at everything but the water.

Her husband understood the reason for her phobia. Years before, when she was at boarding school, she'd been present when a tragic accident had occurred. A girl had drowned in a lake just such as this, and ever since then, she'd been terrified to go near water. Her husband had tried to cure her of her fears without success. She rarely opposed him, but not even for him could she force herself to learn to swim. He would be pleased, though, when she told him she'd walked to the lake by herself.

She wondered if any of the other girls who had been present when Becky drowned were as afraid of water as she. Though she didn't want to think of them, a name registered, *Tessa*, before she could quite suppress it.

One of those rare clouds suddenly covered the sun and again she shivered. The lake took on a sinister aspect. It wasn't a thing of beauty. It was ugly. It was cold and slimy, absorbing everything into itself.

She heard a step on the bridge and jumped. When she saw who it was, she went weak with relief.

"Oh, it's you," she said. "Is it time to go back?"

She felt for the watch at her breast and looked at the time. The first blow caught her on the crown of the head. The second caught her on the neck when she fell to her knees.

An hour later her husband found her lifeless body floating in the pool below the waterfall.

Chapter One

❦❦❦

"*T*essa! It's Tessa Lorimer, is it not?"

The sound of that cultured English accent in the *grande salle* of Alexandre Beaupré's elegant Parisian town house brought a momentary hush to the throng of assembled guests. In the autumn of 1803, England and France were at war, and Frenchmen did not expect to hear the voices of their enemies in their own drawing rooms. Then they remembered that Beaupré's granddaughter was English born, and the young woman who had called out to her might well be another of Beaupré's English relatives, or perhaps the young woman was an American. Either way, no one particularly cared. If she was an American, then she was a friend, and if English, it hardly mattered, not when Beaupré was so highly connected. He was a banker, a financial wizard, and the First Consul was his friend.

At the sound of her name, and spoken in such unmistakable English accents, a look of surprise crossed Tessa's face and she swung round to see who had addressed her. Just inside the glass entrance doors, a young man and woman stood a little apart from the others, as though they were not quite sure of their welcome. The girl was approximately her own age, twenty or so, with light brown hair and a friendly expression lighting up her thin face. Beside her was a gentleman, obviously English from the cut of his garments, who might have been a year or two older.

Tessa leaned down and spoke softly to a white-haired gentleman seated in an invalid-chair. This was Alexandre Beaupré, her grandfather, who, in spite of his infirmities, did not lack presence. Shrewd dark eyes, beautiful eyes, animated a pale aristocratic face that was still handsome though it was deeply lined.

He waved her away. "Enjoy yourself," he said. "This is your birthday. Marcel will look after me." Then, to the footman who stood by his chair, "Fetch me a glass of champagne, Marcel. Yes, yes, I know that the doctor has forbidden it. What has that to say to anything?"

Tessa's smile was warm when she approached the girl who had hailed her, but there was a question in her eyes.

"It's Sally," said the girl. "Sally Turner. Don't you remember me? We were at school together."

"Of course," said Tessa warmly, and she mentally began to sort through the succession of schools she had attended, which were legion, trying vainly to place the girl's face.

Sally added helpfully, "Fleetwood Hall? I suppose I shouldn't expect you to remember me. You were there for only a year or so, then you left to go to relatives in Bath, I believe."

Tessa had been expelled from just about every school she had ever attended, but she tactfully avoided mentioning that unpleasant fact. "That was a long time ago," she said vaguely.

"It was eight years ago," said Sally. "We were twelve at the time."

This did not jog Tessa's memory, but she didn't let her perplexity show. She liked the look of this open-faced young woman. "But how did you recognize me?" she said. "And what are you doing in France?"

Sally began by answering Tessa's last question first. "We were in Reims when the war suddenly started up again, and were taken completely by surprise. So here we are, cut off behind French lines, waiting for Bonaparte to decide what is to become of us."

Tessa nodded. She knew that there were many English visitors in the same position. Some had taken matters into their own hands and had made a dash for freedom across the English Channel. Some had succeeded. Others had not, and were now under house arrest or were languishing in French prisons.

"As for why I recognized you," said Sally, "it's your hair. I've never seen anyone with hair that particular color." At a nudge from her escort, she remembered her manners. "Tessa, may I present my brother, Desmond? Des, this is . . ." She broke off with a laugh. "Why, for all I know, you may be married by now."

"No. I'm not married. I'm still Tessa Lorimer."

Desmond Turner was very glad to hear it. The young woman in the high-waisted, square-necked muslin ball gown who was smiling up at him was so beautiful he hadn't stopped staring since he'd entered the *grande salle*, and that had never happened to him before. Sally had been right about the hair. It wasn't cut in the current fashion, but fell to the girl's shoulders in a cascade of gold that was touched with fire. Her features were regular and classical, and her large eyes were neither violet nor blue, but somewhere in between, an almost perfect match for the nosegay of violets that was pinned to the bodice of her gown.

His sister's elbow connected with his ribs, and he quickly came to himself. He asked Tessa how she had come to be cut off behind enemy lines.

Tessa looked at him curiously. "I live here," she said. "This is my grandfather's house."

"*You* are Monsieur Beaupré's granddaughter?" said Desmond. "But you're so . . . English."

"My mother was French, but she died when I was very young." Not wishing to go into all the convoluted details of how she had finally escaped her guardians' clutches in England and had arrived half starving on her grandfather's doorstep two years before, she voiced the thought that had been puzzling her. "I'm surprised my grand-father didn't tell me that he had invited you."

Desmond replied cautiously, "Actually, Monsieur Beaupré didn't invite us. It was Mr. Trevenan."

At the mention of the American's name, something flashed in Tessa's eyes but was quickly subdued. "Oh, Mr. Trevenan," she said in the same warm tone. "Well, he is practically a member of the family. He has the freedom of the house. He's here somewhere." She gave the room a cursory glance. "Why don't I find him for you?" And with another dazzling smile, she moved away.

Desmond said, "She doesn't have a clue to who you are, Sal."

They were both watching Tessa's progress through the crush. By the time she reached the glass doors that gave onto the terrace, she had collected a cluster of young men who hovered around her like moths to a flame.

Sally responded thoughtfully, "Well, she wouldn't, would she? Besides, she was never in one place long enough to make lasting friendships. Did you notice, when I mentioned the school, she didn't blink an eyelash?"

"What I noticed was that her eyes flashed with fire when I mentioned Ross's name. I don't think she cares for him."

This was said with so much satisfaction that his sister laughed. "Don't let her beauty fool you, Des. She's rich, vain, and spoiled beyond redemption."

"Now you're beginning to sound like Ross. I prefer to make my own judgment about Miss Lorimer."

"Don't say you weren't warned."

Tessa paused at the doors to the terrace to reply to the appeals of the young men who swarmed around her, demanding that she show them her dance card. There were two dances left, but she was saving them for Paul Marmont, who had yet to put in an appearance. She'd had a note from him earlier saying that he'd been called away to Rouen, but he hoped to return before her ball ended, and if not, he'd try to meet her in their usual trysting place. Not to have Paul at her birthday was a great disappointment to Tessa, but he'd softened the blow by sending his note with the posy of violets that was pinned to her bodice.

Though she liked all the young men she had invited to her ball, none of them could compare with Paul. He was older, twenty-four or twenty-five, and all the girls were mad for him. He was divinely handsome, possessed the grace of a dancer, and one look from his bold black eyes could make her blush like a silly schoolgirl. What was incomprehensible to Tessa was that though he could have had his pick of any girl he wanted, he never failed to single her out. She was almost sure he was going to ask her to marry him.

She laughed when her card was snatched out of her hand and passed around for inspection. "I've promised you one dance each," she said airily. "What could be fairer than that? My card is full."

This was no lie, for though Paul hadn't exactly asked her to save him any dances, she knew, hoped, he would be disappointed if he arrived to find her card full, and she had taken the precaution of writing his name down for him.

Belatedly remembering her errand, she looked back at the Turners with a helpless shrug, then stiffened when she saw that her errand was no longer necessary. He was there, Ross Trevenan, and he was watching the antics of her admirers with amused contempt. Then his cool gray eyes lifted to hers in an impertinent appraisal and he dismissed her with a flick of his lashes.

Tessa's gaze, with a will of its own, remained on the man who, in a few short months, had become the bane of her existence. He was, she reluctantly admitted, a fine figure of a man, tall and powerfully built, with blond good looks that made him stand out in a crowd of Frenchmen. Not that she ever looked at him if she could help it. Perhaps because of her own coloring, she'd never been partial to men with blond hair. And he was a man. In fact, he was quite old, thirty or thereabouts, and whenever their eyes locked, she could feel his censure as though he'd rapped her on the knuckles.

It was strange, but he'd disliked her from the moment

he'd set eyes on her. She remembered it well. Her grandfather had called her into his study to meet his new secretary. Her first impression of Trevenan had been favorable, and her heart had skipped a beat. Then she'd looked into his eyes and seen the naked dislike staring out at her before a shutter had descended, concealing what he was thinking. After that, she could never be comfortable with him.

He looked upon her as a vain, empty-headed schoolgirl whose ambitions went no further than to be the belle of the ball. She would have snapped her fingers at his opinions if they had not carried such weight with her grandfather. Ever since he'd taken up employment as her grandfather's . . . she didn't know what to call him. Secretary? General factotum? Man of business? All she knew was that Ross Trevenan had become as indispensable to her grandfather as Marcel, the hefty footman who wheeled Alexandre Beaupré about in his invalid-chair.

Although Trevenan had not exactly displaced her in her grandfather's affections, he had wormed his way into Alexandre Beaupré's good graces to such a degree that his influence now eclipsed hers. When Trevenan made suggestions her grandfather listened to them, and acted on them. Her manners and deportment had suddenly come under the keenest scrutiny. Her laugh was too loud. She was too much the flirt. Her gowns were too daring. She had too much pin money for a young girl. The list was endless, but she knew this wasn't her grandfather speaking. And if she could have found a way to get rid of Ross Trevenan, short of murder, she would have seized on it with relish.

She'd tried to warn her grandfather to be cautious. This wasn't spite on her part, or a desire to even the score. There was something about Trevenan that she deeply distrusted. He said that he was an American, but how could they be sure? He was always vague when answering questions about his origins. For all they knew, he might be an English spy, or one of Fuché's French spies, or a smuggler, if not worse. She could not believe that a man of his arrogance and conceit could be a mere secretary. He must always be the master. And there were those absences that sometimes stretched into days and were never adequately explained. Ross Trevenan was a man of mystery and she was determined to get to the bottom of it. Then, when her grandfather had dismissed him from his post, things would go back to the way they were before. It was a pleasant reverie, and she smiled as she contemplated it.

She wasn't aware that she was still staring until she found herself impaled by his hard gaze. Then those slashes of brows rose just a fraction, mocking her, and he smiled in that unpleasant way of his. He was reading her mind, that look told her, and was vastly amused.

Flinging him a look of loathing, she turned her attention to the young men who hemmed her in. She would show Ross Trevenan that she didn't give a straw for his good opinion. Certainly, these young men did not find her lacking, nor did their sisters, nor any of the young women who were present that evening. This was her birthday party, and she would not be satisfied unless everyone had an enjoyable time, with the exception, of course, of one thoroughly detestable, provoking man.

The orchestra struck up, and her next partner came to claim her. Then she forgot about Ross Trevenan as she was swung into the dance. Her eyes sparkled and a soft, dreamy smile curved her lips. She felt like the luckiest girl in the world. This was her very own ball. She was dressed in a beautiful ball gown. She was dancing under the lights of a thousand candles in the crystal chandeliers overhead. Around her were her friends, young men and women who liked and admired her, and there was one special person to love her. She wasn't thinking of Paul. Her eyes traveled over the sets of dancers until she found the familiar figure of her grandfather. She raised her wrist, flashing the velvet ribbon with the ruby rose pinned to it, the first expensive piece of jewelry she had ever owned, her grandfather's present to her. He caught the gesture, and raised his glass of champagne in a silent tribute.

She was twenty years old and this was the happiest night of her life.

Chapter Two

〜〜〜〜

When he heard the knock on his study door, Alexandre Beaupré opened his eyes. Ross entered and Beaupré immediately composed his features so that the lines of pain were not so evident.

Ross wasn't fooled for an instant. "When did this happen?" he asked, addressing his question to Marcel.

"Before the ball, sir," the footman answered. "He wouldn't let me tell anyone, but insisted on remaining till the end."

"Mademoiselle Therese?"

The footman shook his head.

"Especially not Therese," protested Beaupré. "What could she do? Believe me, it's nothing at all. I've taken something for it." He flexed his left arm. "See, the pain is easing now."

Ross turned on his heel. "I'll send for the physician."

"No!" Beaupré's exclamation stopped Ross before he had taken a step. In a softened tone, Beaupré went on, "A physician is of no use to me. I'm an old man. My heart is finished. You know what my doctors say. They've given me six months at the most. And Latour told me this is what I must expect."

At a nod from his master, the footman left the room. When the door closed behind him, Ross propped himself against the desk and studied the older man while he waited for him to speak.

Though he and Beaupré were poles apart in their political persuasions, in the short time he'd known him, he'd come to admire and respect the man. A fall from a horse almost thirty years before had crippled Beaupré so badly that he could never afterward walk unaided. If that were not enough, his wife had run off with an English diplomat, taking their only child, a girl of ten, with her. It was this child who was Tessa's mother.

A lesser man would have sunk into despair. Beaupré, on the other hand, had risen above his tragic circumstances and had not only weathered the storms of the French Revolution but had emerged as a man of influence. He was a financier, and Bonaparte and his armies had need of his influence to finance the war.

"It's getting worse," said Beaupré at length. "I don't think I'll last the six months."

There was a long silence, then Ross said, "Was it wise to allow the ball to go forward? You should have canceled it."

"And disappoint Therese? This is her birthday, Ross."

Ross's tone was dry. "You spoil her, Alexandre."

Beaupré looked at him quizzically. "Do you blame me? I had no part in her childhood except to pay for her education and upkeep. The terrors of the Revolution kept me from bringing her here, and I could not go to England as I am. I tell you candidly, these two years she has been with me have been the most rewarding of my life."

"Rewarding? That's an odd word to use."

"You wouldn't think so if you'd known Therese two years ago. She has blossomed, Ross. She is a lovely young woman, full of spirit and life." When he saw Ross's expression, which betrayed nothing, he chuckled. "You English set such store by deportment. That will come in time. I beg your pardon. I must remember to think of you as an American."

"It's safer that way."

"Yes, but you'll forgive me for saying that it's not easy to forget you're an English aristocrat. You need not look so surprised. You're just not humble enough to be a common secretary, as my granddaughter never tires of telling me."

Ross grinned. "I shall try, in future, to act with the proper degree of humility. What is it you wished to say to me?"

The soft white hands in Beaupré's lap fisted and unfisted. He said abruptly, "You see how my health is deteriorating. You must get Therese away from here sooner than we anticipated."

Ross spoke quietly. "I've been having second thoughts about our plan, Alexandre, and I see now that it is fraught with difficulties."

"It was always fraught with difficulties. What's on your mind?"

"Your granddaughter opposes me at every turn."

A twinkle kindled in Beaupré's eyes. "You have only yourself to blame. You're too hard on her."

"I won't change."

"And neither will she. But I understand what you're saying. You're going to have your hands full. But I have every confidence that you can manage a mere girl."

Beaupré glanced assessingly at Ross and wondered if the Englishman was as unaware as he pretended to be of the source of his frustration with Therese. A Frenchman would have known. But that was the English for you. They were so wise in some things, and so backward in others. One thing was certain: the carnal pleasures to be found in the Palais Royal were not making an appreciable difference to the Englishman's tolerance for Therese's little foibles.

He felt a momentary pang for Therese, then dismissed it. There was more to consider than her feelings. Ross Trevenan might keep her on a tight leash, but that was precisely what was required at this point in time. As for himself, there was no other man he would have trusted half as well with his granddaughter's welfare. The blond good looks hardly made an impression on him. What he saw and envied was the powerful physique that clearly indicated Ross's athletic pursuits. What he admired was the strength of character evident in that hard face with its square jaw and the intelligence reflected in the deepset gray eyes.

Conscious of the silence that had fallen between them, he said, "What about those friends of yours, the Turners?"

"Only time will tell. Tessa seemed to like them well enough."

"They went into supper together, did they not?"

"They did, and agreed to meet tomorrow at the Palais Royal. This was Tessa's suggestion, of course."

"And you don't approve?"

"The Palais Royal is the known haunt of prostitutes and gamesters."

"As you should know."

Ross grinned. "As I should know. But that doesn't make it a suitable rendezvous for ladies of quality."

"Miss Turner could have refused."

"That's the thing about Tessa. Her recklessness is infectious. Sally jumped at the chance of visiting this notorious scene of debauchery, and Desmond could not talk the girls out of it."

Beaupré chuckled. "You're making too much of it. It's at the close of day that the Palais Royal displays its worst side. In the daylight hours, it's quite harmless. The shops and cafés are full of respectable people. Therese knows this. All the same, I'm glad she and Miss Turner seem to like each other."

"Yes. It will make things simpler all round. Alexandre . . ." Ross hesitated as he put his thoughts in order. Rising, he took a few paces around the room. "There's another reason I'm reluctant to take Tessa to England. He looked down at his companion. "She'd be safer in France."

"Doing what? Hiding in some hole like a terrified rabbit? Always looking over her shoulder, wondering who is after her? I won't have her live like that."

"I could be mistaken, you know. It's possible she isn't in any danger."

"You don't really believe that!"

"No. Nevertheless, the villain I'm after is English. It would be easier to detect him in France."

Beaupré expelled a quick breath. "What I know is that when I'm gone, I'd rather have my granddaughter under the protection of a capable man I trust than left to fend for herself in a foreign country, and I mean France, Ross. She's not French, she's English, and no matter how hard she tries, she'll never be anything but English. It might be different if I could remain with her, but I have no choice in the matter. In fact, my choices are appalling. But I've calculated the odds, and I regard you as my best bet."

He shook his head vigorously when Ross tried to interrupt. "No, hear me out. What do you think would happen to Therese when I am not here to protect her? She will be an heiress, possibly the richest woman in France. It's not the fortune hunters I worry about, it's my friend Bonaparte. He'll make her his ward so fast that the ink will hardly have had time to dry on my death certificate. Then he'll marry her off to one of his poor Corsican relatives who will leave her to rot in some godforsaken backwater. Who will protect her, then, from this terrible threat that is hanging over her? Certainly not Bonaparte. It wouldn't matter to him if anything happened to Therese."

Ross voiced one of the solutions that he'd gone over in his mind scores of times, ever since his conscience had begun to prick him. "What about Paul Marmont? She seems quite taken with him. She could marry him. The sooner the better, if what you say is true."

Beaupré's brows lifted. "You think Paul is man enough for my Therese?"

It was on the tip of Ross's tongue to say that nothing short of a drill sergeant was man enough for Therese Lorimer, but he caught himself in time. "That's not the point. He could take her to America. I think she would be safe there."

"You think? You *think*? That's not good enough for me. Besides, if Bonaparte wants her for one of his poor relations, which he has already hinted to me, he'd soon dissolve the marriage. No, no. I won't have her marry Marmont. I want her to be safe, yes, but I also want her to be happy, and she could never find happiness with Paul Marmont. He doesn't love her. It's her fortune he wants, to prop up his father's failing business enterprises. And if that were not enough, young Marmont is fast becoming a confirmed libertine. He is a womanizer, Ross, and that won't do for my Therese. Sit down. You're giving me a crick in my neck, staring up at you."

Ross took an upright chair, moved it in front of Beaupré, and straddled it. "Perhaps we should discuss this later," he said. "You look as though you are on the point of collapse."

Beaupré waved away his suggestion. "There may not be a 'later' for me. I want to say my piece so there can be no misunderstanding between us." He paused, then went on, "I see no good reason to change our plans at this late date. All the arrangements have been made, all the relevant papers have been signed. It only remains now to inform Therese of my decision."

"What are you going to tell her?"

"No more, no less than we agreed." His voice had turned husky, and he cleared his throat, then waited a moment before continuing. "You think you are taking advantage of an old man for your own ends. That's why you're having second thoughts. Put it out of your mind. You're not taking advantage of me. If I were younger, if I were not a helpless invalid tied to this chair, I would map out the same course that you have chosen."

A light had come into Beaupré's eyes, and they burned with determination. "I understand the risks involved, but they're worth it if they lead to a permanent solution. I am putting my granddaughter's life in your hands. Swear to me, by everything you hold holy, that you will never betray my trust."

Ross looked at the trembling hand that was held out to him and grasped it." I swear," he said.

"Swear on the soul of your dead wife."

There was a moment of hesitation, then Ross replied in a firm, clear voice, "I swear."

Beaupré fell back in his chair, and though the lines of exhaustion in his pale face had deepened, a faint smile touched his lips. "It is good," he said. "Now, send Marcel to me."

After Marcel and another footman had carried Beaupré upstairs, Ross lit a cheroot from one of the candles and wandered out to the terrace. There were still plenty of servants about tidying up after the ball, but Ross hardly noticed them. Deep in thought, he stood at the balustrade, smoking his cheroot.

He hoped to God he knew what he was doing. He hoped to God that Alexandre's trust in him was not misplaced. He couldn't help admiring the old man's acuity. Alexandre had known his conscience was bothering him. Now that they'd become friends, it seemed wrong to hope that Tessa Lorimer was the target of a murderer. But he couldn't change what he was feeling. Without Tessa, he hadn't a hope of catching his man. And because he felt guilty, he was absolutely determined to fulfill all his promises to Alexandre with respect to the girl.

At the end of the terrace was a flight of white marble steps descending to the gardens. Ross idled his way down the steps and stood at the entrance to a stone gazebo with a view of the Seine. The lights of a few boats winked at him from the river, but there was little else to see at that time of night. He drew on his cheroot and let the smoke out slowly, his thoughts still engrossed in the interview just past.

It was obvious Alexandre's time had run out. The old man was right. They had to act quickly, and Ross was his best bet. Tessa's welfare was now his responsibility.

Responsibility wasn't the word for it. Chore, task, labor, problem—those were more the words that came to his mind. Tessa Lorimer was a law unto herself. Alexandre did not know his granddaughter half as well as he thought he did, and Ross had not wanted to disillusion him, not when there was so little time left to his friend. But *he* knew, because he'd made it his business to find out.

A picture formed in his mind. Tessa as he'd seen her on the dance floor, floating down the set with her partner. There was a sparkle in her eyes, and a soft, inviting smile on her lips. She hadn't been merely beautiful, she'd been breathtaking, all the more so because her beauty seemed to come from some inner light. Before he could prevent it, the thought had flashed into his mind that Tessa's beauty was far more interesting that Cassie's had been because there was fire beneath it, and he'd felt, in the next instant, as though he'd betrayed his wife's memory, and he'd been furious with himself.

Tessa's beauty might well be impossible to eclipse, but in other respects she was dismally lacking. The aunt and uncle in England who'd had the raising of her had described a girl who bore little resemblance to the charmer who had, in so short a time, wrapped Alexandre Beaupré around her little finger. In England she'd attended a number of schools, first-class establishments, every one of them, but she'd soon overstayed her welcome. All the people he'd interviewed who'd ever had charge of her told the same story—Tessa Lorimer was rebellious, defiant, incorrigible, and they'd all heaved a great sigh of relief when they'd finally seen the back of her.

It was her last escapade that had made the uncle and aunt wash their hands of her, not that they'd confided in him. They were too ashamed. He'd had it from one of the servants that Miss Tessa had run off with a handsome young footman, and after that Mr. and Mrs. Beasley never wanted to see her again, which surprised no one since they had two innocent young daughters of their own whom they did not wish contaminated by Tessa's influence.

No one knew what had happened to the footman. Shortly after eloping, Tessa had arrived on her grandfather's doorstep and she had lived like a princess ever since—indulged, petted, and pampered, until there was no restraining her.

She'd had the good sense not to say too much about her early years, and not one word about her handsome young footman. The story she had concocted was that the Beasleys were insisting she marry some odious cousin, and she'd fled to France to throw herself on her grandfather's mercy.

In the strictest confidence, Alexandre had told him the rest of the story with unmitigated pride. Therese, he said, had disguised herself as a boy and had bribed a band of English smugglers to smuggle her into France. Part of Ross applauded her audacity but another part was appalled. England and France were at war and anything could have happened to her. A French warship could have blown her smugglers and her with them to smithereens. If she'd been caught, she could have been strung up as an English spy. And if her smugglers had discovered that she was a female, it was highly unlikely that they would have spared her innocence.

If she were an innocent.

He thought of her handsome young footman and a wave of anger surged through him. How dared he leave a young girl to fend for herself? If Ross could have laid his hands on him, he would have torn him limb from limb. The thought startled him and he drew on his cheroot, then exhaled a stream of smoke.

A movement on the terrace alerted him to the presence of someone else. When he saw a shadow move, he took a cautious step back into the gazebo, then another.

"Paul?"

Tessa's voice. There was a rustle of skirts as she descended the steps. Ross threw his cheroot on the ground and crushed it under his heel.

"Paul?" Her voice was breathless, uncertain. "I saw you from my window. I wasn't sure it was you until I saw our signal." Her voice took on a teasing note. "Or perhaps I was mistaken. Perhaps you weren't signaling me but simply slipped into the gazebo for a quiet smoke."

Ross said nothing, but he'd already calculated that he'd stumbled upon the trysting place of Tessa and her French lover and had inadvertently given their signal merely by smoking a cheroot.

Tessa entered the gazebo and halted, waiting for her

eyes to become accustomed to the gloom. "I wanted to thank you for the spray of violets. They really are lovely. But I had to burn your note." She laughed. "You mustn't write such things to me, Paul. My cheeks burned so hot, my maid feared I was coming down with a fever." She paused, and her voice turned husky. "Paul, stop playing games with me. You know you want to kiss me."

It never crossed Ross's mind to enlighten her about his identity. He was too curious to see how far the brazen hussy would go. She had, quite literally, backed him into the darkest corner of the gazebo.

Her hands found his shoulders and curled around them. "Paul," she whispered, and she lifted her head for his kiss.

Tessa was no stranger to a man's kisses. In France, she had discovered, young gentlemen were not so circumspect as their English counterparts, nor were French girls the least bit prudish. Her female friends weren't wicked, far from it, but they saw nothing wrong in indulging in a little kissing. They reasoned, and Tessa agreed with them, that it was foolish for a girl to keep herself in total ignorance of what awaited her in marriage. Now, after two years in France, Tessa considered herself quite knowledgeable about men and their passions.

She also knew that by trysting with Paul in the gazebo, she was overstepping the boundaries of what a French girl would allow. But Paul was different. He was courting her. Perhaps tonight he would ask her to marry him. Then their kisses would be sanctioned by his ring on her finger. And if that were not enough to tempt her, there were Paul's breathtaking kisses. When he molded those experienced lips to hers, something peculiar happened to her insides, and that had never happened to her with any other boy. He made her feel quite giddy.

It was exactly as she had anticipated. His mouth was firm and hot, and those pleasant sensations began to warm her blood. When he wrapped his arms around her and jerked her hard against his full length, she gave a little start of surprise, but that warm, mobile mouth on hers insisted she yield to him. She laughed softly when he kissed her throat, then she stopped breathing altogether when he bent her back and kissed her breasts, just above the lace on her bodice. He'd never gone that far before.

She should stop him, she knew she should stop him, but she felt as weak as a kitten. She said something—a protest? a plea?—and his mouth was on hers again, and everything Tessa knew about men and their passions was reduced to ashes in the scorching heat of that embrace. Her limbs were shaking, wild tremors shook her body, her blood seemed to ignite. She was clinging to him for support, kissing him back, allowing those bold hands of his to wander at will from her breast to her thigh, taking liberties she knew no decent girl should permit, not even a French girl.

When he left her mouth to kiss her ears, her eyebrows, her cheeks, she got out a shaken whisper, "I never knew it could be like this. You make me feel things I never knew existed, sensations I've never experienced before. You seem so different tonight."

And he did. His body was harder, his shoulders seemed broader, and she hadn't known he was so tall. As for his fragrance—

Then she knew, she *knew*, and she opened her eyes wide, trying to see his face. It was too dark, but she didn't need a light to know whose arms she was in. He didn't wear cologne as Paul did. He smelled of fresh air and soap and freshly starched linen. Outrage rooted her to the spot, but only for a moment longer. Those clever hands of his had slipped and were beginning to massage her bottom.

"Trevenan!" she gasped, and fairly leaped out of his arms.

He made no move to stop her, but said in a laconic tone that grated on her ears, "What a pity. And just when things were beginning to turn interesting."

She was so overcome with rage, she could hardly find her voice, and when she did find it, it was high-pitched and unnatural. "*Interesting?* What you did to me was not interesting. It was *depraved.*"

As he advanced she retreated. Though she felt a leap of

alarm, she was too proud to run away. When he halted beside the stone steps, so did she, but she was careful to preserve some space between them. The lights on the terrace had yet to be extinguished, and she had a clear view of his expression. He could hardly keep a straight face.

"Depraved?" he said. "That's not the impression you gave me. I could have sworn you were enjoying yourself. 'I never knew it could be like this,'" he mimicked. "'You make me feel things I never knew existed.'" He began to laugh.

"I thought you were Paul," she shouted. "How dare you impose yourself on me in that hateful way."

He arched one brow. "My dear Miss Lorimer, as I recall, you were the one who imposed yourself on me. I was merely enjoying a quiet smoke when you barged into the gazebo and cornered me. I didn't kiss you. You kissed me." His white teeth gleamed. "Might I give you a word of advice? You're too bold by half. A man likes to be the hunter. Try, if you can, to give the impression that *he* has cornered *you*."

The thought that this depraved rake—and he had to be a rake if his kisses were anything to go by—had the gall to give her advice made her temper burn even hotter. She had to unclench her teeth to get the words out. "There is no excuse for your conduct. You knew I thought you were Paul."

"Come now, Miss Lorimer. That trick is as old as Eve."

Anger made her forget her fear, and she took a quick step toward him. "Do you think I'd want your kisses? You're nothing but my grandfather's lackey. You're a secretary, an employee. If I were to tell him what happened here tonight"—she pointed to the gazebo—"he would dismiss you."

"Tell him, by all means. He won't think less of me for acting like any red-blooded male. It's your conduct that will be a disappointment to him." His voice took on a hard edge. "By God, if I had the schooling of you, you'd learn to obey me."

"Thank God," she cried out, "that will never come to pass."

He laughed. "Stranger things have happened."

He had argued her to a standstill. The thing to do now was to exit with as much dignity as was left to her. She wasn't going to leave him with the impression that she had followed him into the gazebo knowing who he was.

She breathed deeply, trying to find her calm. "If I'd known you were in the gazebo, I would never have entered it." His skeptical look revived her anger, and she said, "I tell you, I thought you were Paul Marmont."

He shrugged. "In that case, all I can say is that little girls who play with fire deserve to get burned."

She said furiously, "You were teaching me a lesson?"

"In a word, yes."

Her head was flung back and she regarded him with smoldering dislike. "And just how far were you prepared to go in this lesson of yours, Mr. Trevenan? Mmm?"

He extended a hand to her, and without a trace of mockery or levity answered, "Come back to the gazebo with me and I'll show you."

He was serious, and the knowledge was like a slap in the face. This was the man who never tried to conceal his contempt from her, who never so much as asked her for a dance at her own ball. He disliked her intensely, but that wouldn't stop him taking her like a common trollop. Then he would discard her. She'd never been so humiliated in her life. With an exclamation of hurt pride, she wheeled away from him and went racing up the stairs to the house.

Ross gave her a few minutes before he followed her in. Her reckless disregard for rules was dangerous and he hoped he had taught her a lesson. In any case, he'd learned something about Tessa Lorimer that pleased him enormously.

She was still an innocent.

His lips quirked when he remembered her words. *I never knew it could be like this. You make me feel things I never knew existed, sensations I've never experienced before.* So much for Paul Marmont and her handsome young footman, he thought, and snapped his fingers.

He'd learned something else, something about himself

that did not please him half as well. If she had not put a stop to it, he did not know where it would have ended.

Scowling, he felt in his coat pocket and withdrew his watch. It wasn't too late to visit Solange. A few minutes later he was in a cab and on his way to the Palais Royal.

Chapter Three

~~~~~

*I*n the enclosed gardens of the Palais Royal, outside the Café de Foy, tables and chairs had been set out for people to enjoy the last lingering days of a late summer. Tessa and her new friends, Sally and Desmond Turner, sat here after exploring the shops that lined the galleries on all sides of the gardens. A colorful crowd thronged the gardens, fops and fashionable ladies, soldiers in uniform, nursemaids out walking with their charges, and well-dressed residents, mostly gentlemen, who rented apartments on the upper floors of the palace. It went without saying, Tessa had just confided to Sally, that ladies who resided in the Palais Royal were not exactly ladies.

Desmond Turner sipped his wine as he observed the passersby. This was the first time he had visited the Palais Royal during the day, and he was relieved that there was no sign of the painted prostitutes who brazenly plied their trade at dusk. There was no violence, no brawls, no drunken voices raised in anger. Bonaparte had requisitioned one of the wings of the palace for his Tribunal, and there were bound to be secret police patrolling the area. On that thought, Desmond looked over the idlers and strollers with professional interest, trying to detect which of them might be a member of Bonaparte's secret police.

Tessa and Sally were speculating on the gentlemen who were exiting, at odd intervals, from a door to the right of the Café de Foy.

"Gamblers," said Tessa. "The gambling goes on all night. Just look at their faces. It's not hard to tell who won and who lost. Or it could be"—she winked at Sally and dropped her voice to a confidential whisper—"that they are returning home after spending the night with a *chère amie.*" To Sally's blank look, she elaborated, "Mistress."

The waiter arrived with their order, and the conversation went on to other matters.

Tessa had discovered that in spite of her aversion to Mr. Trevenan, she liked his friends, especially Sally. The girl might be English, but she was anything but stuffy. When they'd come across those naughty prints in the bookshop in the Gallerie de Valois, Sally had not even blushed. In fact, Sally had tried, humorously, to persuade her brother to buy them. He hadn't of course, but what intrigued Tessa was the easy camaraderie between this brother and sister.

"What exactly is your profession, Mr. Turner?" Tessa asked. "I don't believe you mentioned it."

Sally answered, "It's more of a hobby than a profession. If he wanted to, Desmond could practice law. He was once a barrister."

"Dull," responded Desmond. He was taking minuscule sips from the demitasse of almost black coffee the waiter had just placed in front of him. Deciding it was undrinkable, he set it aside. "I investigate crimes," he said. "You know, chase down bank robbers, apprehend murderers and felons, that sort of thing."

"You're a constable, then? An officer of the law?"

"Oh, no," he replied. "That would hardly be worth my while. My services are for hire."

Tessa couldn't hide her astonishment. She couldn't imagine anyone employing Desmond Turner to track down bank robbers and murderers. She couldn't even imagine him as a barrister in a court of law. For one thing, he looked too young, no more than twenty-three or twenty-four. For another, he didn't look the part. He wasn't hard-faced and forbidding. He was a pleasant-looking young man who reminded her of the young vicar of the small parish church in Arden.

Sally let out a laugh. "You wouldn't know it to look at him," she said, "but Desmond is quite famous in certain circles." And in spite of her brother's protests, she began describing some of the cases he had solved.

Tessa had heard of some of them: the bank in Pall Mall that had been robbed of twenty thousand pounds; the theft of paintings from Lord Hawser's house in York; the ring of procurers that abducted beautiful young girls and sold them into sexual slavery; and last but not least, the vicious murder of a wealthy young lord that was at first attributed to gypsies and later, after Desmond's investigation, pinned on his adulterous and spendthrift wife.

In answer to a question from Tessa, Desmond explained how he had become involved in his hobby, a very lucrative one as it turned out. It was in the blood, he said. He had two uncles who were Justices of the Peace. As a young boy, he'd often helped them out on cases. Later, as a barrister, he'd discovered that his real interest wasn't in defending felons but in catching them.

"Fascinating," said Tessa. "Are you always successful in solving your cases?"

"Oh, no," he said. "There's one in particular that has totally baffled me."

He looked up at her and his kind brown eyes were now as hard as granite. Without being aware of what she was doing, Tessa adjusted her shawl to cover her bare arms. She studied him now and saw that she had misjudged his age. He looked closer to thirty, and she no longer had any trouble seeing him as a barrister in a court of law. There was a lot more to Desmond Turner than nice manners and a pleasant smile.

The granite in his eyes softened, and he said easily, "The young woman who was murdered was only twenty-two years old. Her name was Margaret Hemmel."

"You say that as though I should know her."

"It's possible you do. She was at school with you."

"I was at so many schools, I hardly remember one from another."

Sally was demolishing an ice, turning it to slush on her plate. "Fleetwood Hall," she said, "but I don't remember her either." She looked up at Tessa. "We were in the first form and Margaret was one of the senior girls. In fact, she was the head girl."

"Fleetwood Hall? That doesn't . . . wait a moment. What was the name of the headmistress?"

"Miss Oliphant," said Sally.

Tessa's heart began to pound. Fleetwood Hall. Now she remembered it. The school was housed in a stately, neo-classical mansion set in a beautiful park. There were woods and walks and a picturesque man-made lake that had been out-of-bounds to the girls unless they were accompanied by one of their teachers. The rules had never stopped Nan and her from going down to the lake, but they'd always waited till the house was locked up and everyone was asleep. She hadn't thought about Nan in a long time and wondered where she was and what she was doing.

She nodded. "Miss Oliphant's Academy—that was the name of the school. Fleetwood Hall was the name of the house. It was left to Miss Oliphant by some reclusive old gentleman for the purpose of converting it into a school."

Sally toyed with the melted ice in her plate. "Now that is something I had forgotten." She looked up at Tessa. "What I remember is that dreadful accident where one of the girls drowned."

"What accident?" asked Desmond.

"I'm sure I've mentioned it before," replied Sally, and went on without a pause. "At any rate, just before the summer holidays, four of the senior girls broke the rules and slipped out in the dead of night to party and swim in the lake. Trouble was, none of them knew how to swim. Unbeknownst to them, they weren't the only girls there—" She stopped abruptly. "But I shouldn't be telling you all this. Tessa was there. She should tell you what happened that night."

Tessa's heart pounded harder. "I wasn't there," she said. "I know what the senior girls said, but they were mistaken. It was dark. They didn't really see me. They thought they recognized my voice. But I wasn't there. I was in bed with a fever. I was delirious for three days. Miss Tanner, my house mistress, said so at the inquest."

"Well, whatever," said Sally. "One of the senior girls got into trouble and drowned. It was a tragic business."

"Becky Fallon," said Tessa.

"That's the girl. Poor Becky."

"Yes," said Tessa, and her fingers tightened around her cutlery. Several years had passed since Becky Fallon had drowned, but she couldn't think of it without feeling horribly, horribly guilty. She didn't know why she felt guilty. She hadn't lied to Sally. When the accident happened, she was in her bed. Perhaps she felt guilty because she had never liked Becky Fallon. But she hadn't wished for her death. When she'd heard the dreadful news, she'd been as stunned as everyone else.

Suddenly realizing that two pairs of eyes were watching her, she said, "But you were telling me about Margaret Hemmel. You said she was murdered. When was this, and how did it happen?"

Desmond answered, "It happened almost three years ago. It appeared to be a carriage accident, but her parents were not satisfied with the coroner's verdict, and neither was I. However, I couldn't prove otherwise, so you see, that case remains one of my dismal failures."

"But that's awful," said Tessa.

He flashed her a smile. "I haven't conceded defeat. One day I hope to catch the person responsible."

A shadow fell across the table, and Tessa looked up into the thin smiling face of Paul Marmont. She was quite shaken by the conversation, and her hand instinctively reached for him. Paul had been in Rouen for three days, attending to some business on behalf of his father. Like her own grandfather, Henri Marmont was in banking.

The introductions were made, and as conversation went on about her, Tessa's heart slowed and the events of Fleetwood Hall gradually receded from her mind.

"I missed you at my ball," she said.

"I was unavoidably detained," he replied. "Your maid told me I would find you here."

Paul never apologized, never explained, not even as a formality. It was one of the few things about him that irritated Tessa. In every other way, she admired him, from the casual way he wore his elegant garments to the easy charm that made him so popular.

Tessa watched Paul turn that charm on Sally, and was startled to see that Sally was completely immune. Her credit rose substantially in Tessa's estimation. Most women fell like skittles when Paul made them an object of his gallantry. Paul was French, and the trait seemed to be inborn in all Frenchmen. Unfortunately, Tessa wasn't French, she was English, and she couldn't quite suppress her jealousy when Paul's gaze roved to other women, as it frequently did.

Paul waved the waiter over and ordered a glass of wine. When the waiter left, he said, "I presume you are looking for a way out of your predicament."

"If you mean," said Desmond, "that we want to return to England, you are right."

Paul said, "I may be in a position to help you."

There was a moment's silence, then Desmond said slowly, "That's very kind of you, Monsieur Marmont, and we may yet take you up on your offer."

Paul smiled. "Ah, so it's already arranged. When do you leave?"

A long look passed between brother and sister. "That has yet to be decided," said Desmond.

Paul's wine arrived. He raised his glass and spoke in a voice that did not carry. "Then, I wish you both 'bon voyage.'"

Tessa looked at Sally and tried not to let her disappointment show. "I shall miss you," she said. The absurdity of her remark suddenly struck her, and she shrugged helplessly. She'd only met the girl the night before at her ball.

Sally said, "Perhaps we shall meet again in England."

"I shall never return to England," said Tessa.

"No, indeed," said Paul. "Therese's future lies here with me."

The words thrilled Tessa, but when she looked at Paul, he gave no hint that he'd said something significant. He was looking at his glass of wine.

The Turners did not remain long after that, but before they left, it was arranged that they would meet Tessa the following afternoon at the Louvre museum. Paul declined the invitation for himself, as usual, without explanation.

He watched them go with a thoughtful look on his face. "It wouldn't surprise me," he said, "if your grandfather has arranged for them to get back to England."

"Paul, my grandfather hardly knows them. They're Ross Trevenan's friends."

"Then I'll wager he is the one who is helping them."

"Why should an American run such risks? They're not exactly friends of the English."

"For the money, of course. And I'm not convinced Mr. Trevenan is an American. If he is running an escape route, it would serve his purposes to pass himself off as an American. Then he could move freely around France."

"You think he's English?"

"It's possible."

Tessa let the thought circle in her mind, but when she looked up, she found Paul's bold black eyes upon her, and all thoughts of Ross Trevenan immediately evaporated.

"I had a particular reason for seeking you out," he said. "I must return to Rouen at once and feared I might miss you."

"What is it?"

He took her hand, turned it over, and traced her life line with his thumb. Releasing her hand, he said, "My father wants me to take over the Rouen branch. That could mean we might not see each other as often as I should like."

"Oh." She swallowed hard.

"It wouldn't be convenient for me to post back and forth to Paris, not when I'm settled permanently in Rouen. My family owns a house there."

She nodded, hardly daring to draw air into her lungs.

"If we were to marry—?" He left the question dangling.

Tessa couldn't speak for the lump in her throat. Everything she had ever wanted was within her grasp. She would have a husband and children. She wouldn't be rootless. Her place would be secure, even when her grandfather was no longer there to provide it. She would have a home of her own and Paul to love, as he loved her.

"Do you understand what I'm saying?" he asked gently.

She found her voice. "You're asking me to marry you?"

"Ah no. Not yet, *chérie*. First I must speak to your grandfather. That's how things are done in France. When I have your grandfather's permission to speak to you, then I shall ask you to marry me."

"When are you going to speak to my grandfather?"

He grinned at her eager tone. "I thought I would leave it for a week. That should give you time to prepare the way for me."

"Is that really necessary? Why not speak to him today?"

He shook his head. "I'm not certain that your grandfather would encourage my suit. But if you were to put in a good word for me, you know, let him know that this is what you want, I think he will be more receptive to the idea."

She thought that Paul was being overcautious, but this, too, was the French way. In any case, a week wasn't so very long to wait, and whatever Paul said, she was sure her grandfather would be delighted with the match. Then Paul would propose to her in a more private place, where they could say all that needed to be said between lovers.

Someone hailed Paul from a nearby table.

"Old Dumont," Paul murmured. "He used to manage the Paris branch. This won't take a moment."

While Paul went to speak with Monsieur Dumont, Tessa began to pull on her gloves, her mind sifting through Paul's many fine qualities that she would extol to her grandfather during the coming week. Alexandre Beaupré, she knew, would not be impressed by the fact that Paul was the most eligible bachelor in Paris, and that he was handsome and charming and could have any girl he wanted. Her grandfather would want to know about Paul's character and whether or not he could make her happy.

She would tell him that Paul was one of the kindest gentlemen of her acquaintance. She would never forget the night they'd met. It was the first party she had attended, only months after she'd arrived in Paris. Her grandfather had it in mind that she would take Paris by storm. For his sake, she'd tried to appear confident, but inwardly she was quaking. Her French wasn't fluent. She was gauche on the dance floor. Her appearance was against her. She didn't talk easily in large groups of people.

She'd conducted herself as she always did when she was afraid. She'd held her head just a little higher and pretended that she didn't care that she was sitting with the dowagers at the edge of the ballroom with only her chaperon to talk to, while other girls her age were dancing their feet off. Her one consolation was that her grandfather wasn't there to see her.

Never would she forget her first sight of Paul. The ball was half over, and she'd been looking down at the floor, watching the progress of a small spider that had somehow avoided being crushed beneath tramping feet, when a pair of glossy dark pumps stopped right in front of her. She slowly raised her eyes, inch by inch, taking in muscular legs clothed in white satin breeches, dark cutaway coat over a silver tissue waistcoat, broad shoulders, and finally, jerking her eyes up, a darkly handsome young man who was smiling down at her.

He'd asked her to dance, and afterward had introduced her to some of his friends, both male and female. She'd sensed that he'd known how uncertain she was and had taken it upon himself to see that she enjoyed herself. That night was only the beginning. Paul had become something of a mentor, advising her on what to wear and what not to wear, and had persuaded her to let her hair grow. He actually *liked* the color, and said it made her distinctive.

It was because of Paul that she now had the confidence to make her own way in society.

She was gazing into space, staring at nothing in particular, when her eyes focused on the doorway she and Sally had been watching earlier. Ross Trevenan had just stepped through it, and he wasn't alone. An auburn-haired woman in a froth of transparent gauze that revealed a large expanse of bare flesh was smiling up at him. One slim white hand was caressing his arm while she listened intently to what Trevenan was saying. Then her head went back and she laughed.

That's when Tessa recognized her. Ross Trevenan's companion was none other than Solange Guéry, the most celebrated courtesan in Paris. She had her own box at the opera, her own distinctive carriage, and she was the arbiter of fashion, even among respectable women. Tessa knew all this because Miss Guéry and her comings and goings was a topic of intense interest to Tessa and her friends, if only because it made them feel quite sophisticated to talk about such things. She couldn't imagine what had brought her grandfather's secretary to Solange Guéry's apartment.

Her question was answered when the woman curved one arm around Trevenan's neck and brought his head down for an openmouthed kiss. Tessa could not tear her eyes away. Images were flashing inside her head. Sensations she never wanted to think about in connection with this man were making her go hot all over. And the humiliation she had felt afterward when he had mimicked her words precisely, was as fresh as it had been then. Then the humiliation gave way to a burning resentment.

When the kiss was over and the woman turned to go back inside, Trevenan gave her a smack on the bottom. This brought more laughter. As he turned to leave, his gaze traveled over Tessa, slipped by her, then jerked back. The foolish grin on his face died instantly and he made his way through the tables toward her.

She was covered in confusion, as though she had been caught in the act of committing some particularly nasty piece of mischief. Pride rallied, and her head went back as she stared unflinchingly into his eyes. Knowing that whatever he was going to say to her wouldn't be pleasant, she spoke first.

"You should smile more often, Mr. Trevenan. I swear you look almost human." If she hadn't known better, she would have said that a smile was tugging at the corners of his mouth.

"I smile when the occasion demands it," he replied. "Weren't the Turners supposed to accompany you this morning?"

She breathed slowly, inwardly seething. She knew what he was implying. He thought she was unchaperoned, and was finding fault with her when his own conduct was nothing short of scandalous.

Anger made her reckless. "This isn't morning, it's afternoon, Mr. Trevenan. Perhaps you and Miss Guéry were smiling so much you didn't notice the time passing."

Not a flicker of a smile this time. "Miss Guéry is no concern of yours. Where is your chaperon, Tessa?"

"My chaperon is no concern of yours," she snapped back.

When his gray eyes turned wintry, she felt a stab of alarm. "We'll see about that," he said and reached for her.

"Paul is escorting me," she blurted out, expecting at any moment to feel those strong hands grab her shoulders and yank her to her feet like a naughty child. "Paul Marmont. He's over there."

She glanced over her shoulder and almost sagged with relief when she saw that Paul had finished his conversation with old Dumont and was on his way back to her. Her fear ebbed, and she glared up at the man who was intimidating her. "You remember, Paul Marmont, don't you? He's the man I'm going to marry. I have no need of a chaperon for Paul is an honorable gentleman."

She was taunting him with his own dishonorable

conduct, and she braced for a sharp retort. What he gave her was a look that betrayed what might have been pity, then his expression became inscrutable and he abruptly left her.

In a private parlor in a small inn on the edge of the Faubourg St. Germain, Sally and Desmond Turner were seated at a table taking tea.

"Sorry about the gaffe I made earlier," said Sally. "I should have remembered that the school was named after Miss Oliphant."

"I don't see how you could have remembered when you were never a pupil there. And all the locals refer to it as Fleetwood Hall, in spite of Miss Oliphant. At any rate, I don't think Tessa made anything of it."

"No. She's so trusting, it makes me feel guilty for deceiving her. Poor girl."

"Poor girl? I thought you said she was vain and full of her own conceit."

"That was only a first impression, and I wouldn't have thought so if I hadn't listened to Lord Sayle."

"Sal," Desmond began in a warning tone.

"Ross! I meant to say 'Ross,' of course."

"You mustn't even *think* of him as Lord Sayle until we are in England again. If the French were to find out who he really is—"

"I know, I know. They would lock him away until the war is over. As I was saying, if I hadn't listened to *Ross*, I would have formed an entirely different opinion of Tessa. And she likes me. She really likes me. That's what's so horrible."

Desmond sat back in his chair and studied his sister. She'd helped him on other cases, though this was the first time as an equal partner, and she knew that subterfuge and trickery were often necessary in order to apprehend criminals. But it didn't come naturally to either of them, not when their father was a vicar.

He chose his words with care. "You don't have to go on with this, you know. If you want to, you can stop right here. Tomorrow, we'll go to the Louvre, then bid Tessa adieu in hopes of seeing her someday in England. Then you can go back to keeping house for me, and I shall work alone with Ross."

Sally thought about this for a long time. Looking up, she said, "Couldn't we tell her the truth?"

"At this point, we're not sure what the truth is."

"But as much as we know?"

"What? That we think there is a madman among us? That he's already murdered all the other witnesses to Becky Fallon's drowning and we think Tessa will be his next victim? What young woman could live with that hanging over her?"

"You've left out the most important point," she said. "One of those witnesses was Ross's wife. If Cassie were alive today, we wouldn't be here."

"True," he said mildly.

She leaned forward in her chair. "Do you really think Tessa witnessed the accident?"

"Ross thinks so. His wife told him so, shortly before she died. And at the inquest, the three senior girls who were present that night insisted that Tessa was there."

"But they didn't see her?"

"No, it was too dark, and Tessa was on the other side of the lake. But they recognized her voice. She was splashing around, crying for help. The senior girls weren't alarmed. They thought it was one of Tessa's practical jokes. She'd done this kind of thing before, you see, and the water in the lake wasn't deep."

"So they all went back to the school, all except Becky Fallon?"

"Evidently. At the inquest, everyone was vague about who was exactly where that night. At any rate, Cassie realized Becky was missing and went back to look for her. That's when she saw Tessa coming from the other side of the lake."

"That part didn't come out at the inquest though."

"No. I suppose Cassie thought she was doing the girl a favor by not mentioning it."

Sally sighed. "I don't know what to make of it."

"Think about it, Sal. Of the girls who were present that night, Tessa is the only one left."

"But why would someone wait all these years before doing away with all the witnesses to some tragic accident that hardly made a ripple outside the village of Fleetwood?"

"If I knew the answer to that, I would know who the murderer is. And you're forgetting something, Sal. Ross and I were not the only ones who were trying to locate Tessa. Someone else had been asking questions about her. We were lucky to get to her first. She's the last witness left. We can't let anything happen to her."

She looked at him bleakly. "Poor Tessa," she said.

"Poor Ross is what I'm thinking," he retorted, and won a smile from her. "Well, what's it to be, Sal? Are you with me on this or what?"

After replenishing her cup, she took several refreshing sips of tea and replied, "Nothing is going to happen to Tessa if I have anything to do with it, and if that means I have to deceive her, so be it."

Chapter Four

❦

O ut on the terrace, Tessa was seated at a small table, waiting patiently for her grandfather to appear. This was her favorite hour of the day, just before dinner, when they would talk, or read together, or sometimes merely sit in the silence of their own thoughts, contemplating the view. Laying aside the book she was reading, she went to stand beside the balustrade. The sun was low on the horizon, and a red glow had spread across the sky, fading to pink as it spilled onto the river. Across the Seine, the tiled roofs of the Louvre glowed bloodred, and the muffled sounds of carriages carried to her from the Pont Neuf.

This was her world now. She waited for the familiar sense of peace to wash over her, as it always did when she contemplated this view from the terrace, and though she found a measure of comfort, she was far from composed. Some vague fear that couldn't be reasoned away made her ill at ease, and she groped in her mind, trying to determine the cause.

Nothing much occurred to her, only a series of small things that were hardly worth bothering about. Her grandfather had been closeted with his attorneys for two days in a row. Whenever she mentioned Paul's name to him, he was noncommittal. She'd caught him staring at her with a sad, reflective look on his face that he'd veiled when he became aware of her scrutiny. Conversations with Ross Trevenan faded away whenever she came within earshot.

She stood there unmoving, unseeing, thinking about Ross Trevenan. She'd never had a moment's unease until he'd appeared on the scene. She couldn't explain it, but she sensed that all her fears would be resolved if only he would go away, back to where he came from.

There were secrets here, dangerous secrets, that everyone was keeping from her, something to do with Ross Trevenan. Even Sally and Desmond Turner spoke warily whenever she casually mentioned his name. Desmond had told her he'd met Trevenan, quite by chance, in one of the gaming houses in the Palais Royal, and they'd struck up a friendship. It didn't seem credible. Secretaries didn't make enough money to squander it on gaming. Then again, no secretary she knew could afford the services of someone like Solange Guéry.

Could Paul be right? Was Ross Trevenan English and secretly running an escape route for people who wanted to get out of France? If that were true, it would explain a number of things. His money, for one. His unconscious air of authority for another. It would also explain his odd relationship with her grandfather. Perhaps they were in this together.

If that's all it was, she had nothing to worry about.

She turned from the view and gave a start when she saw Ross Trevenan only a few feet away, watching her with one of his closed expressions. He was dressed informally by her grandfather's standards. His cutaway coat of dark blue broadcloth was unbuttoned and worn over gray knit trousers. His feet were shod in the finest black calfskin. He had the look of a man who had just been out riding. His blond hair was windblown and fell across his forehead, and his skin was ruddy. She couldn't think of him as a secretary. He was too athletic, too masculine, and far too sure of himself.

"I didn't meant to startle you," he said. "Your grandfather would like a word with you."

"Why isn't he here? I was waiting for him."

"What he wishes to say to you is best said where no one can overhear. He's waiting for you in his study."

All the misgivings she'd reasoned away rushed back. With dread filling her heart, she allowed him to lead her to her grandfather's study.

Ross halted at the door and turned to face her. "A word of advice before we go in. Try to remember that your grandfather is not in the best of health. I don't want you overtaxing his strength."

She quivered with resentment. "I don't need any advice from you, Mr. Trevenan. I know about my grandfather's health."

Alexandre Beaupré was seated behind his desk. The candles were lit, and there was no sign of Marcel. Tessa anxiously scanned his face. He was pale, but there was nothing new in that. What alarmed her was the gravity of his expression. He motioned her to a chair, while Ross stood looking out one of the windows.

As soon as she was seated, she said, "Grandfather, what is it?"

The gravity of his expression dissolved, and he smiled at her. "Good news and bad, *ma petite*, but certainly nothing to put that look on your face. I shall come right to the point and begin with the bad news first." His clasped hands were resting on the flat of the desk and he looked at them as he began to speak. "I've known for some time that Bonaparte has had his eye on you, not for himself you understand, but for his brother Jerome." He looked up at her. "And I have wracked my brains for a way of keeping you safe. I have influence, it's true, but against the power of the First Consul, I'm as helpless as a babe."

None of this made sense to her, and she looked over at Ross as though he could help her understand. His back was to her, and that silent, unknowing gesture unnerved her. She would get no help there.

She looked at her grandfather. "What has Jerome Bonaparte to do with me?"

"You are my only heir. If you marry Jerome Bonaparte, all I possess will pass into your husband's hands, or perhaps I should say into Napoleon Bonaparte's hands."

"Marry him!" She gave a disbelieving laugh. "I would never marry him. I don't even know him."

"You wouldn't have a say in the matter. Nor would the young man. To the First Consul, you and his brother are nothing but pawns, a means to enrich his own coffers. Don't look like that, my dear. I have devised a way of outwitting my good friend Napoleon."

Tessa held perfectly still. Her grandfather was watching her with a blank expression, the one he wore when he was playing cards for high stakes. Whatever he was about to say, she knew she didn't want to hear it.

She rose to her feet, and extended her hand, palm up, as though to halt the flow of his words. The soft scrape of leather on parquet warned her that Trevenan had at last condescended to look at her, but she did not spare him a glance.

"Grandfather," she began, and waited a moment to steady her voice. "I'm going to marry Paul Marmont. We were going to tell you on Saturday, when Paul returns from Rouen. Don't you see what this means? If I'm married to Paul, I can't marry Jerome Bonaparte, or anyone else, so the First Consul's schemes will come to nothing."

"Sit down, Therese."

She slowly sank into her chair, knowing that her words had had no effect. Every muscle in her body tensed for a blow.

"I would never give my consent to a marriage between you and Paul Marmont, but even if I did, it wouldn't make the slightest difference. Things are not what they used to be. Divorce is easily come by. Do you think Paul Marmont would stand in the way of the First Consul if he decided he wanted the marriage dissolved? Paul is not such a fool. He knows that Bonaparte would ruin him."

After a long pause, he went on, "Now may I be permitted to tell you how we are going to outwit the First Consul?"

She strove for dignity, though what she wanted to do was storm from the room. It was evident to her that the news of her proposed marriage to Paul came as no surprise to her grandfather. Ross Trevenan had been carrying tales, and she wondered what else he had told her grandfather about Paul. Nothing good by the sound of it. None of that mattered now. What mattered was that she thought she saw where this was leading, and she was going to put a stop to it.

Her tone was acid. "Save your breath, Grandfather. Nothing on God's earth can persuade me to marry Ross Trevenan."

There was a moment of profound silence, then a look passed between both gentlemen, and they began to laugh. Tessa was conscious that she'd made a terrible gaffe, and she wished that she could melt and disappear through the cracks in the parquet floor.

"My dear Miss Lorimer," drawled Trevenan, "rest assured, such a thing never entered my mind. Forgive my frankness, but we would not suit."

She shot him a look of loathing. "I'm not suggesting that it's me you want. I'm an heiress, Mr. Trevenan. Need I say—"

"Therese!" Her grandfather's voice drowned out her words.

She edged forward in her chair. "Then why is he here? What does Ross Trevenan have to do with you or me, Grandfather?"

"I'm coming to that if you'd only let me explain. Therese, get a hold of yourself. You're behaving as if this were a Greek tragedy, when in fact you are being offered the opportunity of a lifetime."

"If I can't marry Paul . . ." Hearing the petulance in her voice, she stopped in midsentence. She sounded childish. But this wasn't childishness. Her heart was breaking.

Beaupré let out a sigh. "Therese, may I go on?"

She was silent.

"As I said, this is something to look forward to. Ross has carried messages to England, and the widow of a good friend has come to our rescue. You are to have a season in London, Therese. Lady Sayle will sponsor you. You'll live with her as a daughter of the house. This is not forever, you understand. When things have had a chance to cool here, when the First Consul sees that he is wasting his time, then you may return to me. And if you still feel the same way about Paul, I promise I won't stand in your way. As for Ross, he will escort you to England. He is acquainted with Lady Sayle and can tell you about her."

England. He was sending her back to England. After everything she'd gone through to come to him, he was sending her back. It was all so reminiscent of her childhood, when she, an orphan, had been sent away to school like a piece of baggage nobody wanted to claim. But her grandfather wasn't like her Beasley relatives. He loved her. He wouldn't send her away if he knew how she felt.

Her eyes were misting over, and she knew that at any moment she would disgrace herself. Clinging to the shreds of her control, she said, "Mr. Trevenan may tell me about Lady Sayle at some other time. Grandfather, I must speak to you alone."

A long look passed between Ross and Beaupré and finally Ross's gaze moved to Tessa, and their eyes locked.

"I shall be on the terrace if you need me," he said.

His eyes still held hers, then, nodding briefly, he left the room.

As soon as the door closed, Tessa was out of her chair, and she went to kneel beside her grandfather. Her head was bowed, and he reached over with one hand to cup her chin, bringing her face up. Tears shimmered in her eyes.

There was a catch in her voice, but her words were fluent and impassioned. "Don't send me away. France is my home now. Everything I love, everyone I love, is here. A season in London means nothing to me. Don't you see—if you send me back, I may never see you again. France and England are at war. No one knows what the future may hold. And I hate England. I really hate it. I was never happy there. Grandfather"—she paused to dash away her tears—"if you would only let me stay—hide me in a convent, I don't know, there must be something we can do—I could bear it. But I don't want to leave you."

One hand stroked her hair. "I've often wondered," he said, "what your life was like in England. You've told me very little."

What could she tell him? The Beasleys hadn't been deliberately cruel to her. They'd been strict and indifferent, but most of all appalled at how her parents had raised her. She'd gone to them when she was six years old and for the next six years they'd tried to break her spirit and teach her, so they said, the fear of the Lord. It had been a great relief to them all when she was old enough to be sent away to school. But school wasn't the escape she'd hoped it would be. It seemed she couldn't do anything right there either. Only one thing had sustained her. She knew she had a grandfather in France, and she was determined that one day she would go to him.

Tears made speech impossible, and she shook her head.

"Do you think, *ma petite*, that I would send you away if I had a choice in the matter? Dry your tears. This isn't the end of the world."

He produced a handkerchief, and Tessa obediently dabbed her face and blew her nose.

"Listen to me, Therese." His voice had taken on a different color, not soothing now, but forceful, and she raised her head to look at him. "I know you don't want to go back. I know you're afraid, but I have confidence in your ability to meet this challenge. And do you know why? Because Beaupré blood runs in your veins. We Beauprés know how to make the best of things, even when life deals us a cruel hand. You're like me in that."

She knew he was thinking about the accident that had crippled him, but she didn't see how it applied to her. She wasn't brave like her grandfather. When adversity struck her, she didn't stand up to it. She tried to find a way around it, and if that didn't work, she pretended that things were not as bad as they seemed. Sometimes, she even came to believe it. She tried to explain her thoughts, but he stopped her after she'd said only a few sentences.

"That's exactly what I mean, Therese. We Beauprés are survivors. We don't give up easily. And when things are against us, we put on a brave face. That's what I'm asking you to do now. It's imperative that you leave France. I know it's not what you want, but it's the only prudent course to follow. Won't you put a brave face on it, for my sake?"

"Oh, Grandfather," she whispered brokenly.

"There is one other thing I want to say to you. I'm sorry that you have taken a dislike to Mr. Trevenan. Oh, I know you think you have good cause. He doesn't pet and spoil you as I do."

"Mr. Trevenan," she protested, "is always finding fault with me. I can't do a thing right in his eyes."

Beaupré smiled. "Yes, I've watched your spats with a great deal of amusement. However, I think you're reading too much into it. But that's not important for now. What matters is that he is a man of integrity. I trust him, Therese, and I want you to trust him too. Always remember, he has your best interests at heart. Don't keep secrets from him. If you are ever frightened, or don't know where to turn, remember what I've told you."

She sat back on her heels and gave him a long, searching look. "I don't understand. What does Mr. Trevenan have to do with me? I thought I was going to Lady Sayle, and that Mr. Trevenan was to escort me."

"That's true. But there are business matters that must be attended to. I've arranged for moneys for you and so on. Ross will take care of the details."

This gave rise in her mind to a host of questions that had been nagging at her. "Does he intend to stay on in England? And how can an American know Lady Sayle? Grandfather, do you think it wise to trust this man when you have known him for only three months? I've heard things about him. He doesn't act like a secretary. He has too much money. He goes to gaming houses, and—" She thought of Solange Guéry and closed her mouth with a snap.

"And?" he prompted.

"It doesn't matter."

"I think it does."

Her cheeks reddened. "I don't think Mr. Trevenan is a suitable escort for any respectable lady."

Beaupré's brows rose and he chuckled. "You've been listening to the gossips, Therese. What have they told you?"

She said nothing.

He eyed her for a moment, then said, "You're young, but not too young to know that a man has needs, appetites. And there are women who are willing to sell their bodies. Ross is a single man. It means nothing. He would not dream of taking advantage of an innocent girl."

Her grandfather was doing it again, defending Trevenan when the man's conduct was indefensible. It was the old double standard coming into play. A man could take a string of mistresses and still be considered honorable, but if a lady was seen in public without a chaperon, her reputation would be in tatters.

Beaupré said, "At any rate, you won't be traveling alone. The Turners are going too. You like them, don't you?"

"So it's true what Paul told me about Mr. Trevenan!"

"What did he tell you?"

"That your secretary runs an escape route to England."

"That is an exaggeration. But yes. From time to time, Ross has helped certain acquaintances to escape to freedom, acquaintances like the Turners, for example. I thought you would be pleased to hear they were to go with you."

For one thoughtless moment, she *was* pleased at the prospect of traveling with her new friends, and she nodded. Her pleasure, however, was short-lived. She wouldn't be traveling with Sally and Desmond. In spite of her grandfather's persuasions, she wasn't ready to give up yet. Already a plan was forming in her mind. If it really was necessary that she leave France, she didn't see why Paul could not go with her. They could be married in England, if only her grandfather would give his permission.

This wasn't the moment to broach the subject. Much as she hated to admit that Ross Trevenan could be right about anything, her grandfather did appear to be tiring. And there was still so much to say. It wasn't only her marriage to Paul she wanted to talk about. The business about Jerome Bonaparte didn't ring true. Once again, she was struck with the feeling that there was more to this than they were telling her. In the morning, when her grandfather was refreshed, she would talk to him again.

"Grandfather," she said, "is there nothing I can say to make you change your mind?"

Beaupré shook his head. "My dear, I wish it could be otherwise."

She got to her feet. "I shall see you at dinner then. Shall I send Marcel to you?"

"No. Tell Ross I want to see him. There are still matters that he and I need to discuss."

A sad, reflective look was on Beaupré's face as he watched her leave the room.

Ross saw her through the open glass doors as she exited from her grandfather's study. He was on the terrace, leaning against the balustrade, smoking a cheroot. The soft gauze of her gown clung provocatively to every womanly curve; her hair, touched by gold from the candlelight, was swept back from her face revealing the long sweep of her throat. She was a vibrantly beautiful young woman who possessed an inherent sensuality. And he could never look at her without feeling irritated.

He wanted her, and the knowledge rankled. She was headstrong, defiant, proud to a fault, and completely ungovernable. If he suggested one thing, she must do the opposite. She possessed none of the womanly virtues that had attracted him to Cassie. Sweet and yielding were hardly the words that came to mind when one thought of Tessa Lorimer. Yet, she invaded his thoughts, tantalizing him, at odd moments of the day. He didn't know what the devil was the matter with him.

She hadn't moved from the door to Beaupré's study and he wondered what was going through her mind. Suddenly she bowed her head and covered her face with both hands. Perversely, he didn't want to see her like this, with her spirit crushed. He had taken a step toward her before he checked himself. He was the last person she would take comfort from. And he couldn't fault Beaupré for the action he had taken.

He blew out a cloud of smoke. When it cleared, he saw the Tessa he knew striding toward him. Her brows were slashed in a mutinous frown and her bottom lip was pursed in a belligerent, though not unattractive pout. He had yet to see the color of her eyes, but he knew they would be shaded in violets and blues, and as turbulent as a whirlwind. He grinned.

She did not waste words on niceties, and that, too, came as no surprise. "Damn you, Ross Trevenan! What did you tell my grandfather about Paul?"

"Nothing he did not know or already suspect."

Her voice rose shrilly. "You told him we were to marry?"

"Was it a secret? Forgive me. You gave me the impression that it was public knowledge."

"You—!" She couldn't find words scathing enough to describe this grinning-faced scoundrel, and her hands balled into fists. "It won't make a bit of difference. Paul and I shall marry in spite of your interference."

The smile left his face and his eyes narrowed unpleasantly. "Oh? And when is this happy event to take place, Tessa?"

She wanted to shout that it would take place as soon as it could be arranged, but she managed to restrain herself, and abruptly changed the subject. "You put my grandfather up to this, didn't you? It's because of you that he wants me to go to England. What's your interest in this, Trevenan? What's really going on? And how is it that you, a mere secretary, are acquainted with a titled English lady?"

Tessa was also, he belatedly recalled, no sloth at putting two and two together. It was something he had better remember for the future. "I served for a while as her man of business," he answered truthfully.

When he said no more than this, she threw her hands up in sheer frustration. "Will no one tell me what is really going on? You must think I'm a fool if you think I believe all that faradiddle about Jerome Bonaparte. If it's my grandfather's money the First Consul is after, he'll find another way to get it."

Again, he answered truthfully. "Your grandfather knows it, and has already transferred a large part of his assets to English banks." He saw that some of the wind had been taken out of her sails, and he went on in an amused tone, "What has that lurid imagination of yours been conjuring up, Tessa, besides the absurd notion that I want you for my wife?"

Her face flamed scarlet and she whirled away from him, then she swung back to face him. "I never thought . . . it never occurred to me that you wanted *me*. I know you care for me as little as I care for you. But some men will stoop to anything for money."

He flicked the stub of his cheroot into the shrubbery. "My dear Miss Lorimer, allow me to set your mind at rest. There isn't enough money in the world to tempt me to marry an unruly, argumentative child. You may have observed, I prefer the society of grown women."

She resisted the impulse to argue that she was not an argumentative child, resisted the almost overpowering temptation to slap the smirk from his handsome face. "You, sir, are a rake," she retorted, "and if ever I should decide to travel to England, it would certainly not be under your protection."

She loved the way his eyes darkened to slate. Satisfied that she had won that skirmish, she turned to go, flinging over her shoulder in an imperious manner, "Oh, and now that I remember it, my grandfather would like to see you in his study, Mr. Trevenan."

Rough hands closed around her shoulders and wrenched her round. She cried out, and shrank from the fury that blazed from the eyes of the man who towered over her.

"If you decide to travel to London, Tessa? *If?* Let's get one thing clearly understood. Your grandfather has entrusted me with your welfare. I have given him my word that I will follow his instructions to the letter. You are going to London, my girl, if I have to shackle you to my wrist all the way. I mean what I say. Once you leave your grandfather's house, you answer to me. You are in sore need of a firm hand, and I am just the person to administer it. I mean that quite literally. Do you understand, Tessa?"

He released her so suddenly, she stumbled back. Eyes trained on his, she slowly retreated.

"Tessa," he said in a different tone, and reached for her.

"Go to blazes," she snapped, and turning on her heel made a shaky though dignified exit.

Chapter Five

❧❧❧

Tessa was lost in a dream. They were running through the woods, and Nan was out in front. "Hurry, Tessa," cried Nan, "or we shall miss them." They were on one of their midnight adventures, then everything went wrong. She was in the lake and she was drowning. Ross Trevenan had her by the shoulders, and he was holding her under. She tried to fight him off, but her arms were confined to her sides.

"No!" she cried out. "No!"

"Wake up, mademoiselle. Wake up!"

She came awake with a start. The grip on her shoulders relaxed, and she quickly drew herself up. It was dark outside, and her maid, Lucille, stood over her. One of the candles had been lit.

"What's happened?" cried Tessa. "Is it my grandfather?"

"It is Monsieur Trevenan who wishes to speak with you. You are to dress and come with me."

Tessa glanced at the clock and saw that it was only a few minutes past midnight. "I don't understand. What's going on, Lucille?"

Her maid shook her head. "Please, mademoiselle." She

held out the garment she'd been told to dress her mistress in, a blue serge round gown that Tessa sometimes used as a riding habit.

Her heart pounding furiously, Tessa began to dress.

Ross Trevenan was waiting for her across the corridor, in the small yellow salon that she had for her own use. She asked him the same questions she'd asked her maid.

"Your grandfather is waiting for you downstairs," he replied. "There's no need to panic. I wanted a word with you in private before you see him."

"Just tell me what's happening!"

Ross's voice was quiet and matter-of-fact. "We start on the first leg of our journey tonight. Everything is ready. All that's left is for you to pack and say your farewells to your grandfather."

Confused, she looked at her maid, then looked back at Ross. "Journey? What journey?"

"To England, Tessa." A spark of sympathy warmed his eyes, but he went on in the same vein, "It's better if we leave Paris when it's dark, because of the patrols. Once we are out of the city, things will be easier. In a few hours you'll be in a warm bed in Vernon. Then you can sleep."

Tessa gaped at him in horror. They were leaving tonight, before she'd had a chance to get word to Paul. Only a few hours had passed since her grandfather had sprung the news on her that she was going to England, and now this.

Her eyes darkened with fury. "This is intolerable! I'm not going anywhere with you at this time of night. I can't believe my grandfather would allow such a thing."

At a word from Ross, the maid hurried from the room. Tessa made to follow her, but Ross stepped in front of her and closed the door with a slam.

His eyes were like flint. "You listen to me, Tessa Lorimer," he said. "You will do exactly as I tell you. You are going to pack a change of clothes and you are going to come downstairs and speak to your grandfather as though you are reconciled to your fate. I'll not have him upset by a childish temper tantrum. For once in your life, you will think of someone besides yourself. He is not a well man. The last thing he needs is a spoiled child causing a scene. It wouldn't do you any good. This journey is going to happen one way or another. Make up your mind to it. All you will achieve otherwise is that you and your grandfather will part with regrets on both sides—bitter regrets. Is that what you want, Tessa?"

Her heart seemed to coil and uncoil within her chest, and her mind raced, sifting through everything he'd said. One thought emerged. "What about my grandfather? What are you saying? Dr. Latour assured me that his constitution is strong and he has many good years ahead of him yet."

"No one can be sure of such a thing."

"You're only trying to frighten me," she cried out.

"No. What I'm trying to do is make you see reason. You know very well his heart is not strong. With proper care, there's every hope he will have many good years ahead of him. I'm asking you not to upset him."

His eyes remained fixed on her face for a long time, then, as if satisfied with what he read there, he turned and left her. A moment later Lucille entered.

"Come, mademoiselle." She held out her hand.

Tessa allowed herself to be led back to her room. She was aware that Lucille was packing a small leather grip, but she took no interest in what her maid packed for her. Thoughts were crowding into her mind. Everything was happening so fast, she didn't know what to do for the best. She didn't trust Ross Trevenan, but she wasn't going to take the chance of putting him to the test. What if her grandfather was not as well as she'd been led to believe? She needed time to consult Dr. Latour, but time was something she did not have.

Lucille draped a warm woolen cloak over her mistress's shoulders, buttoned it, and handed her her gloves. "It is not so bad," she said. "Monsieur Trevenan is a very kind gentleman."

The careless remark brought color back to Tessa's cheeks. "Oh, very kind," she snapped. Realizing she was taking her temper out on the wrong person, she smiled.

"Take my bag down, Lucille, and tell Mr. Trevenan I shall be with him in a moment."

She spent the next few minutes pacing the room, trying to think of a way to make her grandfather change his mind. But nothing came to her. She would only cause a scene, and that would not work with either her grandfather or Trevenan.

She descended the stairs as if every step were her last. Her grandfather and Ross Trevenan were waiting for her in the hall, talking softly. Suddenly aware of her presence, they looked up. Her gaze never wavered from her grandfather's face. It was only a trick of the candlelight, she told herself, that made his face look tired and drawn. His eyes were huge and black against the pallor of his skin, and the lines in his cheeks stood out more prominently.

He was an old man, older than she wanted him to be. Why hadn't she seen it before?

"Tessa," he said, and held out his arms to her.

She ran down the last few stairs, knelt by his chair, and grasped his hands, bringing them to her face. Words could not get past the lump in her throat, and she simply looked up at him with a plea in her eyes.

"My English rose," he murmured, and his gaze wandered over her as though to impress every feature in his memory. "This is the last thing I want. You know that, don't you?"

"I know, darling, I . . ." She couldn't say more.

"Remember our conversation. Remember you are a Beaupré."

She nodded.

He cleared his throat. "Kiss me and say good-bye."

She was in a state of shock, and obeyed him mechanically, not really believing that this could be happening. Slowly she got to her feet.

Her grandfather snapped his fingers, and Marcel appeared out of the shadows. Beaupré's last words were for Ross. His voice shook and seemed to come from a long way off. "We've said all that needs to be said. I know you'll take good care of her. Now go, quickly, and may God go with you."

Tessa was too numb to protest when Ross's arm went around her shoulders and he began to herd her to the door. She felt lost and desperate. Everything was happening so fast, she couldn't seem to get her bearings. She couldn't leave her grandfather like this.

"No!" She shook off Ross's restraining arm and turned to go back. The hall was empty. "Grandfather!" she called out. "Grandfather!"

"Tessa!"

Ross Trevenan's voice drew her up short. His expression was grave but not unkind. "Leave him to his sorrow, Tessa. He needs time to be alone. You did well just now. I'm sure your grandfather was proud of you. I know I was. Don't spoil it now."

She was buffeted by conflicting emotions and very close to tears, but even in her confusion she was gripped by the conviction that this man was responsible for ruining everything. If he had never come to France, none of this would be happening.

Her tears dried. "Frankly, Mr. Trevenan," she said, "I don't give a damn what you think of me."

She strode to the side door that gave onto the stable block. Behind her, Ross raked his hand through his hair, cursed under his breath, and went after her.

Two grooms were waiting outside with five horses in tow. Tessa made straight for the mounting block and was soon mounted. She heard Ross's voice issuing orders, and she automatically fell into place behind him as he led the way through the great iron gates. The grooms followed her with the packhorse in the rear.

Already, she was blocking out all the sights and sounds around her. They weren't out of France yet, and there still might be time to think of a plan.

They rode through woods and fields, keeping close to the road but rarely traveling on it. Though the pace was comfortable, Tessa was not sorry when they entered Vernon. She was drooping with fatigue and drained of all emotion, at least until they halted in the courtyard of Les Trois Frères, a small hostelry on the west side of town, and Ross appeared at her side to help her dismount.

"I can manage," she told him coolly.

"You're almost falling off your horse."

"I can manage!" she insisted in a loud carrying voice.

Shrugging indifferently, he went to see about their lodgings.

Because of the rough terrain they'd had to travel, she wasn't riding sidesaddle, and dismounting was no easy task, but with two grooms watching her, grooms who had overheard her proud boast, she was determined to dismount as well as any man. Willing her weary muscles to obey the commands of her brain, she swung her leg over the saddle. It was a perfectly executed movement, and she was congratulating herself as she slid to the cobblestones when, before she was quite steady on her feet, she felt herself slipping. She tried to right herself, but only made matters worse and tottering back she fell heavily on her rear end. The odor of fresh horse manure wafted up and Tessa groaned.

This was how Ross found her when he came out of the hostelry. "You can manage," he said irritably. Getting behind her, with his hands hooked under her armpits, he hauled her to her feet. Then he sniffed, sniffed again, and let out a bark of laughter. When the grooms joined in, Tessa's face flamed scarlet. She did not wait to hear more, but sweeping by them, she entered the inn. Ross delayed only long enough to unfasten her grip from the packhorse, then he went after her.

In the inn's lobby, Tessa was conversing with the landlord and though the stench of manure was ripe on her person, she gave no sign that she was aware of it. She might have been wearing a costly perfume from Arabia for all the notice she paid to old Fécamp's obvious dismay.

Ross tried to keep a straight face. He reminded himself that the parting with her grandfather had been heart-wrenching, and she'd ridden the fifty or so kilometers to Vernon without a word of complaint. He admired her pluck. At the same time, there was a baser side to him that took satisfaction in seeing Miss Tessa Lorimer brought down a peg or two. She had refused his offer of help out of sheer bad temper, and she had only herself to blame for the result.

There was no delay in getting a room for the night. Ross had arranged things well in advance. This was the sort of hostelry where no questions were asked, and he and the landlord, who was also a smuggler, were well acquainted.

Tessa refused the wine that was offered, and Ross did likewise with the glass of brandy, but not without regret. He knew it came from old Fécamp's private stock, and was the finest to be had in France.

"Thank you, no, Monsieur Fécamp. My wife and I are ready for our bed." He heard Tessa's sharp intake of breath, and he gave her a warning look. "Come along, my dear. Don't keep Monsieur Fécamp waiting. I'm sure he is longing for his bed too."

The landlord led the way up the stairs and ushered them into the small room they were to share. As soon as the landlord left, Tessa pounced on Ross.

"How dared you tell the landlord I was your wife! I won't share a room with you, Trevenan, so you'd best make some other arrangement."

"This was the only room available," he lied. He wasn't letting Tessa out of his sight, but she didn't need to know that.

"And I thought Sally and Desmond Turner were coming with us. Where are they?"

"They are already at Rouen waiting for us to catch up to them. We should be with them tomorrow night."

He was watching her closely. This was the first time he'd told her the route they were to take, and he knew full well that Paul Marmont was in Rouen. A flicker of something came and went in her eyes, and he inwardly sighed. It had been too much to hope that she would go to England without a fight.

Her little foot began to tap. "Why can't you share a room with our grooms?"

"They are bedding down in the stable. Someone has to be here to protect you."

"What will they think when they discover that we've spent the night together?"

"They won't think anything. They know that we are only playing a part. You don't seem to understand that this is a dangerous business. How else can we travel through France without arousing suspicion? And it's only for tonight."

She flung up her chin. "I don't care where you sleep, just as long as you don't sleep with me."

Ross dropped the leather grip he was carrying onto the nearest chair. His tone, though controlled, carried an edge. "Now you are being ridiculous. I won't be sleeping with you. I shall sleep on the floor. And don't pretend you care for the proprieties. Your grandfather told me how you came to France. You were the only female in a crew of cutthroats."

"That was different."

"How was it different?"

She gave him a superior smile. "They were gentlemen," she said.

To her great disappointment, he didn't take offense. After a moment's silence, he roared with laughter. Eyes dancing wickedly, he asked, "Is that what this is all about? You think I may have designs on your virtue? Once again, I can only marvel at your lurid imagination. Even if I were not a gentlemen, Tessa, you'd be quite safe from me. Unlike some scoundrels I could name, I've never been attracted to little girls. Besides, this time you've given yourself one air too many for my taste." He sniffed delicately. "Horse manure," he added, as though she were witless and might have missed the point.

Not for one moment did she think he had designs on her virtue. All she'd wanted was to gain a little privacy. She started to protest, then thought better of it. He would only say something nasty, to the effect that the lady was protesting too much.

She looked around the room and wondered how people could stand to be married. This was intimacy with a vengeance. There was no screen to undress behind. There was a washstand in one corner, in open view, and she was perfectly sure if she looked under the bed she would find the ubiquitous chamber pot. When she married Paul, she was going to insist on separate chambers.

She darted Ross an uneasy glance. His gray eyes gazed steadily back at her, and she had the uncanny feeling that he was reading her mind.

He spoke in a flat, even tone. "I'm going to look around outside to make sure everything is all right. By the time I return, I expect you to be changed and in bed. Leave your garments outside the door and I'll arrange to have one of the maids take care of them."

As soon as he left, she dived for the grip he'd dropped on the chair. A few minutes later, she had deposited her gown and cloak outside the door, and she was in bed with the covers pulled up to her chin. It was several more minutes before she heard his tread outside the door.

When he entered, he made straight for the washstand without looking at her. To her dismay, he began to strip, and she buried her face in the pillow to shut out the sight of him. She heard water splashing, then she heard nothing. She waited, and waited. Finally, she turned her head, and cautiously opened her eyes.

He was standing at the foot of the bed, in only his tight-fitting knit trousers, toweling himself off. With a will of their own, her eyes moved slowly over him. Now she knew where his strength came from. Rock-hard muscles rippled along his arms and shoulders as he dried himself with the towel; a profusion of tawny hair sheathed his broad chest; his waist was lean and supple; his form-fitting trousers did nothing to conceal the long muscular legs, the tight thighs.

She found herself swallowing. It was one thing to match wits with him in the salon, where his clothes made him appear civilized, but now, seeing him as he really was, she felt horribly intimidated.

He took a step toward her, and her gaze flew to his face. His eyes were alight with amusement.

"What the devil is that thing on your head?" he demanded.

She bristled. "What does it look like? It's my nightcap, of course."

"Nightcap?" Chuckling, he came right up to her and fingered the fragile confection that tied under her chin with satin ribbons. "I've never slept with a woman who wears a nightcap. I suppose there's a first time for everything. Now, don't take offense. Really, it's adorable. You look just like a little doll."

Outraged, she slapped his hand away. Not only was her nightcap none of his business—and it was the prettiest, daintiest nightcap she owned—but she didn't care for the crude tone of his remarks either.

"Good night!" she snapped furiously, and pounding her pillow with her fist, she turned her back on him and composed herself for sleep.

I've never slept with a woman who wears a nightcap, she mouthed into the pillow. Just how many women had Ross Trevenan slept with anyway? Plenty, she'd wager. She didn't know how they could bear it. He was all hair and muscles. She'd sooner bed down with a gorilla.

You look just like a little doll. She was becoming thoroughly bored with his frequent references to her lack of years—*adolescent, little girl,* and now *little doll.* She wasn't *that* young. It was simply that he was old. He was about ten years her senior by her reckoning, but he acted as though he were as old as Adam.

Paul wasn't like Ross Trevenan. He had excellent manners and he always treated her with respect. *He* didn't think she was a little girl. He was incredibly handsome, with the pure classic features of a Greek god. Perhaps she was exaggerating, but only a little. He was more handsome than Ross Trevenan and that's what counted.

The light suddenly went out, and she heard him padding about the room. The door to the closet opened and closed, and she sensed from the sounds he made that he'd found a blanket to cover himself.

"Nightcap!" he said under his breath. "Good Lord, what next?"

She could well imagine the smirk on his face, and wished, very badly, that she could do something to wipe it off. But if she tried anything, he would undoubtedly make her sorry for it. Well, soon, Mr. Ross Trevenan would discover he wasn't going to have everything his own way.

On the long ride to Vernon, she'd had time to put her thoughts in order, and it seemed to her that Ross Trevenan had panicked her grandfather into sending her away. That business about Jerome Bonaparte . . . that may have been sheer invention from beginning to end. She wasn't sure of Trevenan's motives, but she thought it might have something to do with the assets her grandfather had transferred to English banks. It wouldn't be the first time someone had wormed his way into an old man's confidence, then proceeded to rob him blind.

If she'd had time, she would have consulted Paul and they could have decided together how to approach her grandfather. But Trevenan had been too crafty to give her time, and then he had played on her fears for her grandfather's health to convince her to leave without making a fuss.

She was so confused. She couldn't leave France, wouldn't leave France, unless there really was no other way. Now that she knew their route would take them to Rouen, her hopes had revived. Together, she and Paul would decide what to do.

"Tessa, are you awake?"

"No," she said.

He laughed. "I've been thinking about the story you told your grandfather. Tell me the truth. Did you really cross the Channel with a band of smugglers?"

"I can't believe my grandfather told you about the smugglers. He told me that no one was to know."

"He told me in the strictest confidence," replied Ross. "And you can trust me not to tell. Well, is it true?"

"What if it is?"

"Can't you answer a simple question without debate?"

"Yes," she said. "I crossed the Channel with a band of smugglers. Why do you ask?"

"Weren't you afraid to trust them?"

She thought of Ben and Harry and Lou, all of whom worked the land in and around Arden, a small village on the south coast of England, and who augmented their meager incomes by smuggling contraband from France. Smugglers they certainly were, but they were also as gentle as lambs, at least with her, but then they'd played together as children.

"I was *terrified*," she said. And she had been, but not of her smuggler friends. It was crossing the Channel that had caused her worst terrors, and after that, the weeks she had traveled on the road, alone, sleeping in haystacks or under hedges, with barely enough money to keep from starving. But it had all been worth it.

A long silence followed, an intimate silence that Tessa found vaguely disturbing. She could hear every breath he inhaled and exhaled; she could hear every slight movement as he adjusted his body on the hard floor. Gradually, she became aware of other things. She could tell that when he'd left her to look around outside, he'd smoked one of those thin cigars to which he was so partial.

She inhaled slowly and smiled. Yes, and he'd also taken the landlord up on his offer to sample his best brandy. Brandy and tobacco always made her think of her grandfather. They were such comforting scents, such masculine scents, and she invariably took to any gentleman who smelled of them.

The thought brought her up short, and she scowled into the darkness.

"Tessa?"

"What is it now?" she asked irritably.

"Whatever happened to your handsome young footman?"

"What footman?"

"The one you eloped with."

"How did you find out about Robbie?" She hadn't told her grandfather about the footman.

"I have my sources."

She presumed he meant Sally Turner, or if not Sally,

someone else who'd been at school with her and whom he'd run into in Paris.

He yawned. "I quite understand if you don't want to talk about it."

She didn't want to talk about it.

"Tessa?"

"Robbie," she said, "had a mistress he wouldn't give up for me, so we parted company in Brighton."

He grunted, as if not entirely pleased with her answer. Gradually, his breathing evened and she knew that he slept.

Her eyelids felt heavy, and they drifted down. She hadn't thought about Robbie in a long while. He'd been a footman at her great-uncle Lorimer's place in Norfolk, not far from the last school she'd attended, the name of which escaped her for the moment. Once again, she'd been in disgrace, and was to be sent back to her guardians in Bath. This time, she had exhausted their patience, and they were marrying her to some ghastly cousin who had already buried two wives. Robbie had saved her from a fate worse than death.

He hated being a footman. The sea was his mistress and he couldn't wait to get back to her. When she heard that he'd given notice and was leaving to take ship at Portsmouth, she'd begged him to take her with him, at least as far as Brighton. The village of Arden, the only real home she'd ever known, was only six miles along the coast, and her parents' cottage, hers now, was still standing on the cliffs looking out over the sea.

She'd stayed there for only a few weeks, long enough to renew old acquaintances and arrange her escape. She'd known that it would be a while before her relatives thought to look for her there, because she'd left a note to Uncle Lorimer advising him that she and Robbie were eloping to Scotland.

She really must be incorrigible as they all said she was, but if that were the case, she didn't see anything wrong with it. If she'd done what her guardians wanted, she never would have come to know her grandfather. She'd be married to one of her beastly Beasley relatives, whose only interest in her was the dowry her grandfather had settled on her. Her guardians had made no bones about the fact that no man would want her for any other reason.

They didn't know about Paul.

A weary sigh escaped her. It had been the longest night of her life, and the most harrowing. The interview in her grandfather's study, when she'd learned that he was sending her to England, seemed to have taken place in a different age. She knew that her grandfather had her best interests at heart, but in this she had to follow her own heart.

She glanced toward the window and saw that dawn was stealing over the horizon. Her last thought before sleep claimed her was that soon it would be time to get up.

Chapter Six

~~~~~~

*T*hey traveled to Rouen in easy stages, setting out at dusk and arriving at their lodgings in the early hours of the morning. Tessa did her best to keep a guard on her tongue because she wanted Trevenan to think that she was resigned to going to England. She had a plan of sorts, but she could only pull it off if she caught him off guard.

The idea had come to her when she'd found a red velvet *pochette* her maid had packed in her grip. Inside the *pochette* were odd pieces of jewelry, and wrapped up in white satin was the red ruby broach her grandfather had given her for her birthday. "My English rose," he'd said as she'd opened the box at the breakfast table. The important thing was that Ross Trevenan had been there when her grandfather had given it to her, and he would know that she would not want to lose it.

She had worn it for two days, pinned under the lapel of her cloak, and every now and again she would finger it, as if it reminded her of her grandfather. She'd made sure that Ross Trevenan had seen this gesture. He hadn't said anything, but those hard gray eyes of his had softened. This was exactly what she wanted.

As their horses clattered over the cobblestones toward the inn where Sally and Desmond Turner were reputedly waiting for them, she surreptitiously glanced around, trying to get her bearings. She'd never been in Rouen at night, but it was hard to get lost if one could only find the cathedral. During the daylight hours, Notre Dame was a landmark that couldn't be missed. Its great towers loomed above the medieval town like a mighty fortress. Now, she could see no more than the half-timbered wattle buildings that lined one side of the street, and the lights from the many boats that were tied up at the docks. One of these boats was going to take them downriver all the way to the sea.

Not if she could help it.

Rouen was a busy commercial center, and the many taverns along the quay seemed to be doing a brisk trade, in spite of the late hour.

They drew a few looks as they cantered down the length of the quay, but no one challenged them. At last she saw what she was looking for—the sign to the road to Amiens. Just up that hill was the cathedral. It was like being handed a map. Now she knew exactly where she was.

Luck was with her. A brawl broke out between two river men and an old soldier in a tattered uniform. While everyone's attention was distracted, she tossed the broach she was clutching in her gloved hand—not the broach her grandfather had given her—as far behind her as she could manage. The sound of it bouncing on the cobblestones was quite distinct.

"My broach!" she called out, and reined in her mount. "I've lost my broach. Back there."

Ross and the grooms had also halted, and Tessa was a little behind them. She looked back. "I think I see it. Yes. There it is!"

She turned her mare's head and cantered back a few paces until she was directly opposite the road to Amiens. She was aware that Ross's gaze had narrowed on her, but she didn't allow that to panic her. Dismounting, and keeping her mare's reins in her hand, she walked toward the entrance to the street. She couldn't see the broach anywhere nor did she care, just as long as she could convince Ross Trevenan that she'd found it. She stooped down and made as if she'd picked something up.

"I found it," she called out, and she mounted up.

Ross nodded and turned away.

Tessa put heels to flanks and spurred her horse forward. With a few leaps and bounds, they made the cover of the houses and were out of Ross's sight. She heard his bellow of alarm and knew that he would be after her in a flash. Her ruse had gained her a head start of only a few seconds and she had to make the most of them. She could never hope to outrun him, but perhaps she could outwit him.

Almost at once, she reined in. Her mare reared up, and Tessa slipped from her back. Then, with a smart slap on the rear, she sent her mare careening up the hill. She had just time to dart into a side street and flatten herself against the wall when Ross and the grooms went thundering by.

Picking up her skirts, she turned in a flurry of motion and ran like a hare, expecting at any moment to hear the sounds of pursuit at her heels. Her heart was thundering against her ribs and the air rushed in and out of her lungs. When she came to a crossroads, she turned right, uphill, then left, down a narrow alley that ran behind the Rue de Gros-Horloge. Like an arrow shot from a bow, she went hurtling into the dark. No one tried to stop her. This was a residential district, and the good citizens of Rouen were safely in their beds behind locked doors.

Just as her steps were beginning to flag, to her great relief, she burst out on the market square. To her left, across from the ruins of St. Savior Church, not far from the spot where Joan of Arc was burned at the stake, was Paul's house. She was about to cross to it when she checked herself. The square was lit by lanterns hanging outside every other door, and she saw horsemen in uniform patrolling the area.

She drew back into the shadows and beat a hasty

retreat the length of one alley, coming at Paul's house from the back. Here, she paused. Satisfied that she was free and clear, she found the gate to the tiny back courtyard. It was locked. Groaning with frustration, she looked around for some means of scaling the wall.

Paul Marmont untangled himself from the woman who slept in his bed, and he raised his head to listen. Someone was pounding on the back door, and no one was going to answer it. Cursing his manservant, who slept like the dead, and cursing his friend Robert, who was visiting from Paris, he reached for his robe.

"Paul?" The woman in the bed stirred. "What is it?"

He gave her a lingering kiss. "It must be Robert. I think he has forgotten his key again."

His fingers stroked over the lush swell of her breasts and desire stirred in him once more. The pounding on the door began again. Sighing, he wrapped himself in his robe, took one of the candles from the top of a tall dresser, and went to investigate.

When he opened the back door and his visitor pushed by him, shock rooted him to the spot. "Therese," he stammered.

"Quick, shut the door!"

He didn't move, so Tessa quickly locked and barred the door. "I think I've shaken him off," she said.

"Who?"

Now that she was safe, her spirits began to revive, and she laughed. "Oh, my dear, you look as though you had seen a ghost. Let's go upstairs to the parlor and I'll tell you everything."

She stalked by him into the long, narrow corridor with the spiral staircase common to all such houses, and she made to mount the stairs.

Shaking off his surprise, he hurried after her. "Therese, you mustn't go up there!"

One hand was on the rail of the staircase, and she turned to face him. Her breathing was labored from all her exertions, not least from scaling the courtyard wall, and she took a moment before answering him.

"This isn't the time to worry about what's proper and what isn't." He seemed almost frightened, and she realized she must look like a wild woman. Not only that, but she'd roused him from his bed in the middle of the night. At the very least, he must think she'd murdered someone.

Retracing her steps, she walked into his arms. "You were right about Ross Trevenan. We were supposed to be leaving tonight. I had to see you, don't you see?" Tears began to burn her eyes, and she sniffed. It was such a relief to lay all her burdens on his broad shoulders. "Hold me, just for a moment. Oh, Paul, if only you had been there, none of this would have happened."

He was beginning to recover his wits. "My poor darling," he soothed, "you look as though you are ready to collapse." He took her firmly by the elbow and began to steer her toward the small waiting room at the front of the house. "I'll pour you some wine, shall I, and while you drink it, I shall get dressed. Then I'll join you and you can tell me all about it."

She turned her head to look at him and smiled, then her gaze went past him to the figure on the spiral staircase. A woman with red hair, dressed in nothing but a man's shirt, was leaning over the banister.

"Paul?" the redhead murmured. "Was it Robert? Did he forget his key?" She saw Tessa and drew back. "Oh," she said.

Surprised, Tessa stared at the woman curiously.

"Get back to bed, Catherine," Paul said tersely.

Without a word, the woman did an about-turn and ran up the stairs.

Tessa jerked her arm free and took a step back.

He looked at her uneasily, then his expression cleared and he grinned sheepishly. "This means nothing. She is just a diversion. You are the only woman who matters to me."

Her heart felt as though it were in a vise. She put her hand on the doorjamb to steady herself. Humiliating tears began to well, and she swallowed hard. In that moment it became crucial not to humiliate herself further, and she strove to master her emotions.

He put his hands on her shoulders. "Therese, you know I love you, only you. I was lonely without you. Catherine . . ." He shrugged carelessly. "Our relationship would have ended just as soon as you became my wife."

Her color rose and her eyes blazed. "Have you no shame? This was to be our home. You were going to bring me here as a bride. How many other women have you brought here . . ."

He said quietly, "You're not yourself. When you've had time to think about it, you'll see that has nothing to do with us. Let me get you that glass of wine. It will calm your nerves."

He was the same Paul that she remembered, handsome, soft-spoken, and the soul of kindness. He was going to give her a glass of wine to calm her nerves. This was the façade she had fallen in love with, but it was a fraud. If he cared about her, he wouldn't have betrayed her.

When he offered her the glass of wine, she began to laugh, but stopped suddenly when she detected hysteria in her voice. She inhaled a long, calming breath. "Do you think a glass of wine is going to make me feel better? I don't want to feel better, because what I feel is contempt for you, yes, and for myself. *You* drink the wine, and I hope you choke on it."

She turned smartly on her heel and made for the front door. Paul set down the glass of wine and went after her. She had pulled back the bolt when he called her name, and she turned to face him. Pride was all that was left to her, and even if it killed her, she wasn't about to let him see how desperately he had hurt her. "What is it?"

"For God's sake, calm yourself! You can't go tearing around Rouen, unescorted, at this time of night. Besides, you haven't explained why you came here."

She was a naive fool, that's why she had come here, but she wasn't going to wallow in self-pity in front of this man. "I'm going to England with Ross Trevenan," she said. "My grandfather has asked his good friend, Lady

Sayle, to sponsor me in society. I came to say good-bye. I was going to ask you to wait for me, but under the circumstances, that would be pointless, wouldn't it?"

His voice sharpened. "Trevenan is here, in Rouen?"

"I have nothing more to say to you, Paul." She was shaking when she unlocked the door and opened it. His hand reached past her and he slammed it closed. Turning, she regarded him with raised eyebrows. Temper had hardened his eyes, and the color was high on his cheeks.

"You're not going anywhere with Mr. Trevenan. I've invested too much time and trouble in you to let that happen." He softened his tone when she recoiled from him. "Therese, there is more to our marriage than what you think. We have so much in common. Don't you understand? Beaupré and Marmont—our financial assets will make us the most powerful institution in France. Think of it! We'll be fêted and cultivated by important people. What can the odd indiscretion matter compared to that? Think of the legacy we shall pass to our children."

Her expression was calm, but inwardly she writhed. "I am thinking of it, Paul, and frankly, the prospect doesn't appeal to me."

"You'll change your mind when you've had time to think about it."

His expression had taken on a sensual cast, and she knew he was going to take her in his arms and try to persuade her with kisses. He had just come from the arms of another woman. His cruelty was past bearing. With a cry of despair, she lashed out with her balled fist, catching him on the chin. As he went stumbling back, she threw the door wide and went tearing into the night.

She'd run the length of several houses when she stopped. Her heart was breaking, her knuckles were aching, and she didn't know where to turn or what to do next. All her hopes had been pinned on Paul. She pressed the heels of her hands against her eyes to stem the flow of tears.

A voice she recognized brought her head whipping up. "That took you long enough," said Ross Trevenan. "I was sure, once you had met the delectable Catherine, you would be out of there like a shot."

He was in the shadow of the overhang of the house on the corner, mounted, leaning forward slightly in the saddle, very much at his ease. In one hand, he held the reins of her own horse.

She took the few steps that separated them and looked up. "How did you know I would be here?"

"Where else would you go?"

Her voice rose. "And you knew what I would find? But how could you know?"

"Let's just say I made it my business to find out."

Her temper exploded. "You might have warned me what to expect! You might have stopped me!"

Though she was distraught, she caught the odd look in his eyes—watchful, wary, as though he couldn't make up his mind about something. Then the look was gone, and he was his old, infuriating self.

He grinned. "You never listen to anyone, Tessa, least of all me. As for stopping you, believe me, I tried. This was no part of my—"

He broke off as Paul Marmont, in breeches and white shirt, came running out of the house. Ross looked down at Tessa. "Well, which is it to be? Do you stay with Marmont or do you come with me?"

Tessa glanced from one man to the other, and she didn't know which one she hated more. In a moment of blind desperation, she reached for her horse and mounted up. All she wanted was to get away from both of them.

"Stop!" Paul cried out. "Therese, come back to the house."

Ross positioned himself between Tessa and Marmont, his attention riveted on the pistol the other man was holding. "Don't be a fool, Marmont. You've lost her, and her fortune. She'll never marry you now."

Paul Marmont's face was livid with fury. "You arranged this, didn't you?"

"No. You brought it on yourself."

The pistol was suddenly jerked up, and Ross bellowed, "Tessa, run for it!"

As her mount sprang forward, a shot from Marmont's pistol plowed into a wooden beam close by Ross's head. Infuriated by this cowardly act, he made to run Marmont down but he checked his horse when he realized that Tessa had changed direction, and was now galloping across the square, uphill, away from the docks. Cursing his own carelessness, and cursing Tessa Lorimer for putting them all in danger, he wheeled his mount to go after her.

As he went cantering across the square, windows on the upper levels were flung wide, and irate house-holders demanded to know who had awakened them from their beds. Two other riders, drawn by the report of the shot, entered the square. From their tunics, Ross recognized them as French police. He heard Paul Marmont's voice screaming something about abduction, and the next thing he knew, the police were bearing down on him with pistols at the ready. As they drew close, he saw they were little more than boys and looked frightened to death.

"Bloody farce!" he muttered, and reached in his waist-band for his own pistol. With a bellow that resembled a battle cry, he fired a warning shot over their heads. It was enough to scatter them, and he gathered his horse, then flashed between them in a leaping bound. A moment or two later he was out of the square and pounding through the narrow street Tessa had taken to the out-skirts of the city.

She was going north to Amiens. Ross bit down on a furious oath. The fool woman was actually trying to escape him! This was the last thing he'd expected after she'd discovered what her lover was up to. He'd thought she would be glad to come with him. He felt a twinge of conscience and swiftly stifled it. He hadn't planned it this way. In fact, she'd taken him by surprise when she'd bolted. In another minute or two, it would have been too late. It was fortunate for him, fortunate for them both, that he knew where Marmont lived. And now that she knew what Marmont was like, he couldn't understand what she was up to. She had nowhere to go. Then where the devil was she?

Then he saw her, a blur of motion on the road ahead. A cloud obscured the moon, and droplets of rain began to fall. As the rain increased in intensity, Ross's fury began to mount. He'd sent the grooms to the boat with their bags, but if he didn't turn up soon, he knew his friends could cast off without them. The next rendez-vous would be in Honfleur. They weren't going to make it back in time. That meant they'd have to spend the next few days on the road when they could have been settled comfortably in a warm bunk. And all this because of one unpredictable slip of a girl who didn't know when to give up.

The rain was driving so hard he could no longer see her, but he could hear the sound of her horse. He was gaining on her. A touch of his spurs had his great roan lengthening its stride, closing the gap between them.

The driving rain whipped at Tessa, tearing at her skirts, plastering her hair to her head. The slim crescent of moon had disappeared behind a cloud and she could see nothing beyond vague shadows as she followed the open road. Cold embraced her, numbing sensation, but it could not numb the tumult inside. She felt as if a splinter of glass were lodged in her heart.

It was some time before she became aware that she was being followed. She turned in the saddle and though she saw nothing, she heard the pounding of hooves. It had to be Ross Trevenan.

Spurred by this new threat, she gave her mount its head. The road dipped down into a valley and she leaned forward in the saddle, almost burying her face in her horse's mane. The little mare was swift and surefooted, but she had been ridden many hours that night, and her pace began to slow. Gradually, Trevenan's great roan drew level. Tessa touched her heels to her horse's flanks but it made no difference. Her horse was beginning to falter, and Tessa was powerless to stop Trevenan reaching over and wresting the reins from her hands. Moments later he turned both horses off the road and into an overgrown track. Behind a hedge of undergrowth, he drew rein.

When he lifted her from the saddle, all the pain and anger inside her found expression in a torrent of words. He was to blame for everything. If he hadn't come to France, none of this would have happened. He should have told her about Paul, warned her what to expect. But no, he liked nothing better than to gloat over all her misfortunes. She hated him, and would go on hating him to her dying day.

Ross heard her out in tight-lipped silence, but when the spate of hatred gave no sign of drying up, he put his hands on her shoulders and administered a rough shake. "Will you be quiet? We're not free and clear yet. Those police may have followed me. I shot at them. If they catch me, they'll shoot first and ask questions later."

His words hardly registered. He could have prevented her humiliation, but no, he had gloated afterward, when he must have known her heart was breaking. She was beyond caring what happened, beyond everything but a frenzied desire to be rid of him.

She struggled to free herself, and as his grip tightened, she lashed out with every ounce of her strength. His arms went around her, and he wrestled her to the ground. When she opened her mouth to scream, his hand clamped over her mouth and he rolled on top of her, subduing her with his weight.

"Listen!" he hissed in her ear. "Listen!"

She heard the pound of approaching hoofbeats and renewed her energies to free herself. She had done nothing wrong. If she got away from him, the police would return her to her grandfather. The more she struggled, however, the more he tightened his grip. She couldn't breathe, she couldn't see. Her heart was racing out of control. If he didn't release her, she would die.

When she stopped struggling, the pressure of his arms eased slightly. Above her, his face was a white blur. She heard the hoofbeats slow, then halt just beyond the hedge, and two voices spoke in an undertone. She couldn't make out what they were saying, but when the riders turned their horses and rode back toward Rouen, she knew they had given up the chase.

She lay there in the long wet grass, eyes closed, spent of all emotion. Nothing mattered anymore. Everything worthwhile was lost to her—her grandfather, her life in France, Paul. Ross Trevenan would take her to Lady Sayle in England. Then she hoped she would never set eyes on him again.

His hand left her mouth and he rolled off her. She remained as she was, shivering, with the rain beating down on her, wondering if she had the strength to rise, when his hands grabbed the lapels of her cloak and she was yanked to her feet. She had seen him in many moods, but never had she seen him so violently angry. He was white with it, and his eyes blazed down at her.

He had her by the scruff of the neck and he shook her with enough force to rattle her teeth. "You bitch!" he said fiercely. "You wanted them to find me. You wanted them to put a bullet through my brain."

She was dropped so suddenly, she went sprawling on the ground. Shocked at his violence, she lay there trembling.

"Up," he told her. She moved too slowly for his temper, and once again she was hauled to her feet.

She bit back a cry. This wasn't the Ross Trevenan she knew. This man was barely civilized. A picture flashed into her mind—Trevenan, naked to the waist, and muscles rippling along his powerful arms and shoulders. She had been right to fear him. One wrong move on her part, and she did not doubt he would unleash all that brute strength against her.

"Move!" he commanded, and she moved.

She didn't know where the path led, but she followed it blindly. Though she heard him behind her and the soft tread of the horses, she did not dare turn to look or ask questions.

As they came out of the undergrowth, a small squat building loomed out of the darkness. The door was hanging off, and grass and weeds choked the garden. For a moment she stood shivering, peering into the dark interior. A push sent her over the threshold, and she carefully moved deeper into the shadows, putting as much distance between herself and her captor as possible.

Chapter Seven

❦

It was some time before she heard his step, and when she saw him silhouetted in the open doorway, in spite of her chilled and sodden state, she began to perspire. Though she could barely see him, she was acutely aware of his every movement. There was no hesitation. He seemed to know exactly what he was doing, just as though he had the vision of a night predator. She heard flint striking, and Ross cursing, and after a long time a flame appeared.

Tearing her eyes from him, she chanced a quick glance around. The place was a one-room hovel, and looked as though it had been converted for use as a barn before it was abandoned. There was a broken-down feeding trough beside the hearth, some stone crocks in one corner, and a three-legged stool. The massive central post that supported the ceiling had tethering rings with long strips of rawhide attached to them for, she supposed, tying up animals. The only other sign of habitation was a rickety ladder that went up to the loft. The droplets of rainwater that leaked through cracks in the ceiling and dripped on the hard-packed earth floor only added to the dismal appearance of the place.

Her gaze jerked back to Ross. He had lit a lantern and was crouched in front of the stone hearth, absorbed in getting a fire going in the grate. He'd removed his cloak and there was an open saddlebag lying at his feet.

She found his preoccupation with this ordinary task quite comforting, and as her fears subsided, she sagged against the post with the hitching rings on it. Her eyes never wavered from him as she tried to gauge his mood. She was not left in doubt for long. Suddenly straightening, he reached for the broken trough, smashed it violently against the stone hearth, and fed it, piece by piece, to the feeble flame in the grate. When the fire blazed up, he turned his attention on her.

His lips were tightly compressed as though he were holding his temper in check. His jaw was rock-hard, and his eyes were narrowed. She found her own gaze faltering.

"Come here," he said.

"I am perfectly—"

"I said, come here."

With a confidence she was far from feeling, she slowly approached him.

"Get out of those wet things and spread them in front of the fire to dry."

She was loath to give up her cloak, not for any sane reason, but because she felt defenseless without it. She was also soaked to the skin. Shrugging out of her cloak, she did as he'd told her.

"Now the gown."

Her eyes flared in alarm, and she shook her head.

"Spare me your modesty," he snapped. "There are consequences to your actions, Tessa Lorimer, and it's your fault that we have nothing to wear but the clothes on our backs. It may suit you to come down with a lung fever, but it doesn't suit me. Now, do as I say, or I shall remove your gown for you."

Her eyes darted past him to the door.

With an expletive, he seized her, stripped the gown from her, and threw it in a heap in front of the fire.

Shamed by her near nakedness and the intimate touch

of his hands as he'd wrested the gown from her, she glared up at him with hate-filled eyes. No man had ever treated her like this. No man had ever seen her in only her underthings.

His eyes flashed with a fire to match her own. "Have done with the melodrama, Tessa. I have no interest in you as a woman, not even if you were willing. When will you stop imagining that every man is a slave to your beauty?"

When he lifted her in his arms and began to carry her to the post in the center of the room, a fresh wave of panic engulfed her. Twisting, writhing, she sought wildly to free herself. One of her blows landed and he grunted. Her satisfaction was short-lived. He set her roughly on her feet and, swiftly capturing her wrists, tethered her to the hitching ring with a long strip of rawhide.

Now that she was free of his hateful hold, she stopped struggling. They were both breathing hard, their eyes warring, his implacable, hers wildly resentful.

He spoke in a voice that was all the more menacing for being soft. "I made a promise to your grandfather and I intend to keep it. I've been too lenient with you, but that's a thing of the past. You forfeited any claim to my sympathies by the trick you just pulled."

"Now you're talking in riddles," she burst out.

"You know perfectly well what I'm talking about. You tried to attract the notice of those French police! If you'd had your way, right this minute, I would be lying in a ditch with a bullet in my brain."

"That's a lie! I wanted to escape you, yes, but I never thought . . . it never occurred to me . . ."

"You *never* think! When you are in the throes of a temper tantrum, you don't think about what damage you might do. Where were you going? What did you hope to gain?"

She'd been distraught, crushed by Paul's betrayal, and she'd acted on impulse. She shook her head, and rested her cheek against the rough beam. "I don't know where I was going," she said tonelessly. "I didn't care. I just wanted to be by myself."

"Don't start wallowing in self-pity," he snapped. "We have a long journey ahead of us, thanks to your childishness, and I'm in no mood for argument. When I say move, you'll move. What I say goes. Do you understand, Tessa?"

A moment before she'd felt a pang of remorse, thinking that he had a reason to be angry. Now, stung by his scorn, she flung up her head. "Oh, I understand," she said scathingly. "I've never doubted your capacity for violence."

"Good! See that you remember it." He stared at her for a long interval. When he spoke, his tone had softened. "It doesn't have to be like this, Tessa. Promise me that you won't try to escape again and I'll release you."

Pride dictated only one answer. "I never make promises under duress."

"Fine. Then you'll suffer the consequences."

When he turned away, she rested her cheek against the post. She heard him rummaging in the saddlebag, then jumped when she felt the soft folds of something drape around her shoulders. It was a man's coat.

Her instinct was to throw it off. She didn't want any favors from this man. Logic prevailed. The coat was dry, and it covered her scantily clad body. Not that he had spared her as much as a glance. She might have been dressed in a tent for all he noticed.

He was waiting for her to say something. Though it almost choked her to say it, she managed a terse, "Thank you," but she was looking at a point over his shoulder. He made one of those incomprehensible sounds she was becoming used to, and moved away.

She felt a quiver of uneasiness when he left her to go outside. She didn't care for the idea of being left alone, bound to a hitching post like a farm animal, with no means of defense. He returned in only a few minutes with a stack of kindling and what looked like broken fence posts. He didn't say where he'd found them and she didn't ask. When he'd banked the fire, he went up to the loft. A moment later a bale of hay came tumbling through the open trap door, then another.

In the space of a few minutes, he'd transformed that cheerless hovel into a comfortable refuge. A fire burned cheerily in the grate; the ladder with their clothes spread out on it was now on its side, angled close to the hearth; and in front of the grate, he'd spread out the straw to make a bed.

She regarded him darkly, wondering whether he was going to leave her tethered to the post all night while he stretched out on the soft bed of hay. Something else was bothering her, but she tried not to think about it.

He caught that look and came toward her. To her great surprise, he began to untie her hands. "There's a privy behind the lean-to where I've tethered our horses," he said, "but I wouldn't recommend it. Come, I'll show you where you can relieve yourself."

She didn't care for the way he could read her mind, and she answered sharply, "I don't need your escort. I'm perfectly capable of going by myself."

"Then promise you won't try to escape me again."

Having defied him once, she felt compelled to go on with it. "I told you, I never make promises under duress."

"Have it your own way. Well, don't dawdle. Let's go."

Her eyes spitting her utter disdain for him, she stalked out the door. He led her to a clump of bushes, and though he stayed close by, he had the grace to turn his back. The color was high on her cheeks when she entered the cottage, but it soon faded when he indicated that not only were they to share the bed of straw, but he was also going to bind their wrists together.

One look at his expression convinced her there was no point in arguing. If she resisted, he would only impose his will on her. He was waiting for her to back down, to promise to be a docile, spiritless cipher, then he would allow her some freedom. He could wait till Judgment Day.

With a look she hoped conveyed her utter contempt for him, she held out her wrist. When he had bound her to him, he plucked the coat from her shoulders and told her to lie down.

She crawled onto the straw awkwardly, feeling the tug on her wrist as he followed her down. A moment later he covered them first with his coat, then his cloak. She was huddled as far from him as she could manage, but it made no difference. She couldn't put any distance between them. His bound arm encircled her shoulders, and she could feel the hard length of him pressing against her flimsy drawers, the heat of his body as warm as the blaze in the grate.

This was intolerable. Their position was too intimate. She would never sleep a wink all night. But if she said anything, he would only demolish her with scathing references to her lurid imagination. He'd made it plain enough that to him she was only a child. He'd told her he wouldn't have her even if she were willing, and she believed him. Then why couldn't she be as unaffected as he?

Time passed and her eyelids grew heavy. Other thoughts began to intrude: Paul, her grandfather, Lady Sayle. She was far too weary to sort things through.

Ross locked his jaw and tried to ignore the numbness in the arm that was draped across the softly sleeping girl. It had been one hell of a night, and it wasn't over yet. She was sleeping like a babe and he was left to suffer the torments of the damned. He'd never taken a more perfect specimen of femininity to his bed, and he was constrained by circumstance and honor to act the part of the eunuch.

It might have been easier if he hadn't disrobed her. The trouble was, though they'd shared a room last night, he'd been as circumspect as a clergyman and hadn't a clue as to what she wore beneath her demure frocks. He'd taken it for granted that she would dress like a modest English girl—stays, linen shift, and reams of starched white petticoats. When he'd stripped her of her gown, what he'd got was an eyeful. She'd adopted the French custom of discarding petticoats in favor of silk drawers, clinging silk drawers that were almost transparent, and left nothing to a man's imagination. The same could be said of her frilly chemise. Just thinking about what he'd seen brought a wave of heat surging to his loins, and he was aghast at his body's response to her.

Tessa, he reminded himself, was not only a perfect specimen of femininity, she was also the most irritating female of his acquaintance. She defied him at every turn. She was a born rebel. If she'd had a grain of common sense, she would have given him the promise he'd asked for. There was no reasoning with her. The only thing that Tessa Lorimer submitted to was a strong hand and a will that was greater than her own.

He exhaled on a low groan. If his grandmother ever discovered how he'd manhandled this slip of a girl, she would be appalled. This wasn't the Ross she knew. He liked women. He respected them. He'd never been known to lay his hand in anger on a member of the weaker sex. But he'd never met a woman who hated him so much that she'd wanted to see him dead.

For several long moments he nursed his wrath, keeping it at boiling point by remembering how Tessa had tried to call out to the French police. By degrees, his wrath lost its hard edge. She'd been under a great deal of strain. He and her grandfather had decided together that the best way of handling her was to catch her off guard. They hadn't wanted to give her time to think, fearing that she would find some way of circumventing their plans. So he'd carried her off in the middle of the night. And then there was the episode with Paul Marmont. Perhaps he should have warned her. But it hadn't occurred to him that she'd run away like that. Evidently, her feelings for Marmont went much deeper than he'd imagined. Too bad he hadn't had a few minutes more to teach that adolescent Romeo the lesson he so richly deserved.

Suddenly she turned into him and he went as rigid as a board. Her free arm went around his waist and she nestled closer. "Ross?" she queried softly.

It was the first time she'd used his Christian name, and he gazed down at her as though she'd taken leave of her senses.

When no one answered, her eyelashes fluttered. "Tell me it was a bad dream," she whispered brokenly. "Ross?"

Something moved inside his chest, and he couldn't resist pressing a chaste kiss on her brow. "It was a bad dream," he said softly. "Hush now. I'm here. Everything will be all right."

His answer quieted her and she relaxed against him. Ross was anything but relaxed. Her softness, her scent, her susceptibility, were wreaking havoc with his control. He wanted to kiss the tears from her lashes. He wanted to lay his hand on her satiny skin and know her intimately. He wanted to gather her close and protect her from everything.

Liar, an inner voice chided. He wanted to protect her from everything but himself.

Appalled by that thought, he reached over and swiftly untied their bonds. Then he rolled free of their makeshift covers and rose to his feet. He was breathing heavily, and that, too, appalled him. Turning away with a scowl, he banked the fire and stood with one arm braced against the mantel, staring into the flames, trying to think of anything except Tessa.

It was almost a relief to think of Cassie. His wife had been the antithesis of Tessa. He'd never heard her speak a word in anger. She was sweet and soft-spoken and had never once irritated him. It wasn't that she was spiritless. It was simply that Cassie had delighted in pleasing others. He thought about Cassie for a long time, and the pain he'd learned to control suddenly flared up as though everything had happened yesterday.

He'd been twenty-eight when they'd wed, and Cassie had been seven years younger. He hadn't been in love with her then. He'd married because it was the duty of a man in his position to marry and produce heirs, and Cassie was an ideal choice for a wife. She came of good family, she was well mannered and dutiful, and sweetly lovely, with dark hair and eyes as blue as cornflowers. In Cassie, he'd found more than he'd bargained for. He'd found love.

Love was something he'd never expected. In his world, marriage was an alliance, a means of consolidating a dynasty; couples lived separate lives and pursued their own interests. He'd never questioned this arrangement because he hadn't known anything different, not until after he'd married Cassie.

He had loved Cassie, and she had loved him. Life couldn't get any better. They'd been married for almost a year when Desmond Turner first approached him.

He'd heard of Desmond Turner and his unusual occupation, and his curiosity was roused. Desmond began by telling him of a strange coincidence. In the summer of '95, he said, when he was a temporary clerk to his uncle, who was the Chief Justice for the county of Esher, he'd been present at the inquest into the drowning death of a young girl, a pupil at Fleetwood Hall. There were three witnesses to this tragic event, possibly four, all of them boarders at the school.

This meant nothing to Ross until Desmond began to reel off their names. One of the girls was Ross's wife, Cassie Mortimer, as she was then called. It was the only name Ross recognized.

Time passed, said Desmond, and the facts surrounding the inquest slipped to the back of his mind. Then about three months ago, he was employed to investigate the accidental death of a young woman, whose grief-stricken parents were not entirely satisfied with the coroner's verdict. The dead girl's name was Margaret Hemmel, and she had been one of the witnesses to the accident at Fleetwood Hall.

At this point in Desmond's narrative, Ross was beginning to feel uneasy. It was becoming clear to him that Desmond felt Cassie was in some kind of danger.

Of the three known witnesses to the drowning accident, Desmond said, only one was still alive—Cassie, Ross's wife. The other two had died in the last year, and in each case the coroner had brought in a verdict of accidental death. Desmond, however, was not satisfied with this. He had nothing concrete to go on, but he'd never felt comfortable with the "accident" at Fleetwood Hall, and now all his instincts warned him that things were not as they seemed. That's why he had decided to approach Ross. There was one other girl, Tessa Lorimer, who might or might not have been a witness to the drowning, but so far he had been unable to trace her.

Ross had been skeptical. It didn't make sense to him.

Why would anyone wait four or five years before eliminating witnesses to an accident that everyone had forgotten? He'd questioned Cassie about the accident, but since he didn't want to frighten her, he had not mentioned Desmond's suspicions or the girls who had died. The more he thought about it, the more convinced he was that Desmond Turner was making too much of a series of coincidences.

Two months later, Ross had been the one to find Cassie's body floating in the pool beneath the waterfall.

It had been her birthday and he'd planned a surprise celebration. He'd told Cassie to make herself scarce for an hour or two. He could still remember that moment. She'd laughed up at him, knowing full well what he was up to. And he'd kissed her cheek carelessly, not understanding the significance of the moment. He would never see her alive again. When two hours had passed and she had not returned, he went looking for her.

He couldn't remember much of the days that followed, except that he'd been like a man demented. He wouldn't accept that it was an accident, though that was the consensus. It seemed that Cassie had taken one of the small punts out on the lake and had overturned it. He knew she wouldn't do such a thing. She was terrified of water.

He remembered what Desmond Turner had told him. He'd been skeptical of those suspicions, and Cassie had paid the price.

For weeks after, he'd locked himself in his library, drinking himself into a constant state of oblivion. The guilt was a brutal weight he had never succeeded in shaking off. He hadn't blamed only himself. He'd cursed the powers that be for taking Cassie. So much loveliness, so much kindness snuffed out, and he could not see the reason for it. When he'd buried Cassie, he'd buried more than his wife. He'd learned by that time that she carried his child. He remembered the unreasoning resentment he'd harbored against Tessa Lorimer, the girl who had been spared.

When he emerged from the library, he'd been a changed man with only one thought. He was going to find the monster who had killed Cassie and bring him to justice. Desmond Turner agreed to help him. They had only one lead, and that was Tessa Lorimer, and she seemed to have disappeared off the face of the earth. And so they started the painstaking task of tracking her down. As their investigation progressed, they were electrified to discover that someone else was trying to find her, someone who was one step ahead of them. If Tessa had not escaped to France, she might have met with the same fate as Cassie.

It sobered him to think that he was taking her back to England where a murderer was, in all probability, waiting in the wings, but he couldn't see a way around it, not if Tessa were ever to be free of the threat that was hanging over her. It was what her grandfather wanted. It also suited Ross's purposes since he would never rest until he had brought Cassie's murderer to justice.

Tessa was the key to unlocking the mystery to what had happened all those years ago. Cassie had been sure that Tessa had been present that night. Not only had Cassie recognized Tessa's voice, but she'd also seen her later. He didn't know why Tessa denied being there.

He stared unseeing into the fire, going over in his mind the sequence of events at Fleetwood as described by both Desmond and Cassie. It had been the end of term. At Miss Oliphant's, it was a tradition of the senior girls who were leaving to bathe in the lake. This was more than just a prank. These girls were going out into the world and this was like a sacred ritual. Which explained why Cassie had taken part. He couldn't imagine her breaking the rules under any other circumstances.

Four senior girls went out that night. When they were bathing, they discovered that someone was spying on them. They heard someone splashing around in the water on the other side of the lake, then they heard a girl crying for help. They didn't see Tessa—it was too dark—but they recognized her voice and assumed she was playing one of her famous practical jokes on them. They weren't alarmed. She'd done this kind of thing before, and the water in the lake wasn't deep. So they all went back to the school, all except Becky Fallon. When Cassie realized Becky was missing, she went back to look for her. That's when she'd seen Tessa, coming from the other side of the lake.

What had Tessa seen that made her deny being there? He knew he'd never get anything out of her, but he hoped that Sally Turner would manage it. Tessa seemed to like Sally as much as she disliked him.

It didn't matter how she felt about him. He had promised her grandfather that he would protect her with his life and so he would, with or without Tessa's cooperation.

After Cassie's death he'd changed in more ways than one. He'd gone through hell when he'd lost her, and he never wanted to love anyone like that again. There had been women since then, many women, but no one who could touch his heart, and if he'd found such a woman, he would have avoided her like the plague. He knew he must marry again for the sake of an heir, but this time he would keep his heart intact. His wife would preside with grace over his many establishments, but otherwise they would lead separate lives and pursue their own interests. It was enough.

Tessa moaned in her sleep and he crossed to her. She'd kicked off the covers and lay revealed in her decadent French underthings. *Minx*, he thought, and wondered why the hell he was grinning.

After he covered her with the coats, he positioned the ladder so that he could tie her wrist to it securely, but not too tightly. He was weary and if she awoke when he was sleeping, he wouldn't put it past her to creep out and take off with both horses, leaving him stranded. She'd have a hard time creeping out with a ladder attached to her wrist.

Her cloak was dry, and he wrapped himself in it, then stretched out in front of the fire. He was remembering how she'd said his name, *Ross*, like a trusting child who looked to him for protection. It was all in his imagination, of course. In full possession of her faculties, Tessa wouldn't take a crust of bread from him if she were starving.

He let out a long sigh. Somehow, they'd got off on the wrong foot. When he'd first seen her in her grandfather's house, something had moved deep inside him. Then a different emotion had moved him. He'd been bitter, thinking that it was so unjust that she lived while Cassie lay in her grave. It was an ugly thought that he'd instantly crushed, but perhaps he had betrayed himself. For whatever reason, Tessa had taken an instant dislike to him, which made things difficult, since now the only way to control her was to break her will.

Rising on one elbow, he looked over at her. In sleep she looked like an angel. It was too bad it couldn't last. He huddled down and closed his eyes.

Chapter Eight

❧❧❧

*I*t took them three days to reach Honfleur, three days of hard riding and sleeping rough with little protection from the elements. Ross had only a little money in his pockets, and he used it to buy food from isolated farmhouses. Because he had no way of knowing what story Paul Marmont might have told the authorities, he was keeping his distance from towns and villages, fearing the police might be watching for them. There was also the problem of Tessa, who could not be trusted.

She was silent and uncomplaining, however, and though at first this was a relief, he began to be uneasy about the change in her. She barely looked at him, and when they stopped for the night, he had to snap at her to get her to eat. She seemed detached, as though she'd removed herself to a faraway place where nothing could touch her. It made him feel helpless. He wanted to comfort her, but he knew she would never accept that from him.

They arrived in Honfleur after dark. He went straight to the livery stable in the marketplace where he stabled the horses. After paying his last few coins to the attendant, he took Tessa by the wrist and hustled her out the door. Already, his spirits were lifting. Soon, they would be with friends. They would bathe and change their clothes and have something hot to eat. That ought to make Tessa feel better. Then, they would slip away to England.

Keeping to narrow passageways, he made for a small tavern at one end of the dock. The taproom was smoky and crowded with patrons. Ross passed it and, with Tessa in tow, made for the stairs. He rapped on a door and was almost immediately admitted.

It was a small parlor, shabby but cozy, with a fire burning in the grate. Three people were there to greet them. Tessa was expecting to see Sally and Desmond Turner, but all the same, she nearly broke down at the sight of their friendly faces. All the anguish of lost love, all the emotions she had ruthlessly frozen these last several days began to thaw as Sally's arms went around her. Then Sally remarked that she'd seen better dressed scarecrows, and Tessa found herself laughing.

As she was pushed into a chair beside the fire, and Sally thrust a glass of something into her hand, she looked curiously at the third occupant of the room. At first, she had taken him for a *contrabandier*, one of the daring French smugglers who plied their trade between France and England. He was of medium height, dark, and dressed in a homespun jerkin and grubby twill trousers. But now she saw that she had been wrong. His English was flawless and he and Ross Trevenan were laughing and pounding each other on the back, talking about mutual friends. It came to her then that Paul had been right. Trevenan wasn't an American; he was English. He'd only played the part of an American so that he could move freely around France.

Trevenan then greeted Desmond almost as warmly as he'd greeted the man he called "Julian." Somehow, she'd never pictured Ross Trevenan as anybody's close friend. He'd always been so aloof and distant. This reunion made him seem almost human.

When the greetings were over, in answer to a question, Ross explained that the reason they'd missed the rendezvous at Rouen was because Tessa's horse had bolted and when he'd caught up to her, they'd had the bad luck to run into a French patrol.

Ross then introduced Tessa to his friend. His name was Julian Percy, and it was he who had helped Ross arrange their escape, something they'd done several times before for others.

"But never," said Julian, "have I had the pleasure of assisting two more lovely and charming ladies."

He then captured Tessa's hand and raised it to his lips. His was another friendly face, and she couldn't help giving him a warm smile. He wasn't handsome. His nose was too big; his mouth was too generous. But his eyes were beautiful, dark blue and thick-lashed, with a wicked twinkle lurking in their depths.

He released her hand. "Ross," he said, "you have been misleading me. You told me your ward was little more than a child."

Tessa's smile became even warmer. Here was a gentleman who knew how to treat a lady! But how like Trevenan to relegate her to the unflattering role of ward.

She didn't correct Mr. Percy, but she threw Ross a barbed look. He wasn't looking at her. He was looking at Mr. Percy, and his expression was no longer so friendly.

But before she could think about this, Trevenan took charge and began issuing orders. She was to go with Sally, and when she was bathed and changed, they would all sit down together and have something to eat. Desmond was to order their bathwater and dinner and inform the grooms where their horses were stabled. The grooms were heading back to Paris early the next morning. Tessa was so tired she hardly listened. All she wanted was to curl up on a soft feather bed and sleep.

Julian led Ross to a small bedchamber across the hall. As soon as the door closed, Ross began to peel out of his clothes.

"Her horse didn't bolt," he said. "She tried to escape me. However, it's true that we ran into a French patrol, and they cut us off. It's been a damned uncomfortable journey, let me tell you," and he launched into a description of the episode with Paul Marmont, as well as all the discomforts he'd suffered because of one infuriating girl.

He broke off when his bathwater arrived, and was not pleased to discover that all that could be spared after the young mademoiselle's bath had been drawn was a kettle of tepid water. Sloshing it into the china basin on the washstand, he began to soap himself with a coarse cloth.

Julian lounged on the bed and eyed his friend curiously. After Cassie had died so tragically, no woman had meant much to Ross, not even the ones he took to his bed. Now, however, Julian had watched his friend with Tessa Lorimer and was both amused and awed at how much emotion the "infuriating girl" had stirred up. And he hadn't missed the jealous look Ross had shot him when he'd flirted with Tessa.

He spoke now with studied casualness. "I met Amanda Chalmers just before I left for France. She's curious about your absence from town. In fact, I'd say the lovely Amanda is downright suspicious."

"Suspicious?"

Julian grinned. "She thinks you're involved with another woman."

"I'm not. Not that it has anything to do with Amanda. I ended our affair months ago."

"I'm surprised."

"Why are you surprised?"

"I don't think she knows it. It might be best if you ended the affair again, so there's no doubt in the lady's mind where you stand. I'd advise you to be careful, though. It always pays to be chivalrous."

Now it was Ross's turn to grin. "I am chivalrous," he said. "In fact, chivalry is my middle name."

"I'm glad to hear it, because Amanda Chalmers has all the instincts of a viper, from what I've observed. And don't forget, she has friends in high places. If she wanted to, she could make life very uncomfortable for you."

Ross had soaped his face and his razor was in his hand. He turned to look at Julian. "I know how to look after myself."

"I wasn't thinking of you so much as Tessa. If Amanda began to suspect that you were in love with the girl—"

"In love? *With Tessa Lorimer?*" Ross laughed. "You must have sawdust where your brains should be." He turned back to the mirror and began to shave.

After a moment Julian said, "Is this Paul Marmont likely to be a problem?"

Ross nicked his jaw. Muttering, he dabbed at the blood with the washcloth.

"Was that yes or no?"

Ross snorted. "How can he be a problem when he's here and she will be in England?"

"He might come to England looking for her. It wouldn't be hard to do, with all the French refugees in England right now."

"If he shows his face in England, I'll call him out so fast the bastard won't know what's hit him."

Julian came off the bed tisking. "You've nicked yourself again. Here, let me do it before you turn your face into beefsteak."

Ross sank down on the bed, and Julian began to shave him with the finesse of a barber. "Do you know, Ross, those words have the ring of a jealous lover? Hold steady! I almost sliced off your nose. Don't worry. It's only a small nick. It's hardly bleeding."

Ross's hand came up and he grasped Julian's wrist, preventing him from plying the razor. "Let's get one thing straight, Julian. Tessa Lorimer is my responsibility and I'm going to guard her as though my life depended on it. It's what I promised her grandfather."

Julian's brows rose. "And that's your only interest in the girl?"

"Oh, for God's sake!" Ross jumped to his feet. "Tessa Lorimer means nothing to me. How many times do I have to say it? She's a tiresome baggage. I feel responsible for her, and that's all there is to it." He strode to the mirror above the washstand and eyed the nicks on his face. "Beefsteak!" he muttered, then turned to look at Julian. "Tessa Lorimer is—"

"Yes, yes, I know!" Grinning unrepentantly, Julian

lolled on the bed and mocked Ross's glare. "She's a spoiled beauty, full of her own conceit. Isn't that how the litany goes?"

Ross opened his mouth, then thought better of what he was going to say. In the three days he and Tessa had been on the road, she'd ridden as hard as he, had shared his meager rations, and not once had she complained. She hadn't acted like a spoiled beauty then. It was perverse of him, he knew, but he couldn't help feeling mildly irritated. She hadn't complained because she saw him as an insensitive brute.

He sighed, wondering if she would ever soften toward him. There'd been odd moments, when she'd said his name with an appeal in her voice. *Ross.* Now *that* Tessa was one he could warm to. When he felt his lips turn up, he frowned and glanced at Julian to find that his friend was watching him as a cat watches a mouse hole.

"What I think of her is irrelevant," Ross said. "She's in my charge, and that's what matters."

"How much have you told her?"

"Only what we agreed—that I'm escorting her to Lady Sayle's for a season in London." He reached for the set of fresh clothes that were laid out on a chair and began to dress. "Once we are home, I'll explain the details."

"Why not tell her now?"

Ross pictured Tessa in a full-blown temper, and he suppressed a shudder. "Because," he said, "she'd only try to escape me again. Things will be different in England. She can't just hop back to France at the drop of a hat. Now what the devil are you laughing at?"

Julian bounded from the bed and flung an arm around Ross's shoulders. "Everything. Nothing. If you don't know, I can't explain it."

Ross gave his friend a hard stare. "Careful, Julian. Two can play at that game."

"I don't know what you mean."

"Don't you?"

The smile left Julian's eyes. "If you're suggesting that there is anything between Sally Turner and me, you need your head examined."

This time, the smile was on Ross's face. "I'm not suggesting anything," he said. "Shall we join the ladies?"

They ate in the small parlor, a hearty supper of vegetable soup and rabbit stew with thick slices of coarse black bread washed down with a glass or two of wine. Ross's gaze frequently flitted to Tessa, and though he was pleased that the wine had brought the color back to her cheeks, he also saw that she was merely toying with her food. He hoped her listlessness was nothing more serious than fatigue.

Her listless manner disappeared when they rose from the table and Julian indicated that it was time to go.

Tessa's face paled, and her eyes went wide. She spoke in a faltering tone. "Go? Where?"

"To the boat that will take us to my yacht," Julian replied. He was checking his pistol and hadn't noticed Tessa's reaction. "Wear your warmest cloaks, ladies. It can get very cold at night in the middle of the ocean."

Tessa steadied herself with both hands braced against the table. "You're taking a boat out in the dark? Wouldn't it make more sense to wait till morning?"

The edge of panic in her voice brought all eyes to her. Sally moved first. With a reassuring smile, she linked her arm through Tessa's. "You and I think alike," she said. "I'm a landlubber too. But really, it's quite safe. And I'll be with you."

Julian said, "You'll be fine, Tessa. My yacht has all the comforts of home."

Tessa barely glanced at him. Her eyes were wide and fixed on Ross.

He said gently, "Why don't you all get started and Tessa and I will catch up to you? We'll meet you at the jetty. This won't take long."

There was a moment's awkwardness. Sally made a halfhearted protest but was silenced by a look from her brother, and with a last lingering look at Tessa, she followed the gentlemen from the room.

When the door closed, Ross said softly, "What is it,

Tessa? Why are you so afraid? You crossed the Channel when you came to France, didn't you?"

She moistened her lips. "That was different. It was daylight."

"How strange. I thought smugglers plied their trade under cover of darkness."

She pressed a hand to her eyes. "I don't know. We were supposed to be a French fishing boat. We let down nets and caught fish, and sailed into the harbor with the fishing fleet."

"That was a clever ploy, but it won't help us. Julian's yacht is waiting for us off the coast of France. If we don't make the rendezvous it will return to England without us, and there won't be another rendezvous for three days. We must leave tonight."

"You don't understand," she cried out. "Even in daylight, I'm terrified of water, but at night—" She shook her head. "I can't, Ross. Please don't ask it of me."

"Why?" he queried in the same soft, persistent tone. "Why are you afraid of water, Tessa?"

"I don't know why. There's no explaining it."

He did not reply to this, and she saw that he didn't believe her. Still, she hesitated. She's never confided her fears to anyone, and this man was the last person she wanted to confide in.

He made a half turn toward the door. "We haven't got time for—"

"Wait!" She saw that her fingers were curled like talons, and she made an effort to uncurl them. She looked up at Ross, took a deep breath, and began to speak. "There was a girl at school who drowned at night while she was out swimming. Her name was Becky Fallon. Ever since, I've had nightmares about it. I'm with her in the water, you see, and suddenly I can't find her." She folded her arms across her breasts and hugged herself. "I'm hoarse with calling her name. Then I start to call for help. There are people there, but they walk away laughing. My lungs are fit to burst, but I keep on diving, trying to find her. But all I come up with are reeds and debris. I just can't find her. It's so dark, you see, I can't see anything. Then I go under, and I'm the one who is drowning. And no one will help me."

Ross waited and when she remained silent, he said, "Who are these people who refuse to help you?"

She shook her head. "People I've met during the day. They could be anyone at all. You. Sally and Desmond. Anyone."

"Then what happens?"

"That's when I wake up."

"Are you sure it's a dream, Tessa?"

She cried out, "I wasn't there when Becky drowned! I swear I wasn't! Why will no one believe me?" Her passionate outburst shocked them both. Coming to herself, she gave a shaken laugh. "I beg your pardon. None of this can mean anything to you. But you must see that I can't go with you."

His voice was kind, but his words were relentless. "If I had known about your fear before now, I would have arranged things differently. As it is, we have no choice. Come, Tessa. The others are waiting for us."

She saw from the hard set of his face that nothing she said would make him change his mind. For a few moments she debated defying him. She could scream for help, and when the landlord came running, she would demand his protection, but even as the thought occurred to her, she dismissed it. The last time she'd defied him, she'd only put his life in danger, and that wasn't what she wanted. She just wanted to be free.

"Come!" said Ross, and he held the door for her.

One of the grooms was waiting in the corridor. He handed Ross Tessa's cloak. She made no protest as he draped it around her shoulders and fastened it under her chin.

"Good girl," he said, and smiled.

The urge to spit in his handsome face crossed her mind, but only briefly. She'd bared her heart to him, and shared something she had never shared with a living soul. And this was all she got for it. Squaring her shoulders, she followed the groom down the stairs.

At the jetty, the others were already sitting in an open rowing boat. Tessa clenched down on her teeth to stop their chattering. Ross handed her in and quickly followed her down. He maneuvered her into the seat in the bow and sat beside her, crowding her into the corner.

Everyone had been warned not to make a sound for fear of rousing the watch. The oars dipped soundlessly into the water, and the boat slipped into the stream. Tessa stared straight ahead, using every ounce of will to control the rising panic. Already she was breaking out in a sweat, and her lungs were tightening horribly, as though they would burst. Ross put an arm around her shoulders and she shivered convulsively.

"It will be better when we reach the yacht," he whispered. "I'm here, Tessa. Nothing can hurt you."

She couldn't find the breath to throw his words back in his face. The dream was closing in on her. She could feel the slime at the bottom of the lake, hear Becky thrashing as she screamed her name. There was a roaring in her ears, and a mist blinding her eyes. She grasped something solid, and held on as though her life depended on it.

Ross made no protest as her nails dug into his hand. He tightened the arm around her shoulders, bringing her closer to the warmth of his body. It was so dark, he could not see her face, but he felt her tension. He had not understood the depth of her terrors, and was cursing himself for putting her in this situation.

When they came to the yacht, Julian quickly climbed the ladder, then reached down to take Tessa from Ross's arms. Though not a word had been spoken in that short journey, it was obvious to everyone that something was wrong with Tessa. When Ross landed on the deck, he gathered Tessa in his own arms and went directly below.

She hadn't fainted, but she seemed to be in shock. His heart was hammering as he deposited her gently on the bunk and went to fetch a glass of brandy from the bottom drawer of Julian's desk. A moment later he held her head steady while he forced her to drink it.

As Ross tilted the glass, brandy entered her mouth and burned a path down her throat. Her eyes stung and she weakly tried to push the glass away. "No," she protested.

"More," he told her. "Only a little more and you'll feel much better."

She had no choice but to obey him. Gulping, sputtering, she drained the glass. Only then did Ross release her. For a long time she remained as she was, propped against the pillows, eyes tightly closed. Gradually, her breathing evened and her lashes fluttered open. Ross's face hovered over her, white as chalk and strangely anxious.

Ross tried for a smile. He gestured with one arm. "It's just like being in your own bedchamber," he said. "See, all the comforts of home."

There was no answering smile from Tessa. "Don't leave me," she whispered.

He grasped her hand. "I wouldn't dream of it."

With a little sigh, she turned her face to the wall. Ross sat on the edge of the bunk, staring down at her. From time to time he smoothed back tendrils of red-gold hair that curled on her cheek.

This was how Julian found them when he entered the cabin some time later. Ross put a finger to his lips, and ushered Julian into the gangway, leaving the door open.

"We're free and clear," said Julian. "How is she?"

"Asleep."

"What brought this on?"

"She's terrified of water."

Julian looked over Ross's shoulder at the sleeping girl. "Like Cassie," he murmured. He looked at Ross. "So apparently she was there the night Becky Fallon drowned?"

"I'm almost sure of it. But she truly believes she wasn't there. She has nightmares about it, and that's as much as she is willing to admit, even to herself."

Julian let out a low whistle. "So she's not going to tell us anything we don't already know?"

"She may, in time, if the memory comes back to her."

A movement from the bed silenced them. "Ross?" Tessa's voice.

"I'm here." Ross slowly, and quite deliberately, shut the door on his friend's face, shutting him out of his own cabin. He crossed to the bunk. Tessa was restless, but she had not wakened. When he put his hand on her brow, she quieted.

He discovered that whenever he moved away from her, she became restless again. Eventually, giving up all pretense at chivalry, he stretched out beside her.

He dozed. When he wakened, she was nestled against him. Her lips were so close to his that he couldn't resist kissing her.

When he set his mouth to hers, she opened to him, warmly, willingly, and he was tempted to take the kiss deeper. Sanity prevailed. If he didn't take care, he would find himself making love to her in earnest, then he would be forced to marry her, which was the last thing he wanted. Tessa was the kind of woman who would demand a man's heart . . . and he didn't have a heart to give.

She was soft, warm, willing—with a muffled curse, he extricated himself from her arms and slid from the bed. For all he knew, she might be dreaming she was in Paul Marmont's arms.

She sighed and whispered a name, *his* name. Moments later she was making snuffling sounds that came perilously close to snoring.

Damn and blast the woman! His body was on fire for her, and she didn't even wake when he kissed her. Even her snoring didn't put him off.

Smiling in spite of himself, he gently drew the covers over her, and wrapping his cloak around himself, he stretched out on the hard, uncomfortable floor.

Tessa came awake on a cry. Her heart was racing. Her skin was slick with perspiration. She'd had the dream again. It had started on a happy note with Nan and her setting off from the chapel on one of their midnight adventures. But it had ended up at the lake, as it always did.

Nan Roberts had been her special friend at Miss Oliphant's, but until recently, she'd mostly forgotten about her. Now, suddenly, she was dreaming of Nan, and the old nightmare had come back to haunt her.

Sighing, she turned on her side. Bright sunshine was streaming through a porthole window. For a moment she didn't know where she was, and she lay there, quietly, contemplating the window. Something stirred at the back of her mind. Ross Trevenan had kissed her and she had wanted him to.

Sickening!

Then everything came back to her in a rush, and she jerked to her elbows. When she saw that she was the only one in the cabin, she sighed in heartfelt relief. She had a vague recollection of begging him not to leave her and hoped it was all part of her dream.

When she went on deck, she found the others standing in the prow, looking out toward England. Ross caught sight of her first and came to meet her. There was a moment of awkwardness, when she feared that her dream might have been rooted in reality, but his expression seemed the same as always and she was reassured.

"How do you feel?" he asked.

She looked out at the choppy sea and waited for the trembling to begin. Nothing happened. She filled her lungs with refreshing sea air. She could feel the boat rolling beneath her feet and hear the raucous call of gulls overhead. She wasn't the least bit panicked. In fact, she felt no fear.

He was smiling at her. She gave him back a brilliant smile before she remembered he was her mortal enemy. "How do you think I feel?" she snapped. "I have a headache from the brandy you forced down my throat. I see nothing to laugh at in that."

"No, you wouldn't," he replied, but the foolish grin was still on his face.

Tossing her head, she went to join Sally at the rail.

"Look," said Sally, and pointed. "Home."

The white cliffs of Dover rose up majestically in front of them.

"England," said Tessa, and all the brightness went out of the morning.

Chapter Nine

The dowager Marchioness of Sayle was not in her usual, happy frame of mind, though she was careful to hide this from her guests. She was worried. She'd come up to London to get the house ready for her grandson's arrival. Ross should have returned from France three days ago with Miss Lorimer. His carriage and coachmen had been waiting for him in Dover for the past week. But there was no sign of him, so she'd asked her dear friend, George Naseby, if he would go down to Dover and see if there was any news. She wasn't sure if Ross would approve of her taking George into her confidence, but she'd felt she had no other choice. She'd known George for close to fifty years and trusted him implicitly.

As much as possible, she had done exactly as her grandson had told her, which was to stay out of the public eye until he and Miss Lorimer had arrived in England. No one was supposed to know he was in France. There were too many French spies around and an incautious remark in the wrong ear could lead to disaster. If she had to, she could say that he was touring the west country, and he would be bringing his ward with him when he returned.

Her first caller that afternoon was Ross's brother-in-law, the Viscount Pelham. As Cassie's step-brother, Larry was family. He was an engaging character whom she truly liked. Ross, on the other hand, frequently lost patience with the boy. He was Larry's trustee and it did not sit well with him that Larry could not live within his means. The viscount was forever running up debts and turning to Ross to settle them.

Mrs. Amanda Chalmers and her cousin, Mr. Bertram Gibbon, were also visiting that afternoon, but had been admitted only because they'd arrived on the heels of the viscount. Lady Sayle could not insult them by turning them away.

Now, the dowager was sipping her tea and watching Larry flirt with Amanda. There wasn't much hope that anything would come of it. Not that the dowager wanted it to. She really liked Larry and was convinced that the right woman would be the making of him, but that woman was not Amanda Chalmers. Besides, Amanda had set her sights on Ross.

Lady Sayle did not like Amanda Chalmers. There were many reasons for this, not least the dowager's odd notion that one could tell a lot about a person's character just by studying his or her face. Though Ross poked fun at her, she insisted she'd made a science of it, and was rarely proved wrong.

As she covertly examined Amanda's face, she felt mildly repelled. The beauty was flawed by a certain coldness of expression. The green eyes were wide and luminous, but they could narrow suddenly with a cold, calculating light. Amanda's smooth complexion was never marred by a freckle; her coiffure of raven-black ringlets was always impeccable, even when there was a wind blowing. All that aside, Amanda's bones were in the wrong conjunction, and that settled the matter in the dowager's mind. Lady Sayle summed up that beautiful face as shrewd, ambitious, and intimidating, and everything she knew about the lady supported that view.

Amanda Chalmers had been the driving force behind her late husband's successful political career. Poor Freddie would have been just as happy spending his days in the country with his horses and dogs. Amanda had had other ideas. She'd wanted a milieu where she could hold center stage. She'd wanted to be one of the lionesses of political circles. And she had succeeded. She could number among her friends the Prince of Wales himself. But the prince was not on the marriage mart, and Amanda's eye had fallen on Ross.

There was a momentary lull in the conversation, and Amanda's eyes suddenly narrowed on her hostess in a way that made the dowager hope she had all her wits about her. Amanda said, "I hear that your goddaughter is expected to arrive in town at any moment. I don't believe I've had the pleasure of meeting her."

Tessa's visit was no secret. In fact, on Ross's advice, the dowager had mentioned it to some of her cronies before she'd come up to town, to prepare the way for Tessa's arrival. But now that she didn't know whether Ross and Tessa were still in France, she needed to be cautious. Tessa, she began, wasn't exactly her goddaughter, she was Ross's ward.

She told the story much as Ross had told it to her, leaving out references to France and Tessa's escapades. She knew only the bare facts, which was that Ross had become a close friend of Tessa's grandfather, who had asked Ross to take care of the girl.

"As far as I know," she concluded, "Tessa has never been to London, so of course you have never met her." There was a twinkle in her eye. It had struck her that Amanda had misconstrued the situation. She knew a jealous woman when she saw one.

"Tessa Lorimer?" Bertram Gibbon, Amanda's cousin, polished his quizzing glass with a snowy white handkerchief. He was in his early thirties, had light brown hair that was receding at the temples and a muscular physique that a younger man would have envied. Lady Sayle liked him no better than Amanda. She'd heard that he mistreated his wife. In addition to this, the dowager had made a study of his face, and she didn't care much for it either.

"Lorimer?" he repeated. "Would those be the Norfolk Lorimers? I met an Admiral Lorimer once."

"The Sussex Lorimers," answered the dowager.

"I don't think I know them."

And Lady Sayle was not about to enlighten him. Ross did not want anyone prying too closely into Miss Lorimer's background. Tessa, he'd said, in spite of her youth, had managed to acquire something of a reputation. All that was behind her, and he was sure that Tessa, given a firm hand to guide her, would soon settle down.

"Her father was a naval officer, I believe," she said vaguely, "and her grandfather is a banker."

"Are you saying the girl is an heiress, Aunt Em?"

She turned her head to look at the viscount, and couldn't help responding to his rakish grin. "If she were, you would be the last person I'd tell," she retorted.

There was no real censure in her voice. With Larry, everything was a game. He was a self-confessed fortune hunter, but because he was very young, no one took him seriously—no one, except Ross.

He strolled to the sideboard and, very much at home, lifted the sherry decanter, offered it to Bertram, then topped up his own glass. "Wouldn't have done any good anyway," he lamented. "Heiresses can look higher than a mere viscount."

"Whatever happened to Miss Fairchild?" asked the dowager, referring to last season's matrimonial prize whom Larry had shamelessly pursued.

He shrugged. "Her father found a better bargain. Didn't I tell you? She's to marry old Doncaster before the year is out."

"And Doncaster is an earl?"

"Precisely."

"Come now, Larry," interjected Bertram with a smile, "it's no secret that ever since Miss Fairchild jilted you, you have been paying court to Miss Simpson. I hear you have made quite an impression on her."

"My effect on the ladies is not in question," Larry

replied. "Now if I could only make an impression on their fond papas, maybe I would get somewhere." He made a face, and everyone laughed.

Amanda, who had been waiting for an opening, said casually, "There are lots of rumors going around. Take Ross, for instance. Some say he's in Ireland. Another rumor has it he's gone to Cornwall. The only thing we know for sure is that he has deserted all his friends since Lady Brewster's ball, and that was three months ago. What should we make of that, Lady Sayle?"

Lady Sayle had her answer ready, the one Ross had given her. Fortunately, before Amanda could pursue it further, the viscount chose that moment to take his leave. The dowager excused herself for a moment and followed him out.

"I'm sorry about Miss Fairchild," she said seriously as she walked him to the head of the stairs.

His eyes were dancing. "I thought you might be. As I recall, you took a fancy to poor Miss Fairchild's nose."

"It was her bones, you naughty boy, as you well know. Oh, you and Ross may laugh at me, but I know what I know. I've made a study of faces, and I'm usually right."

He grinned. "Good God! I wouldn't dare ask what you think of my face."

She could not help laughing. "And I wouldn't dare tell you! But that's not what I wished to say to you." She laid a hand on his sleeve. "Larry—"

His color heightened. "If it's about the money I owe you, Aunt Em, I'm afraid I must beg for more time. I'm still trying to find a buyer for my team of chestnuts, but I have not been able to get my price."

She replied tartly, "I cannot abide people who finish my sentences for me! What I wished to say is that if you are under the hatches, I would be happy to help you out."

He captured her hand and kissed it. "You are a jewel, Aunt Em. Thank you for the offer, but things are not that bad. No, really, I didn't come to borrow money. I came to see Ross. When do you expect him?"

She couldn't keep the worry from her voice. "I expected him three days ago." Catching his curious look, she steadied herself. "It wouldn't surprise me," she said, "if he has decided to stay on for the shooting."

For a long while after the viscount had gone, she stayed at the top of the stairs, thinking about him. She'd heard rumors that he'd been hopelessly in love with Cassie and had never got over her death, and that that was the real reason he could not bring himself to marry. The thought of Cassie brought her mind back to Ross, and she wondered where he was and what he was doing.

At that moment Ross was only five minutes away. He and Tessa were in a carriage after dropping off the Turners at their modest house in Wigmore Street. His friend, Julian, had gone with them, having conveniently remembered something he wanted to discuss with Desmond.

Tessa was sulking over the discovery that Lady Sayle was actually Ross's grandmother. It was Colonel Naseby, waiting for them at the inn at Dover, who had let the cat out of the bag.

"Sayle," he'd called out in his hearty way. "Your grandmother is worried half to death. Lady Sayle expected you to arrive days ago."

Ross should have expected something like this. His grandmother and George Naseby were so close he sometimes wondered if they were lovers. The old boy hardly looked the part of a lover, though—bald as a coot, the buttons on his coat always looking as though they were ready to pop. Besides, Naseby was going on seventy.

There was one thing, however, that he did know. Naseby had once been the great love of his grandmother's life, and she expected her grandson to treat him with respect.

Of course he had invited Colonel Naseby to have breakfast with them. This had given Tessa the opportunity she'd been waiting for. She'd flirted with poor old Naseby and led him on until there was damn little she didn't know about Ross, the Marquess of Sayle. And the rest of them had sat there, laughing nervously, waiting for Tessa to pounce on them.

They'd parted company with Naseby outside the inn, all smiles and cheeriness, but as soon as they'd entered the carriage, Tessa had turned into ice. Julian had tried to explain why they'd had to conceal their identities, but Tessa maintained a furious silence, hardly saying two words on the whole five-hour journey from Dover.

"Tessa," Ross said reasonably, after the carriage moved off, "I couldn't tell you who I was before we reached England. It was too risky. If the French authorities got wind of a couple of English noblemen running an escape route out of France, they would have left no stone unturned to capture us. I would have told you all this at the inn if that damned chatterbox hadn't got there first."

"I found Colonel Naseby to be a charming, considerate gentleman."

"Well, he is of course, but—oh, hell!"

She glanced at him, then looked away. It wasn't just that he'd duped her but that she'd hoped never to see him again once he had delivered her to Lady Sayle. Since he was Lady Sayle's grandson, this now no longer seemed likely.

"Tessa—"

"Did Sally and Desmond know?" she rudely interrupted.

"What?" The question had destroyed his train of thought.

"Did Sally and Desmond know who you are, who Julian is?"

"They were sworn to secrecy. Don't blame Sally for not confiding in you. She wanted to, but I forbade her to say anything."

"And it didn't occur to you that if you had sworn me to secrecy, I would have kept your secret too?"

Laughter glinted in his eyes. "Frankly, Tessa, no."

She sniffed and turned her head away. He didn't have a high opinion of her character, but that came as no surprise. If he had taken the trouble to get to know her better, he would have known that she would never break a promise.

Ross started again. "As I was about to say, there is one other thing that must be clearly understood between us."

There was something in his voice that made her sit up straighter. "I'm listening," she said carefully.

He gave her a long, steady look. "Now that we are in England, Tessa, you must accept that I stand in your grandfather's place."

"Meaning?"

"Meaning that you will answer to me if you behave recklessly. Do you understand?"

"No!" she snapped. "I don't understand. You are nothing to me."

"Then allow me to explain it to you. For all intents and purposes, I shall be your guardian and you will be my ward."

"Your ward?" She stared at him aghast. "My grandfather never said this."

"He said it to me."

"I don't need a guardian. And if I did, you would be the last person I would choose."

"What you want doesn't come into it." His voice had taken on a hard edge. "Make no mistake about it, Tessa! You will defer to me as your guardian, and I shall look upon you as my ward." She stared at him mutely, and he softened his tone. "Come now, Tessa, I'm not an unreasonable man. If you behave yourself, there won't be any problems."

Tessa could see what was in store for her. This was the man who had complained that her laugh was too loud, that her gowns were too daring, that her manners were atrocious. If she let him, he would make her life miserable.

As her temper began to heat, her bosom rose and fell. "I'd take you to court before I'd submit to such a thing."

"You will only make yourself look ridiculous, and it won't do you a bit of good. I have letters from your grandfather entrusting you to my care."

His words took the wind out of her sails, and she stared at him in silence. Why would her grandfather have concealed this from her? There was no reason, unless he'd been tricked into it.

"I would like to know," she cried passionately, "what game you are playing."

"Would you care to explain that remark?"

"You duped us all, lied to my grandfather, pretending to be someone you are not."

The gray eyes blazed before they darkened. "Your grandfather and I were completely open with each other. I was in his confidence, and he was in mine. There was no pretense between us."

"You're lying!" she shouted. "My grandfather would have told me! He knows I would never have agreed to come to England to live with you as your ward."

"Alexandre understood you better than you think. He gave you his reasons, but you wouldn't listen. He couldn't trust you to do what's right. You know I speak the truth."

Averting her head, she stared out the window. Through the blaze of her anger, she recognized that there was something in what he said. She'd always sensed that her grandfather was keeping something from her, something to do with Trevenan, and now she knew what it was and why. And it hurt.

Her eyes burned and she blinked hard to dispel the incipient tears.

Ross leaned across the width of the coach and grasped her hands. "Tessa," he said, "you must know your grandfather thinks the world of you. He wants to keep you safe. That's why he entrusted you to my care. We told you as much as we dared. Lady Sayle, my grandmother, will sponsor you in society. You might even enjoy yourself."

She looked down at the strong masculine hands that gripped her wrists. Her voice was trembling. "You're hurting me," she said, and her voice broke on the last word.

"Tessa, look at me!"

When her gaze lifted to meet his, he forgot what he was going to say. Her eyes were huge and brimming with tears. She was biting down on her bottom lip to keep it from trembling. He didn't like to see her hurting like this. He couldn't bear to see her hurting like this.

"Tessa," he said, and his voice altered, was deeper, hoarser. "Tessa."

She dragged her eyes from his and said breathlessly, "Please, you're hurting me."

He dropped her hands and pulled back as though he were stepping back from a precipice, as, in fact, he was.

Her hands were trembling, and she hid them in the folds of the blanket that covered her lap so that he would not see how shaken she was. For a moment there, she'd been electrified, thinking he was going to kiss her. It was all in her imagination. He didn't care for her. He didn't even like her. She was a burden her grandfather had foisted upon him, and she'd better remember that.

She didn't know how she could bear it.

"Ah, here we are," said Ross.

She'd been vaguely aware that they'd traveled past what she assumed was Hyde Park and that they were on the road to the village of Kensington. As she looked out the window, the carriage turned into a well-treed estate and she had a view of the house. It was an old-fashioned, red brick mansion with two wings that didn't quite fit in with the main building.

"Sayle House," said Ross. "This is our London residence. It came into the family in the seventeenth century and over the years we've added to it. Greenways, that's my place in Oxfordshire, is quite different. We'll be spending Christmas there."

When the coach drew up outside the main doors, Ross descended first, then helped Tessa down. There was another carriage on the drive with a coachman standing by, holding the lead horses' heads. Ross recognized the equipage and his mouth flattened. Cupping Tessa's elbow with one hand, he ushered her up the stone steps. The knocker was answered by a liveried footman, and they entered a gloomy, wood-paneled hall with portraits of equally gloomy personages staring down at them.

Tessa's heart was thundering and her throat was dry. She felt like a little girl again, when she'd arrived on the Beasleys' doorstep after her mother had died.

"Grandmother?" thundered Ross, then frowned when

two people, a lady and a gentleman, came through the arch that led to the staircase. "Amanda! Bertram!" he greeted them. "I thought I recognized the carriage."

Tessa froze in her tracks, transfixed by the measuring look the woman had thrown her. It was a lightning look, no longer than a heartbeat, but it was comprehensive, and it made her excruciatingly aware of the difference between them. The woman looked like a fashion plate. Tessa felt that she herself belonged in the fields, scaring the crows away.

"Ross," said Amanda, and passing in front of Tessa, offered him her hand. "We've just been visiting your grandmother."

He kissed her hand. "What brings you to London? I thought you were staying in Henley till Christmas."

Amanda replied archly, "And I thought you were joining us to get in some shooting."

Tessa was aware of something else. The woman reminded her of Solange Guéry, the beautiful courtesan whom she'd seen Ross kiss at the Palais Royal. She was a more cultured and elegant version of Solange, but she exuded the same playful air of intimacy with Ross.

"And I would have," said Ross, "if I hadn't been escorting my ward to town." He turned to Tessa, with a warning expression. "Tessa, come and be introduced to Mrs. Chalmers and her cousin, Mr. Gibbon."

Tessa's spine stiffened. Did he think she was a child to be instructed in how to conduct herself in society? Pinning a smile to her face, she obediently came forward and curtsied.

"What a pretty child," said Amanda. Her eyes were still on Ross. "We shouldn't keep you. You must be tired after your journey. Where have you been hiding yourself these last weeks?"

"France," said Ross succinctly. It no longer mattered what people knew. "Miss Lorimer is the granddaughter of a close friend. Until things are more settled in France, he wishes her to live in England."

Tessa stood there fuming. It wouldn't have surprised her to learn that she'd suddenly become invisible. For the sake of pride, she said nothing and kept a vacant smile in place.

Mr. Gibbon was eyeing her through his quizzing glass, and just because here was someone who knew she hadn't vanished into thin air, she flashed him a grateful smile.

"Tessa!"

Her head jerked up. She saw that Ross was watching her and his smile was not reflected in his eyes. "Come along, Tessa. Lady Sayle is waiting for us upstairs," he said.

There was an awkward moment when Amanda tried to delay them, but Ross was firm. They would see each other before long, he told her, and he ushered Tessa under the arch toward the stairs.

A few moments later he said to Tessa in a low, tense voice, "I will not tolerate flirting, and certainly not under my own roof."

"Tell that to Mrs. Chalmers," she retorted and stuck her nose in the air.

He said something else, derogatory of course, but she hardly heard him. In another moment she would come face-to-face with Ross's grandmother, and for some reason that she didn't understand, she wanted to make a good impression.

"Grandmother?" cried Ross when they entered the drawing room.

The lady who came forward was an older, feminine version of her grandson, and Tessa's heart sank. She'd hoped for an ally in this strange house, or at least a friendly face.

For the second time since entering that house, Tessa came under the keenest scrutiny, but this time it was slow and thorough.

"Grandmother!" said Ross in a warning tone.

The dowager waved him to silence and continued with her perusal. Tessa's throat was tinder dry. Those wise old eyes saw too much for her comfort, and she had the strangest urge to hide herself. Then the dowager smiled, and the knot of tension inside Tessa began to melt.

"A strong face," observed the dowager, "and loyal. But above all, tenderhearted. I'd wager that as a child you

collected quite a menagerie of injured and lost animals.
Am I right, Tessa?"

"But how could you know?" asked Tessa, astonished.

Ross answered the question. "You might say my
grandmother is something of an . . . um . . . witch," he
said. Then, laughing, he pounced on his grandmother
and smothered her in a bear hug.

There were no formal introductions. The dowager
enfolded Tessa in a warm embrace and told her grandson
to go away. Linking arms with Tessa, she led her to the
stuffed chairs beside the fire, where, she said, they could
have a quiet coze.

Tessa glanced around wildly to find Ross, arms folded
across his chest, watching them both with an enigmatic
smile on his face.

"Soho Square," Bertram Gibbon told the coachman
before following his cousin inside her carriage.

"Why Soho Square?" asked Amanda after they were
seated.

He gave her a slow, sleepy smile. "That is something
you don't wish to know," he said.

She glanced at him with raised brows. The only subject that they did not discuss openly was Bertram's taste
for the well-stocked brothels that proliferated on the
edges of Mayfair. Amanda had never understood how
men could find pleasure in the sexual act. For herself, she
found the whole business highly distasteful, and never
indulged in it unless there was a greater goal to be
gained. All the same, she was well versed in how to give
men pleasure, having employed the services of a prosti-
tute to teach her all the tricks of the trade. She'd never
wasted these tricks on her husband, but had used them
with men who could advance his career. Now, with
Freddie gone, it was her own career she wished to
advance.

"What did you think of her?" she asked abruptly.

Bertram turned his head to look at her. "That she'll
give you a run for your money. She's very beautiful."

She inhaled sharply. "You think she's a rival?"

"Haven't you got eyes in your head?"

"But Ross hardly looked at her."

"Perhaps not, but there was something different about him, a tension. I could almost feel the fences he'd built around her, and that was before he gave me that murderous look when she smiled at me."

Amanda's fingers curled into claws. "Well? What do you make of it?"

"It's obvious, isn't it? Either he wants her for himself, or he is living up to his new role of guardian." He shook his head. "There's something else, but I can't quite put my finger on it."

"That was the feeling I got from that cow of a grandmother when I mentioned Miss Lorimer. What exactly do we know about this girl?"

His eyelids drooped as he considered her question. "That she comes originally from Sussex, and more recently from France; that her father was a naval officer; that her grandfather is apparently her legal guardian. Other than that, we know very little."

Amanda was frowning. Bertram had no trouble in divining what was going through her mind. They were first cousins, and though they did not look alike, they'd always been close, and had the knack of reading each other's thoughts before a word was spoken.

She would want him to investigate, to find something she could use to destroy the girl, if necessary. In Amanda's shoes, he would do the same. They were both ruthless in the pursuit of their goals. His own ambitions had been thwarted when he'd married a rich wife only to discover that her father had tied up her fortune so that he could not get his hands on it. Sir Thomas had misjudged his man, however, and was now on the point of offering a substantial settlement to free his beloved daughter from a marriage that Bertram had made intolerable.

Amanda said, "Do you think we can ruin her if we need to?"

She hadn't disappointed him, and he smiled. "It's possible," he said. "Everyone has something to hide."

As even he himself did. He'd been in love with Amanda

for years, but he knew better than to let her know it. She was as callous as a cat, and would take pleasure in tormenting him. Bertram Gibbon, he'd long since decided, was one person she wasn't going to get her sharp claws into.

There was a moment of silence, then Amanda said, "I'd like to know all there is to know about Tessa Lorimer. Can you find out for me?"

"My dear, that would be time-consuming."

"I'll make it worth your while."

"In that case, I shall certainly try."

Chapter Ten

～～～

*I*n the act of dictating a letter to his secretary, Ross stopped in midsentence and looked up at the ceiling. The silver chandelier swayed alarmingly and the sound of laughter from Tessa's private parlor could be distinctly heard. In the next instant the knocker on the front door banged with enough force to make him wince. It was two o'clock of a fine afternoon and his ward, as had become her habit, was entertaining her friends.

He heard the front door open, then a voice he recognized greeting his butler, a voice that irritated Ross. His brother-in-law, Larry, was becoming a regular visitor at Sayle House, and it wasn't to consult with Ross, his trustee, about putting his affairs in order. In fact, the last time they'd talked he and Larry had had quite an argument about a painting the viscount had sold, without permission, to pay off his debts. Normally, Larry would have avoided him like the plague after that. But not with Tessa here, Tessa and her fortune.

"Ah, Mannings," Larry cried in a theatrical voice that carried clear to the library where Ross and his secretary were working. "Lead me to the heiress."

The butler's reply was more muted. "You and your jokes, sir."

"Don't tell me she's eloped!"

Ross lifted his head as footsteps went bounding up the stairs.

His secretary chuckled. "Young people!" he said. "It's hard to remember that we were once that age, isn't it?"

"Quite," said Ross, and glanced at the older man. Miles Jessop had been his father's secretary and had passed to him on his father's death eight years ago. The man was almost twice Ross's age, yet he'd spoken as though they were contemporaries.

He wasn't *that* old. He was only eight years older than Larry. It was more than years that separated him from his brother-in-law, though. It was an attitude of mind. Ross had responsibilities. Larry had yet to assume responsibility for himself. He was the eternal adolescent.

Tessa didn't seem to object to Larry's immaturity. No doubt she looked upon him, Ross, as already having one foot in the grave. Perhaps she put him in a bracket with his secretary.

Suddenly conscious that he was riffling through the letters on his desk, letters that represented his many responsibilities as both landowner and peer of the realm, he threw them aside and grinned sheepishly at his secretary.

"I've lost my train of thought," he said. "Where was I?"

He finished his dictation, then after Mr. Jessop had left to go to his own office, he picked up his pen. Before he could dip it in the ink pot, he was distracted again by sounds of laughter from the room above.

Since Tessa's arrival, his quiet, ordered existence was constantly being shot to pieces. He never knew whom he might meet on the stairs, who might be sitting down to dinner, or who might be hammering on the knocker at all hours of the day.

This wasn't entirely Tessa's fault. His grandmother had taken the girl under her wing, as he'd hoped she would, but with a fervor that astonished him. The dowager had visited all her old cronies and had called in her favors. The result was that Tessa had acquired a following—the children and grandchildren of his grand-mother's set—without even leaving the house.

Not everything had been taken out of his hands, though Tessa might think so. Ross made sure that Tessa never left the house without a male escort; never went riding without grooms accompanying her; never received visitors unless she was suitably chaperoned. As for keeping an eye on her friends, he had taken care of that with a little ruse.

Sally Turner had come to stay with them. It was Tessa, in all innocence, who had asked his grandmother if she could have her since Desmond was investigating a case in Yorkshire, and Sally was all alone in London. Tessa never suspected that the situation had been engineered. It was devious, but necessary. He couldn't be everywhere at once, and Sally was levelheaded. At the first hint of trouble, she would know what to do.

When the door knocker sounded again, he cursed under his breath. Rising, he crossed to the door and wandered into the hall. When his butler opened the door, it was Julian Percy, in all his sartorial splendor, who entered.

"Good afternoon, Mannings," said Julian. "How is the gout?"

"Not so bad, my lord, not so bad."

"Glad to hear it. Ah, Ross, just the man I wanted to see. What do you think of my new coat?"

Julian made straight for the pier glass at the foot of the stairs and admired his reflection.

Ross grinned. It was all affectation, this posturing as a dandy. The real Julian possessed one of the sharpest intellects he knew. His gaze traveled over his friend's maroon cutaway coat with silver buttons, his fawn-colored, skintight pantaloons, and Hessian boots that sported high heels.

"What I think," replied Ross, "is that with a little powder and paint, you would look like a fop from our fathers' era."

Julian clicked his tongue and turned to look over at his friend. "Just look at you with that conservative dark coat and beige trousers. You need a tailor who knows how to cut your garments to fit."

"What's wrong with my tailoring?" Ross squared his shoulders and smoothed down the edges of his coat as he led the way into his library.

"Let's just say your coat doesn't fit like a glove."

"That's because it's a coat and not a glove. Besides, when I drop something, I don't want the aggravation of wondering whether my coat is going to split up my back if I try to retrieve it."

"A tricky maneuver," Julian conceded, "but it can be done, and if you should ever acquire a coat like mine, I'd be happy to demonstrate. Now, tell me what's been happening."

They took the chairs by the fireplace. "Desmond has gone into Yorkshire looking for a girl by the name of Nan Roberts," Ross told him. "Sally had it from Tessa that she and Miss Roberts were at Fleetwood together."

"And where does Miss Roberts fit into this?"

Ross shrugged. "She doesn't, as far as I know. This is in the nature of a fishing expedition."

"I see." Julian paused to take snuff. Finally, he said, "You look quite calm and collected, quite different from the . . . er . . . last time I saw you."

"You're referring, of course, to the time you cravenly abandoned me in my carriage to face Tessa's wrath."

Julian smiled. "I thought I would only be in the way." He glanced at Ross. "How are you two getting along?"

"She received a letter from her grandfather. It made a difference. We don't quarrel so much anymore."

"I'm glad to hear it."

A burst of masculine laughter from upstairs scattered their thoughts.

"Good God!" said Julian. "What was that?"

"That," said Ross, "is what I've had to put up with since Tessa became a member of my household. She's turned the yellow salon into her own private parlor and unfortunately it's right above my library. I am telling you, Julian, a posting house could not be noisier than this place."

"A posting house! If I'd known what an exciting life you were leading, I might have turned up sooner! Shall we join the fun?"

Ross glanced toward the pile of letters on his desk. "Why not?" he said, and got to his feet.

When they entered Tessa's parlor, Ross discovered that the reason for the uproar wasn't Tessa, it was his grandmother. Together with a purple-faced Colonel Naseby, she was demonstrating the steps of some boisterous dance of her youth.

"Ah," said Lady Sayle, "Ross! Just the person I was looking for. Poor Colonel Naseby is quite done up. You remember the steps, dear, don't you? I'm sure I taught you the gavotte when you were a boy."

"You're confusing me with Julian," he said. "I was the one with two left feet, remember, Grandmother?" He turned away with a smile, and went to sit next to Sally Turner.

Though protesting, Julian allowed Lady Sayle to lead him to the center of the room.

Ross suddenly noticed that Tessa was not there and asked Sally where she was.

"Oh, she went to fetch Lady Sayle's fan," she replied. "I wonder what's keeping her?"

Ross saw that Larry was sitting on a sofa beside George Naseby's granddaughter. She, at least, was safe from Larry's mercenary ambitions since she had no fortune.

The viscount was avoiding his eyes. He was still smarting, Ross supposed, from the humiliation of having to buy back the painting he had no business selling in the first place. He had no patience with Larry's sulking.

Sally said, "Perhaps I'd best go and see what's happened to Tessa."

"No, I'll go," Ross said. He felt out of place here anyway.

Not many minutes after Ross had left, Julian gave a yelp, clutched the small of his back, and after a short consultation with the dowager, hobbled over to Sally and slowly sank down on the sofa beside her.

Sally watched him from the corner of her eye. He was not so tactful. Raising his quizzing glass, he languidly surveyed her from head to toe. "Good lord," he drawled in a voice only she could hear, "perhaps it's you who should have the name of my tailor."

The smile on Sally's face was as sweet as syrup. She, too, spoke in a soft undertone. "Listen to me, you feather-brained, fatuous fop, and listen well. One more snide remark from you—"

"Feather-brained, fatuous fop! Oh, that's very good. I must record it."

Under Sally's mystified stare, he fished in his pocket and produced a small enamel case with a gold pencil attached to it. Removing a card, he began to write. "Was that 'fop' or 'fribble'?" he asked, glancing up at her. "Oh, no matter. Either one will do."

"What are you doing?" Sally demanded.

"I'm recording your *bon mot* for future reference. At the earliest opportunity, I shall use it and astonish my audience with my cleverness. Oh, don't look so shocked. It's a common practice with gentlemen who are celebrated for their wit. You don't think we make up these witticisms on the spur of the moment, do you?"

Sally's eyes were snapping. "But that's dishonest!"

"Yes, isn't it? Now where were we? Oh, yes. I believe you had just said something to the effect that if I continued to goad you, you would—? Pray continue."

"If you continue to goad me," she said, bosom quivering, "I shall put a wrinkle in your ridiculous coat."

"Oh, not my coat!" He edged away from her. "You really know how to hurt a fellow. Don't you like me, Sal?"

She turned her intelligent brown eyes upon him. "Peacocks have their place in the scheme of things, I suppose," she said. "For myself, I prefer my birds plucked and trussed for Sunday dinner."

He leaned toward her. "Shall I tell you how I like my birds, Sal?"

"If you do," she said, "it will be the last thing you do."

With great dignity, she rose and joined Larry and Miss Naseby on the long sofa.

Julian swung his quizzing glass on its black ribbon. They'd been sniping at each other almost from the moment they'd met, when he'd agreed to take Sally and her brother into France. Even then, she'd looked down her nose at him, and he had been stung into poking fun at her. And so it went on. It was a pleasant way to pass the time—and that's all it was.

Tessa was beginning to know her way around that great convoluted house and she had taken a shortcut, using one of the servants' staircases, to the wing that housed the bedchambers. When she came out on the long corridor, she paused, trying to get her bearings. She knew that the door to Lady Sayle's suite of rooms was opposite the pier glass, but somehow it didn't look right. Shrugging this off as probably just a trick of her imagination, she walked to the pier glass, opened the door opposite, and went in. The blinds were half-drawn, and all the furniture was under Holland covers. Obviously, she'd entered the wrong room.

She tried the next chamber, but it was just the same. In the third chamber, which was also the same, she went to the window and raised a blind to look out. Across the grounds of Sayle House, she could see nothing but trees and fields. Now she understood her mistake. She must have taken the wrong staircase and had come out in the west wing. This part of the house, the dowager had told her, was closed off.

Cursing her stupidity, she returned to the corridor. Row upon row of closed doors, one indistinguishable from the other, seemed to mock her. She had no idea which door led to the servants' staircase. The only thing she could do was try every one.

Just then, down the corridor, a door opened and a maid exited from one of the rooms. She carried mops and dusters, and the pockets of her apron were bulging with what Tessa assumed were cleaning supplies. Tessa hailed the maid and quickly caught up to her.

"It's Jenny, isn't it?" she began.

"Yes, miss. Fancy you remembering my name!" The maid beamed at Tessa.

"I didn't know that this part of the house was in use." The door was ajar, and Tessa couldn't resist pushing it open.

"It isn't used, miss."

Jenny's smile had faded, and she appeared flustered. Tessa's brows rose fractionally, inviting an explanation. The gesture seemed to fluster the maid more, and she stammered, "No one is allowed into these rooms. His lordship has forbidden it."

"Has he?" That was all the challenge Tessa needed to boldly step past the maid and push into the room. "Why, this is lovely!" she exclaimed.

It was a sitting room done in pink and white, but it wasn't sugary or tasteless. It was airy, and elegant, and just the kind of room Tessa would have chosen for herself. Between the two long windows, there was a curio cabinet displaying a collection of antique fans. A vase of hothouse violets graced the white marble mantelpiece. Every chair seat and cushion was done in fine needlepoint. Just off the sitting room, she found a matching bedchamber.

"Whose rooms are these, Jenny?"

The girl glanced uneasily at the door, then looked at Tessa. "Lady Sayle's rooms," she answered.

"The dowager's rooms?" Tessa's brow wrinkled.

The maid shook her head. "His lordship's wife."

"His lordship's wife?" Tessa repeated, not sure if she understood these vague connections. "You can't mean Lord Sayle, the present marquess?"

"That's right, miss. The master. These are his wife's rooms."

Tessa felt as though she had taken a blow to the abdomen. All the breath was knocked out of her, and she put a hand on the back of a chair to support herself.

The maid looked at her curiously, and Tessa made an effort to pull herself together. "I didn't know Lord Sayle was married," she said. "Where is Lady Sayle?"

"She died some years ago."

It was a moment or two before Tessa could absorb this. "How did she die?"

"It was an accident. That's all I know. Please, miss, I must lock up. Mrs. Garvey will be wondering what's happened to me."

"Mmm? Oh, you go along. I'll make things right with the housekeeper."

The maid looked as though she might argue the point, then she bobbed a curtsy and left the room.

Tessa remained as she was, half propped against the chair, staring at that room. This time, however, she was seeing it with different eyes, and she experienced an odd sense of reverence. Without conscious thought, she wandered around, touching first one object, then another. When she entered the bedchamber, she stared at the bed for several long minutes, not knowing what she was thinking, aware only that something had clenched deep inside her. She turned aside and opened the doors of a mahogany wardrobe. Garments of every description and color were stored there—pale muslins and silks, velvet pelisses and warm kerseymere mantles. She skimmed her fingers along them, then slowed to a lingering caress, as if she could take the impression of the woman who had worn these garments by sheer sense of touch.

Tessa next turned her attention to a row of shelves that displayed an array of satin slippers, embroidered silk stockings, and gloves of the finest leathers. She picked up an elbow-length, white kid glove that was obviously meant to be worn to a ball. When she rubbed it against her cheek, it felt as soft as satin. With infinite care, she eased it over her fingers, over her hand, and all the way up to her elbow. It was a perfect fit.

"What the hell do you think you're doing?"

Ross's outraged demand froze her to the spot. She was appalled to be caught in such a position, appalled at her own vulgar curiosity. If she'd been caught desecrating someone's grave, she could not have felt more ashamed.

When the silence lengthened, she slowly turned to face

him. The chambermaid was behind him, looking as though she would rather be anywhere than in that room. Which was exactly how Tessa felt.

His grim expression made her want to run away, but she knew she owed him an apology. She couldn't help stammering. "I'm s-sorry, s-so sorry. I don't know what came over me." She made a feeble gesture with one hand. "These rooms are lovely. Your wife had excellent taste."

A muscle clenched in his cheek. "Do you think I need you to tell me anything about my wife? And what were you doing in Cassie's wardrobe?" For the first time, he saw the glove on her hand. His mouth twisted, and reaching for her wrist, he grabbed it and tore the glove off.

That was too much for the maid. She gasped and looked at her master in astonishment.

"Leave us," said Ross.

Tessa's eyes were unfaltering on the man who towered over her. She did not see the look of apology the maid threw her, or hear Jenny as she quickly left the room.

When they were alone, Ross said, "I asked you a question. What are you doing here?"

Tessa knew she was in the wrong, but she had already apologized. She lifted her chin. "I beg your pardon," she said. "I had no idea these rooms were sacred to the memory of your wife. How should I? You never mentioned a wife to me, and certainly in Paris . . ." She trailed to a halt, afraid that she'd said too much. Defending herself was one thing; provoking him was another.

It was obvious she'd gone too far. His face went white with anger.

"What about Paris?"

Though she was trembling, she kept her voice steady. "With my own eyes, I saw you with Solange Guéry, and I know there were others. That hardly indicates to me that you—"

"That I what?" he asked softly when she hesitated.

She swallowed. "—that you revere your wife's memory."

"You self-righteous little prig! What would you know

about it? What would you know about lying awake, night after night, aching with the pain of loss? You never shed a tear for Paul Marmont."

"That's not true!"

He made a violent motion with one hand. "Don't lie to me! I've been watching you. You've forgotten all about Paul Marmont now that you have a new set of fribbles to flirt with you and flatter you. Yes, I've had women since Cassie died, plenty of them. What of it? There wouldn't be other women if I still had Cassie. Cassie will always have my heart."

Tessa was reeling under his attack, stunned by all the images that were crowding into her head. She couldn't bear to hear about his other women, couldn't bear to think he was right about Paul. She hadn't shed a tear for Paul, but that was because she'd done all her crying weeks ago. And who was he to find fault with her?

"Damn you!" she said fiercely. "There is no defense for your conduct."

Suddenly his hands were on her shoulders, gripping her in a fierce clasp. The door opened but neither of them noticed. They were aware of nothing but the fury in the other's eyes.

"Your lordship!"

The sound of the housekeeper's voice brought Ross's head up. Mrs. Garvey stood in the doorway, and behind her, peeping over her shoulder, was the little maid. When Ross released Tessa, she took a quick step away from him.

"Is everything all right, your lordship?" asked the housekeeper, her eyes darting suspiciously from Ross to Tessa.

Tessa bent to pick up the glove she'd tried on, and handed it to Ross. His hand came up automatically to receive it. She knew she should do her part to smooth over the awkwardness of having servants witness their quarrel, but she was too overwrought to care. With her head down, she quickly made her escape.

Long moments were to pass before Ross moved. "See

that that door is locked at all times," he told his house-keeper, and flinging the glove on the bed, he, too, left the room.

Tessa did not come down to dinner that evening, but pleaded a headache and had a tray sent to her room. It would have choked her to eat a bite, and she did no more than take a few sips from the glass of wine that accompanied the meal.

She paced her room, going over in her mind every moment of that humiliating encounter, when Ross had surprised her going through his wife's things. She didn't know how she could look him in the eye again, or how she could explain what she'd done. There was no explaining it. What had started out as curiosity had ended in a strange compulsion. She'd lost all sense of place and time, all sense of right and wrong.

She'd lost all sense of decency, that's what it amounted to. How could she have done such a thing?

As for the quarrel that followed, if only she could learn to keep her mouth shut and not provoke him! On the other hand, it was a lesson he could learn as well.

Cassie will always have my heart.

He was right. Her grandfather was right. She didn't know anything about anything, and men least of all. If he found solace in the arms of other women, that was his business. It had nothing to do with her.

She had never felt so anguished and uncertain. Dear God, what was wrong with her?

A sudden knock on the door brought her to a standstill.

"Tessa?"

Ross's voice. Her heart skipped a beat.

"Tessa, I wish to speak with you. I know you're in there."

The door handle rattled and she held her breath.

"Tessa!" His voice was louder, more impatient. "Open the door!"

She took a step toward the door, then halted. She

wasn't ready to face him yet. On the other hand, she had to face him sometime.

The seconds dragged by as she stared at that closed door. Finally, she crossed to the door and opened it. There was no one there, but she could hear his footsteps descending the stairs.

Chapter Eleven

Julian teaching Sally to ride was a hilarious spectacle. The trouble was, they were both stubborn. He was determined she would do things his way, and Sally was just as determined she would not. Tessa could predict that by the end of an hour, they wouldn't be speaking to each other.

She patted her mount's neck and turned away with a smile, then waved as the Viscount Pelham rode across the turf to join her. Larry frequently met up with them on their morning rides in Hyde Park.

As the sun filtered through the bare branches of a horse chestnut, she lifted her face. It was a glorious morning with just the slightest nip in the air, and she was impatient for a good gallop. Touching her heels to her sorrel's flanks, she leaped forward. The viscount was taken by surprise when she flashed by him. Reining in, he turned his horse and went bounding after her.

The warmth of the sun on her face, the wind whipping at her riding habit, the swift smoothness of the sorrel, and his instant response to her every touch made Tessa's spirits soar. Neck-and-neck now, laughing at each other, she and Larry raced for the far perimeter of the park.

There were few other riders about. The hour was still early, and there was nothing to dampen their spirits, no lofty matrons of the ton spying on them from closed carriages. Two grooms followed at a respectful distance.

They spurred their mounts to a faster pace. The horses stretched out and seemed to fly over the sward. At the last moment Larry shot forward, then swung his bay in an arc. Tessa followed him. A few moments later they drew rein. Larry dismounted first and came to help Tessa down.

"Well done!" he exclaimed. "That wasn't bad for a girl."

Tessa smiled warmly. "If I hadn't been riding side-saddle, I would have beaten you."

"Why do you think we men invented the sidesaddle?"

Laughing, they began to walk their horses back. When the grooms once again fell into step a few yards behind them, Larry chuckled.

"What's the joke?" asked Tessa.

He looked down at her, his mouth curving in a lop-sided grin. "Our mutual trustee is making sure I don't run off with you. Haven't you noticed how well guarded you are? Lord Harlow and Miss Turner are your constant companions, not to mention the grooms who stay closer to you than your own shadow."

Tessa said archly, "Is that why you've taken to meeting me on my morning rides—to annoy Lord Sayle?"

"The thought never occurred to me!" Noting her raised brows, he shrugged, then laughed. "Well, perhaps at first. But now that I know you, I can say, in all honesty, that I never give my wicked trustee a thought."

Tessa slanted him a sidelong look. He was not much older than she, perhaps three or four years, but he seemed younger. He was very handsome, with light brown hair, and when he smiled, dimples flashed in his cheeks. There was always a tease in his voice, a mischievous glint in his blue eyes, except when he was talking to Ross. He was frank about the fact that he couldn't wait to turn twenty-five so that he could be out from under Ross's thumb. She knew exactly how he felt.

"I'm a little vague," she said, "on your connection to Lord Sayle. The dowager calls you her nephew, but Julian says you're Lord Sayle's brother-in-law."

"Actually, I'm neither. Those are just courtesy titles. I was Cassie's stepbrother. My father married her mother when Cassie and I were both away at school. We called each other brother and sister, but that was only to please our parents. I never thought of her as my sister."

"What was she like?"

He let his breath out slowly. "Beautiful, in her own quiet way. Shy. She never went against Ross or quarreled with him. He always had everything his own way." He turned a self-mocking smile upon her. "I suppose I sound bitter. I was in love with her, myself, but nothing could come of it."

"Is that why you dislike him so much?"

"Not at all. In fact, I used to hero-worship him, but that was before he became my trustee and changed toward me."

"Changed? How?"

Larry shrugged. "He criticizes everything I do. He doesn't like my friends and"—he broke off and grinned at her—"and my expensive tastes, shall we say? You, of all people, must know what it's like."

"Why should you think that?"

"I've seen the way you stiffen up whenever he comes near you. You're no more happy to have him as your trustee than I am."

She shrugged helplessly. "I didn't want to leave France. My grandfather is there, and he is the only family I have left." Ross had told her, and she agreed with him, that the less said about her reasons for leaving France the better.

"Then why did you leave?"

She responded evasively, "Circumstances changed. The war—you know what I mean. My grandfather thought England was the best place for me."

He looked at her, his eyes shrewd and watchful. "Perhaps I was wrong," he said. "Perhaps Ross hasn't surrounded you with guards to keep me away. Perhaps he's afraid you'll try to make a break for it and return to France."

She raised her brows. "Now you are being fanciful," she said.

He laughed. "Possibly. I haven't made up my mind about you yet, Tessa Lorimer."

Not liking where all this was leading, she said abruptly, "We were talking about Lord Sayle's wife. What happened to her? How did she die?"

He looked at her quizzically. "Why don't you ask Ross?"

She wouldn't dare ask Ross the time of day, let alone ask him about his wife. Since he'd discovered her in Cassie's rooms, they'd had only one conversation—if it could be called a conversation—where he had apologized for losing his temper, and she had apologized for her unseemly conduct. Since then, she'd tried to keep out of his way, and it seemed that he was doing the same with her.

Misunderstanding her silence, he said, "So that's it! You *did* ask him and he lost his temper. He still carries on like a man demented by grief even though there has been no shortage of women to replace Cassie these last years."

Tessa knew that they had gone beyond what a gentleman and a lady should be talking about. But she was burning with curiosity, and couldn't stop now.

"You're wrong, Larry," she said. "I couldn't ask him about his wife, especially not how she died. It would be too cruel."

"It was an accident," he said. "Cassie went out boating on the lake. The punt capsized and she drowned."

Tessa halted. "A drowning accident! Oh God, how awful!" She felt as if someone had just walked over her grave, and she shivered.

Larry did not notice her reaction. He was too busy looking at a point over her shoulder. "Well, well, well! Speak of the devil! And look who is with him—I thought their affair was over."

Tessa turned her head. Two riders had just entered the

park by the Stanhope Gate. The gentleman was mounted on a huge black gelding, the lady on a glossy bay. She recognized them at once—Ross and Amanda Chalmers.

She looked enquiringly at Larry.

He grinned wickedly at her. "I've said too much already. Let's move on, shall we?"

When she and Larry were mounted, she glanced back. Ross and Amanda Chalmers hadn't moved, but were still watching them. With a flick of the reins, she urged her mount forward. Larry followed.

The riders who had halted just inside the Stanhope Gate watched their flight across the turf.

"Isn't that your ward and your brother-in-law?" asked Amanda. She turned a speculative look upon Ross, but his expression was inscrutable.

"I don't think there's any doubt of that," he said.

"I'm told they meet here, quite by chance, just about every morning." She paused, and when Ross was silent, said casually, "You don't seem surprised."

He could hardly be surprised when Sally and Julian gave him a daily accounting of Tessa's movements. What he felt was annoyance. Amanda had deliberately arranged things so that he would see Tessa and Larry together. She was testing him, seeing Tessa as her rival. Was he that obvious?

Amanda redirected her attention to the riders who were now cresting a rise. "I suppose," she said, as though musing aloud, "the girl would do very well for Larry." She glanced up at Ross. "Is that why your grandmother has taken her under her wing? Is Lady Sayle playing matchmaker?"

Ross replied easily, "My grandmother has more sense than that. Larry isn't responsible enough for marriage."

"I thought you would approve. You are, after all, his trustee."

"I am also Tessa's guardian, and it's my duty to protect her interests."

"So it's true what they say—she really is an heiress!"

Ross regarded her steadily. "Whether or not Tessa is an heiress is irrelevant. She is not on the marriage mart."

"Not on the marriage mart!" She laughed lightly.

"That's a crude way of putting it. And why, pray tell, is she not?"

"Because I don't wish it."

She looked at him uncertainly, then forced a smile. She was too shrewd, too experienced to press him for answers. The last thing she wanted was to annoy him when she was so close to realizing her ambitions.

They moved off at a decorous jog toward Rotten Row, the path that was reserved for riders. Amanda was conscious that she'd had a rebuff and strove to regain lost ground. She spoke of what she knew would interest Ross, the debate in the House on the progress of the war with France. Try as she might, however, she could elicit no more than monosyllabic replies, and soon gave up.

For his part, Ross was beginning to regret renewing his friendship with Amanda. It could have been worse. He'd meant to resume their affair when he'd turned up on her doorstep after his encounter with Tessa. He'd spent the night carousing with Julian, trying to wipe the picture of Tessa as he'd last seen her from his mind, and when that hadn't worked, he'd decided to replace it with another woman. To his great chagrin, he'd discovered that that didn't work either. He'd been incapable, Amanda had been gracious, and he'd spent what was left of the night in his club in St. James's.

Having turned up on Amanda's doorstep, he could hardly now avoid her as though she had the plague. It was worse than the plague. Amanda had developed an acute case of "marriage on her mind." Though she hadn't come out and said anything, he could read the signs.

Marriage to Amanda. The thought revolved in his mind. He was fond of her. She was an intelligent, interesting companion. In bed, what she lacked in genuine passion she made up for in skill, and that suited him well enough. He wasn't looking for more. His heart wasn't involved, and if he read her correctly, her heart wasn't involved either, but that was all to the good. They'd have the kind of marriage he'd come to accept was all that he was capable of, all that he wanted after Cassie. There was, however, one major stumbling block to committing himself to any woman, and that was the way he felt about Tessa Lorimer.

He didn't love Tessa. He was very sure about that. Love was what he'd had with Cassie. It was kind and gentle and involved all the finer feelings. What he felt for Tessa was far different. It was a primitive and a purely physical response on his part, one that appalled him, something he'd never experienced for another woman and hoped never to experience again.

Tessa Lorimer had damn near become an obsession with him, and had been right from the beginning, only he'd been too stubborn to admit it. He'd hardly been able to look at her without his body becoming hard with desire. He knew how she looked when she was almost naked, and he'd thought of how she'd look, how she'd be in his bed, with her fiery hair wrapped around him. Just once, he wanted to see the surrender in her eyes; he wanted her defiance shattered, her features love-softened after he had taken her to bed.

It didn't matter what he wanted. He was her guardian; she was his ward. He'd made a solemn promise to Alexandre that he would take care of Tessa, a promise he'd made on the soul of his dead wife.

He had a flash of recall—Tessa's expression when he'd torn the glove from her hand in Cassie's bedchamber. He'd lashed out at her because he'd felt so damn guilty, as though by her very presence, Tessa had hurt Cassie. Those other women he'd taken his pleasure with since Cassie's death hadn't mattered. They were no threat to Cassie's memory. Amanda wouldn't be a threat. But Tessa was different. Even though he did not love her he wanted her more than he had ever wanted Cassie, and he resented it like hell.

It was in Cassie's room that the truth had hit him like a thunderbolt. Whenever he'd entered these rooms, which was rarely, he'd always been deeply conscious of Cassie's presence. He'd given her permission to refurbish his whole house, but she'd done no more than her own rooms before she'd been brutally taken from him. The rooms were a reflection of Cassie—unaffected and quietly appealing. There were no strong colors here. Everything was soft and restful. The needlepoint on the chairs had been done by her own hand. It was one of the memories that made him ache—Cassie, her head bent over her needlework of an evening while he lost himself in a book. Occasionally, he would read something aloud to her, and she would look up and smile at him, protesting that she had no head for books. But he had persevered anyway, and she had listened because she'd wanted to please him.

But even that memory was beginning to fade, eclipsed by another, more recent memory. He could see Tessa and her grandfather out on the terrace, in the hour before dinner, discussing some book or other, debating its merits. He'd always found some excuse not to join them. He didn't want to discuss books with Tessa Lorimer. He hadn't wanted anything to do with her.

When he'd met the maid on the stairs and she'd told him where Tessa was, he'd been furious. If it had been anyone else but Tessa, it wouldn't have mattered so much. He'd felt vaguely threatened, and when he'd walked into Cassie's rooms, he'd known why. Tessa's vibrant beauty, her vitality, seemed to fill the room. He'd felt his body tighten in response to her, and his anger had turned inward. Even here, in Cassie's rooms, he still wanted her. To steady himself, he'd looked at the needlepoint chairs and the pictures on the wall. Someone had put a posy of violets—Cassie's favorite flowers—on the mantelpiece. It made no difference. Tessa's presence seemed to diminish his wife's memory. He couldn't even recall Cassie's face, and there was no portrait to remind him of it. They'd been married for so short a time, he'd never got around to arranging it. Then he'd seen the glove on Tessa's hand, and it was the last straw.

Later, when he'd been in a calmer frame of mind, it came to him that if he did not do something to cure himself of his obsession with Tessa, he might do something he would regret. Which was why he had turned up on Amanda's doorstep and was now her most constant companion.

"You look," said Amanda, "as though you are plotting to do murder."

He turned his head slowly, looking at her as though he were trying to remember who she was.

Amanda's poise slipped and she spoke more sharply than she meant to. "Am I boring you, Ross?"

"I am never bored by a beautiful woman," he said, stretching the truth a little. "Why don't we take the fidgets out of our horses?"

And with that, she had to be content.

An hour later Amanda stormed into her house on Hill Street and rudely pushed past the footman who came forward to take her cloak. She made straight for the stairs and her own chamber. Her quirt was still in her hand, and as she ascended the stairs, she lashed out periodically, striking the handrail with enough force to scar the surface.

As she approached the door to her bedchamber, another door at the far end of the hall opened and a maid exited. She was young and pretty and she was crying copiously as she tried to arrange her disheveled clothing. Amanda's temper flared even higher. So this was what the servants got up to in her absence! She was about to call out when the door opened again. This time a gentleman stepped into the corridor. It was Bertram, her cousin, and he was buttoning the closure on his trousers. Both man and maid saw Amanda at the same time. The maid blanched, bobbed a curtsy, and hurried away. Bertram merely raised his eyebrows.

Amanda's nostrils flared. Sweeping into her chamber, she slammed the door behind her. She threw off her outer garments and sat down at her dressing table to brush out her hair. A moment later the door opened and Bertram entered.

She said acidly, "Must you debauch my maids? Surely there are enough brothels within walking distance to satisfy even your voracious appetite."

He shrugged nonchalantly and propped himself

against one of the bedposts. Their eyes met in the looking glass. "I was quite comfortable here, thank you."

"Was the girl willing?"

"Willing enough. Does it matter?"

She swiveled to face him. "For a man who is hoping to secure a favorable financial settlement when he separates from his wife, you run too many unnecessary risks, Bertram."

"Now that's where you are wrong, my dear. Hetty's family is so straitlaced they are practically Methodists. The worse my reputation, the more determined they become to buy me off at any price."

"I don't know how they allowed their sainted daughter to marry you in the first place!"

He gave a low laugh. "For the same reason, I presume, that the sainted Honorable Fredrick Chalmers married you. I went to a great deal of trouble to present myself as a suitable candidate—memorizing Bible verses, religiously attending chapel services. It was all a great bore!"

She frowned at him, then chuckled. "Poor Bertram."

"Poor Bertram, indeed. Not only did I find myself married to a whey-faced pudding of a woman, but the money that was promised to me never materialized. Ah. That amuses you. I'm glad to see that your temper has improved. What is it, Amanda? What's been happening in my absence?"

"Ross Trevenan," she said simply, and her lips compressed.

"I thought that might be it."

"You were right, Bertram. I have a rival. A serious rival."

His eyes narrowed slightly as he studied her face. "He's not the only pebble on the beach, you know. And I doubt you're lusting after his beautiful body. Is it the title?"

She tilted her head and gazed up at him. "I'd be the Marchioness of Sayle, and that's not to be sneezed at. But it's more than that. Everyone knows he's been paying me court. Oh, I'm not counting on him offering me marriage. That's not what's important to me."

"No. What is important to you is your pride. You can't bear to think you may become an object of ridicule."

"How well you understand me." She smiled. "I'm not going to stand by and let some gawky girl who is barely out of the schoolroom take him away from me."

"Gawky girl!" He sank onto the bed. "Are you referring to Miss Tessa Lorimer?"

"Who else?"

"Then I'd advise you not to underestimate her. They're calling her 'The Toast' in my clubs, and she has yet to attend any major function."

Her eyes were very wide, very green when she looked at him. "I'd give anything to be rid of her. I understood you were going to help me. You said you were going to find out everything there was to know about Miss Lorimer. I thought we had a bargain."

"And so we have." He paused to take snuff. "Where do you think I've been for the last week?"

"To see your wife and her parents, to come to terms with them."

"I went to Norfolk to renew my acquaintance with Admiral Lorimer, the only Lorimer I know. I met him once at a shooting party at my dear father-in-law's place. It turns out that Admiral Lorimer is the girl's great-uncle, and a fount of information."

"Then why didn't you say so when you walked in here!" She gave a crow of laughter. "Out with it, Bertram. What skeletons have you unearthed?"

"Plenty." And he went on to tell her about Tessa's succession of schools, and her reputation for waywardness. He told her about the elopement with her uncle's footman and the Beasley relatives who had cast her off. But he wasn't able to shed any light on Tessa's life in France and how Ross had become involved in her affairs.

When he finished speaking, Amanda rose and, deep in thought, began to pace. Suddenly turning, she asked, "This footman she eloped with—did she marry him?"

"Apparently not."

Her face fell.

"I did discover, though, that the Beasley relatives are

still her guardians, at least under English law." He gave her a slow, lazy smile. "Her grandfather was never her guardian. But he did hold the purse strings."

She went very still, but her eyes betrayed her. They glittered brilliantly. "You've done well," she said softly.

"And now await my reward."

Her brows rose delicately. "If you want the maid, I'll turn a blind eye."

"A bargain is a bargain," he said. "Come here."

She sauntered over to him, and stood perfectly still as he began to disrobe her. "Why does it always have to be this?" she asked, and made a grimace of distaste when he filled his hands with the breasts he'd bared.

His eyes were burning with lust as he parted her thighs. "If I were to tell you, my love, you wouldn't believe me."

Chapter Twelve

~~~~~~~~

Ross was late for his appointment and as soon as he pulled his grays to a stop outside the Turners' house on Wigmore Street, he quickly jumped down from his curricle, threw the reins to his groom, and mounted the stairs. He was admitted at once and shown into a small library on the ground floor.

Desmond Turner and Julian looked up as he entered. They were sipping sherry.

There were handshakes all round and the usual conversation between friends who had not seen each other for some time. This was more than a social call, however. Desmond had just returned from Yorkshire and they were meeting to share information.

When Ross was seated, Julian said, "Desmond and I were beginning to wonder if something had happened to you. What kept you?"

"I was obliged to ... ah ... advise my ward on a matter of feminine apparel," said Ross.

This was a blatant lie. He and Tessa had been embroiled in an argument over a stupid triviality, and he'd lost track of the time. It had all started innocently enough. His grandmother had arranged for her hairdresser to call that afternoon to cut and dress the ladies' hair, a harmless occupation, he'd thought, until he'd discovered Tessa meant to have her glorious hair done in the current mode—sheared to a crop and crimped to frame her face. He should have kept his mouth shut. Instead, he'd said something—he couldn't remember what—that had got her temper up. From there, their difference of opinion had degenerated into a ferocious war of words. He was an autocratic fusspot, and she was damn near incorrigible. It was the look on his grandmother's face that had brought him to his senses. Her mouth was open and she was looking at him as though he'd sprouted another head.

Banishing the argument with Tessa from his mind, he accepted Desmond's offer of sherry, then asked what he'd learned in Yorkshire.

"I didn't find Nan Roberts," Desmond replied, "but I did find out quite a bit about her. The interesting thing is, her background is not unlike Tessa's. She was an orphan who was raised by relatives. By all accounts, she was hard to manage and moved from one school to another. The family in Yorkshire died out, and the last anyone heard of her, she had fallen on hard times and had taken a position as a governess. I had most of this from the local vicar, by the way. Vicars always know what there is to know about their parishioners."

"Oh well, even if you'd found Nan Roberts," said Julian, "she probably couldn't have told you much."

Desmond shrugged. "If she was Tessa's best friend at Fleetwood, she might have seen or heard something that didn't come out at the inquest."

"She couldn't have been much of a friend," Julian said. "They never even corresponded."

"Which is what makes it so surprising that Nan Roberts stands out in Tessa's mind," Desmond pointed out.

Ross listened in silence as his friends began to speculate about Nan Roberts. There was so little to go on, it was like playing a game of blindman's bluff.

"Now," said Desmond at one point, "tell me what has been happening here."

"Damn little," replied Ross. "To all appearances, everything is normal. Nothing has been happening."

Julian said, "Perhaps Tessa was telling the truth, and she wasn't there the night Becky Fallon drowned."

"She was there," said Desmond. "We have the the the evidence of witnesses at the time. Also the fact that someone was asking questions about her—someone, remember, whom we feared would get to her first. I'm not saying Tessa is lying. It's quite possible she doesn't remember she was there. You said so yourself, Ross."

"I've heard of that phenomenon," said Julian. "I had an uncle who was thrown from his horse and broke his leg. To the day he died, he couldn't remember the accident or, indeed, that he'd been out riding."

"Then why hasn't someone tried to get to her?" asked Ross.

Julian eyed him askance. "You sound disappointed!"

"Well, of course I'm disappointed. Do you think I want this always to be hanging over her? How will she ever live a normal life if we don't catch this villain?" Ross's pent-up frustration boiled over. "How can I protect her day in and day out for the rest of her life? In less than a year, she'll reach her majority. She'll be free to come and go as she pleases. How can I protect her then? You know what she's like. She'll want to live her own life, and my wishes won't matter."

Julian was studiously polishing his quizzing glass. He said casually, "Then there's only one solution to your problem, old boy. You'll just have to marry the girl."

There was an abrupt and prolonged silence. Gradually, small sounds reestablished themselves. The clock on the mantel ticked; the burning coals in the grate hissed; carriages coming and going in the street rattled over the cobblestones.

Desmond cleared his throat. "It's early days yet," he said. "And let's consider whether our villain suspects a trap. That could explain why he's gone into hiding."

Ross shook his head. "I don't think so. It's true that Tessa is well guarded, but everyone thinks that's because she's an heiress and I'm protecting her from an unsuitable match. I'm sure no one suspects just how vigilant we all really are. One of us is always close by, either Sally or Julian or myself, but we're discreet about it. Take Julian, for instance. Everyone assumes he's smitten with your sister, and that's why he's at Sayle House at every hour of the day."

At Desmond's astonished look, Julian answered easily, "It was the only thing we could think of to ward off suspicion and keep me close to Tessa and Sally. It's all very innocent, Desmond. Don't look at me like that."

"I thought of something else," Desmond said, handing the decanter of sherry around. "What if we take Tessa back to Fleetwood Hall . . ."

"Go on," said Ross. "What are you getting at?"

"I'm trying to think of a way of bringing everything back to her. We could get her to act out what we know took place."

Ross frowned. "But we don't know what happened that night."

"If you think about it," said Desmond, "you'll see that we know a great deal. There are gaps, of course, crucial gaps, but if we made Tessa act out as much as we know, there may be some chance that the rest would come back to her."

Ross said carefully, "But if we did that, she'd have to know that we think she might be the next victim. We'd have to tell her about the other girls, everything, in fact."

Desmond was staring into his glass. "I've been thinking of that too, and it seems to me, it might be the best thing all round." He looked up at Ross. "It would force her to take the situation seriously. Just a suggestion."

Julian was getting impatient. "And I think we're making mountains out of molehills. This could be nothing more than a series of unconnected accidents. Maybe there is no murderer! The only thing that connects all these unfortunate women is that they went to the same school."

Ross's hands clenched into fists, and he deliberately relaxed them before responding to Julian. "Cassie was murdered," he said. "She was terrified of water. She would never have taken that punt out on the lake, especially with no one there to see her."

"Are you sure? She might have, to please you. Isn't it possible that she wanted to surprise you? Cassie was like that."

Ross said fiercely, "I made a mistake with Cassie, but I'm not going to make the same mistake with Tessa. Once, I was as skeptical as you are, and because of it, a lovely young woman died. It's not going to happen to Tessa, not if I have to chain her to me for the rest of her life."

"Ross!" Julian said. "You can't blame yourself for what happened to Cassie! You couldn't have known—"

"I did know, and I did nothing."

Desmond quickly cut in, "That's not true. Even I wasn't sure then. It was only after . . . later . . . that we were convinced Cassie's death wasn't an accident. Don't worry, Ross. One way or another, we'll catch her murderer."

The conversation drifted to other things, but Ross's thoughts were still on Tessa and what Desmond had suggested. He'd never liked the idea of telling her that her life was in danger, and the more he thought of it, the less he liked it. No young girl should have to live with that hanging over her.

He'd once suggested to her grandfather that it might be best if she took up a new life in America, and he was seriously considering this possibility when the front door knocker began to pound. All three men rose as though an alarm had been raised, and quickly went to answer it. Desmond got to the door before his servant and when he opened it a groom in the Sayle livery burst into the hall.

"Your lordship!" He went straight to Ross. "You're to come at once. There's trouble at the house."

Before the groom had finished speaking, Ross was on the move. "Is it Miss Lorimer? What's happened to her?"

The groom ran to keep up with him. "They're trying to take her away."

"Who is trying to take her away?"

The groom's horse was tied to a hitching ring. Ignoring

his curricle, Ross untied the horse and vaulted into the saddle.

"I don't know," said the groom. "There's a magistrate and a constable. And others I've never seen before. Miss Turner told me to fetch you."

Anyone could pass himself off as a magistrate or a constable if he was desperate enough. They'd been expecting some kind of an attack and this might be it. With a slash of the reins, Ross sent his mount leaping forward.

He took the straightest route home, cutting across Hyde Park to the Knightsbridge Road. The hooves of his horse tore up chunks of earth in its mad gallop across the turf. Ross let nothing stand in his way. They leaped hedges and went tearing past startled riders, sending them scattering. The wild, panicked ride fed the irrational fear that had taken hold of his mind. He wasn't thinking only of Tessa, but Cassie also, remembering how he'd felt when he'd found her body in the pool beneath the waterfall at Greenways.

Outside Sayle House there was a carriage and two saddle horses. Ross quickly dismounted and made straight for the door. Knots of anxious servants were standing around in the hall.

"Upstairs, sir," said one. "They're in her ladyship's drawing room."

He took the stairs two at a time. On the next floor, he was met by one of the burly manservants he'd hired as a bodyguard for Tessa. It sounded as though there was a riot taking place in his grandmother's drawing room.

"They've locked the door," said the bodyguard. "But—"

There was a cry of protest from inside the drawing room, a cry that Ross was sure came from Tessa. He removed his pistol from his pocket, and bracing his shoulder for the impact, he charged the locked door. As wood splintered, the babble of voices suddenly ceased. On the second charge, the door burst inward.

Chapter Thirteen

He halted just inside the door, a harsh look on his face, his eyes swiftly assessing the several people who were gaping at him. He found Tessa and stared hard at the red-faced, portly gentleman who was gripping her arm. Under the ferocity of that glare, the gentleman quickly released her and took a step back.

"Ross!" Tessa's voice was so shaken, so teary, he hardly recognized it. "Oh, thank God you're here!" And quickly crossing the room, she threw herself into his arms.

One arm went around her, holding her close-pressed to his body. He still held his pistol, but a second comprehensive glance convinced him that Tessa was in no danger. The only weapons he could see were the scissors his grandmother clutched to her bosom. Two of the people in that room were strangers to him––the portly gentleman who had been grasping Tessa's arm when he'd burst into the room, and a thin, distinguished-looking gentleman with silver hair. There was also a couple in their middle years who looked vaguely familiar. Sally, his grandmother, and Mr. Harris, the hairdresser, were also present.

Ross slipped his pistol into his pocket. Immediately

everyone began to talk at once, but Ross's attention was riveted on Tessa. Teardrops had gathered on the tips of her lashes, and her eyes were huge in her pale face. Her whole body shook with tremors, and he tightened his hold on her.

"They're going to take me away," she said.

He ignored the many voices that were trying to attract his attention and spoke only to Tessa. "No one is going to take you away."

"You don't understand. They have a . . . a writ, or something, that gives them the right. They say they have more right to be my guardians than you, and the law is on their side."

"Who says?"

"The magistrate, Mr. Wade." She pointed to the silver-haired gentleman. "And my aunt and uncle Beasley."

Ross raised his head to stare at the couple who had looked familiar. The female topped her husband by several inches. They were both stout, both in sober gray as though they'd dressed to go to chapel. He'd met Mr. and Mrs. Beasley in Bath when he was trying to trace Tessa. He'd thought them solid, respectable citizens who were ideally suited to be a young girl's guardians. When Tessa had eloped with her footman, they had washed their hands of her. Now they wanted her back. Why?

It didn't matter why. Nobody was going to take Tessa away from him.

Tessa tugged on his sleeve. "The thing is . . . ah . . . Ross, I was forced to tell them the . . . um . . . truth about us."

He liked the soft, appealing look in her eyes, liked the way she said his name, and he particularly liked the way she clung to him.

"What truth is that, Tessa?"

She swallowed hard. "That we were secretly m-married in Paris," she said.

"M-married?" he mimicked. "And whom did we m-marry?" Then the full import of her words hit him, and he stood there, unblinking, as though he'd turned to stone.

"Each other, of course," she said crossly. "This isn't funny."

"Am I laughing?"

She gave him a searching look, and satisfied that he wasn't mocking her, dropped her voice to a confiding whisper. "I had to tell them something. And married women don't have guardians. But they wouldn't believe me and insisted on taking me away. Your grandmother tried to ward them off with Mr. Harris's shears, and when that didn't work, I locked the door and threw the key out the window."

Now he did laugh, but sobered when once again everyone began talking across each other. He held up his hand, and when there was silence, fixed his eyes on the thin, distinguished-looking gentleman with silver hair. "Magistrate Wade," he said, "would you mind explaining why you are here?"

Flattered to be recognized, the magistrate came forward and handed Ross an official-looking document. After many apologies and several silencing looks directed at the Beasleys, he came to the point. "If you are married, my lord, as the young lady says, and can prove it, this doesn't apply. Otherwise, you must relinquish Miss Lorimer into the care of Mr. and Mrs. Beasley. As you can see, it's all perfectly legal. Mrs. Beasley is related to Miss Lorimer by blood and can prove her claims. However, if you contest it, it will be up to the courts to decide who will be her guardian."

Mrs. Beasley's chest puffed up, and she wagged a finger at Tessa. "You wicked, wicked girl!" she exclaimed. "Is this the thanks we get after all we've done for you? We tried to bring you up to be a God-fearing, decent young woman, but you wouldn't have it. A secret marriage in Paris! I've yet to hear his lordship say so. Well, it won't wash. Tell her, Mr. Beasley."

"Shocking," said Mr. Beasley. "We had no idea she was an heiress. I mean, we knew her grandfather paid for everything, but we saw very little of it. He paid us only for her board."

Mrs. Beasley held up a hand, and her husband

instantly stopped speaking. She turned to the red-faced constable. "Constable Porter," she said, "kindly take Miss Lorimer to our carriage."

"I wouldn't lay a finger on her if I were you." Ross's voice was mild, too mild, and everyone froze.

Marriage. He knew that once he spoke the words, there would be no going back. Hell, he really didn't care who he was married to, and maybe Julian had been right. Marriage to Tessa was the perfect solution.

He smiled down at her. "We deserve to be scolded, my love," he said. "I'll take the responsibility, though. It's all my fault."

Relieved that he had decided to help her, Tessa let out a pent-up breath.

"Tessa told you the truth," Ross said, turning to the others. "We were secretly married in Paris, with her grandfather's consent, of course." He ignored the furious protest from Mrs. Beasley, and the gasp of astonishment from his grandmother. "But I wasn't going to announce it until I'd spoken to you, Mrs. Beasley, and you, Mr. Beasley. We owed you that much at least. I'd hoped to post down to Bath to tell you the good news, but first one thing came up, then another—you know how it is. I don't blame you for your lecture. But . . . we really are man and wife . . . and how splendid that you are here and can be the first to congratulate us."

Tessa could not understand why everyone was in such high spirits. As soon as Ross left the room to show their visitors out, Julian and Desmond arrived, and the story had to be told to them. After they'd stopped laughing, Julian rang for a footman and ordered champagne all round. They seemed to think it was a stroke of genius to put the Beasleys off by inventing this fictitious marriage. She didn't share their enthusiasm. The truth was bound to come out and then where would they be? And it was all her fault.

She glanced at the clock, wondering what was keeping Ross. Ten minutes had passed since she'd last checked the time. What was he saying to the Beasleys? What were they saying to him? And, more worrying, what was he going to say to *her* for creating this tangle?

At last the door opened and Ross entered. He, at least, seemed to have retained his sanity. He was unsmiling, and when he observed the long-stemmed glasses from which they were all drinking, his brows lifted.

His serious expression did not dampen the party atmosphere, though everyone drained their glasses and began to file out of the room. Tessa wished she could go with them, but she knew she and Ross had a lot to talk about. Somehow, they had to find a way out of the quagmire she'd landed them in.

Julian clapped Ross on the shoulder and grinned from ear to ear. "This is the first time in years that you've taken my advice," he said. "I presume you're going to ask me to stand up with you at your wedding?"

"You can count on it—if that day ever arrives," said Ross.

"My friend, from what I hear, you practically signed your own—" Julian's eyes flickered to Tessa, and he went on easily, "What I mean is, I don't see how you can get out of it."

Desmond was next. He shook Ross's hand. "I think it's for the best," he said and followed Julian out.

Sally put her hands on Tessa's shoulders and kissed her on both cheeks. "It will be all right, you'll see," was all she said before slipping through the door.

The dowager's parting words were similar. She smiled into Tessa's eyes, kissed her, and said, "I must have been blind. It wasn't until you threatened to have your hair cut that I began to see. Oh, my dear, I couldn't be happier for you both."

When the door closed, and she and Ross were alone, Tessa sank into the nearest chair and pressed a hand to her eyes. "They've all taken leave of their senses," she moaned. "They're acting as though we really are married, or soon will be." She let out a sighing breath, raised her head, and straightened her shoulders. "What are we going to do?"

"What are *we* going to do? You were the one who got

us into this. What do you suggest?" He'd poured himself a glass of champagne and sipped it slowly as he took the chair flanking the fireplace.

"I refuse to go back to the Beasleys," she said.

"Do you mind telling me why?"

"You saw what they're like. They're more religious than the Archbishop of Canterbury. They're vicious with it! They despise everything—singing, dancing, drinking, young men who come calling. The only reading materials they allow in the house, apart from the Bible, are books of sermons and tracts on deportment."

"The Beasleys sound like very sensible guardians to me."

She caught the flash of humor in his eyes, and that got her back up. She rose and began to prowl. "Men are always such hypocrites. It's all right for them to sow their wild oats. But if a female steps over the line, her reputation is tarnished."

"Tarnished?" He chuckled. "I'd say your reputation was rusted through and through."

An angry retort trembled on her lips. That was old history he was flinging in her teeth. Since coming to live at Sayle House, she'd followed all his rules, up to a point.

But guilt over the quandary they were now in held her back.

"Sit down, Tessa," he said. When she did so, he went on, "We really don't have much choice. The Beasleys are your legal guardians, and they have your father's last will and testament to prove it."

She threw up her hands. "Then why did you support my story when I told them we were secretly married in Paris?"

"Because," he said reasonably, "they were going to take you away there and then, and I wanted us to have some time alone to discuss what to do. And you can take that hopeful look off your face. You are not going back to France, and that's flat."

"Please," she said, leaning toward him, "I'll do anything you say, *anything*, as long as you don't send me back to the Beasleys. There's a cousin, a middle-aged glutton of a man they want me to marry. That's why I ran away. If you don't do something, they'll force me to marry him, don't you see?"

"You heard what the magistrate said. If we can't prove that we're married, and we can't, you'll have to go back to them. I suppose there's a chance that the courts might appoint me as your guardian, but I wouldn't count on it. I'm afraid that only a real marriage will solve your problem. Pity."

Her eyes dropped to her clasped hands. She'd had a few wild ideas of how she could escape the Beasleys, but none so wild as the one that suddenly seized her mind. Hot and cold chills raced through her, making her tremble, and her eyes turned a brilliant violet.

She raised her head and Ross's gaze narrowed on those brilliant violet eyes. "What?" he asked.

"N-nothing." It was too bizarre. He would never agree to it.

"N-nothing? Have you developed a stutter, by any chance?"

"N-no."

"I see. Then it's something you're afraid to tell me. What is it, Tessa?"

She spoke before she had a chance to change her mind. "We could get married," she said in a rush. "Oh, not a real marriage, of course, a marriage of convenience. Then, when I go back to France, I'll divorce you. It's easy to get a divorce in France."

There was a moment of stupefied silence, then he began to laugh.

Her brows came down. "I think it's an excellent idea!"

He stopped laughing. "That's easy for you to say, but how can I trust you? What if you decide you don't want a divorce?"

"Are you crazy?" She jumped to her feet and went on the prowl again. "You're not exactly one of my favorite people. You know I can't wait to be rid of you."

In a very different tone, he said, "How do *you* know you can trust *me*? What if I decide I don't want a divorce and refuse to let you go?"

She stopped pacing and turned to stare at him. "Don't make empty threats," she snapped. "I know how you feel about me. To you, I'm just a child. You've told me so more times than I care to remember." Her gaze wavered, then steadied. "And we both know, you're still in love with your wife."

His head went back and his eyes flared. "Tessa—"

He was going to turn her down, and she was too desperate to let that happen. "You listen to me, Ross Trevenan," she said fiercely, drowning out his words. "You made a promise to my grandfather and it's a promise you're going to keep." She was standing by his chair, glaring down at him. "You said I was to have a season in London. You said you would protect me. I demand that you either keep your promise or send me back to France."

He rose without haste and faced her. She had to throw back her head just to keep her eyes steady on his, making her feel at a distinct disadvantage.

"I know what I promised your grandfather," he said, "but the price you are demanding is a little too steep. Tessa, the world doesn't revolve around you. I have my own life to lead."

"Then lead it! Marriage to me won't stop you. You won't even know that I'm there. And it's not as though it's forever. I swear, the first thing I'll do when I get back to Paris is arrange for a divorce."

He shook his head. "If I could only believe you. But you wouldn't be the first woman to try and trap me into marriage."

She wanted to hit him, to scratch his eyes out, to stretch him on the rack and then boil him in oil. That he should think she *really* wanted to marry him. Perhaps he thought she was in love with him. Ugh!

"You puffed-up, conceited blockhead!" she railed. "I was right about you, and my grandfather was wrong. Well, one way or another, I'm going back to France. I've done it once, and I can do it again. Let me tell you, I'd rather be married to Jerome Bonaparte than to that . . .

that drooling Beasley octopus who can't keep his hands to himself."

She turned smartly on her heel.

"Tessa," he said.

"What?"

He sighed. "All right. You win. I'll do it. But on one condition."

Her jaw dropped. "You'll do it?" She turned to stare at him.

"If I marry you, I want it to be our secret that it's in name only and a temporary affair. No one must know, not Sally, not my grandmother, not anyone. We have to make this convincing, otherwise there's no point to it."

She would have promised him the moon to escape the clutches of her Beasley relatives. "I won't tell a soul," she breathed.

"There's more to it than that. I expect you to act like a wife. I don't want you to make me look ridiculous. When I say something, you'll listen. In public, we'll look like a happily married couple. You'll be a sweet and docile wife and I shall be an attentive husband. If you're not up to it, say so now. The Beasleys are staying at the Clarendon. You can be there within the hour."

She smiled through clenched teeth. She couldn't afford to argue with him in case he retracted his offer. She'd won, that was the important thing. "I understand," she said.

Abruptly turning, she made for the door. When he called her name, she looked over her shoulder. "What is it now?"

"Where do you think you're going?"

"To have my hair cut by Mr. Harris. He never did get around to doing our hair. Sally and Lady Sayle are with him now, in your grandmother's boudoir."

"Have you forgotten our bargain so soon? I don't want your hair sheared off."

"Oh," she said. A moment later she gave him a brilliant smile. "Oh, well, I never really meant to have my hair sheared . . . not until you put your foot down." And with a saucy toss of her head and a flounce of her skirts, she was gone.

Ross fell back in his chair with a big smile on his face. That girl would call black white and white black just to annoy him. Well, in this case she was doing exactly what he wanted, only she didn't know it.

Tessa had handed him what he wanted on a silver platter.

He didn't know why he was congratulating himself. It was true that everything had turned out as he wanted, but that was only in the short term. When Tessa learned she could never go back to France, and that in England a French divorce wasn't worth the paper it was written on, things could turn ugly.

That thought led him to Tessa's grandfather. There had been the occasional letter smuggled in and out of France, and Alexandre seemed to be holding his own, but Ross didn't put much faith in his friend's assurances. Alexandre was far from well. The news of his marriage to Tessa was bound to cheer him. He wouldn't tell Alexandre that it was only a marriage of convenience. It cost him nothing to leave the old man with his illusions.

Thoughts drifted in and out of his mind. She'd called him crazy, and he was beginning to wonder if she was right. *A marriage of convenience.* Who in hell's name had invented such an unholy thing? It must have been a woman, or a young man married to an ugly old witch. Tessa wasn't an ugly old witch. A marriage of convenience? Purgatory was more appealing. He didn't know how he was going to keep his hands off her.

In one gulp, he drained his glass. He had enough troubles for the present and the future had a way of looking after itself. Meanwhile, he had a marriage to arrange.

Quickly rising, he strode from the room.

Chapter Fourteen

❦

It had never occurred to Tessa that her friends wouldn't see her marriage to Ross for what it was—a temporary maneuver to keep her out of the Beasleys' clutches. They all acted as though this impending marriage were a cause for celebration. Evidently, they had forgotten that a divorce in France was as easy to come by as buying a loaf of bread. And she couldn't remind them because of the promise she had made to Ross.

There was no time to talk things over with him and come up with another solution to their problem. In the week before the wedding, they barely saw each other and said no more than a few words in passing. Events had rushed in on them like a tidal wave, events she had set in motion and was now helpless to reverse. The notice of their fictitious marriage in France was carried in all the morning papers, as well as the report that the marriage would be privately solemnized again according to the rites of the Church of England, as was proper for a man in Lord Sayle's position. The modiste who had provided her with a wardrobe suitable for a young girl embarking on her first season was called in again, this time to make garments that were more in keeping with Tessa's exalted station as Ross's marchioness. Invitations were sent out for a ball that was to be held at Sayle House to celebrate their marriage. The house was in an uproar with all these preparations, but it wasn't unpleasant. There was a feeling of excitement that seemed to permeate the very air she breathed.

All this had a profound effect on Tessa. Her moods swung alarmingly from one extreme to the other. There were moments when she was so caught up in things that she forgot none of it was real. Then her heart would plummet and her excitement and anticipation would slip away. She wasn't a bride in the true sense of the word. She was playing a part. Why couldn't she remember it?

On the eve of her wedding, the enormity of what she was doing was pressed home to her when Ross's grandmother entered her bedchamber. Tessa immediately knew why the dowager had come. She was going to tell her what she could expect to happen, the following night, in her marriage bed. There was no need. French girls were not as ignorant as their English counterparts. And besides, this wasn't a real marriage. It was a farce, but she couldn't tell the dowager that. The dowager, however, was so uncomfortable, pausing for long intervals, groping for words, that Tessa finally put her out of her misery and explained that she already knew all about such things.

But the dowager had more on her mind. She also wanted to talk about Ross, to prepare Tessa for life with a man who wasn't always easy to live with.

She told Tessa about Ross's parents, and their abysmal neglect. She spoke of Cassie and how Ross had changed after the tragic accident that had taken her life. Tessa absorbed the dowager's words in silence but inside her head a picture was forming. She saw a solitary young man who had been transformed by his love for a young woman, then cruelly crushed by the caprice of fate.

When she was done, the dowager smiled at Tessa and took her hand. "My grandson has a great capacity for love," she said, "but you will need a great deal of patience with him. Give him time to become accustomed to what he feels for you, Tessa. Don't give up too easily and I think you'll be surprised at the result."

Long after the dowager left, Tessa tossed and turned in her bed. The dowager was mistaken. Ross didn't feel anything for her. He still loved Cassie, and he would never get over her.

She wished with her whole heart that she had never met him.

The dowager was still thinking of Tessa when she returned to the drawing room. George Naseby was sipping a glass of port, waiting for her. Everyone else had gone to their own homes or to their beds. He turned at her entrance and her heart warmed, as it always did, when he looked at her like that. He'd once been the great love of her life. When they'd been forced to part, her heart had broken, and so had his. But hearts mend. They'd survived. And now, almost fifty years later, they were content to be the best of friends.

"You seem to have weathered the ordeal well," he said, and chuckled.

She took the chair on the other side of the fireplace. "It wasn't much of an ordeal. Tessa is more knowledgeable than English girls. Don't forget, she spent two years in France."

"What is it, Em? Why do you look like that?"

"Weddings," she said. "They always make me feel sad. But that's not to be wondered at, is it? My own wedding was the saddest day of my life. How long did you hate me, George, after I married Sayle?"

He set aside his glass and came to sit on the arm of her chair. "I could never hate you for long, Em. I knew your parents had forced you to marry him. You were an heiress. My prospects weren't very bright. Our trouble was that we were too young to understand the ways of our world."

"We thought love could conquer all."

He kissed her brow. "Aye, that we did."

"I'm glad you had your Margaret. I'm glad you were happy with her."

"She was a good wife. But I never forgot you, Em."

"Nor I you."

The colonel broke the silence that had fallen between them. "That was an odd business about the girl's guardians turning up, wasn't it?"

She looked at him curiously. "They wanted to get their hands on Tessa's fortune," she said.

"But Ross has control of her moneys?"

"When he brought Tessa to England, her grandfather made him her trustee."

"They're saying in my club that Mr. and Mrs. Beasley are out to make trouble."

"Bah!" she said. "After tomorrow, what can they do?"

"That's true."

Her brow wrinkled. "Ross is not marrying Tessa for her fortune, George."

"Are you sure?" His smile was quizzical.

"He's in love with her," she said. "He just doesn't know it yet."

The colonel laughed. "Still the same Em," he said. "You were ever the romantic."

She smiled. "You rogue! You're no better than I. You won't let your Sophie go to a man she cannot love."

"True. But I'd like to see her settled comfortably as well."

"And so you shall." She patted his hand. "Leave it to me, George. If Sophie isn't betrothed by the end of the season, I shall be very surprised."

Tessa awakened on her wedding day with a feeling of dread hanging over her. Before she could dwell on it, however, the maid arrived with her chocolate. Jenny's eyes glowed with excitement, and she chattered cheerfully as she drew back the curtains and laid out Tessa's bridal clothes.

The dress had simple lines. It was a high-waisted, white muslin with a scooped neck and long sleeves. The gold embroidery on the dress, however, made it unique. All the stitches that Tessa had never mastered—satin stitch, French knots and chain—were there on the embroidered panels of gold vines and roses that trailed from waist to hem and along the edges of the short train. It was a gown any bride would be proud to wear.

Tessa felt a yearning so intense it was almost a pain. She'd never imagined her wedding day would be anything like this. The dress was perfection itself, but everything else was wrong. Her grandfather should have been there to give her away. And she should have been marrying a man who loved her.

She shivered and braced herself for what must be. It would be all right. Ross said this was the only way. And not even to salve her conscience was she willing to return to the Beasleys' tender mercies.

Shortly after she was bathed and dressed, Sally entered. She, too, was in white muslin, her dress almost a replica of Tessa's except that it was devoid of embroidery. In her hand, she held a bouquet of red roses.

"These are for you," she said, "from Ross. It's time, Tessa." She laughed. "If you don't come downstairs soon, I think he'll have a fit. He's been up for hours. I've never seen a more anxious bridegroom."

It was all an act. That was something she must never forget.

"Tessa," said Sally, "you're not having second thoughts."

The words jolted Tessa, and she looked up to see the searching look Sally was giving her. "Second thoughts?" she echoed faintly.

"Because if you are," said Sally, "just say so now and we'll call the wedding off. There's no need to be frightened, Tessa. I'll stand by you. No one can make you do anything you don't want to do."

Tessa wanted to throw herself into Sally's arms and confess everything. Never, in her whole life, had she had such a friend. She trembled on the brink of indecision, but Julian's voice called to them from the other side of the door, and the moment was lost.

"Coming," said Sally. "Well?"

Tessa summoned her composure. "I still can't believe how lucky I am."

Sally's frown vanished and she smiled. "Ross says he knew right from the beginning that you cared for him, and I must say, I began to suspect the truth when I saw how you turned to him when your Beasley relations were trying to take you away. Well, we all did."

Tessa waited for some mention of Ross's feelings for her. When none was forthcoming, she smiled brightly. "Let's not keep the anxious bridegroom waiting." And before Sally could subject her to another searching look, she swept from the room.

When she entered the library, Ross came forward to meet her. He didn't look to Tessa as though he were an anxious bridegroom. He looked remarkably relaxed and there was a twinkle in his eyes.

Taking her by the wrist, he led her to one side. "I have something for you," he said.

She gasped when he fished in his pocket and produced the broach her grandfather had given her. The red rose was now nestled in emerald studded gold leaves. He swiftly fastened it to her bodice, giving her no time to admire it.

"My English rose," he whispered in her ear. "Sweet to look at, but beware the sharp thorns. Don't frown, Tessa. Remember you're the radiant bride, and this is the happiest day of your life."

His ungracious remarks revived her spirits. A brilliant smile lit up her face, and she nodded to the few people who were standing beside the black-robed cleric. The dowager, Julian, Sally, and Desmond were the only witnesses to their marriage. They beamed right back at her.

Ross extended his arm and Tessa obediently slipped her hand through the crook of his elbow. His eyes moved over her in a leisurely appraisal. "You're overdoing it," he said.

Her nostrils quivered and her smile slipped. Without moving her lips, she said, "You are a cad, Lord Sayle." She turned her head and gave him a slow melting smile. "Is this better?"

His lips twitched. "Very convincing. Are you sure you

are playacting, Tessa? You're not, by any chance, in love with me and plotting to turn this into a real marriage?"

She choked back a snort. "Do I look crazy?" she asked. "Shall we get on with it?"

"So eager?"

"I'd like to get back to the book I was reading."

They smiled into each other's eyes for the benefit of their audience, and Ross slowly exhaled a long breath. When she'd first entered the library, she'd looked like a terrified rabbit, a conscience-stricken terrified rabbit if such a thing were possible. He'd known, though, that she might refuse to go through with it. It was fortunate he was beginning to get the knack of how to handle her. This was better, much better. The hand in the crook of his arm had stopped trembling, and the color had come back to her cheeks.

She was beautiful, of course, with her red-gold hair pinned up in a loose knot, and the gold thread in her gauze gown reflecting the highlights in her hair. Beautiful and desirable. And very, very frightened, in spite of her bravado.

He moved his free hand to cover the hand that rested in the crook of his arm and squeezed gently. She looked up, startled. "Trust me," he said softly. "Everything is going to be fine."

The reception later that evening was easier than Tessa had feared. Ross had made sure that someone was always there, by her side, ready to help her field awkward questions.

As the evening went on, perhaps because of the champagne, she began to enjoy the part she was playing. She could see the benevolent envy in the eyes of the ladies who were covertly studying her. She had snared one of the most eligible gentlemen in all of England, and they were sizing her up, trying to fathom what he saw in her.

Ross helped the fantasy along. Even when he was mingling with their guests, his eyes rarely left her. Occasionally, from across the room, he would lift his glass in a silent tribute, and she would respond in kind. And when he danced with her, there would be small, intimate touches, nothing too obvious, just a hand on the small of her back, a feather-light touch on her shoulder or on the nape of her neck. And she would laugh up at him, and flirt with him with her eyes.

It was a game, she told herself, not unlike the fantasies she'd indulged in as a child when she was locked in her room as a punishment. Sometimes, she remembered, the fantasy had become so real to her, so much better than reality, as now, that she hadn't wanted the punishment to end.

Toward the end of the ball, however, reality returned with the arrival of Amanda Chalmers and her cousin, Bertram Gibbon. The malevolence that blazed from Amanda's eyes made Tessa shrink back. She stammered out something, she didn't know what, and looked around for Ross.

If ever she had doubted Amanda's role in Ross's life, it was confirmed for her now. A silence had descended on the guests who were closest to her. There were a few pitying looks. Someone laughed nervously. Out on the dance floor, Julian and Sally abruptly stopped dancing and were dodging couples as they tried to make their way to her. Ross and Desmond were in conversation with a gentleman Tessa did not recognize. Ross's eyes casually lifted to meet hers, then moved to Amanda. Straightening, he, too, began to make his way toward her, leaving his companions staring.

Out of nowhere, Larry appeared at her elbow. The viscount was the last person Tessa expected to come to her aid. He'd been sulking all evening because he had not been invited to the wedding ceremony.

"Amanda! Bertram!" he exclaimed. "Isn't this famous!" He smiled down at Tessa and put a steadying arm around her waist. "My sly brother-in-law has snagged himself an heiress, and a beautiful heiress into the bargain. I wish someone would tell me how it's done." He looked down at Tessa and his smile vanished. "Are you all right?"

Muscles tightened in her throat, and her voice

sounded strange to her own ears. "I . . . I feel light-headed. I don't know what's come over me."

"Probably too much champagne," said Larry, grinning, and he rescued her empty glass from her nerveless fingers.

Ross came up at that moment. "What is it, Tessa?" He deftly detached her from Larry's grasp and anchored her to his side.

"I don't think Lady Sayle is feeling well," drawled Bertram Gibbon, surveying her through his quizzing glass.

They all thought she'd had too much champagne to drink. Perhaps she had, but she wasn't tipsy. She was suffering the effects of coming back to reality.

"I feel fine," she said and hiccuped.

Above the laughter that followed, she heard the dowager's voice. "I think you had best take Tessa upstairs, Ross. I'll arrange for coffee and sandwiches. I don't think the poor child has had a bite to eat all day."

"Say your adieux to our guests, Tessa," said Ross.

She did as she was bid, but she couldn't bring herself to look directly at Amanda. She hadn't given one thought to Ross's mistress when she'd practically forced him into marriage. She could feel Amanda's hatred coming at her in waves, and she could not blame her. But she hadn't meant to hurt anyone. Wasn't that what she always said?

With Sally on one side and Ross on the other, she left the ballroom. For the sake of appearances, Tessa's things had been moved to the bedchamber that adjoined Ross's. When Sally entered, Ross held Tessa back in the corridor and closed the door softly.

"Tears?" he said, and his thumb gently removed an errant tear from her lashes.

"I'm sorry," she said, keeping her voice down so that the footmen who were stationed at either end of the corridor wouldn't overhear her. "I've spoiled everything."

"No. I was proud of you tonight."

There was a strange intimacy in the silence that followed. Her throat ached with all the tears she held in check. "I'm . . . I'm not tipsy, you know."

"I didn't think you were."

She could feel her heart beating and her pulse racing. Before she could make a fool of herself, she reached for the door handle.

"Tessa?"

He was looking at her lips, and she could barely breathe. "What is it?" she asked hoarsely.

His eyes crinkled at the corners. "Wait up for me?"

Then he kissed her, swiftly, and moved away before she could find the breath to answer him.

Julian was waiting for Sally when she finally left Tessa's room. "Too much champagne?" he asked.

"Too much excitement for one day. However, she's eaten the sandwiches, and now she's resting." She frowned. "Julian, what is Amanda Chalmers to Ross?"

He glanced at her quickly. "Did Tessa say something?"

"No. I'm not stupid. I saw how you and Ross dashed to Tessa's side when you saw her in conversation with Mrs. Chalmers."

When they were descending the stairs, and out of earshot of the footmen, Julian said, "Amanda used to be Ross's mistress but she'd hoped to become his wife."

"But . . . but she's a wealthy widow," she said. "Why would she want to become any man's mistress?"

"Guess." A faint smile touched his lips.

Sally said crossly, "You've got that look on your face that tells me that the next word in this conversation is bound to be 'copulation' or something to that effect."

"That's an old-fashioned word, Sal. I was thinking of sex."

"I'm an old-fashioned girl."

"Aren't old-fashioned girls interested in sex?"

Sally exhaled an exasperated breath. "Not particularly."

"I could make you change your mind."

Her eyes narrowed. "I'm not interested in becoming one of your women, Julian."

"Sal, I'm not trying to bed you. All I'm interested in is a light flirtation. Egad, I think I deserve some reward for all I've given up to play nursemaid to Tessa."

She sniffed. "You are referring, I suppose, to all your opera dancers and actresses?"

"And *la dolce Deluca*. Don't forget her, Sal."

"Is she the one who drives all over town in that outrageous carriage with the pink satin trimmings and those great white horses?"

"I thought you were above listening to the gossips! And those horses are match-grays, as I should know. They cost me a pretty penny. You'd best unfreeze your face if we're to keep everyone convinced that you're the reason I visit Sayle House so frequently. I see you're bursting to say something to me. Shall we take a walk in the gallery and admire the pictures before we return to the ballroom?"

In the gallery they stopped before a portrait of a lady in an Elizabethan costume. There were other couples promenading about, but no one tried to join them.

"Smile, Sal," whispered Julian. "We're on center stage."

She turned her face up to him, smiled, and batted her eyelashes, but the instant she turned back to look at the painting, her smile died. "This isn't going to work," she hissed. "No one will believe you are paying court to me, you, a dandy, and me a—"

"Dowd," he supplied.

"Vicar's daughter!" she replied tartly.

"Oh, I don't know. I'm known to be attracted to the unusual. Well, look at *la Deluca*. She's not particularly beautiful. Her talents lie in other directions." He ignored her sharp intake of breath. "Besides, how else can I explain why I hang around Tessa when Ross is away? You and I are smitten with each other, Sal. Better get used to it."

"Why can't you give Desmond's reason for being here?"

"What? That we're involved in devising—what is it Ross and Desmond are supposed to be doing? I forget."

"They're putting together a plan for policing the cities of England, a plan they're going to present to the Home Secretary. And they're not pretending. They really are working on it."

"No one would believe I'd be interested in such a thing. It sounds too much like work. Now skirt-chasing—that's a different matter."

Her bosom quivered. "Life is all a game to you, isn't it, Julian?"

"Not entirely. But I do believe that life is meant to be enjoyed. Don't look now, but Mrs. Abigail Shortreed has just entered on the arm of her betrothed, old Major What's-his-name. I swear those two have the busiest tongues in all London. I'm going to kiss you, Sal, and if you fight me, it will be all over town tomorrow that we've had a falling out, and that would put paid to my coming here again. You wouldn't want that, would you?"

She was swept up in his arms before she could utter a word. The kiss was swift, but thorough, and when he released her she was panting as if she'd just run up ten flights of stairs. He, on the other hand, remained unmoved, except for the twinkle in his eyes.

"It was all in the line of duty, Sal," he said.

She took the arm he offered and couldn't help blushing when they passed Mrs. Shortreed and Major Blake. "Julian," she said dulcetly, "have you ever heard the phrase 'parson's mousetrap'?"

He gave a theatrical shudder. "You mean marriage, of course, the bane of every confirmed bachelor. Why do you ask?"

"Just to remind you, in case you have forgotten, that I'm the parson's daughter."

"But, Sal, my whole object in life is to make you *forget* you're a parson's daughter," he said, and laughed when her eyes began to heat.

Chapter Fifteen

❧❧❧

*T*essa stood at the window that overlooked the courtyard and watched the stream of departing carriages. The ball was over. The servants would be cleaning up. She'd heard Sally and the dowager pass her door some time ago. She really ought to undress and go to bed.

Wait up for me. Perhaps there was some business he wished to discuss. Perhaps he wanted to talk to her about Mrs. Chalmers. She could hardly object if he kept a mistress. She wasn't a real wife, and this wasn't a real marriage.

She touched her fingers to her lips, remembering the pressure of his mouth on hers. She didn't know what she was feeling, what she was thinking.

When someone knocked at the door, she bit down on her lip. After taking a moment to compose herself, she crossed to the door and opened it. It was only a footman.

"This letter arrived for you, m'lady," he said.

"A letter? At this time of night?" She took the letter from the silver tray the footman extended to her.

"It was delivered by hand," he replied.

She wasn't interested in the letter. "Has . . . has his lordship come up yet?"

"I believe he's in the library, ma'am."

She nodded and quietly shut the door. She didn't know who could be writing to her at this time of night, but with nothing better to do while she waited for Ross, she sat beside the candle, broke the seal, and spread out the one-page epistle.

There was no date, no salutation, and no signature. It took her only a moment to scan the message, and in that moment, her whole body began to tremble.

I am glad you came back. I must speak to you about Becky Fallon. You know where to find me.

It was a joke, of course, nothing more sinister than a tasteless, spiteful prank. And she was shaking because she hated to be reminded of the night Becky had drowned. Everyone always thought she had something to hide. Which was a lie.

She read the letter again and again, her mind furiously grappling with who could have written it. Who knew that she'd once attended Miss Oliphant's school?

Sally. And Sally was always introducing the subject of Fleetwood Hall. The last time they'd talked about it, Tessa had told her about Nan Roberts, the only girl she could really remember, and Sally had seemed strangely curious about her.

She read the letter again. Sally couldn't have written this piece of spite. It just wasn't like her. But Nan . . . it was so long ago, but one thing she remembered. Nan was a fiend when it came to practical jokes.

But she had no idea where to find Nan.

She stared into space, the letter forgotten, as she tried to call up an image of Nan. They'd become best friends only because they'd both arrived at the school in the middle of term, when the other girls had already chosen their friends. They were the odd girls out, and they'd pretended not to care. In fact, their bravado became obnoxious; they'd got into all sorts of mischief just to thumb their noses at the other girls.

It was a pattern she had followed in every subsequent school she had ever attended. She'd been her own worst enemy if only she'd known it. But that was all behind her now.

The more she thought about it, the more convinced she became that the note was from Nan. They'd lost touch with each other, but Nan could have found her after Ross had put the notice of their marriage in all the morning papers.

She would show the letter to Ross. He would know what to make of it. There was no reason such a silly prank should frighten her.

She rose and left her chamber, making for the library.

After leaving Tessa with Sally, Ross had returned to the ballroom. He was reluctant to leave his bride, knowing how fragile her emotions were, but he had an unpleasant duty to perform, and the sooner it was over and done with, the better.

The first thing he did was track down his brother-in-law. Larry was in conversation with a group of male friends, and gave a start when Ross touched him on the elbow. When they were out of earshot of the others, Ross said, "What happened with Tessa? Did Mrs. Chalmers say something?"

"Not that I'm aware of," said Larry. He was very stiff and his resentment was obvious. "I saw Tessa's face and knew that something was wrong."

"I see. Thank you for taking care of her."

"Your thanks are unnecessary. I didn't do it for you. I did it for Tessa."

"All the same, I'm grateful. Look, Larry, I know you're upset about not being invited to the wedding ceremony—"

"Why should I be upset? I am nothing to you. I'm not really family."

Ross said calmly, "It wasn't a normal wedding where invitations are sent out. I apologize. You were not deliberately left out."

Larry did not unbend. "Is that all?"

"What else can I say?"

"Nothing. Everything has been said." And Larry turned on his heel and sauntered off.

Ross did not have time to brood on his brother-in-law's hurt feelings. Already people were beginning to call for their carriages. He hastened the end of the ball by dismissing the orchestra and advising his wine steward not to serve any more champagne.

Amanda and her cousin were among the last to leave. Ross quietly arranged a private rendezvous with his former mistress. Not long after, he slipped into the library where he found her waiting with two glasses and a bottle of opened champagne.

Her green eyes were wide and alert, and glimmering in anticipation. She was beautiful, of course, and dressed in a shimmering emerald silk gown that showed off her dark hair and svelte form to perfection. Beautiful, elegant, and poised, and so very different from Tessa. The hellion. The thought made him smile.

Amanda evidently read something in his expression that wasn't meant for her. Her own smile became brilliant, and she gave a sultry laugh. "I sent Bertram home in my carriage," she said, "so you see, I'm completely at your disposal."

He couldn't fail to understand the innuendo. It annoyed him because it showed she hadn't the least understanding of his character. He quelled his annoyance. It was his own fault. He'd turned up on her doorstep in the middle of the night when he was supposed to be secretly married to Tessa. What else could she think but that he'd wanted to take up with her again? He'd been saved from that folly only because he'd had too much to drink.

No. It wasn't the quantity of brandy he'd consumed that night that had made him damn near impotent. It was Tessa he had wanted, and no other woman would do.

He refused the glass of champagne she offered and went to stand by the fireplace. He didn't invite her to sit. He wanted this to be short and to the point.

"I owe you an apology," he said. "I should have made it clear months ago that our connection had to end. There were reasons why I couldn't tell you about my marriage, reasons that no longer exist. I hope you'll forgive me."

Her lashes swept down and when she raised them again, her eyes were moist with tears. Her hand fluttered to her throat. "Ross, I don't know what to say! What you must think of me! I never meant to come between you and your wife. I thought . . ." She shrugged helplessly. "I thought you had married the child to give her a home and that it would not make a difference to us."

"It does make a difference," he said. "That's what I wanted to say to you."

Her eyes fell away from his. "Oh, I know you never loved me, not the way I loved you, but I could have sworn you were fond of me, more than fond."

He had hurt her, really hurt her, and that surprised him. It also made him feel horribly guilty. "I can't tell you how sorry I am," he said sincerely. "I've behaved like a scoundrel."

"No, you haven't, Ross!" She crossed to him. "I was foolish. Oh, I never expected you to marry me, or anything like that. I didn't mind, just as long as I had some small part in your life. I should have known how it would be. Your wife is lovely, Ross. She has youth and innocence on her side. I hope you will be happy together. I mean that sincerely."

"You're very generous, Amanda."

Her eyes were huge with misery. "I hope we can still be friends?"

"That goes without saying."

"And . . . and you'll visit me now and then?"

There was a short silence. Finally, he said, "That would be awkward, Amanda."

"You're thinking of your wife, of course. But I didn't mean to exclude her. You must bring Lady Sayle to my next salon. Mr. Fox will be there, and it should make for an interesting evening. Oh, how foolish of me!" she exclaimed. "As though a young girl would be interested in what old people might have to say!"

Ah. This was more like the Amanda he expected. Though it was veiled, he recognized the spite in her remark. Tessa was too young, too immature for him. Hell, he was only one and thirty! And the odd thing was, Amanda was wrong. It was true that there was much of the child in Tessa, but she wasn't childish. She saw everything through an unprejudiced eye. And there were occasions when he'd caught a glimpse of another Tessa, sadder and wiser beyond her years.

Amanda was looking at him through the sweep of her lashes. "No, not one of my boring salons! A house party! That would be the very thing! There's much in and around Henley of interest and I would be sure to invite young people of her own age."

It was time to bring this little tête-à-tête to a close before Amanda said something that really got his back up. "Did you say something to Tessa in the ballroom?" he asked abruptly.

Her eyes filled with pain. "Do you think so little of me that you believe I would deliberately hurt an innocent girl? What would be the point? It would only make you hate me, and I couldn't bear that, not after everything we have been to each other."

It irritated him to hear her talk as if theirs had been a grand passion. They'd shared a few carnal nights in her bed, and that's all it had amounted to.

He said, "I trust that I can count on your discretion over something that touches me so closely." It was a veiled threat, and they both knew it.

She gave a tremulous smile. "You must love her very much."

He inclined his head, a vague response that made her brows wing upward.

"I shall arrange for my carriage to take you home," he said.

She held out both hands. He felt he had no choice but to take them and raise them to his lips. She let out a shivery sigh, and swayed into him, and before he could prevent it, she was kissing him on the mouth.

Suddenly she pulled back and gasped, staring in

horror at a point over his shoulder. He turned swiftly only to see Tessa taking to her heels.

"The poor girl," moaned Amanda. "Oh, I should go after her and explain everything."

"Don't be ridiculous," snapped Ross. Her fingers were curled around his wrist like talons and he was trying to pry them loose. Giving up the attempt, he wrenched out of her grasp and made for the door.

"But, Ross," she cried out, "you can't leave me here like this. What will your wife think? Please, you must call your carriage for me."

The delay took only a few moments, then he took the stairs two at a time.

Tessa raced into her room and quickly locked the door. Thinking this cowardly, she unlocked it and retreated as far as the bed. The letter in her hand was crumpled into a tight ball. It didn't matter now. Nothing mattered. Flinging it aside, she stared at the door, waiting for him to enter.

What was keeping him?

What a stupid question! And why did she care? He wouldn't be coming after her. She might as well lock the door.

Her hand was reaching for the key when he entered by the door that adjoined their two chambers. Tessa whirled to face him.

Ross propped himself casually against the door frame, not because he felt casual, but because he could tell that she was angry and primed for a fight. He didn't want to fight with her, not on this night of all nights.

"Tessa, it's not what you think," he said gently.

She said quickly, "You don't have to explain anything to me. Larry told me about Mrs. Chalmers. So you see, there's nothing to apologize for."

His mouth flattened. "Oh, Larry told you, did he? And what exactly did my dear brother-in-law have to say?"

"That Mrs. Chalmers is your mistress."

"Was! She *was* my mistress, but that was many months ago, before I ever met you."

"I'm not accusing you of anything." She was proud of her calm tone. "I told you I wouldn't interfere in your life, and I meant it. You won't even know I'm here."

He was tempted to laugh. Not know that she was here? That's where all his troubles had started. He couldn't be unaware of her. What he hadn't been able to accept was that he'd wanted her more than he'd wanted Cassie. Now, he'd come to terms with what he was feeling. Cassie was locked away in his heart, where no one and nothing could touch her. He would always love her. But that didn't mean he couldn't make a life for himself with Tessa, and it would be a damn sight better than the life he'd have had with Amanda Chalmers and women like her.

"You don't care if I take a mistress?" he asked whimsically.

She swallowed the painful lump in her throat. "Yes. No. Oh, you know what I mean. Ours is a marriage of convenience. I'm not really your wife. The same rules don't apply."

"Now that's where you're wrong. The same rules do apply." He spoke evenly and slowly, to impress every word upon her. "I would never shame my wife by taking a mistress. Do you understand?"

"But our case is different."

"Not to me, not as long as you're my wife."

Her chin lifted. "I see. Then the sooner I return to France, the sooner you can return to the arms of Mrs. Chalmers."

"That's not what I meant. I made a mistake with Amanda," he said. "I was sure she understood that our affair was over, but she didn't. She does now. That's why we were together in the library. The kiss didn't mean anything."

"I understand. That's what Paul said when I found him with that woman."

When he came away from the door frame, she sucked in a sharp breath.

"I am not Paul Marmont," he said.

Now she'd roused his temper, and she really didn't feel like quarreling. She just wanted him to go. "I don't care about Mrs. Chalmers," she said. "She didn't do anything wrong, or say anything out of turn. There was no need to speak to her on my account."

"Then why did you look so stricken, there in the ballroom, when you were talking with her?"

Stricken. The word humiliated her, but it was the right word. She'd almost died of shame at the look Mrs. Chalmers had blazed at her. She'd stolen Ross from the beautiful widow, unthinking of the pain she might cause. She'd felt guilty, and jealous, and utterly mortified when she'd seen how some of their guests pitied her, coming face-to-face with her husband's beautiful mistress at her own ball.

She'd had enough humiliation for one night. If she had to go on much longer like this, she would do something stupid, like brain him with the poker that lay conveniently on the hearth.

"Look," she said, "it was the champagne. I'm not used to it. I was feeling ill. That's all it was. Please, I'm tired. Haven't we said everything that needs to be said?"

He looked at her set jaw and the squared shoulders, and he swore under his breath. She had set her mind against him.

The hell she had! he thought, and moved swiftly. He caught her in his arms and dragged her against him, then his mouth came down on hers.

She told herself not to respond, if only for the sake of her pride. What she hadn't counted on was that her brain didn't come into it. Her whole body softened in response to the hard pressure of his, and she clung to him as the kiss became deeper, hotter, more and more demanding.

When he drew away, she was dazed and breathless, and could only stand there, staring up at him.

He waited a moment, until he was sure his breathing had evened. "Haven't you figured it out yet?" he said. "This is what all our quarreling is about."

She still hadn't come to herself when he released her and walked to the door of his own room. On the threshold, he turned back to look at her. "Why did you come to the library tonight?"

It was his self-confident smile that jerked her back to her senses. She deliberately squared her shoulders and jutted her chin out, challenging him to contradict her. "I couldn't sleep. I thought if I read for a while, it would help."

"No one told you I was there with Amanda?"

"I wasn't in a jealous rage, if that's what you're hinting at."

"It was only a thought. Sweet dreams, Tessa."

When the door closed softly on his smiling face, she let out a shivery breath. Why did he have such power to confuse her? She picked up the crumpled letter she'd received earlier, the letter that had caused her so much distress, and she threw it in the smoldering fire without giving it another thought. Then she absently yanked on the bellpull to summon her maid.

When Jenny entered, she took one look at her mistress's face and her smile vanished. "Whatever is the matter, m'lady?" she asked anxiously.

Tessa pressed a hand to her eyes. "It was the champagne," she said. "The champagne."

And she almost believed it.

Amanda Chalmers kept her smile in place until she entered the privacy of her boudoir. Her cousin was not there, nor had she expected him to be. Bertram had supposed, as she had, that tonight she would be sharing her bed with the noble Marquess of Sayle. Bertram had even toasted her triumph.

It wouldn't have ended there. She would have played with Ross, toying with him as a cat plays with a mouse. Then she would have humiliated him, publicly, as he had humiliated her by throwing her over for that nobody of a chit. Nothing less would satisfy her thirst for revenge. But he had turned the tables on her. Well, she wasn't done yet. No one made a fool of her and got off scot-free.

She raised her arm to sweep the crystal bottles and porcelain pots from the top of her dressing table and checked herself, swiping at air. What she wanted was to go on the rampage. Only one thing stopped her. The noise would bring the servants running, and servants sometimes carried tales out of school. No one was going to say that Amanda Chalmers's nose was out of joint because Ross Trevenan had chosen a pasty-faced, gormless girl over her.

She could almost hear Bertram laughing, and that infuriated her more. He had warned her not to bring the Beasleys into the affair, but even he had not foreseen the outcome. That Ross should have married that creature in Paris! That he should have done so without a by your leave! He would regret it. She never forgot an affront.

Not since she was a girl growing up in Henley had she felt so humiliated. Her father had been a country squire, but he wasn't rich and he didn't have a title. She'd fallen in love with Jack Fenton, the heir to the greatest landholder in the area, and he had fallen in love with her, or so he'd said. But at the Christmas ball at Henley House, his betrothal had been announced to Lord Melrose's daughter.

By God, she had learned a lesson from that. There were two kinds of people in this world, players and spectators, and she knew which one she wanted to be. She'd made something of herself, and when Freddie Chalmers had come into her orbit, she'd made her move. He'd been betrothed to another lady, but she hadn't let that stand in her way. And she'd had her revenge on Jack Fenton. Henley House was now hers, bought for a song when Jack wasted his wife's fortune on gaming and wenching.

She'd shared that triumph with Bertram. Nobody else understood her as he did. They'd both learned their lessons the hard way. For people in their position, there was only one way to raise themselves out of obscurity and that was to marry for money and connections.

Ross Trevenan was another Jack Fenton, but she wasn't the gullible girl she'd been all those years ago. Just remembering that scene in the library made her feel better. Bertram would have been proud of her. She hadn't lost her temper. Instead, she'd deliberately softened Ross with tremulous smiles, and tears, and long speaking looks. He didn't know it yet, but now they were playing the game by her rules.

She thought of Tessa and tears of rage welled in her eyes. She should have known how things stood when Bertram told her what they were saying in all his clubs. The Marquess of Sayle had lost his head over the girl. The wardrobe he'd ordered for her was reputed to be worth a king's ransom. Her pelisses were lined with sable; the gold thread in her gowns was real gold. As for the priceless collection of Sayle gems, every last piece was in the process of being sized for his bride. Then she'd seen the Sayle diamonds glittering on the girl's throat when she'd entered the ballroom, and she'd wanted to scratch her eyes out.

He'd trifled with her. He'd come to her house in the middle of the night and had tried to bed her. And afterward, he'd singled her out and paid her a great deal of attention. He'd made her believe that he was ready to resurrect their affair and she'd boasted to her friends that the Marquess of Sayle was in her pocket.

He would pay for it. She didn't know how, but she knew she was going to make him pay.

A picture formed in her mind—the look on Ross's face after she'd kissed him, and he'd realized his wife was watching. It wouldn't surprise her if he was already paying for his sins.

It wasn't enough. It wasn't nearly enough. She wouldn't be satisfied until she had brought him to his knees. The only thing that remained to be seen was how she was going to do it.

Chapter Sixteen

❦

When Tessa entered the drawing room, she found the others already there. Sally was playing the piano; the dowager was embroidering at her tambour frame; Desmond and Julian were playing checkers; and Ross was reading a book. She'd brought her own book with her, and without disturbing the others, she settled herself in a chair close to the fire and began to read.

It wasn't long before her thoughts began to wander. She felt comfortable here, among friends who accepted her as she was, spending a quiet evening at home for a change. It wasn't like this when she went out in society. People looked up to her, deferred to her, not for her own sake but because she was the Marchioness of Sayle. In her lighter moments, she sometimes wished she could throw a ball for all those former teachers who had predicted she would come to a bad end. The fantasy never lasted for more than a few minutes. She was well aware that if they knew all the circumstances leading up to her marriage, they would shake their heads and say that Tessa Lorimer was incorrigible and this escapade was just what they would have expected of her.

She didn't care a jot for the good opinion of high society or her former teachers. But she did care for the people in this room and she hated to disappoint them, and they would be disappointed when they discovered she and Ross weren't really married.

Her marriage was a masquerade, and Ross was far more adept at carrying it off than she. In fact, he even seemed to enjoy embarrassing her with all his little marks of attention. Sometimes she was downright mortified. He would come barging into her bedchamber while her maid was dressing her to go out, and then stand there watching her, talking of trivialities while she hardly knew where to look. In private, when she'd protested, demanding that he give her the key to the door that separated their chambers, he'd pointed out that the marriage had been her idea, and she'd promised to play by his rules. The servants would think it odd if he did not share a few intimate moments with his wife, and they would be scandalized if they found out the door adjoining their rooms was locked. He didn't know why she was making such a fuss. For a girl who had crossed the English Channel in a small boat with only a band of smugglers as chaperons, she was making much ado about nothing.

Fortunately, Christmas was almost here, and many families were away at their country estates, so their audience was limited. There was concerts and musicales and the odd ball, but not the round of parties they could expect when the real season got under way. All the same, it was a great strain, remembering to smile and simper when Ross took liberties that in another man would have earned him a black eye. And he took many liberties. She was seeing a side of his character she had never seen before. He'd kissed her once in the gazebo in St. Germain, but he'd been different then. Now he was playful and flirtatious, and she was forced to follow his lead. It was important to remember that they were playing a game, and one day soon it would have to end.

It was the thought of her grandfather that gave her her worst moments. She didn't know how she was going to face him. If she'd been thinking straight, she would have guessed that Ross would write to him immediately about their marriage. She had hesitated, trying to decide how to describe the situation, and the delay had proved to be a costly mistake. Her grandfather had replied warmly that he'd known from the very beginning that this was meant to be, and they'd brightened an old man's dreary days. There was more in the same vein, and each word she'd read had felt like a dead weight pressing against her heart. She dreaded to think what the divorce would do to him. And because she could not yet face disappointing him, she had penned only a vague reply.

It was all such a muddle. And as each day passed, she became more entangled in the web of deceit. The dowager was teaching her how to manage Ross's house. There could be only one mistress, the dowager said, and it must be the lord's wife. There were menus to plan and accounts to go over as well as the ordering of supplies that came in twice weekly from Ross's country estate. And this was as nothing to what she could expect when they went down to Greenways. The odd thing was, she seemed to have a natural aptitude for running a large house, and took more satisfaction from the sparse praise the housekeeper paid her than she did from all the flowery compliments she received in the drawing rooms of Mayfair.

She would miss the dowager when she left here. She would miss them all. Though she'd tried not to become too fond of Ross's friends and family, it was impossible not to become involved in their affairs. Ross didn't always appreciate her meddling.

There had been another argument when Ross discovered that Larry was secretly selling off some silver plate that belonged to Repton, Larry's estate in Kent. Later, after Larry had stormed out of the house, she had hesitantly suggested to Ross that if Larry could manage more of his own affairs, the result might be surprising. Ross had dismissed this as a naive suggestion. But she wasn't naive. She saw something of herself in Larry. At school, her teachers had expected the worst of her and she had tried not to disappoint them.

One thing she couldn't fault Ross on. He'd gone out of his way to make amends for not inviting Larry to their wedding. Larry had unbent enough to visit them now and again, but his manner toward Ross was still frigid.

Julian was another regular visitor, and everyone knew what drew him. He'd taken a fancy to Sally, but Sally was keeping him at arm's length. She'd confided to Tessa that she wasn't convinced Lord Harlow would make a suitable husband for any woman, let alone a vicar's daughter, and she was even less sure of her own feelings. Tessa hoped Sally would make up her mind soon because if there was going to be a wedding, she wanted to be part of it.

That was the problem. She was becoming too caught up in her friends. She was beginning to think of them as her own little family. Their troubles were her troubles, what interested them interested her. Even Desmond had got her fired up over the project he was working on with Ross. Establishing a comprehensive police force! How could she be interested in something like that? But she was. Desmond's passion was infectious. Now if only she could get him to fire up Colonel Naseby's quiet little granddaughter, she would be happy.

Sophie Naseby would be perfect for Desmond. The girl was shy, but behind her calm gray eyes was a keen intelligence. She was well read. Though she didn't say very much, Sophie wasn't easily swayed by the opinions of others. In fact, Sophie . . .

She came to herself with a start when her book slipped from her fingers and fell with a thud on the floor. She was doing it again, becoming too involved. After retrieving the book, she looked up to see Ross staring at her. There was an odd moment of intimacy as their glances locked, then his expression cleared and he smiled.

"You don't seem to be enjoying your book, my love," he said. "What are you reading?"

My love! That was for the benefit of the others, of course. She had to look down at the book in her lap to see what it was. "One of Mr. Sheridan's plays," she said. *"The School for Scandal."*

"It's supposed to be a comedy."

She knew it, and would normally have been giggling her way through it if her thoughts hadn't been elsewhere. "I'm not sure I care for how Mr. Sheridan portrays his female characters," she said lamely.

Ross closed his own book. "Did you know that Mr. Sheridan based those characters on real people?"

She took a moment to think about this. "Do you mean Lady Teezle is someone he knew?"

"She was inspired by Lady Melbourne. There are others. The Duchess of Devonshire, for instance. You'll meet them soon enough, when Lady Melbourne gives her opening ball of the season. You'll meet Mr. Sheridan, too. Of course, the play was written a long time ago, so you might not recognize them."

"Don't you believe it, Tessa," the dowager joined in. "Georgina Devonshire and Elizabeth Melbourne are as silly now as they were then."

Tessa liked the idea of meeting the characters from a play she'd been reading, and she turned to say so to Ross, but he was looking at her this time with a closed expression, and she forgot what she was going to say.

Their glances parted when a footman entered with the tea tray. Soon after, Desmond and Julian went home and the ladies retired to bed, leaving Ross to enjoy a glass of brandy while he finished the novel he'd been reading.

As soon as she was ready for bed, Tessa dismissed her maid, donned a warm woolen robe, and sat down at her writing table. She'd been thinking a great deal about her grandfather these last few days, partly because some time had passed since she'd received a letter from him, and partly because she'd been troubled by guilt. And the longer she put off the unpleasant task of telling him that her marriage was a fraud, the more guilty she felt.

She picked up her pen, dipped it in the ink pot, and began to write. After several false starts, she realized that it was almost impossible to put the thing delicately. Her attention was diverted by the sound of the door knocker. She heard Ross's voice, then the house became silent again. Crumpling the page she'd already written, she threw it aside and started over.

As unhappy with this attempt as the others, she threw down her pen, sat back in her chair, and let out a frustrated breath. Just then, there was a knock on the door from Ross's chamber and before she could call out, Ross entered. He had a letter in his hand, and his expression was grave.

"I saw your light under the door," he said, "and knew you were still up."

The words were innocent enough, but her mind was making lightning connections—the door knocker sounding so late at night, the letter in his hand, his grave expression, the fact that she hadn't heard from her grandfather for some time. She couldn't breathe, couldn't speak, wouldn't dare let her thoughts complete themselves.

He came to stand a few feet away from her. "Tessa," he said gently, "you must prepare yourself for a great shock. I just received this letter. It's from your grandfather's attorney." He paused, giving her time to absorb his words. "Alexandre," he said, "died in his sleep last Thursday night. It was pneumonia. He didn't suffer. His last words were of you."

She felt all the blood drain out of her face and the room began to spin. "No." Her voice was no more than a painfully constricted whisper. "There must be some mistake. There *must* be."

"There's no mistake, Tessa. Alexandre was not a well man. He didn't want you to know how ill he really was."

Ross threw aside the letter he was holding, sank down on his haunches, and took her trembling hands in his. "I'm sorry, Tessa. I'm so sorry."

Her eyes searched his face, then she gave a little cry and buried her head on his shoulder. "Last Thursday night!" Her voice broke. "I was at Lady Uxbridge's musicale. And my grandfather was dying." She looked up at Ross. "I can't bear to think of him all alone, with no one to tend him but servants. Oh, God, how can I ever forgive myself?"

"He died in his sleep. Even if you had been there, he wouldn't have known it."

She was shaking her head. "But my grandfather's doctors assured me he had many good years ahead of him. I wouldn't have left him if I'd known, suspected, that this might happen. I swear I wouldn't."

Her hair was loose, and he caressed it idly with one hand. Her face was ashen. She was trembling.

"Listen to me, Tessa," he said. "Alexandre knew that this would happen. First and foremost, he wanted you safe. He didn't want you to be alone in France when he died and that's why he asked me to take care of you. By coming here, you made his last months happy. And when he heard of our marriage, he was deeply gratified. You are not to blame yourself for anything, do you understand?"

The tears she'd been checking spilled over. "I've been enjoying myself all these months, while he . . . what must he have . . . while I . . ."

Ross straightened. "You're in shock," he said. "Don't move. I'm just going next door to get you a glass of brandy."

He had taken only a few steps when she called him by name. He turned and saw that she had risen to her feet. Her breathing was shallow and fast, and she was supporting herself with one hand braced on the flat of her writing table.

She said, "Am I to understand that you knew how seriously ill my grandfather was when you brought me here? You knew I would never see him again?"

A muscle tensed in his cheek, and he answered her question with a slight inclination of his head.

Her shoulders began to heave and she had difficulty articulating her words. "D-damn you! Who gave you the right to m-meddle in my affairs? I would not have l-left my grandfather for the w-world. He should have confided in *me*. I could have borne it. But no, you think I'm a child, to be dragged here and there at your whim. I'm a g-grown woman. I should have been consulted. The decision to leave him was mine to make."

"The decision was Alexandre's," he said quietly.

Her reply was passionate. "You could have persuaded him to change his mind. He would have listened to you. You could make my grandfather do almost anything. Don't you realize what you've done? You've robbed me of something precious. I should have been told. I should have been there. I shall n-never forgive you for this!"

Ignoring her outburst, he said very gently, "Let me get that brandy for you. You'll feel better after you drink it."

She watched him go, her breath shuddering in and out of her lungs as she tried to master her emotions. How could he have done this to her? How could he have kept from her something that so closely touched her? A season in London! As though she cared about that! They had both treated her like a child, both Ross and her grandfather. They should have consulted her. No matter what the outcome, they should have consulted her.

She looked down at her writing table and saw the several unfinished letters she'd crumpled into balls. Never again would she write to her grandfather. She moved before she knew what she was going to do. With a sweep of one hand, she sent letters and writing materials tumbling to the floor, then she whirled around and rushed from the room.

In the act of pouring out a glass of brandy, Ross heard the commotion next door and called out Tessa's name. When there was no answer, he set down the decanter and glass and quickly crossed to the open door. There was no sign of Tessa, but on the floor were several crumpled sheets of paper, the pumice pot, her pen, and an ink pot that was spilling its contents onto the carpet.

A few quick strides took him into the corridor. He looked over the handrail. On the floor below, the brawny footman whose duty it was to rouse him if anything unusual occurred looked up at him. Tessa evidently had not passed that way. Swiftly turning, Ross made for the servants' staircase. As soon as he opened the door, he could hear the click of her slippers as she rushed headlong down the stairs.

"Tessa!" he bellowed.

She did not answer. Then he heard the outside door opening and closing and he raced after her.

A crescent moon barely illuminated the gardens and park of Sayle House. Tessa plunged into the darkness. She'd walked in these grounds so many times that she could have found her way blindfolded. She didn't know consciously where she was going. Her actions were purely reflex. She was making for one of her favorite walks, a sheltered grove on the far side of the west lawns.

Her feet flew over the parterre with its invisible formal shrubs and barren flower beds, and in a few minutes she had reached the lawn. There were no obstacles here and she took off like a hare. She wasn't looking for a place to hide. It never occurred to her that Ross would pursue her. Her thoughts were so chaotic that she was barely conscious of what she was doing.

Her flight was checked suddenly when a hand closed around her wrist and swung her round. She could tell it was Ross even before he spoke. He caught her in his arms and steadied her.

"Tessa, Tessa! This is foolish. You must come back to the house with me."

"Let me go, damn you! I shall never go anywhere with you again."

The naked pain in her voice shocked him and he relaxed his hold on her. In the next instant she lashed out with her clenched fist catching him off guard with a blow to the shoulder. When he released her, she whirled away from him.

She veered from her course and plunged into a thicket of briers and brambles. Branches slapped at her face and as she pushed them aside, thorns tore at her hands. Her gown caught. She yanked it free and went stumbling over a tree root. He caught her from behind, and with all the panic of a cornered wild thing, she turned on him. He made no effort to protect himself from her attack other than to gather her in his arms in a close embrace. Kicking, arching away from him, trying to claw him despite the confinement of his arms, she strove to free herself.

His words were soothing. Hers were almost incoherent. He had betrayed her. He should have told her about her grandfather. There were things she had never told him, things that should have been said, and now it was too late. But he had always despised her. He didn't care if he hurt her. He didn't believe she had feelings. He hated her.

There was more in this vein, much more, and he held her till the heedless words had ebbed to choked sobs. When she quieted and went limp against him, he swung her into his arms and nestled her against his chest. Without prompting, she put her arms around his neck and turned her face into his shoulder. Not a word was spoken as he carried her back to the house.

When they entered the house, she lifted her head from his shoulder, but she didn't say anything. He carried her to his own chamber and laid her on the bed. She made a halfhearted protest, then turned her face to the wall.

She wanted to hide from him in shame. She felt exposed, as though she'd bared her soul. In her despair, she'd said too much, things that she was afraid to acknowledge even to herself. Dear God, what must he think of her?

He sensed her deep mortification and spoke casually to spare her feelings. "I'll ring for a servant to tidy your room. Meanwhile, you still have to take the brandy I poured out for you. Yes, I know you don't like brandy, but in this case, it's necessary. And you have some deep scratches to your hands. Those will have to be treated so they don't become infected."

His calm, reasonable words went a long way to restoring her composure. After a few moments, with an effort of will, she pulled herself up and sat on the edge of the bed. He was adding coal to the fire, and barely looked at her, and for that she was grateful.

"The brandy is on the table beside the bed," he said.

She looked at the glass, picked it up, and set it to her lips. The first swallow made her gasp. The second was easier, and she sipped slowly. Her eyes were downcast, nor did she lift them when she heard Ross answer the knock at the door. He spoke in an undertone to the footman who was on duty, and not long after a pitcher of hot water was delivered.

When he put a basin on the table by the bed and poured the water from the pitcher into it, she looked up.

"You can drink the brandy later," he said, and took the glass from her. "Now, let me see your hands."

Faint color tinted her cheeks, but she did as he said. He took one hand in his and uncurled her fingers. He didn't look at her as he bathed the scratches.

"You have every right to be angry with me," he said. "It's true that I didn't think much of you at first. I hope you will believe that I've known for a long time that I was wrong." He dried her hand and started on the other. "It was all my fault. You thought me cold and unfeeling, when actually the reverse was true. I cared much too deeply. Which is why I did everything I could to destroy your power over me."

She looked up at him, startled. His eyes were unguarded, with a warmth she had rarely seen directed at her.

He looked down at her hand, and traced one of the scratches with his thumb. A lump wedged in her chest. She wanted to believe him, but she was afraid to.

In the same quietly persuasive tone, he went on, "As for not telling you about the state of Alexandre's health . . ." He smiled slightly. "You have a will of your own, and nothing your grandfather or I could say would have persuaded you to leave him. But you had to leave. I'm sorry you were hurt by our decision."

He had dried her hand, but he did not release it. He reached over and captured her other hand and seemed to be completely absorbed in studying it.

"I'm sorry about your grandfather, Tessa," he said. "There wasn't a man I admired more. And I know how much you loved him, and he you. There's one more thing I want to say. You're not alone. You have me. It's what your grandfather wanted, and I think it's what we want too."

He kissed her hands and rose from the bed. "Come," he said, holding out his arms. "I'll take you to your own chamber."

Her throat was working, and her eyes were red-rimmed and raw with pain. "I don't want to be alone," she said. "Ross, will you stay here with me, and talk to me about my grandfather? No one knew him as you did."

"Of course I'll stay, if you want me to."

One despairing cry tore from her throat, then she was in his arms, clinging to him like a lost child.

Chapter Seventeen

～～∽つ～～

Tessa awakened not knowing where she was. Outside, it was dark, and the candles were still lit. It was warm in that room, too warm, and the thought flitted through her mind that it would be better if she opened a window to let in some fresh air. Her throat was tight, as though she were suffocating, as though . . . Then everything came back to her and she pulled herself up. When she saw that Ross hadn't left her, she gradually relaxed.

He was slumped in a chair close to the grate, eyes closed, his chest rising and falling regularly in his sleep. He had discarded his coat and neckcloth, and she could see the strong column of his throat and the steady pulse that beat there. A lock of blond hair fell across his brow. In sleep, his features were softened. He looked younger, less intimidating.

She nestled under the covers, keeping to her side so that she could watch him. Just knowing he was close by was a comfort to her. At the same time, she dreaded the moment when he would awaken and she would have to face him. Last night, she'd cried in his arms like a babe.

She wasn't ashamed of her grief. She was ashamed of laying her heart bare.

With a soft moan she closed her eyes. In a weak moment she had told him things about herself she'd never told another soul. The shock of her grandfather's death had unbolted a door she'd hoped was locked forever. And Ross had been so compassionate, so patient, that all the slights, all the despair of her childhood had spilled out of her.

She didn't want his pity. The last thing she wanted was his pity.

You're not alone. You have me. It's what your grandfather wanted, and I think it's what we want too.

She was so afraid she was reading too much into his words.

She opened her eyes and found that he was watching her. Her chest and throat still ached from all the crying she'd done, but that wasn't why she didn't say anything. His eyes held hers in an unsmiling stare, and her heart began to pound. It picked up speed when he rose from the chair and came to stand by the bed. She couldn't look away. He wouldn't let her. And now she was aware of him in a different way. This time, he wasn't going to comfort her. She could see it in his eyes.

"A few hours ago," he said, "you told me that when you went to live with your grandfather, you felt you'd made a fresh start." He searched her face, then slowly leaned toward her, bracing his weight with one hand on either side of her. "Will you do as much for me, Tessa? Will you give me and our marriage a fresh start?"

She couldn't move, couldn't say anything. A huge swell of emotion lodged in her throat, bringing tears to her eyes. He read the answer he wanted, and, lowering his head, brushed her lips with his own.

He knew he was taking advantage of her. He'd debated with himself half the night, trying to be fair to her, while she slept like an exhausted child. He'd always known she was susceptible to him. But now she was vulnerable, confused by the storm of emotions her grandfather's death had unleashed. A better man would give her time to come to herself. A better man would take a step back and wait for her to come to him, if and when it was right for her. Once he had been such a man, but that was before last night, before she'd allowed him to get close to her. He'd never doubted that he lusted after her beautiful body, but now he wanted so much more. He wanted everything that made her who and what she was.

When his hand cupped her face, she closed her eyes, absorbing the feel of his warm fingers on her skin and the throb of her pulse as it began to race. Then she felt his hand tremble, and she drew back, looking up at him with a question in her eyes. His gray eyes were clouded with uncertainty, as though he were having second thoughts.

"You've been through a lot tonight," he said. "This can wait."

She slipped her hands over his shoulders and around his neck. "Ross," she whispered, "I need you. I need this. Don't leave me now."

He drew her to him on a moan, and his lips found hers again. He kissed her once, twice, and as her lips softened, he asked for more, but not too much, not yet. He didn't want to frighten her. He didn't want to hurt her. No one and nothing was going to hurt her ever again.

His control was tested when she made a small sound of arousal. Her breathing was irregular and his own breath quickened in response. But that was as nothing when she ran the point of her tongue along his lips and timidly penetrated his mouth.

When he pulled back, her eyes were anxious, as though she'd done something wrong.

"That was nice," he said. "Do it again."

Her arms went around his neck and she drew his head down for her embrace. She felt the smile on his lips, and she smiled too. This was so easy, so natural. She didn't know why English girls went in terror of their wedding night. There was nothing to fear here.

She wasn't quite so confident when he slipped first one arm and then the other from the sleeves of her night-gown. For a moment she stilled, but the caress of his hands on her back was so soothing, so comforting, that she sighed her contentment into his mouth.

Following her example, he ran the tip of his tongue over her lips and entered her mouth. "Am I doing it right?" he murmured.

"Open your mouth wider," she said. "Yes, that's better. See how nice it can be?"

Ross buried his face against her throat. He would have laughed if he hadn't been so shaken. The minx really did know a thing or two about kissing. The blood was pounding in his ears, his hands were shaking. If she tipped him her dainty little tongue one more time, he was sure he would explode. She was such an innocent that she couldn't know what was going through his mind when she invited his tongue into her mouth. He wanted to be inside her. He wanted to show her where all this was leading. No, he was desperate to show her where all this was leading.

Control, he reminded himself, and took her lips again.

Desire crept up on her slowly. Kisses weren't enough for her. She wanted to get closer to him. She wanted to press her body against his and crawl inside him. She was hot. She was cold. She was restless. She didn't know what was the matter with her. Her breasts were aching with a fullness she'd never experienced before.

"Ross?" she said, appealing to him. "Ross?"

She sighed with relief when he pulled back the covers and stretched out beside her. This was better. This was what she wanted, to be held by him, breast to breast, thigh to thigh. Nestling closer, she kissed his lips, his eyes, his cheeks, his throat. She wanted this to go on forever.

He touched her then, a lean hand cupping her breast, but he did not linger. He forced himself to keep his touches casual. This was her first time, and he wasn't going to do anything to frighten her. He murmured soothingly, his hands gently arousing, betraying none of the desperation that was building inside him.

"Tessa?" He tugged on her nightgown to free her of

its confining folds. "We don't need clothes between us, do we?"

She murmured something unintelligible, but she didn't try to stop him. She was wallowing in the sensations that held her in thrall. Her limbs felt heavy. Her brain was foggy. She could have sworn she was floating on a warm current of air. All her senses had heightened. She could smell the faint lavender that scented the starched linen sheets, hear the hiss of the coals in the grate, feel the flickering warmth of the candles against her bare skin. But most of all, she was aware of the scent and taste of the man who lavished her with caresses.

When he moved away from her, she stretched languidly, then jolted in shock when he rejoined her on the bed and molded his naked body to hers. She could feel the ridge of his swollen sex, there, cradled between her thighs. There was a moment of blind panic as it suddenly became clear to her that there was more to going to bed with a man than she'd been told. Her fingers curled into his shoulders conveying her alarm.

Ross lifted his head. "What is it, Tessa? What's wrong?"

She swallowed. "I didn't know . . . that is . . . no one told me . . . Ross, what exactly is going to happen?"

He searched for his control, found it, and mentally took a step back. Her eyes held traces of arousal, but there was fear there too. That steadied him as nothing else could. "I thought," he said, "you already knew. Certainly, that's what you told my grandmother when she came to your room the night before our wedding. Girls in France, you told her . . ."

"I know what I told your grandmother," she said crossly, "but obviously I was mistaken. Ross, are you laughing at me?"

"Believe me, Tessa, laughter is the farthest thing from my mind."

"Then tell me—"

"It's better if I show you. Trust me. Don't be afraid. I would never do anything you didn't want me to."

The words hung between them for a long moment,

then she smiled up at him and draped her arms around his neck. "Then show me," she said.

And he did. He stole her breath with slow, intimate caresses and kisses that set her blood on fire. Sighs became moans; half-formed thoughts floated away on a haze. She had never known such pleasure and she was ravenous to know more.

While she abandoned herself to every new sensation, Ross ruthlessly bridled his own desire. Sweat beaded his brow and he clenched his teeth. Again and again, he reminded himself he had to be careful with her. He deliberately gentled his touch, kept his kisses soft and easy, but the more he held back the more she demanded. Her hands became greedy, her kisses wilder. When he touched her and found her wet and ready for him, he almost lost the struggle to hang on to his control

He rose above her, and at his nudging, she opened for him.

"It's all right," she said, seeing something in his eyes that made her reach up and kiss him.

"Tessa . . ." He couldn't say more. It had never been like this.

Then she arched beneath him, and he gave her what she wanted, what they both wanted. He felt her body resist him as he slowly entered her, but she didn't cry out. She wrapped her arms and legs around him, locking him to her. Then he was past the barrier and he began to move.

At the back of her mind, she sensed that whatever skill and patience he possessed, he used for her sake. She had no skill and less patience. She moved instinctively. She wanted to tell him . . . she didn't know what she wanted to tell him. She thought her heart would burst. She thought her body would shatter. At the end, she cried out and buried her face against his neck.

He felt her slip from the bed, heard the rustle of her gown and robe as she donned them, then her soft foot-pads as she moved to his dressing room. A moment later the door closed and he heard nothing. She would want to be private, to wash all traces of their lovemaking from her thighs. This time, he would allow it, but he was not as fastidious as she. It gave him pleasure to think of his seed invading her body.

He was on fire again, and as his sex hardened like a ramrod, the damn sheet rose up to rebuke him. He shifted to his side. Nothing could come of it, so he had better get a grip on himself. She would be tender; she wouldn't want him, and even if she did, he would be no better than a savage if he took her twice in one night.

When the door to his dressing room opened, he raised his lashes and quietly watched her. She was plaiting her hair, and in the candlelight it appeared more gold than red. Her skin was flushed from their exertions. He knew that her lips would be red and swollen and he wondered if the vivid violet in her eyes had faded to a calmer hue. He couldn't see. She was standing by the window looking out.

Tessa turned from the window, saw that he was awake, and gestured with one hand. "There's someone out there on the grounds, someone with a lantern."

He heaved himself up and adjusted the pillows at his back. "That will be one of the groundsmen. They patrol the gardens at night with dogs, to warn off housebreakers, you know what I mean."

"I wasn't aware of that."

"No, I don't suppose you were, but then, how often have you been up in the middle of the night?"

"I . . . I usually sleep like a babe," she said, and blushed.

He grinned. "There you are then."

Flustered, she babbled, "I didn't see any groundsmen earlier, I mean, when I ran out of the house and into the parterre."

No, and someone's head was going to roll for it. But he would deal with that problem later. "Didn't you? I did, but you had other things on your mind."

He was propped against the pillows, with the covers to his waist, and she could hardly tear her eyes from him. She had a vague recollection, when she'd been lost in passion, that she'd reveled in his hard, muscular strength. She'd taken that impression with her fingertips, as her hands had raced over him. Now, she was seeing exactly what had excited her. He was magnificent—broad shoulders, tight waist, and muscles that seemed to ripple as he moved.

He said, "You looked so pensive when you were staring out the window. What were you thinking?"

She'd been thinking of many things, him most of all. "My grandfather," she said, "and . . ."

"And?"

She shrugged. "And how you let me run on about him. I don't know why, but it makes the pain easier to bear."

He patted the bed, and when she obediently padded over, he took her hands and helped her up beside him. "Do you know what I think?" he said. "I think that, right this minute, Alexandre is having a good laugh at our expense. He knew that this is how things would turn out for us. You know it's what he always wanted. We were just too stubborn to admit it."

The tightness around her heart eased and she chuckled. "When I think of it, my grandfather was a very devious man. He was always singing your praises, till I was ready to scream."

"It was the same for me."

"Perhaps he wasn't so very wise after all. Look how we hated each other."

"He was wiser than us. Look at us now."

She felt her breath catch, and she searched his face. He'd said a number of things to her in the last few hours that she'd been afraid to believe. But now, by every look and gesture, he was making it plain that he really did care for her.

His hand slowly lifted to cup her cheek. "Why so pensive?"

"I don't understand myself," she said. "A few hours ago, I was grieving for my grandfather. He was all I could think about. And now . . ."

He kissed her swiftly. "You shouldn't feel guilty," he said. "Alexandre wouldn't want you to. Besides, this is how it's supposed to be between husband and wife. The act of love involves more than pleasure. It brings a man and his wife closer together." She was looking at him with wide, serious eyes and he said, less confidently, "You're not sorry that I"—he discarded the word "seduced"—"made love to you, are you?"

"No."

He grinned at her emphatic reply. "Good. Because I intend to make love to my beautiful wife every chance I get. That's also how it is between a man and his wife."

She stared, she blushed, she stammered, then laughter bubbled up. "Forgive me," she said, "I don't know how it's supposed to be between a husband and wife."

"I should hope not."

"I can't believe how ignorant I was."

"This, coming from a girl who spent two years in France?"

She gave him a sideways glance. "I know a lot about kissing," she said.

"Now that I can't deny."

"I had good teachers." She smiled archly.

His eyes darkened. "Paul Marmont, I suppose?"

"Oh, he was only one among many."

Though he knew she was only flirting with him, he was remembering the first time he'd kissed her. Kissed her, and touched her, and practically had his way with her. If other men had kissed her like that, he would kill them.

"Who were they?"

Her eyes danced. "Now, Ross, if you promise not to ask me about my past lovers, I promise not to ask about yours."

"It's that kind of talk that earned you the reputation of being fast."

The more they talked, the more confident she became. She heard the edge in his voice but thought he was feigning it to indulge her humor. "I prefer to think of myself as an adventuress. You said so yourself. How many ladies of your acquaintance have eloped with footmen, yes, and crossed the Channel with a boatload of swarthy pirates?"

"None that I recall. And I thought they were smugglers. Where is this leading, Tessa?" He knew where it was taking him. He could hardly believe it of himself, but he was beginning to feel like a sulky schoolboy.

She smiled into his eyes. "Ross," she said softly, "when you made love to me just now I felt . . . cherished. It was wonderful."

He smiled. "I'm glad."

"But . . ."

"But?" he prompted, dangerously quiet.

"But I couldn't help sensing that you were . . . well . . . holding yourself back."

"You noticed that, did you?"

She nodded. "Oh, yes. Quite distinctly. You made me feel like a piece of priceless porcelain. Oh, I'm not ungrateful. I just want you to know I'm not as delicate as all that. I don't break easily." She laughed self-consciously. "You'll think I'm . . . too bold." She peeked up at him and was reassured by his bland smile. "But, as I've explained, I'm not a complete innocent. And I'm not easily shocked. So you see, there's no need to hold back on my account."

When she rose from the bed, he snagged her wrist. "Where do you think you're going?"

"To blow out the candles." She looked at the clock. "We'll be lucky if we manage a few hours' sleep before it's time to get up."

He yanked on her wrist and sent her sprawling on the bed. When he reared up over her, she sucked in a shocked breath. His eyes were heated and intensely gray, reminding her of the time he'd sent her running from the gazebo after he'd kissed her.

"You're wrong, my love," he said, and he lowered his face to within an inch of hers. "I can safely promise you there'll be no sleep for us tonight."

"Ross," she began.

He cut her off. "That is, if you meant what you said. Did you mean it, Tessa? You don't want me to hold back?"

A hot, dizzying tide washed over her. It wasn't only his words that sent blood pumping through her veins. It was the sensual slant of his mouth, the cast of his countenance, and her own wicked, wicked imagination.

Her breath shuddered through her lips. "I meant it."

"Then you shall have your wish."

There'd been a few sleepless nights when he'd suffered the tortures of the damned, fantasizing about taking her the way he really wanted. It would make a good beginning.

Where before he'd been considerate of her innocence, now he was reckless. He allowed her no modesty. Her clothes were torn from her and thrown aside. She wasn't fighting him, but with one hand he pinioned her arms above her head. Then he looked down, feasting his eyes on her naked flesh.

And became lost in his own fantasy.

"Perfect," he said. "I knew you would be."

He caught one nipple between his thumb and finger and smiled as he coaxed it erect. "That's better," he said, and did the same to the other.

Her head was swimming, her body was throbbing. "Ross," she said hoarsely, "what . . . what are you going to do to me?"

"I'm acting out my darkest fantasy," he said. "I thought it's what you wanted. You told me not to hold back. Have you changed your mind?"

"I . . . I don't know."

"Perhaps this will help you decide." He lowered his head and blew a warm stream of air over her breasts. "You have beautiful breasts," he said, and cupped one, molding his fingers in a voluptuous caress. "They fill my hands as though they were made for them. Your nipples are blushing. In fact, they're flirting with me. They're just begging for my mouth. Here, give me your hand." He took her fingers and pressed them to first one nipple, then the other. They were as hard as pebbles. "Are they begging for my mouth, Tessa?"

Her nipples? In his mouth? The thought was so erotically exciting that her whole body jerked. "Are you sure you want to?" she quavered.

"Oh, I want to. If only you knew . . ."

He shifted slightly and kissed her breasts, then his lips closed over one distended nipple and he sucked hard. A wave of heat engulfed her. "Ross," she panted, "Ross."

He held her breast in his hand as he took full suckle. He squeezed, he kneaded, he pumped, he moved from one to the other. And all the while his voice bewitched her. She was beautiful. He'd wanted to do this for a long, long time. He was glad she was beyond shocking, for this was only the first of many fantasies. But all in good time.

He'd shown her passion before, but nothing like this. Her body was vibrating like a finely tuned instrument, its one object to give him pleasure. Modesty had never been her strong point, but she'd cherished a few inhibitions. Now he'd taken those away from her. She had no will of her own. Whatever he asked of her she would gladly give.

He turned her over and trailed kisses from her nape to the back of her knees. His hands squeezed the cheeks of her bottom, then gentled to one of his voluptuous caresses. His fingers brushed and sank into her soft flesh, making the pleasure almost unbearable.

When he rolled her on her back and she looked up at him, she saw that she wasn't the only one to suffer. His nostrils were flared. His eyes were glittering. His chest rose and fell as he tried to control his breathing.

"Open your legs for me," he said, and she obeyed. "No, my love, like this."

He raised her knees so that the soles of her feet rested on the sheets. His fingers were warm as they brushed the insides of her thighs. "Easy, easy," he murmured as she moved restlessly, anticipating the moment when his fingers would enter her.

She said his name in an agony of desire, and he laughed softly. "My fantasy isn't over," he said, "not nearly over. But I'll stop if you want me to."

A faint shake of her head gave him the answer he wanted.

He opened her legs wider. "Soon," he whispered in the same beguiling tone. "Soon, I'll give you what you want. Only let me, let me . . ."

He slipped a finger inside her, and stilled when her

breathing stopped, then started up in a long, keening moan. He dipped into her again and again, not deeply, but enough to drive her wild with wanting. When he was certain that she was past caring, he spread her legs wide, on either side of his shoulders, and he dipped into her with his tongue.

Through a daze of passion, she realized what he was doing and she tried to tighten her knees against him. It was out of her power. His shoulders were lodged solidly between her thighs. His tongue thrust deeply, and her whole body contracted, then began to shudder as she edged closer to climax.

He heard her sobbing his name, felt her nails scoring his shoulders, and all the suppressed passion exploded through him in a wild uncontrollable wave. He reared up over her.

He found her mouth and thrust deep with his tongue just as his sex thrust deep into her body. He gave her no respite, but set up a rhythm of thrust and withdraw that sent her soaring over the edge. When he felt her sheath convulse in hard rhythmic spasms around him, he threw back his head in sheer animal arousal. Then he let the pleasure take them both.

He was lying on his back, one arm covering his eyes. She was on her side, facing away from him. The silence had lengthened, and he was cursing himself for a fool. She'd barely got over the shock of hearing the sad news about her grandfather, and this was how he had used her.

A man did not act out his darkest fantasies with his wife, not even if these fantasies were all woven around her and no other woman would do. He'd been married before. He knew the score. A wife deserved a husband's utmost restraint. And Tessa was his *bride*.

It had never been like this with Cassie. Then why was it so different with Tessa?

He reached out a hand to touch her, then thought better of it. He slipped into his shirt and rolled from the bed. That got her attention.

"Where are you going?" she asked.

He looked at the clock. "To blow out the candles. We may manage an hour or two of sleep before it's time to get up."

He saw that her eyes were dancing in that mischievous way he was coming to know.

"I distinctly remember," she said, "that you promised there would be no sleep for us tonight."

He loved the sparkle in her eyes, loved the way her lips turned up. She offered him her hand and he automatically grasped it. When she tugged on it hard, and he stood there as though rooted to the spot, she puffed up her cheeks and blew out a long exasperated breath.

"Consider yourself tumbled on the bed," she said. "Well, what did you think? You're not the only one who indulges in fantasies. And now it's my turn."

For a moment he was thunderstruck. Then, with a great whoop of laughter, he charged her and they went rolling on the bed.

Chapter Eighteen

~~~~~~

Tessa was not completely happy about spending Christmas at Greenways, though the company could not have pleased her more. Sally, Desmond, and Julian would be there for a few days, but the Turners would be leaving early to spend Christmas with their own parents. The dowager had invited Colonel Naseby and his granddaughter, as well as Larry. These were Tessa's special friends, and she wanted to be with them. But Greenways itself was a different matter.

It was at Greenways that Cassie had lost her life, and Tessa feared that the memories would make a difference to Ross. There was a new intimacy between them that she was afraid to put to the test. They were lovers now, but it was so much more than that. They were also companions. He talked to her about the things that interested him, and he wanted to know about her interests. He made her laugh by telling stories of all the mischief he and Julian had got up to as schoolboys, and she told him about some of the hilarious practical jokes she'd played on her teachers and fellow pupils. Though their tastes were different, they both shared a passionate interest in books, and could argue for hours on the merits of various authors. They talked endlessly, but there was one subject they never broached. Cassie.

Patience, the dowager had cautioned on the eve of her wedding, and though it had never been one of her virtues, Tessa found new depths in herself. What she wanted was worth a little patience. She was in love, and she was almost certain that Ross loved her too, though he'd never said so. In the deep of the night when she was sated with love, she would turn into him with the words aching to be said, but she held off, unsure of how he would respond. And so she'd made up her mind that the words would have to come from him first. Once she knew that he loved her, once he had given her the words, Cassie would no longer come between them.

The odd thing was, Cassie wasn't a problem for her. The more she heard about Ross's first wife, the more she liked her. And it seemed to her that Cassie would never have begrudged Ross his chance at happiness. It was Ross who could not let Cassie go, and Tessa did not know if he ever would.

It was the dowager, who seemed to have a sixth sense where Tessa was concerned, who relieved Tessa's worst fears. Cassie, she said, had not cared for Greenways and had rarely set foot in it. There were no wings here that were closed off from the rest of the house. As for the lake and waterfall, they no longer existed. A month after Cassie's death, Ross had hired an army of laborers to drain and fill in the site and plant trees. Afterward the park had been hardly recognizable.

In the days that followed, Tessa saw no indication that Ross was haunted by ghosts. On the mornings when none of the gentlemen wanted to go out shooting, he would go riding with her and seemed to enjoy showing her around the estate. On one of those mornings, as they were resting their horses on top of a rise with a view of the house and stables, Tessa asked him about the lake. If a shadow crossed his face or came and went in his eyes, she could not detect it.

He answered easily, "All the walks and paths have

been changed. It's hard to say where the lake used to be, but I would guess it was right here, where we are now."

He went on casually, "I'm glad there's no lake, and not only for my own peace of mind. I remember how terrified you were on Julian's yacht when I brought you to England. Tell me what you were so afraid of."

She found his words too casual, and she looked at him curiously. They'd had this conversation before. "I told you," she said. "There was an accident at the school I attended. A girl drowned. I used to have nightmares about it."

"Yes, you've said that before. But you've also told me since that your early years were spent in a house that overlooked the sea, and you would spend hours on the beach when the tide was out, gathering crabs and winkles. It seems strange that a child brought up in that environment would be afraid of water."

Her heart was beginning to pound and she didn't know why. "It's only at night that I'm really terrified of water. I told you that too."

"Do you still dream about the accident?"

"No."

"It was a strange dream as I remember. You're drowning and though there are several bystanders, no one will help you."

"Must you go on like this?" She gave a feeble laugh. "If that nightmare keeps me awake all night, I'll know who to blame for it."

His eyes were intense on hers and she felt the fine hairs on the back of her neck begin to rise, then the look was gone and suddenly he cupped her neck, and leaning over, he kissed her.

He drew back and smiled down at her. "That won't happen," he said.

"What?" She had trouble putting her thoughts in order. His kisses always did this to her.

"The dream won't keep you awake all night. I will."

The obscure fear that hovered at the back of her mind quickly faded. He was flirting with her, and this was one area where she definitely excelled. "You've got that wrong, Trevenan," she said. "I'll be the one to keep *you* awake all night."

"Not with kisses you won't," he said. "My love, you're too shy for me."

Her eyes sparkled. "Say that tonight after I've practiced what I learned from that book I found in your library."

"What book?"

"The one you keep tucked away behind your books on animal husbandry, you know, on the top shelf where no one can reach it?"

Baffled, he stared at her, then a hot tide of color ran into his cheeks.

"Yes, that book," she said. "Frankly, Ross, I was shocked. I wouldn't have believed it of you!"

"That book has been there for years! I'd forgotten all about it! Tessa, every young man collects such books. It doesn't mean anything. And as I said, I haven't looked at it in years."

"Oh, I believe you. Sally and I almost choked when it toppled to the floor and a cloud of dust shot into the air, and that was before we opened it and came across those decadent sketches."

"Sally? You're making this up!"

"Didn't you see how she blushed this morning when you entered the breakfast room?"

"Oh, God!"

"Too shy for you, am I? We'll see." And with a saucy smile, she brought her quirt down on her mount's back and went leaping away.

Torn between laughter and chagrin, he followed after her. The laughter won out. She was such a pleasure to him now, this impossible girl. When they got back to town, he was going to have her portrait done, but no portrait painter he knew had the skill to capture that provocative look. She was part sprite and part siren.

There had been a moment or two there, though, when the light had gone out of her eyes, and she'd looked really afraid. He still wasn't sure if she was hiding something from him or if she truly couldn't remember the night

Becky Fallon had drowned. The one thing he never doubted was that Tessa had been there.

On this glorious, crisp morning, none of it seemed to matter and he regretted now that he'd pressed her to remember Fleetwood Hall.

Larry arrived on Christmas Day, and he was on his best behavior. There were no jokes about eloping with heiresses, no provocative remarks to get Ross's back up, and no flirting with the only eligible girl present, Sophie Naseby. This suited Tessa just fine, because she'd already decided that it was Sophie and Desmond who were made for each other.

Julian stayed on for one more day, but Desmond had invited him down to his family home in Kent, and Julian decided to take him up on his offer. Tessa strongly suspected that what Julian really wanted was to meet Sally's parents, especially her father, and ask for permission to court Sally.

As the days slipped by, she began to feel more and more secure of her place as Ross's wife. She was thinking about this on the evening before everyone's departure for town. Only she and Ross were staying on for another week. His excuse had been estate business, but he'd told her privately that he wanted to spend time alone with his wife.

They were in the drawing room, whiling away the hours before bedtime. She was sitting at a small table, going over the stillroom ledgers and making notations of supplies that had to be ordered. Ross was reading the papers, and the others were at the card table playing a game of whist.

The house was her domain. That thought had been endlessly drummed into her by the dowager, and she'd done her best to master all the intricacies of being chatelaine of two great houses. She still had a lot to learn, but she didn't begrudge the time she gave up in making her daily rounds with the housekeeper while the others were out shooting or catching up on their correspondence or going for long walks. Even now, they were all enjoying themselves while she was doing her homework. If the house was her domain, then she had the right to make changes.

With that thought, she snapped the covers of her ledger together, bringing all eyes to her. "This drawing room," she said, "has a much nicer view than the one in Sayle House."

"That is very true," said Colonel Naseby. "But that's because Greenways is surrounded by parkland."

"So is Sayle House," she responded, "except on one side. The east wing looks out over several rows of houses that separate us from Hyde Park. Not only that, but the east wing gets the morning sun. I prefer the afternoon sun, especially in winter."

Ross lowered his newspaper. "What are you getting at, Tessa?"

A stillness had crept into the room. The dowager laid aside her cards. No one else moved.

Tessa breathed deeply and plunged on. "When we return to Sayle House," she said, "I thought I'd make some changes. The west wing looks out over the countryside." It was also the wing with Cassie's rooms, and everyone there knew it. She took a quick look at Ross, and her voice lost some of its animation. "It makes more sense to live in that wing, at least in the winter months. In summer, it doesn't matter so much. When the trees are in leaf, the houses bordering Hyde Park aren't visible from the east wing."

Ross slowly got to his feet. "There will be no changes," he said.

"Why not? You made changes at Greenways, didn't you? Why not at Sayle House? In my opinion—"

He cut her off. "No one has asked for your opinion! When I do, you may give it to me."

Every vestige of color washed out of her face, and she looked down at her hands. She had put him to the test, and he had failed her. Not only that, but he had publicly rebuked her. Now she knew where she stood, and so did everyone else.

"Ross," chided the dowager, "Tessa made a perfectly

sensible suggestion, and I agree with her. You're not being reasonable. In fact, though it pains me to speak so plainly, I think you're being morbid."

There was a moment of charged silence. Someone coughed.

Ross threw down his newspaper. "If you'll excuse me," he said. "There is some estate business I must attend to," and he left the room.

Tessa hardly knew where to look. It was Colonel Naseby who smoothed things over. "Sophie, my dear," he said, "it would please your old grandfather if you would take a turn at the piano. Tessa, would you mind taking over Sophie's cards? No, I won't take no for an answer. Sophie would rather do anything than play cards."

"How true," said Sophie, and seating herself at the piano, she launched into a lively air.

Tessa sat down at the card table. George Naseby, she reflected, not for the first time, was one of the kindest gentlemen she knew. Her eyes lifted to meet Larry's, and a look passed between them. He was telling her that he knew exactly how she was feeling because he'd frequently been in the same position.

"Hearts are trumps," he said, and smiled.

Tessa picked up her cards.

Tessa did not wait up for Ross. This was one night she did not want her husband in her bed. She was too shaken, too crushed by his rejection. And behind the hurt was a festering resentment. This wasn't the kind of marriage she wanted. She wanted a man who was free to love her, but he still loved Cassie. He should have sent her back to France, and now it was too late.

She blew out the candles and crawled into bed. It was a long time before she slipped into sleep, and when she did, the old dream was waiting for her. She felt the strong masculine hands holding her under the water, but this time she knew whose hands they were. It was Ross who was trying to drown her.

She came awake on a cry of terror, but her cry was smothered against her lips. Terrified, disoriented, she began to struggle and the crushing pressure was instantly released.

"Tessa! I didn't mean to frighten you. It's me, Ross."

The reassuring words brought a momentary relief. She was in her own bed. Ross was beside her. It was the unremitting darkness that had confused her. As her senses returned, all the hurt and resentment she'd experienced since he'd walked out of the drawing room rushed back.

She fought clear of his arms, and hauled herself up. "Why are you here?"

"That's a strange thing for a wife to ask her husband."

His amusement acted on her like brandy on an open sore. She slipped from the bed, lit the candles on the mantelpiece, then turned to face him.

What she felt was too deep for anger. It was closer to despair. She hadn't lost him, because she'd never had him, not the way she wanted. And because she thought there was no hope for her, she didn't care what she said.

"You've got the wrong woman, Ross. I don't think there's any doubt of that now."

"I don't know what you mean."

"*Cassie!* There! I've said the forbidden word."

"Tessa, leave it."

"Why? What's going to happen to me? Am I going to be struck by a thunderbolt if I dare to say that holy name? Will I be consumed by fire? Will there be an earthquake? Or perhaps the world will end." She looked up at the ceiling. "Are you there, Cassie? If you are, you'd best come and take your man away, because I have no use for him."

Her voice broke on the last word. Ross leaped from the bed and jerked her into his arms. To be held close to him, to have him pity her, was the last thing she wanted. The more she struggled, however, the more his arms tightened. She had her own way of fighting back.

"Cassie," she chanted. "Cassie. Cassie."

She saw the blaze of violence in his eyes, then his mouth came down on hers in a punishing assault. When he released her, he buried his face against her hair. His voice was hoarse, ragged. "Why can't you accept what we have? I give you as much of myself as I'm capable of giving. Why can't you be satisfied with that?"

She turned her head away so that he wouldn't see the pain in her eyes. She shouldn't be blaming him. No one was to blame. She couldn't command him to love her. Love was too capricious for that.

She made a choked sound, and he pulled her to the bed. When he stretched out beside her and gathered her in his arms, she could feel him trembling. His face was pale.

"I need you," he said. "I need you *now*. I need this."

His hand cupped her breast and he kissed her, softly at first, then more ardently as she relaxed against him. Her hands moved slowly over his back, feeling his muscles clench. She couldn't help responding to him. She loved him. It was as simple as that. He wanted her passion, and passion was so much easier than love. She wound her fingers through his hair, pulling him closer.

It was a swift, violent coupling that seemed to Tessa to have little to do with pleasure. Ross was like a man driven. Once wasn't enough for him. Each time he turned to her, she surrendered herself, but it wasn't the same for her, and she sensed his frustration.

When she was drifting into sleep, he grasped her by the shoulder and shook her awake. "Why, Tessa?" he demanded. "Why won't you give in to me?"

She didn't deliberately try to hurt him, but the words came without volition. "I give you as much of myself as I'm capable of giving."

After that, he left her alone.

They stayed on at Greenways for one more week, but the honeymoon was over. They had nothing to say to each other, and it was awkward with no guests there to take up the slack in the conversation. Ross spent most of his time on estate business, and Tessa immersed herself in household duties. But every night, he came to her bed and claimed his conjugal rights.

She never tried to turn him away. And he gave her pleasure. He was very sure about that. But it was like making love to a different woman. There was no playfulness in her now. She didn't tease him or say outrageous things. There was a reserve there that he wanted to smash into smithereens.

She asked for too much from him. Not even for her would he obliterate all traces of Cassie. The lake was different. It had taken Cassie's life, and so he had destroyed it. Cassie's rooms in Sayle House were all that was left of her. What difference could it make to Tessa?

He should have known that Tessa would never be satisfied with locked doors. She would want all of him, heart, body, and soul. He wasn't ready for that much intimacy, and he would never be ready for it. He saw no contradiction in demanding more of Tessa than he was willing to give. It was her nature to give herself completely. He wasn't the one who had changed. She was.

It was a relief to them both when they finally returned to Sayle House. Ross watched as Tessa ran to his grandmother's arms with the first genuine smile he'd seen on her face in a week. His grandmother gave him a perfunctory greeting over the top of Tessa's head, then arm-in-arm, his ladies ascended the stairs, talking their heads off as though they hadn't seen each other for a year.

For the first time in a week, he, too, had a genuine smile on his face. Tessa belonged here. She was his wife, and though their marriage might not be perfect, there were other bonds that tied her to him. Her affection for his grandmother for one. And in time there would be children. But long before that, she would give him what he wanted, because Tessa was Tessa. She could no more dole out her love in miserly driblets than he could hold back the ocean at full tide.

He would give her another week.

The low murmur of voices coming from his library put an end to his reveries. When he entered, he found Julian and Desmond ensconced in the chairs flanking the fireplace. They were drinking coffee. He hadn't expected to see them quite so soon. They'd decided that the time had come to take up their own lives. They couldn't always be at his beck and call, and if they continued to spend every waking moment at Sayle House, people might begin to ask questions, especially the dowager and Tessa.

Ross helped himself to a cup of coffee and after a bare exchange of news, Julian came to the point.

"I heard it in my clubs," he said. "The most damnable thing, Ross! There's a whispering campaign going on. Everyone is talking about Tessa."

"What are they saying?" Ross asked sharply.

"They're saying that scandal has followed her from the day she was born. They know about her school record. They know about the footman she eloped with, yes, and the smugglers who helped her escape to France."

"Did you hear anything, Desmond?" asked Ross.

"No. Not until Julian told me, but I don't move in the same circles as he."

"And," said Julian, "they're vicious with it. They've exaggerated everything." He paused, searching for words that would give the least offense. Finding none, he went on, "There's no point in trying to conceal anything from you. They're saying that she sold herself both to her footman and to the smugglers to pay for her passage. They also say that she was your mistress before she was your wife. I've tried to scotch these rumors, but people believe what they want to believe."

Ross's face was starkly white. "Who started these rumors?"

"Almost certainly Mr. and Mrs. Beasley of Bath, Tessa's erstwhile guardians. They're not in town, but they have connections, and they've made the most of them."

"I'll find a way to make them pay for it."

"That," said Julian forcefully, "will only make matters worse. What we must do is find a way to restore Tessa's reputation. Otherwise, with this scandal hanging over her, she'll be cut wherever she goes. No one will receive her."

"I suggest we fight fire with fire," said Desmond.

Ross stared at him hard. "What does that mean?"

"It means," said Desmond, "that we ruin the credibility of the Beasleys. I have connections. It wouldn't be difficult to arrange for the Beasleys to be thrown into prison, or to be charged with theft, that sort of thing. But I wouldn't want to go that far unless I was perfectly sure they are the culprits."

"This," said Ross, "from a vicar's son?"

Julian laughed. "Oh, don't let Des's innocent face fool you, Ross. He may look like his father, but the resemblance ends there. His mind is as devious as a labyrinth."

Ross now stared hard at Julian. "Then you really did go down to Kent to meet Sally's parents?"

"I met them, yes, but I went as Des's friend."

"I see," said Ross, and smiled.

Julian glowered at him. "What do you see?"

"Nothing. It was just a manner of speaking. How much does my grandmother know?"

"Everything," said Julian. "Now don't look at me like that. When she returned to Sayle House, there were so few invitations that she became suspicious. I had to tell her. Besides, she'd have found out soon enough."

"Then," said Ross, "the sooner we fight fire with fire, the sooner everyone's peace of mind will be restored." He looked at Desmond.

"I'll get onto it," he said.

Upstairs, Tessa had yet to remove her wraps.

"Who is the letter from, Tessa?"

Tessa slipped the note she had just read into a drawer of her writing table and turned to the dowager with a smile. "It's from an acquaintance I met at the Uxbridge musicale," she said. "Charlotte Sandys."

"I don't think I know her."

"She was reminding me about the dinner at the Opera House on Thursday. I'm looking forward to seeing her again."

The dowager's smile slipped. "Do you think that's wise, my dear? I mean, you are in mourning, and if you feel you're not up to it, well, I'm sure your friend will understand."

Tessa sat down at her dressing table and looked at the dowager in the mirror. "My grandfather loved music, did you know? When I'm at the opera, I feel he is close to me."

"In that case," said the dowager, "we must certainly go. Are you tired from your journey? You should rest, and in an hour or so I'll send one of the maids to you with tea and biscuits."

"Thank you. I am a little tired. I think I'll do that."

When she was alone, Tessa rose and got the letter from her writing table. Taking it to the window, she quickly scanned it.

> *Dear Thor,*
>   *Opera House Dinner, Round Room, Thursday.*
>   *Look for me there. I need your help.*
>
> *Odin.*

Thor. Odin. She hadn't thought of these Teutonic gods since she was a pupil at Miss Oliphant's Academy. She was Thor, and Odin was Nan Roberts. It was a secret code. The letter should be destroyed before it fell into the wrong hands.

Several minutes passed before she crumpled the note into a ball and threw it on the fire.

Chapter Nineteen

〜〜〜

Within minutes of entering the Opera House, Ross began to suspect that he had sent Desmond to Bath on a wild goose chase. The Beasleys were not behind the whispering campaign to ruin Tessa's character. It was Amanda Chalmers.

She had positioned herself on the gallery that overlooked the entrance hall. Bertram Gibbon was on one side of her, and she was laughing and talking animatedly with a group of acquaintances while her cousin scanned the crush of patrons below with an opera glass. When he sighted Ross and his party, he touched Amanda on the shoulder and passed the glass to her. All conversation in her vicinity immediately ceased as Amanda trained the glass on Ross. Then she passed the glass to someone else.

Still staring at Ross, she threw back her head and smiled brilliantly. Ross knew that smile well. It was a victory smile, and one that he'd seen often enough on Amanda's face when she'd routed anyone foolish enough to try to get the better of her. But that was in debate, at one of her salons. Tessa had done nothing to deserve Amanda's hostility.

Hard on that thought came another. Amanda wasn't

punishing Tessa. She was punishing him for having the gall to end their affair.

Her laugh rang out, and with a provocative bow, she turned her back on him. Ross's rage rose like bile in his throat. He looked down at Tessa, but she was oblivious of Amanda's performance. She was looking about her, as though searching for someone. But Julian had caught Amanda's performance, and his brow was like thunder.

Few people stopped to speak to them as they made their way to their box. Though Ross was highly aware of this, he was sure Tessa hardly noticed.

She was pale tonight, but that might be nothing more than the contrast between her white skin and her black mourning gown. Then again, she wasn't entirely herself either. She seemed subdued, fragile, and he wondered if she'd heard something of the rumors that were circulating.

They were forced to pause on the gallery when Amanda and her train of friends chose that particular moment to cut in front of them. It was all deliberately done, a blatant snub to Tessa for the world to see. Ross was ready to throttle Amanda when Julian laid a hand on his sleeve, distracting him.

"I do believe," Julian murmured, "that reinforcements have arrived."

Ross looked where Julian had indicated. Among the crush outside the boxes, he spotted a number of friendly faces. Some of them belonged to Julian's friends, some of them were his own, couples whom he'd sadly neglected since Cassie's death. In a matter of minutes they were surrounded by well-wishers. Introductions were made and Ross edged out of the way as Tessa became the focus of attention. He smiled foolishly, touched that his friends had not deserted him. It was a beginning, a good beginning, but it wasn't nearly enough. He would not be satisfied until Tessa's character was completely vindicated.

He glanced along the corridor and saw Amanda poised to enter her box. She was looking back at him with that smile he thoroughly detested. Then, with a flick of her lashes, she dismissed him and the friends who had stood by him and she entered her box.

The performance was over. They were making their way to the Round Room and Tessa felt every nerve strain in anticipation. That enigmatic note from Nan Roberts had stirred up loose ends, threads—she didn't know what to call them—things she'd pushed to the back of her mind until Nan's secretive little note had brought them sharply into focus again. It had filled her with dread, but what she feared was beyond her comprehension.

It all went back to Fleetwood Hall. She'd barely thought of the school in all the years she'd been away from it, then suddenly, within the space of a few months, she'd been reminded of it at every turn, and not only Fleetwood Hall, but the fatal accident that had claimed Becky Fallon's life. Even the old dream that she'd thought she was getting over had begun to lie in wait for her every night. And how could she explain the pounding of her heart and the acceleration of her pulse when she was reminded of that fatal accident? She was becoming so unhinged that she was beginning to suspect something sinister was going on. Perhaps they were all involved in a conspiracy against her—Ross, Sally, Julian, and Desmond. They were all hammering away at her, forcing her to remember Fleetwood Hall.

It was preposterous. Her mind was playing tricks on her.

If she believed that, then why hadn't she confided in Ross? She didn't know what she was thinking.

Look for me, Nan had written. She'd been looking all evening, but she didn't know what to look for. Brown hair and big brown eyes—that much she remembered, and Nan had been small for her age. But that was years ago, almost another lifetime ago. Yet she and Nan had once been inseparable. They'd told each other everything, as young girls do. She'd never had another friend like Nan.

As they edged their way into the Round Room, she tried to look for Nan, but she was hemmed in on every side by men who might as well have been mountains. It was a great relief when they were finally seated at the table and she had a clear view of the company. It was hopeless. There were several ladies there who caught her eye, but whether or not they were Nan she couldn't say.

In the act of filling her glass with champagne, a footman somehow dislodged her napkin. With a murmured apology, he straightened it and moved on. She gazed at that napkin for a moment or two before shaking it out. A small piece of paper fell into her lap. She waited several minutes before smoothing it out to covertly read the few words on it. Then she raised her eyes to look for the door to the footmen's entrance.

Ross chose his moment with care. The dinner was over and footmen were clearing and dismantling the tables before the dancing got under way. He and Tessa would not be staying for this part of the evening, not while she was in full mourning. He'd sent her off to the cloakroom with some of their party to retrieve their coats. As soon as he saw them pass through the doors, he turned aside and made straight for Amanda Chalmers.

As he approached, Amanda's train of admirers fell back. Only Bertram Gibbon stood his ground. He surveyed Ross languidly through his quizzing glass, and Ross was tempted to ram it down his throat.

Bertram turned to Amanda with an amused smile. "Shall I stay, Cousin, or shall I go?"

Amanda let out a low laugh and plied her fan. "Why, Bertram" she said, "you know that Lord Sayle is one of my dearest friends."

With that, Bertram bowed and sauntered off.

Ross held out his arm, and when Amanda laid her gloved fingers on it, he led her to one of the window alcoves.

His tone was polite. His eyes were murderous. "What do you hope to gain by ostracizing my wife?"

She didn't pretend to misunderstand him. "A little revenge?"

"Careful, Amanda. Two can play at that game."

Her brows winged up. "Threats, Ross? Now this is

becoming interesting. I'm beyond your power, and you know it."

A muscle in his jaw tensed. Amanda Chalmers was not in the same class as the Beasleys. She didn't frighten easily, and with good reason. She had powerful friends in high places, not least the Prince of Wales. Desmond's methods would not work here.

"The woman scorned, Amanda?" he said softly. "I would not have thought that role to your taste."

Anger flashed in her eyes and was quickly subdued. "I think you will find, Lord Sayle, that it is your wife who is the woman scorned. I'd call that poetic justice, wouldn't you?"

His hands itched to wrap themselves around her beautiful throat and choke the life out of her. Instead, he gave her one long insulting appraisal from head to toe before raising his eyes to her face. "You are a beautiful, intelligent woman," he said, "but you have no soul."

She flicked open her fan and peeked over it, as though she were flirting with him. "What would you know about a soul?"

"Not very much. In fact, you and I probably deserved each other. But I, thank God, have been blessed with a wife I don't deserve. I won't let you hurt her. If you don't put a stop to this whispering campaign, I'll find a way to ruin you."

She laughed, genuinely amused, snapped her fan closed, and tapped him on the arm with it.

"Dear, dear! Such strong words! But I won't take offense. I understand how you must feel. Only think—an elopement with a footman! And the doxy of a band of smugglers! I don't see how Lady Sayle will ever live this down."

He was losing the battle. Nothing could shake Amanda's poise.

"I should have listened to my grandmother," he said.

"I beg your pardon?"

"Your bones. Did you know they're in the wrong configuration?"

"You're talking in riddles."

"I'm sorely tempted to bend them into shape."

She looked at him uncertainly. "Bend what into shape?"

"Your bones. Like this."

He plucked the fan from her fingers and carefully and slowly snapped every spine, before roughly shoving it into her hand. "That's what I'll do to you, Amanda, if you don't sheathe your claws."

Turning on his heel, he walked away from her, but her gloating laugh at his back had the last word.

He met Sally and Julian just inside the entrance hall.

"Isn't Tessa with you?" asked Sally, her eyes anxiously searching his face.

"We've lost her," said Julian. "One moment she was there and the next she'd vanished into thin air."

All was in confusion on the other side of the footmen's door. Tessa entered one slow step at a time, keeping well out of the way of the stream of footmen and maids who were scurrying to clear places on tables as more dirty dishes were brought in from the Round Room. One of the maids caught sight of her and hurried over.

"I'm sorry, ma'am," she said, "but you can't come in here."

Tessa looked over her shoulder, through the open door to the Round Room. "I'm looking for someone," she said.

The maid came closer. "Lady Sayle?"

Tessa nodded.

"Please, come with me. Your friend is waiting for you."

With the maid leading the way, they went through a door and passed through a room where the musicians for the ball were tuning their instruments. There was so much coming and going, so much of a party atmosphere, that no one gave them a second look. They went through another door, down a hallway, and came out backstage. Things were quieter here. Maids and seamstresses were folding away costumes; cleaners were sweeping floors. The maid led her up a circular staircase, and they came out on the wings looking out to the stage.

Tessa edged onto the stage and looked out. Many of

the lights had been doused, but not all, for there were cleaners here too, picking up the debris of the patrons who had watched the performance a short while ago. Tiers of empty guilded boxes surrounded the stage.

She walked back to the maid. "There's no one here," she said, "leastways not the lady I'm looking for. Are you sure this is where we were supposed to meet?"

"Tessa," said the maid, "don't you recognize me?"

The wings were not well lit, and Tessa took the few steps that brought her to within an arm's length of the other girl. "Nan?" she said. "Is it you?"

"Have I changed so much? I would have known you anywhere. I don't think I've ever seen hair that color, except on you."

It *was* Nan. She could see that now. She had full, round eyes, dark coarse hair peeping out from her muslin cap, and the kind of skin that tanned easily. At school, some of the girls had taunted her with being a gypsy. This was something Tessa had forgotten until now.

She felt a lump in her throat and swallowed hard. She and Nan had once been close. They'd talked endlessly, sharing all their secret hopes and desires. Now they stared at each other awkwardly, not knowing how to bridge the gulf of the years that separated them. All the questions that had been hammering inside Tessa's head since she'd received Nan's cryptic note quietly slipped away.

"I wrote to you," she said, "but you never answered my letters."

Nan lifted her shoulders and let them fall. "I left Miss O's shortly after you. No one forwarded your letters, and I didn't know where you were."

Tessa swallowed another lump that had risen in her throat. "Nan," she said, hesitating a little, "why are you wearing that maid's getup?"

Nan looked down at her black dress and white muslin apron. "Because I've run out of money, and I have to eat." She looked up at Tessa. "I don't work here, though. No. I had to find some way of speaking to you alone, and this is the best I could think of. I've tried to get close to you, Tessa, but you're never alone. I've watched you walk in the grounds of Sayle House, but even there, you're well chaperoned."

"You've watched me?"

Nan nodded. "But the gardeners always chased me away."

"But why didn't you come to the front door?"

Nan said, "It's a long story, Tessa, but the gist of it is, I was afraid someone would see and recognize me. I've fallen on hard times, Tessa, and was hoping, for old times' sake, that you would help me out. We're blood sisters, remember?"

Tessa nodded. That was one thing she'd never forgotten. "We went to the chapel," she said, "when all the other girls were asleep. You pricked your wrist and I pricked mine. Then we mingled our blood over the altar, and chanted some nonsense. I can't remember what."

"A gypsy spell," said Nan. "We swore never to turn our backs on each other or our spirits would wander the earth till the end of time. And as a reminder of our sacred oath, we signed a pledge and hid it in our hallowed hiding place."

Tessa smiled. "I wonder what happened to it, and all the other treasures we hid there?"

"I expect they're still there," said Nan. She reached out and briefly touched Tessa's sleeve. "I'm in trouble, Tessa, terrible trouble. I need money to get out of London and start a new life. I don't know who to turn to. If you don't help me, I don't know what I'll do."

"Of course I'll help you. But you must tell me what's wrong. Your notes told me nothing at all."

"Notes? I sent you only one note." Nan's voice betrayed her rising alarm. "Did someone else write to you using our code?"

Tessa spoke calmly, soothingly. "No, no. Someone was playing a trick on me, but they didn't use our code."

"You didn't tell anyone you were meeting me here?"

"Of course not, not when you asked me not to. But you must tell me what's going on."

Nan looked over her shoulder, then back at Tessa. "This isn't the time or place to go into it. Will you help me, Tessa? Two hundred pounds would do it, a hundred if that's all you can spare. I must get out of London. It's too dangerous for me here."

"Of course I'll give you the money, but you must tell me what kind of trouble you're in."

Nan shook her head. "Not here. Can you bring the money tomorrow night?"

"Tomorrow night? Yes, I'm sure I can." Tessa wasn't really thinking about the logistics of raising two hundred pounds and bringing it to Nan. She was too impatient to know more.

Though they'd kept their voices down, Nan's voice now fell to little more than a whisper. "You won't have to go far, Tessa. I live in Kensington, in the little house right opposite the church. I've watched from my upstairs bedroom window as you've attended church services, but I was afraid to show my face in case you recognized me and said something. You mustn't tell anyone you've seen me. You mustn't tell anyone about the money. You do realize that, don't you? That's why I was afraid to say too much in my letter." Again she looked over her shoulder. "Tomorrow night then. Use the back door. And be careful. Make sure you're not followed."

She was on the point of turning away, and Tessa reached out to grasp her by the arms. The suddenness of the movement took Nan by surprise, and she flinched away, but Tessa did not let go. "Nan, if someone is trying to hurt you, we'll go to my husband. He'll help you."

"Your husband! He's the last person I'd go to. Your husband would kill me if he knew what I'd done."

She was struggling in earnest, trying to free herself, but Tessa's fingers only tightened. Suspicions that had once seemed irrational were beginning to solidify into convictions.

"This all goes back to Becky Fallon, doesn't it?" When Nan didn't answer, she gave her a shake. "Nan, what have you done?"

Tears welled in Nan's eyes and spilled over. "I thought I was safe because he didn't see me that night. He thought I was one of those other girls." The words that had begun as a trickle now became a flood as though a dam had burst. "I'm almost sure he killed them, Tessa. I never thought . . . I didn't know . . . I thought they were accidents! You were safe because you were in France. Or maybe he knows you had nothing to do with it. But we mustn't be seen together, and that's why I couldn't approach you openly. Not only for my sake, but for yours. Let me go, Tessa! Let me go!"

"Nan, calm yourself! If we go to the authorities, they'll help you."

"They're after me too! That's why I have to get out of London. There's a man, Desmond Turner, he's been asking questions about me. He works hand in glove with the police. Can't you see what will happen to me? It's because of me that he killed those girls. If they don't hang me, they'll transport me to the colonies."

She tore out of Tessa's grasp and stood there shivering, rubbing her arms where Tessa's fingers had dug into them. "They won't do anything to you," she said. "You were very clever, Tessa, to pretend that you weren't there that night. But I was too clever for my own good. And now he's looking for me, and he'll kill me if he finds me, just as he killed those other girls."

Tessa pressed her shaking fingers to her temples. There was no coherence to her thoughts. They buzzed inside her head like a swarm of angry bees. "You're not making sense," she said, and looked up. "Nan, who is trying to kill you?"

Their heads lifted as a ghostly echo suddenly filled that huge interior, then dwindled to an eerie whisper. "Tessa . . ."

Like a startled deer, Nan darted away, leaving the door to the circular staircase open.

"Tessa?" The voice was closer, recognizable. It was Ross's voice.

She wasn't ready to face him yet. Turning blindly, she made for the circular staircase. More by instinct than anything else, she retraced the route Nan had taken her. She pushed into the room where the musicians had been tuning their instruments and ran straight into the arms of the Viscount Pelham.

"Larry," she breathed, and collapsed against him.

His arms felt solid and safe. He wasn't like her husband and Desmond and Sally and Julian, hammering away at her, trying to make her remember the night Becky Fallon drowned. He'd never asked her about Fleetwood Hall or Nan Roberts. He was like a solid footing she'd stumbled upon in the middle of a treacherous quagmire. Even his angry words reassured her.

"Where the devil have you been, Tessa? Ross is in a terrible temper and we're all suffering for it. He has us all out looking for you." He held her at arm's length, and the anxious look on his face subtly changed. "You're as white as a sheet. Did someone insult you? If they did, I'll make them pay for it."

"No." She shook her head. "Larry, I'm glad it's you who has found me, because I need your help."

"Go on," he said cautiously.

"I know I have money of my own, but I don't know how to get to it. Do I just go to the bank and ask them to give it to me? I've never needed money before now. Ross always takes care of everything."

"Tessa, what do you need the money for?"

"Please, Larry"—she clutched the edge of his coat— "just answer my question."

"Married ladies do not have bank accounts, not generally speaking. You will have to ask Ross to act for you. Now will you tell me what's going on?"

She thought for a moment, then said, "When you're short of funds, Larry, how do you get money?"

His brow darkened. "Has Ross been talking to you about me, because if he has—"

"No, no. You don't understand and I can't explain it. Just tell me how I can raise two hundred pounds without my husband knowing about it. You've done it often enough, I know."

His grin was crooked. "I usually sell something or pawn it. But I'm warning you, Ross *always* finds out. Look, why don't I lend you the money?"

Her eyes burned and her throat ached. "Would you do that for me, Larry?"

"I'd be happy to. It may take me a few days to raise such a sum—"

She put a hand on his sleeve. "This can't wait. But thank you for offering. Larry, will you do something for me? Will you call for me tomorrow morning in your curricle and take me driving?"

He looked at her for a long moment, then shook his head. "Tessa," he said, "I know what you're thinking, and I don't think it's such a good idea. Look, Julian has plenty of money. He'll be glad to lend you two hundred pounds."

"No." Her voice was becoming stronger as her nerves steadied. "You're the only one I can trust. No one else would understand. Now give me your arm and take me to Ross."

Ross followed Tessa into her bedchamber and quietly shut the door. He hadn't had a chance to say anything to her on the drive home, not with his grandmother listening to every word. He watched her now as she walked slowly across the room, unfastening her sable-lined cloak as she went, then absently throwing it across a chair before going to stand at the window to look out.

"Tessa," he said, "what happened tonight? Why did you go off by yourself without telling anyone where you were going?"

Her voice sounded far off, hollow. "I told you. The heat was too much for me and one of the footmen showed me to a room where it was cooler." She parted the muslin curtains. "Is that the church where we attend Sunday services? Of course, it must be. It's very close to our park, isn't it? I suppose I knew that before, but it just didn't register."

He came to stand beside her and slowly turned her to face him. Her eyes were blank, shading her thoughts from him. "Tessa," he said gently, "did someone say something to upset you? Did you overhear something at the opera that made you run away?"

"Like what, for instance?"

He cupped her face in both hands and pressed a kiss to her lips. "Don't let it distress you," he murmured. "They're small-minded, mean-spirited people who have nothing better to do with their time. Amanda Chalmers will be silenced, I promise you."

She shivered and took a step back, out of his arms. "Amanda Chalmers?"

"She's behind the whispering campaign. She admitted it to me quite openly. I'm beginning to see things I didn't see before. She must be getting her information from your Beasley relatives. I'm sure it was Amanda who sent for them to take you back to Bath. We took care of her then, Tessa, and we'll do it again. No one who knows you will believe these exaggerated tales that are going around."

His words puzzled her at first. "Oh, I see," she said at length. "My unsavory reputation has finally caught up with me. Is that it? Well, there's nothing new in that."

He frowned, and his eyes narrowed on her face. "You didn't know? You didn't hear the gossip?"

The paralysis that had gripped her mind ever since seeing Nan gradually began to thaw. He didn't believe she'd slipped away because she'd been overcome with the heat. He thought she'd overheard some silly gossip someone had dredged up about her past. If she'd been thinking straight, she would have let him believe it. Now, he had that look on his face that told her he was going to probe until he got some straight answers.

Nan's words drummed inside her head. *Your husband would kill me if he knew what I'd done.* She couldn't tell him anything, not until she had some straight answers herself.

She had the strangest feeling that she couldn't shake off. She felt as though she'd been caught up in a wonderful dream and now it was about to end. Unseen enemies were marshaling their forces against her, and she couldn't fight them because she didn't know who they were.

She didn't want to know who they were because she

was afraid, so terribly afraid that the knowledge would shatter her.

The lie came easily to her lips. "I was thinking about my grandfather. At the opera? I was thinking about my grandfather. He loved music. We would have had so much to talk about after the performance. I . . . I couldn't stop the tears coming and slipped away until I could come to myself."

His expression softened and she knew that he believed her. "Tessa," he said and held out his arms.

Her mind told her to be cautious, but her heart told her something different. She wanted to trust him, oh, how she wanted to trust him. But she was afraid and didn't know why she was afraid.

With a little cry, she stepped into his arms. "I don't want to think anymore. It doesn't do any good. I just want to forget. Help me, Ross. Make me forget."

Thinking she wanted comforting, he held her in a loose clasp and pressed soothing kisses to her brow, her cheeks, her eyelids. It wasn't enough for her. She pressed her soft contours against his hard length and kissed him with all the pent-up love she couldn't hide. He tasted the longing, and behind the longing, a sense of desperation. Something was far wrong.

His fingers brushed through her hair, spilling pins as he tried to calm her. "Tessa, what is it? Tell me. Talk to me."

Talking was the last thing she wanted. She slipped her hand between their bodies and touched him intimately. His response was immediate. "Yes," she said, "yes," and pulled him to the bed.

He wanted to take his time with her, but she wouldn't allow it, and she knew just how to break down his control. She tempted him with kisses and intimate caresses until he was wild to have her. He pulled her beneath him and positioned himself to take her. Their eyes met and held, his uncertain, wanting answers, hers veiled.

"Make me stop thinking," she whispered, and raising her head from the pillow, she took his lips in a hungry demand.

She cried out when he entered her and they both stilled. Then he began to move, building the pleasure slowly, carefully, until she could think of nothing but this. Again and again, he brought her to the brink of climax, then held off, giving her time to recover before building the pleasure again. At the last, when she lay shuddering in his arms, and they were both spent, he tried to talk to her.

"Tell me what's troubling you," he said.

"I miss France. I'm homesick."

Tessa fell asleep almost at once. Ross lay there brooding for a long while after.

Chapter Twenty

❧❧❧

Ross was working in his library when a letter arrived for him. It had been hand delivered, and the boy who had brought it was waiting downstairs for a reply. Ross could see from the signature that it came from Mr. King, a well-known moneylender whose premises were on Clarges Street. There had been letters from moneylenders in the past. In fact, Ross had made a point of warning them in person that if Lord Pelham showed up on their doorstep and tried to peddle any item that belonged to the Pelham estate, he wanted to know about it. Most of them had taken the hint and had refused to have further dealings with Larry.

To his knowledge, Larry had never had dealings with Mr. King. This was no ordinary moneylender. His customers came from the highest reaches of the peerage and included one or two of the royal dukes. Larry and gentlemen like him were very small fry to Mr. King, and Ross had never bothered to warn him off.

Settling back in his chair, he began to read. Mr. King wrote that he had received a necklace that morning, one that he recognized as part of the Sayle collection. There was something else he thought his lordship should know.

The lady who had pawned the necklace had also tried to pawn a ruby and emerald broach but had withdrawn it when she learned the necklace alone would raise the amount she wanted.

Ross's mind instantly made the connections. That morning, Larry had taken Tessa driving in his curricle. The plan was that he would drop her off at the Turners' house and she would spend the afternoon there with Sally and Julian. Later he was to send the carriage for them so that they could all dine together at Sayle House.

Gritting his teeth, he crushed the letter in his hand and tossed it aside. It was perfectly obvious to him what had happened. Larry must be in debt again, and had persuaded Tessa to give him the necklace so that he could pawn it. Ross didn't know who enraged him more—Tessa for doing something like this behind his back, or Larry for putting her up to it.

Tessa was soon pardoned. Too many things had happened to her all at once and she wasn't herself. She wouldn't realize that it would be a long time, if ever, before Larry had the money to redeem the necklace. Larry had probably told her a pack of lies.

When he thought some more about Larry, his wrath gradually cooled to an impatience that was edged with anxiety. He didn't know what to do with the boy. There had been a time when they'd been able to talk to each other, but now he could talk till he was blue in the face, but Larry still went his own way. He was addicted to gambling, spent money like water and had nothing to show for it, nothing but his flashy curricle and an even flashier team of chestnuts.

With a muffled curse, Ross scraped back his chair and went in search of the boy who had delivered the letter.

Sally poured out the tea and Tessa handed Julian his cup and saucer, then took her own to the chair beside the fire. They were in great spirits, having just spent an hour in Hyde Park, walking their hearts out for the sheer pleasure of it.

Tessa sat there quietly now, thinking how ordinary it

all seemed. They were in Sally's parlor, enjoying the cheerful coal fire that burned in the grate; the maid had just set down a plate of seed cake, and Sally and Julian were sniping at each other as usual.

But it wasn't ordinary, not really. All she had to do was slip her hand into her pocket to feel the bank note she'd received that morning from Mr. King, a bank note made out to the bearer in the sum of two hundred pounds.

Just thinking about that encounter made her nervous all over again. Larry had driven her there, but she'd insisted on going in by herself. She didn't want Ross's fury directed at Larry, if he were ever to find out about what she'd done.

But it wasn't going to get back to Ross. For one thing, she'd used a false name. For another, she was going to redeem the diamond necklace before the week was out. She had money of her own. All she had to do was find out how to get to it. It was appalling that she hadn't given any thought to it before now. Men knew about such things, and so should women, and so she would just as soon as this nightmare was over.

She glanced at the clock. In a few hours she would be with Nan, and all the questions that churned inside her head would finally be answered. The uncertainty was unbearable. It made her suspicious of her friends. It made her suspicious of her own husband! Her imagination had taken hold of Nan's words and was making something terrifying out of them.

Your husband would kill me if he knew what I'd done.

It was just a figure of speech. People said such things all the time. Nan didn't mean it literally. Then what did she mean by it, and how was she connected to Ross?

There's a man, Desmond Turner, he's been asking questions about me.

Ross, and now Desmond. What in God's name did it all mean?

She took a sip of tea, waited until her nerves had steadied, then began on the script she had rehearsed. "When do you expect Desmond to return?" she asked Sally.

"Tomorrow or the next day," answered Sally absently. She was refilling Julian's cup.

"Is he on a case?"

Sally looked up. "A case?"

"Wasn't he in Yorkshire recently on a case?"

"Yes," said Sally. "His work takes him all over the place."

Tessa took another sip of tea. "I remember in Paris, when we first met, he told me about one of his more interesting cases, one that baffled him. Desmond said he would never give up on it."

"I remember," said Sally.

"Well, of course you would. Didn't the girl go to our school? I forget her name."

"Margaret Hemmel," said Sally. She looked at Julian, then looked away.

There was no tea left in Tessa's cup, but she continued to sip at it all the same. It wasn't all in her imagination. Things were not as they seemed. Julian and Sally were like frozen sculptures waiting to come to life if she said the right words.

He thought I was one of those other girls. He killed them. I thought they were accidents.

Tessa said, "I remember Desmond saying that the girl died in what appeared to be a carriage accident, but he was convinced it was murder."

"That sounds like Desmond," said Julian, and laughed.

Tessa laughed along with him. Sally smiled.

"Do you know," said Tessa, "I have no recollection of Margaret Hemmel? Do you know who her friends were, Sally?"

"No," said Sally. "I don't remember her either."

Julian said, "What's brought this on, Tessa? Have you met someone who was asking about Miss Hemmel?"

He was all casualness now, but his eyes were avid with interest. Tessa curled her fingers around her cup to stop them from shaking.

"No," she said, "Larry was asking me about Desmond." And that was no lie. "He'd never heard of anyone hiring himself out to solve murders."

244 / Elizabeth Thornton

"Larry?" said Julian, and a look passed between him and Sally. "Yes, he was asking me too."

It was time to change the subject. Without meaning to, she'd cast suspicion on poor Larry. But suspicion of what? She looked at the clock. Her meeting with Nan could not come soon enough for her peace of mind.

"Sally," she said, "your seed cake is delicious. You must give me the recipe so I can pass it along to our cook. Might I have another piece?"

She had a plan for slipping away unseen, but it wasn't a good plan. If Nan had not been so terrified of discovery, she would have had Larry drive her to the front door in broad daylight. But Nan *was* terrified, and now she had to choose her moment with care.

The trouble was, she was never alone for more than a few minutes at a time, and it was beginning to dawn on her that this was no accident. Not only was she suspicious of her husband and his friends, but they were also suspicious of her. Suspicious wasn't the right word. Watchful. Wary. She didn't know what to call it.

She squirmed in the bed, dislodging Ross's arm. He did not waken, and after a moment or two, she inched to the edge of the bed and soundlessly rose to her feet. It took only a moment to don her dressing gown.

"Tessa?" murmured Ross. His voice was husky with sleep. "Where are you going?"

"I can't sleep," she said. "I'm going to the library to find a book to read."

"Mmm." He turned on his side, away from her.

She waited for a moment, listening to the even rhythm of his breathing. Satisfied that he'd gone back to sleep, she crept from the room.

When Ross heard the click of the door latch, he hauled himself up. Not for one moment did he believe that she was going to the library to find a book. Something was going on, and he meant to discover what it was.

All evening, he'd resisted asking her about the necklace she'd pawned. After seeing Mr. King, he had tracked down his brother-in-law, and after a few violent words, he had become convinced that Tessa had not pawned the necklace for Larry. Ross wasn't sure if she'd done it for herself. What he knew was that she now had a bank note worth two hundred pounds and he wanted to know what she was going to do with it.

He'd been sure that she would make her move tonight. She'd hardly been able to look him in the eye all evening. She was by turns distracted, then the life and soul of the party. And when he'd come to bed, she hadn't wanted to make love, which suited him just fine, because he knew if he made love to her he wouldn't be able to conceal his anger. Then he might never find out what was going on.

Throwing back the bedcovers, he strode into his own chamber and quickly donned his clothes. Within minutes, he had gone through the concealed door to the servants' staircase and was making for the ground floor.

Tessa entered the morning room and set down her candle. The footman on duty had seemed startled by her confidence that she couldn't sleep and had decided to read a book in the cozy morning room, where the candle wouldn't disturb her husband. Normally, she wouldn't have bothered explaining herself to a footman, but she didn't want him wondering what was keeping her.

Her warm woolen coat and half boots were in the sideboard where she'd stowed them earlier, when no one was looking. She quickly slipped into them, felt in her coat pocket, and closed her hand around the folded bank note. Leaving the candle burning, she moved to the window. It opened easily, as she knew it would, having tested it before she went to bed.

She climbed over the windowsill, dropped onto the hard-packed earth, and held perfectly still, crouched down, taking her bearings. The church, St. Mary Abbots, was off to her right, and she could just make out its silhouette.

So far, so good, but there were groundsmen out there, patrolling the park, groundsmen with lanterns and dogs.

She saw the lanterns, heard the dogs. They were moving away from her, turning the corner of the house.

Taking a deep breath, she began to run.

• • •

The distance was greater than she'd anticipated, and when she came to the church, she was clutching her side and gasping for breath. She immediately took cover under the cloisters and pressed herself hard against the wall. One of the groundsmen had caught sight of her in her mad dash across the turf, but she was sure she had lost him when she'd dived into the wilderness that bordered the park.

Her hand was pressed against her mouth to stifle her harsh breathing; her ears were straining for every sound. A dog barked somewhere off in the distance. She heard shrubbery rustling as some small creature moved through it. The wind soughed through the bare branches of the trees and ruffled her skirts. Then there was nothing.

Many minutes passed before she began to move. It was dark under the cloisters, so dark that she could hardly see her hand in front of her face. She groped her way, inch by inch, until she came to the end of the wall and looked out on Church Lane.

It was a winding country lane, well treed, with cottages and houses separated by stretches of pasture or garden plots. The lanterns that were lit at every other house gave off a pale, watery light. There were no lights in any of the windows. There was no one about.

She took a moment to study Nan's cottage. It was directly opposite the church, with a dense stretch of spiky black trees on one side and pasture on the other. There were no lights that she could see shining from inside the house, but the lantern above the front porch had been lit. Two small windows flanked the front door and there was one dormer window in the roof. This must be Nan's room. The small garden was enclosed by a hedge and entered by a white wooden gate.

Everything appeared very ordinary, very quiet, just as it should be at this time of night.

Tessa shuddered and pulled back into the shadows. A fear that was almost crippling had suddenly taken hold of her. It was too ordinary, too quiet, as though someone had engineered everything to make her feel safe.

She knew that her fear was irrational and she remained as she was, arguing with herself until she had finally mastered it. She had to go on, not only for Nan's sake, but for her own as well. She had to know, she had to find out and put her horrible suspicions to rest.

Without giving herself more time to think, she picked up her skirts and dashed across the lane. Her fingers fumbled with the latch on the gate, then she was through it and swiftly veering across a patch of grass to the back of the house. There was no lantern here, but through one of the small windows she saw a candle burning in what appeared to be a small scullery.

She rapped on the door with her knuckles, then looked fearfully over her shoulder. It wasn't as dark here as under the cloisters, and she could make out the shape of the outhouses. There would be a washhouse, of course, and the coal cellar. Everything was just as it should be. Then one of the outhouse doors creaked. She thought she heard footsteps and fear gripped her throat.

Hurry, Nan! Hurry!

She rapped on the door again. When she tried the handle, the door opened, and she flung herself inside the house, then quickly shut the door. She would have locked it, but there was no key, and she stood there trembling in an agony of indecision.

"Nan?" she whispered. "Nan?"

No one answered.

Logic told her that Nan had given up waiting for her and had gone to bed. The missing key meant nothing. This was practically the country, and it was well known that country people did not lock their doors. But logic could not calm her sheer animal terror. Every fine hair on her body, all her senses, were telling her to run for her life.

She had to get Nan out of here.

Through sheer willpower, she forced her limbs to obey the commands of her brain. Moving swiftly but soundlessly, she entered the scullery and snatched the candle and its holder from a cutting block.

"Nan?" she said again, but this time her voice was less tremulous.

Convinced that there was no one to hear her on this floor, she made for the stairs. "Nan," she whispered urgently, mounting the stairs. "Where are you?"

Still no answer. The silence and the flickering shadows cast by the candle made everything seem eerie, and her heart beat frantically against her ribs. There was a door at the top of the stairs that stood open. Her steps slowed. She was afraid to enter that open door, afraid of what she would find.

"Nan?"

She halted on the threshold and her fear ebbed. God only knew what she'd expected to find—Nan murdered in her bed; something dreadful. But there was no sign of Nan, and the bed was unmade. As her eyes moved over the rest of the room, however, the fear that had ebbed rushed back in a flood. The room had been wrecked. Every drawer had been turned out and the contents spilled on the floor; the upholstery on chairs had been slashed and the stuffing pulled out. Pictures on the walls were askew. And the bed wasn't unmade. It was wrecked too. Someone had been desperate to find something.

There was another door off that bedchamber, and it, too, was wide open. She approached it cautiously. There was a small landing just beyond the door with a steep flight of wooden stairs going straight down to the ground floor. It was a maid's staircase and would lead to the back of the house, most probably to the scullery where she'd found the candle.

She turned back into the room, trying to decide what to do next. She had to get help. Anything could have happened to Nan.

Her hand was on the rail of the main staircase when she heard a door close. She heard the tread of footsteps approaching the stairs.

"Nan?" she called out, not recognizing her own voice. "Nan, is that you?"

The footsteps stopped. That ghostly silence had fallen

again. But it wasn't an absolute silence. She could hear someone breathing.

And she knew it wasn't Nan.

When she heard the first tread on the stairs, she moved. There was no thought of concealment, no thought of anything but escape. Her irrational fear had turned into panic. Whisking herself around, she bounded across the room, through the door to the maid's stairs, and she flung herself down the steps. She came out in the scullery, still holding the candle, and dashed toward the back door.

A hand struck out at her and the candle went flying to the floor, plunging the hallway into darkness. She cried out and dodged to the left, then came to a standstill. Her assailant was between her and the door. Her brain made lightning deductions, as though every cell in her body had been charged with electricity. Behind her were two doors, but which one led to the exit at the front of the house, she had no way of knowing. And she didn't have time to find out.

He sprang at her. She smelled his sweat and the faint aroma of tobacco. She felt his breath, and before she knew what she was going to do, she had lashed out with the hand that still clutched the candleholder. The force of the blow almost snapped her wrist and she cried out as the holder fell from her nerveless grip. Her attacker groaned and staggered back. She leaped past him, wrenched the door open, and sped out of the house.

She did not once look back. Blind instinct drove her on and she was aware of nothing but the will to survive. She tore through a hedge and went leaping into the grounds of Sayle House. She kept running. There was nothing else she could do. Then she heard the dogs and saw the lanterns and a great sob of relief tore from her throat.

The dogs reached her first. She ran for a few yards more before she collapsed on the turf. On her knees, hunched over, she sucked great gusts of air into her burning lungs. The dogs jumped around her, licking her face, whining.

She looked up as two burly groundsmen came up to

her. They were carrying guns. She tried to speak, to tell them about Nan and how they must hurry, but the sounds that came out of her mouth sounded like gibberish.

One groundsman lifted the rifle to his shoulder and fired a shot in the air. Many minutes passed before she heard shouts and saw other groundsmen carrying guns and lanterns all converging on her. Ross was with them. Heaving herself up, she ran into his arms.

Ross sent Tessa to the house with two of his men. He'd wanted to go with her, but she was so distraught, so insistent that he find her friend, that he'd given way just to calm her. He hadn't asked her any questions, but she'd told him enough to go on. The two hundred pounds had been meant for Nan Roberts, a friend who had fallen on hard times. She'd arranged to go to the girl's house late at night to deliver it. And while he had been out of his mind combing his own woods and grounds for her, she'd been attacked by an unknown assailant.

He knew a fury so profound that if he'd come face-to-face with the man who had terrorized her, he would have put a bullet in his brain without a pang of conscience. There was another emotion at work in him. He was alarmed for the safety of Tessa's friend. Nan Roberts. He remembered the name well. This was the girl Desmond had failed to trace. She, too, had once been a pupil at Fleetwood Hall. He didn't understand where she came into it, not yet, but he knew that everything tied together.

After sending one of his men to fetch the local magistrate, he and the others, about ten in all, some with lanterns, some with guns, fanned out with the dogs and made for the church, just as though they were a shooting party and they were flushing out game. Tonight, they found no game.

It took them about thirty minutes to come to Nan Roberts's cottage, and when his men had surrounded the place, he tried the front door. It was unlocked, and there were no signs that it had been forced.

He entered the narrow hallway with four doors leading off it. Holding his lantern high, he tried the door on his right. It gave onto a small dining room, and the room was in total confusion. Every drawer had been pulled out; chairs were overturned; upholstery was slashed. He found the same in the front parlor. The last room he tried was a bedchamber. One step over the threshold, he halted. This room, also, was in total disorder, but what riveted his attention was the huddled heap on the floor by the bed.

She was an elderly woman and someone had quite evidently strangled her. He didn't touch her other than to move aside the bedclothes so that he could see the marks on her throat. Whoever had strangled her hadn't used his bare hands but a silk scarf or something like it. It didn't look as though she'd put up much of a struggle.

Moving quickly, he opened the door that led to the back of the house. Mounting the stairs, he came to an open door. His breathing steadied when he saw that the room beyond it was empty. Taking his time now, he made a more thorough inspection. The door to this room had been forced. The lock was broken, and one of the hinges was hanging half off. There were also dents and scratches below the lock, as though someone had kicked at it repeatedly.

In his mind's eye, he could follow the unfolding chain of events. Whoever had broken into the house had probably strangled the old lady first. And whoever was in this room was either sleeping behind a locked door or had locked the door in fear of her life.

But Nan Roberts couldn't have been asleep. She would have been waiting up for Tessa, waiting for the money Tessa had promised to bring her. And it was more than likely she would have waited downstairs. Had she heard something? Had the intruder cut off her escape, making her take refuge in her bedchamber?

He now examined the door to the maid's staircase. There was no sign of a forced entry here, but on the landing he found a satin slipper. He picked up the slipper and regarded it thoughtfully. Whoever had worn this slipper had descended the stairs in great haste.

"Your lordship! Your lordship!"

The voice came from the floor below. Ross took the maid's staircase down to the scullery and the back of the house.

"We've found something, sir," said the groundsman.

He led the way out the back door to one of the outhouses.

"In the washhouse, sir," he said.

Ross knew at once that he was looking at Nan Roberts. She was lying on her back, her eyes hideously staring, and the unsightly flush of death deformed her throat and face. One leg was bent under her, and a satin slipper was on the floor, kicked into a corner.

He knelt down and touched her wrist. He wasn't feeling for a pulse, but testing the temperature of the body. She was cold, but so was the washhouse. He couldn't tell how long she'd been dead.

"Get a blanket," he bit out, "anything, something to cover this poor girl."

When she was covered, he rose to his feet. He couldn't go to Tessa before seeing the magistrate. It was going to be a long night.

Chapter Twenty-one

~~~~~~~~~

Tessa took a long swallow of the tea in her cup. It was scalding hot and burned her tongue, but she was hardly aware of it. Nan was dead, murdered, and so was the old lady who lived with her. Ross had seen them with his own eyes.

She began to shake and took another swallow of tea to try and steady her nerves. Just looking at Ross made her feel better. He looked solid, and strong, and good, and as different from the man she'd encountered in Nan's cottage as heaven from hell. He had one foot on the brass fender and was poking the fire to get a blaze going. They were in her bedchamber. She was in her nightclothes but he was still fully dressed. It was late, very late, but the house wasn't silent. She heard a door close softly and whispering. It seemed that Ross had roused the whole house when he'd found she was missing. The dowager had left to go to her own rooms just a few minutes ago, but there were still servants around.

She didn't know why her mind was dwelling on all these trivialities. Nan had been murdered. That's what she should be thinking about. She couldn't seem to take it in.

Ross looked down at her. She was shaking and her face was pale with confusion and weariness. He spoke to her gently as if he were soothing a frightened child. "The magistrate and constables are there now," he said, "but they will come here tomorrow morning to question you."

She nodded, but she wasn't really taking in what he was saying. "Nan said nothing to me of an old lady who lived with her. Who was she?"

"Mrs. Conway. Your friend worked for her, as a maid-companion. The magistrate learned that from their neighbors."

The neighbors, who had been roused from their beds, had also said that Mrs. Conway was as deaf as a door. She wouldn't have heard a housebreaker coming into her house. As for Miss Roberts, she hadn't been with Mrs. Conway for very long. By Ross's reckoning, she'd taken up her post shortly after the notice of his marriage to Tessa had appeared in all the papers. This was too much of a coincidence to be credible in his view. Nan Roberts had wanted to be close to Tessa, and he had yet to discover why.

"How did Nan die?" Tessa asked softly.

"Tessa—"

Her voice rose sharply. "I have to know."

He hesitated, then said, "They were both strangled. Mrs. Conway was in the downstairs bedchamber, and your friend was in the washhouse."

He wasn't going to tell her what he and the magistrate had pieced together. Nan Roberts had locked herself in the washhouse but the murderer had broken in there too. Unlike Mrs. Conway, Miss Roberts had not died quickly. The surgeon who had accompanied the magistrate and his officers could tell by the discoloration and marks on her throat that she'd been strangled slowly, as if the murderer had released the pressure a time or two, either to torture her or to force her to tell him something.

Then he'd torn the house apart looking for something, but Tessa had already told him she had no idea what it could be.

"Mrs. Conway was in the downstairs bedroom when I

was there!" Tessa said, and the shaking began anew. "And Nan was in the washhouse! Oh, God! I heard something, a door opening, footsteps, when I was waiting for Nan to let me in."

Just thinking about the risks she'd run made his fear blaze to a white-hot fury, and the volume of his voice rose dramatically. "What the devil induced you to enter that house when there was no one there to let you in? Don't you realize you could be dead too?"

His words made her flinch. "I don't know . . . there was a light in the scullery. I thought Nan had left it for me."

"He was very clever."

"Oh, no," she said. "Why would he do such a thing?"

"He wanted you to enter the house. It would be easier for him to cut off your escape."

"But why should he want me? No, I'm sure you're mistaken."

Her refusal to face facts made him angrier. "He was waiting for you. He must think you know what he's looking for. He knew that you were coming. He'd been smoking cheroots in the washhouse. We found the stubs . . ."

He broke off when she cowered back in her chair. Her eyes were brimming. His anger died, but the fear was still churning inside him, making him more abrupt than he meant to be.

He said, "Tell me exactly what happened when you reached the house."

She told her story in a few stark sentences, and when she was finished, he was more shaken than she.

"He trapped you in the house!"

She nodded and gulped.

"And you escaped by striking him with the candle-holder."

"Yes," she whispered.

"Would you know him again?"

"No. It was too dark."

In his mind's eye, he was seeing himself kneeling down beside Nan Roberts's body, but it was Tessa's lifeless face that stared up at him. He said the only thing he could manage at that moment. "Why, Tessa, why?"

She knew exactly what he meant. He wanted to know why she had done everything in secrecy and stealth. There were some things better left unsaid. She didn't want him to know that her overactive imagination had made her begin to distrust everyone who was close to her. He'd rescued her tonight, roused the whole house when he'd found her missing. Now, she felt terribly ashamed of ever having doubted him.

After a moment she came up with a rational explanation that was, at least, part of the truth. She said quietly, "You must understand how it was between Nan and me. She was the only friend I ever had at school. We were blood sisters. We promised to help each other. She needed money. She was frightened out of her wits, so frightened that she was terrified to approach me openly. She would come to the edge of our park, hoping to find me alone, but I was always surrounded by people. So she sent me a letter."

He had his answer to one question—why Nan Roberts had come to work for Mrs. Conway. She'd been waiting her chance to approach Tessa, but he'd made damn sure that no one could get close to Tessa. He hadn't foreseen that Tessa would circumvent all his careful stratagems.

"Ross," she said softly, appealing to him, "I couldn't let her down. Surely you can see that?"

He turned to stare at her. His face was hard and unfriendly, almost hostile. "Tell me about Nan Roberts," he said. "Tell me how you came to meet up with her again. I want to know everything. Don't leave anything out."

She looked down at her cup and turned it aimlessly in her hands. His coldness chilled her, but she forgave it because she felt that she had brought it on herself. As she began to relate the sequence of events, her words came slowly, not because she had trouble remembering, but because she was choosing her words to spare his feelings.

"It began, I suppose, with the first note I received," she said, "though later, Nan denied that it had come from her."

"Two notes?" he asked sharply.

"The first one must have been a prank. I don't know."
As closely as she could remember, she told him what was
in the note. When he was silent, she said, "What do you
think it means, Ross?"

"I . . . don't know, Tessa. Let's leave that for now. What
did the second note say?"

As she spoke, he paced, stopping to interrupt her when
he wasn't clear about something. She became less
coherent when she tried to recall what Nan had said to
her at the Opera House.

At one point, he rounded on her and exclaimed, "She
said I would kill her if I knew what she'd done? What did
she mean by that?"

"She didn't mean it literally. I suppose she meant that
she'd done something that would make you very, very
angry. I told you, she also said the authorities would
transport her if they knew what she'd done. Obviously,
she'd done something bad, Ross, and it worried her.
Haven't you any idea what it was?"

He combed his fingers through his hair. "No, I haven't
a clue."

"And she mentioned Desmond by name. She said that
he'd been asking questions about her. Do you know anything about that?"

He didn't answer at once, but reached into his pocket
and produced a cheroot. Lighting it from the fire, he
inhaled and blew out a stream of smoke. "Only Desmond
can answer that question," he said, "but I'm sure there's
nothing sinister in it."

"But . . . but don't you think it's strange? Too much of
a coincidence?"

"What's strange about it? Your friend had obviously
done something reprehensible, even criminal. Desmond
is paid to find such people. There's nothing strange about
that."

Her eyes dropped away. "I suppose you're right."

He didn't give her time to dwell on it. "I'm far more
interested in what your friend was afraid of, and why
someone should wish to kill her and ransack the house.
What did she say to you?"

"There wasn't time to go into it. She was going to tell me tonight. But one thing she did say." She looked up at him. "She said that he knew she was there that night, the night Becky Fallon drowned. You remember, I told you about the girl at my school who died in a drowning accident."

"Yes, I remember. That's why you're so terrified of water." He looked at the cheroot in his hand, thought of the stubs he'd found in the washhouse, then threw it into the blazing coals.

A strange reluctance made her hesitate to voice her next thought, but she forced herself to go on. "Ross, she seemed to think I was there too." She shook her head. "No, she didn't think it. She was sure of it. She said I'd been very clever to pretend I was never there that night. She said . . . she said . . ." The rest came in a rush. "She said that I was safe because I'd been in France. And she mentioned other girls too. Oh, Ross, it was horrible."

"Other girls?"

"Nan said he may have murdered them too, though their deaths looked like accidents. She said—oh, I can hardly believe it."

He said sharply, "Believe what?"

"She said that it was because of her that he'd murdered those other girls, but she wasn't sure."

He said incredulously, "And you were going to hand over two hundred pounds, just like that, and help her escape?"

"Of course not! I wanted to talk to her! I thought she was exaggerating! I don't know what I thought, but I wanted to see her first before I did anything."

His pacing had taken him to the window. He turned suddenly so that his back was to her. She could no longer see his expression, but every line in his body, every muscle, was rigid with tension.

Ross sensed he was frightening her, but he couldn't turn and face her, not yet. His emotions were in a turmoil, and he knew he couldn't speak to her until he had mastered them. Tessa's words stabbed at him, until he had to grit his teeth against the memories they stirred up.

If only he hadn't let her out of his sight he might have been talking to Nan Roberts right now and getting answers from her. Nan had been right to fear him; if Cassie had died because of something she'd done, he would have wanted to kill her.

He felt helpless, deeply shaken by everything Tessa had told him. He couldn't make sense of it, didn't know which way to turn. He and Desmond had questioned witnesses, they'd examined coroners' reports. There had been no mention anywhere, not even a hint, that Nan Roberts had been there that night. They weren't getting closer to solving the case. They were lost in a maze. At one time, he'd hoped that Tessa would be the key to lead him out of it, but she was just as lost as he was.

He breathed deeply, slowly, and as he regained a measure of calm, something came back to him, a conversation he'd had with Desmond when he'd expressed his frustration. He could hear Desmond's calm voice, as if he were at his shoulder.

What if we take Tessa back to Fleetwood Hall. If we made Tessa act out as much as we know, the rest might come back to her.

When he turned to face her, he forced himself to relax. "Just so that I have things clear, tell me again what your friend said about the night Becky Fallon drowned."

She watched his face for a moment before she answered him. "I don't remember her exact words. She said that she was there, and now he knew it."

"And what did she say about you?"

She moistened her lips. "She said I was there too, but it was very clever of me to pretend that I hadn't been."

"And were you there, Tessa?"

The denial rushed to her lips and stopped there. She wanted to say no, but at this crucial moment, she couldn't fight against a truth she now saw she had always suspected and feared.

"I think I must have been," she whispered.

A look of surprise crossed his face, then his eyes met hers directly. "Why do you say that?"

Her throat was aching, but she managed to get out the

words. "Whenever I think of that night, my heart begins to pound and I can't breathe. I'm terrified of someone or something, but I don't know who or what. And I have dreams, terrible dreams, but you know about those." Her voice began to shake. "Do you know what I think, Ross? I think that maybe I was there that night and I don't want to remember it. Everyone says I was there." She shrugged helplessly. "And I have this feeling that if only I could remember, I would understand everything Nan told me, and we would know who had murdered her."

He was careful not to betray himself. He didn't want to say or do anything that would frighten her off. If there had been some other way to unmask his man, he would have gladly taken it. But Tessa was the only card he had to play.

Straightening, he came away from the window, crossed to her, and went down on his haunches beside her chair. "Listen to me, Tessa," he said. "When you went to your friend's house, the murderer was waiting for you. There's no doubt in my mind that he'll try again. He's got to be stopped, do you understand? If there's a chance that you can remember what happened that night, we've got to take it."

She looked at him with huge, trusting eyes. "What is it you want me to do, Ross?"

Her sleep that night was dreamless. It wasn't a natural sleep. Left to herself, she wouldn't have slept a wink. But before going to bed, she'd drunk a glass of warm milk to which Ross had added a few drops of laudanum. It did the trick.

The following morning, when the magistrates and constables came calling, the lingering effects of the laudanum were still obvious. She felt groggy, and answered all their questions calmly, if a little dully. It wasn't an ordeal, and not only because of the laudanum. No awkward questions were put to her, but this might have been because during the whole of the interview, the dowager fussed around her like a brood hen with her little chick, and Ross, with arms folded, stood over her like a watchdog.

It was not until they were in the carriage and on the way to the village of Fleetwood that her brain began to clear a little, though she still felt inordinately sleepy and couldn't stop yawning.

"Nervous?"

She turned her head and looked at Ross. They were going to Fleetwood Hall in hopes that something there would jog her into remembering the night Becky died. "Yes. No. A little."

He smiled with real humor and patted her hand.

After an interval of silence, she sighed and said, "Ross, last night, this seemed like a good idea, but now I'm having doubts about it." When he raised his brows, she responded, "If I *was* there that night, why haven't I remembered something about it in all these years?"

"Don't think about it now. If you remember something, well and good. If not, our journey won't be wasted. We'll make a holiday of it. I've sent a man ahead to engage rooms at The Bell, so we'll be quite comfortable, and the walking in these parts is supposed to be excellent."

"Walking? In January?"

He grinned wickedly. "If you don't want to go walking, I'm sure we can think of something else to do."

She smiled, but a stray thought intruded, a horrifying thought, and the smile shattered. "I can't stop thinking about Nan,"she whispered.

At heart, he wasn't a cold-blooded man, he told himself, but these were exceptional circumstances. He couldn't give in to his natural inclination to take her in his arms and try to distract her. They were here for a purpose.

He picked up her hand and squeezed gently. "Don't think about last night," he said. "Think about happier times. Tell me about your friendship with Nan. Tell me about Fleetwood."

She pressed her lips together and nodded. Her fingers wandered to the fur collar at her throat and absently stroked it. "Nan and I didn't fit in. The other girls came from the ranks of your class, Ross, and they looked down on us. Miss Oliphant's Academy was very select. I don't know how Nan and I ever got into it."

When she paused he said, "I understand that Miss Oliphant had very progressive ideas, and didn't believe in class distinctions."

"Well, Nan and I didn't know anything about that. All we knew was that we seemed to be the poor relations. Nan was a very clever girl, you know. She was there on a scholarship, and of course, my grandfather was footing the bill for me, though at the time I never gave it a thought."

She smiled as something came back to her. "Nan and I were really quite atrocious. We were forever getting into mischief and being punished for it. I remember one night we crept into the chapel when everyone was asleep and rang the bell. Of course, the whole school was in an uproar. It was great fun. Unfortunately, we were found out, and after that, we were put into different dormitories and forbidden to associate with each other."

"But that didn't prevent you and Nan getting together?"

She laughed. "Good Lord, no! We sent secret, coded messages. I was Thor and she was Odin. But I've already told you that."

She went on at some length, but despite her humorous description of pranks and practical jokes, he found it more moving than funny. He was beginning to form a clear picture of just how ostracized these two young girls had been. They'd turned to each other for friendship because none of the other girls would allow them into their circles.

He thought of Amanda Chalmers and her attempt to ostracize Tessa, and his blood boiled. More than ever now he was determined to put a stop to her. No one was going to ostracize Tessa ever again.

When she said a name, he straightened. "Cassandra Mortimer?"

"Do you know, I'd forgotten all about her? She was one of the senior girls, and she didn't give herself airs and graces. She was one of the few girls Nan and I liked. But she was so much older than us that we couldn't really call her a friend."

He was electrified and looked out the window so that his expression wouldn't betray him. Cassandra Mortimer. Cassie. His wife.

Tessa let out a long sigh and yawned. "I know I shouldn't speak ill of the dead, but Becky Fallon, well, she wasn't a nice girl. She'd taken a dislike to Nan and she was downright spiteful."

"Why had she taken a dislike to your friend?"

"Nan said it was because Becky was a scholarship girl as well, but she didn't want anyone to know it. I think their families knew each other. I'm not sure. Anyway . . ." Another long yawn.

After a while he prompted, "You were telling me that Becky was a scholarship girl but didn't want anyone to know it."

"So Nan said. Anyway, Becky told everyone that she was an heiress and that her family was connected to the Dukes of Northumberland. Nan said it was all a lie, and told her so to her face."

She sighed again and rested her head on his shoulder. "Becky was always carrying tales to the teachers, you know, 'Nan and Tessa were outdoors and they weren't wearing their bonnets.' That sort of thing. We had more detentions because of Becky Fallon than any of the other girls who broke the rules. And it wasn't as though Becky were a saint herself, or so . . . so . . ." Her voice faded to nothing and her eyes fluttered closed.

Ross shook her awake. "What did you mean by that, Tessa? Becky, you said, wasn't a saint. Go on."

"Did I?" She brushed a hand over her face. "Nan said that if our teachers ever found out what Becky was up to they would expel her."

Suddenly realizing that she'd said something important, her eyes flared and she looked up at him. "I had forgotten that," she said.

"When did Nan say this?"

"I . . . I don't remember."

He quelled his rising excitement. She was beginning to remember things. If he did this right, if he set the stage with the right props and the right cues, there was a chance, a faint chance, that it might all come back to her.

Julian and Sally might not like all that he had in mind, which was why he hadn't told them that he was bringing Tessa to Fleetwood. As for Desmond, he was just as obsessed as he was with bringing that black-hearted monster to justice. And they had to succeed if Tessa was ever to lead an ordinary life.

He looked down at her and though all he could see was the top of her head, he knew that she slept. She was curled into him like a trusting child. His hand balled into a fist and he stared out the window.

It was dusk when they arrived at The Bell, and Tessa was still sleeping. When he gathered her in his arms and carried her up the stairs to their rooms, she made small, mewling sounds of protest, but she lapsed into sleep again as soon as he laid her on the bed. He untied her bonnet, slipped it from her head, and tossed it on a chair. He then undid the buttons on her coat. Holding her in a sitting position, he tugged her arms free. More mewling protests that lapsed into silence when the coat was off and she was allowed to fall back against the pillows. Smiling, shaking his head, he removed her half boots and set them aside. She was wearing a short spencer. He undid the buttons on that too, and pulled back the edges to expose her throat. Her skin was warm to the touch. He rested his hand lightly on her breast. Her breathing was slow and even.

He felt the familiar fear tighten his chest. Life was so fragile, and she took too many senseless risks. Last night, she'd put him through hell. She had deceived him, stolen from him, lied to him, and had damn near fallen into the hands of a murderer. And later, while she had slept like a babe the whole night through, he had prowled the house. He hadn't been able to sleep a wink for thinking about Nan Roberts, knowing it could just as easily have been Tessa he'd found on that washhouse floor.

There was nothing he would not do to keep her safe.

His hand shook. Abruptly rising, he threw off his coat and neckcloth and went to the washstand. The water was cold, and that's what he wanted. Leaning over the basin, he poured the pitcher of cold water over his head, then shook off the excess droplets of moisture before toweling his hair dry.

It didn't help. He threw the towel aside and looked back at the bed. She was so small, so defenseless. A fierce determination flooded through him, and in its wake, a sense of his own helplessness. A man shouldn't feel like this. A man should know that he could protect his woman. But he had learned a harsh, unforgiving lesson in the school of life, and he was afraid.

He went back to the bed and sat down beside her. He inhaled her perfume, listened to the even tempo of her breathing and the slow pulse of her heart. She had no conception of what she had put him through with her rash, thoughtless exploit. He wanted to shake some sense into her. He wanted to teach her that she could not disregard his wishes with impunity.

His fingers slid through the fiery strands of her hair, clenched, and trembled.

She came awake slowly. Her lashes lifted, and she looked up at him. His face was pale, and dark frustration burned in his eyes. "Ross, what is it? What's wrong?" she cried out.

There was a moment of blind panic when he dug his fingers into her hair and forced her head up for his kiss. She put a hand out to restrain him. Beneath her fingertips, she could feel his heart thundering. His body was trembling. She tasted stark desperation on his lips, and something raw and primitive.

The lover in her came alive. He wasn't himself. Something was wrong. He needed her, needed this. Without conscious thought, she surrendered herself to his embrace. Her hands ran ceaselessly over his back, his shoulders, into his hair, gentling him of the demons she sensed were driving him.

He responded to her surrender by crushing her

beneath him with the full press of his weight. He wasn't asking, he was taking, his kiss told her. He was her husband and she would submit to him. And in those few explosive moments, she gave and gave and gave.

Groaning, he drew back his head. "It's not this simple," he said fiercely.

"I know, I know." Helpless with love, she drew him back to her.

He resisted. "There is nothing I won't do to keep you safe, even if I have to make you afraid of me, Tessa."

In answer, she held his face with both hands and kissed his mouth. "So make me afraid of you," she said.

He savaged her lips, crushed her with arms of steel, showing her how easily he could conquer her.

She seduced him with ravishing caresses and words he had never had from her before. "I love you, love you, love you," she cried. She couldn't stop.

"Tessa—"

"Hush."

She was pulling up her skirts, squirming, positioning herself so that he could take her.

"Oh, no!" He shook his head to clear his mind of the fog that had gathered there. "Not like this." Belatedly, he searched for his control and sucked in a breath when he felt her nimble fingers begin to unbutton the closure on his trousers.

"No," he said again. "Wait—"

"It's all right," she soothed.

His fierce protest turned into a groan when she guided his sex to the entrance to her body. For one moment more he struggled to assert his better nature, but she wouldn't give him a choice. She pressed herself to him, and with a groan that was half roar, he drove into her.

She wrapped her arms and legs around him, locking him to her. Then she began to move. When she kissed him, she felt the smile on his lips.

"Tessa," he said, "you witch! Only a woman could be this ruthless!"

Then there was only sensation, and at the end, the sweet abandoned release.

• • •

Tessa entered the private parlor where their dinner was to be served. This room adjoined their bedchamber, and since it was very late, she had changed into her nightclothes. Ross was waiting for her, but he was fully clothed.

She caught the warmth in his eyes and she smiled, then abruptly the warmth was gone and his eyes were blank. He held a chair for her, and when she was seated, he took his own place at the table and began to ladle something savory from a steaming tureen. There were other servers on the table with a selection of vegetables.

"Hungry?" he asked.

"Famished."

There had been few moments in Tessa's life when she'd felt shy, but this was one of them. When they'd made love, she'd bared her heart to him. Now she wanted to hear the same words from him, but she had too much pride to ask for them.

Everything was suddenly wrong, his reserve, his forced smile, the way he was looking at her. Uncertain, and hurt to the quick by the distance he had put between them, she picked up her knife and fork and cut into a piece of meat.

He poured her a glass of wine. "I'd advise you to dress warmly," he said. "Wear your fur-lined pelisse. We may have a long walk."

She studied his face. "What are you talking about?"

"Fleetwood Hall," he said. "It's quite a walk from the house to the lake."

"But we're surely not going there tonight!"

"Why not?"

"Because . . . because it's dark."

"We'll take a lantern. Don't worry, Tessa, we won't lose our way."

"But it's so late."

"Not as late as it was the night Becky Fallon drowned."

She set down her knife and fork. "I thought we would go in the morning," she said. "We can see more when it's light."

"That's true. But that's not the point of the exercise, is it?" He helped himself from several of the servers. "The point of the exercise is to force you to remember everything that happened that night."

She didn't like the set of his features; she didn't like the sound of his words. Her heart was beginning to pound. Her breath was rushing in and out of her lungs. She looked down at her plate and knew she couldn't eat a bite.

He was watching her with narrowed eyes, and she read his cold determination. This time, she couldn't get round him and it was useless to try.

With trembling fingers, she picked up her glass of wine and drank deeply.

Chapter Twenty-two

~~~~~~

They left the carriage on the approach to the house and set off on foot. Tessa was surprised that the gatekeepers had allowed them to pass, and mentioned it to Ross.

"They were expecting us," he said.

"Expecting us!"

"I arranged it when you were asleep."

A shiver ran over her, but she managed to say lightly, "And did you also arrange with Miss Oliphant to allow us to trespass all over her park in the dead of night?"

"No," he said. "We want everything to be just as it was the night you and your friend stole out of the house and crept down to the lake. You would have been afraid of being discovered. Whatever you felt that night, I want you to experience now."

His words jarred her, and she quickly looked up at him. The lantern he was carrying cast odd shadows, making his features seem misshapen, masklike. If she hadn't known him, she would have taken him for a stranger. Even his voice sounded odd to her ears. It was hard and uncompromising.

To steady herself, she darted a glance over her

shoulder, to the small group of men on foot who formed their guard. There were six of them in all, all armed like Ross, and all carrying lanterns. The sight of them should have reassured her, but their lanterns cast frightening shadows too, and they looked more like a band of desperate ruffians than the Sayle coachmen and grooms she had come to know and like.

The night was cold, but she wasn't uncomfortable. Her coat was lined with fur and the exercise of walking helped keep her warm. Moonlight silvered the dense stands of leafless oaks and limes that flanked the drive, and filtered down to a paler glaze on the shrubbery that lay in the shadows. From time to time they passed lanterns that were hung on poles. No one spoke, nothing broke the silence but the crunch of leather on gravel and the odd creak of a branch. The landscape was as still and unmoving as a painting.

It wasn't like this the night Nan and I went out.

Before she could prevent it, her mind was swamped with images, trees in full leaf, swaying in a warm westerly breeze and soft fragrant grass beneath their feet. She was hot, too hot, and knew she was coming down with a fever. Nan giggling in anticipation. A secret! Tessa had to see it with her own eyes or she would never believe it.

The memory meant nothing at all. She'd gone out with Nan on many nights. Perhaps it wasn't a memory. Perhaps just knowing how desperate Ross was for her to remember made her suggestible.

"Fleetwood Hall," said Ross, and her mind instantly cleared.

They halted under a great, spreading horse chestnut tree and silently studied the house. It was not unlike Greenways. There was a main building with two wings running off it. Her dormitory had been in the west wing and Nan's in the east. There wouldn't be many girls here until the beginning of the new term. A few lights could be seen through the windows, showing that the house was not completely deserted, and the lantern above the portico was lit.

Ross said, "This is where it begins, Tessa."

He was watching her to see if she understood him, and she nodded. Whatever the truth of the matter, he wanted her to act as though she'd been there the night Becky drowned. She'd told him the account the senior girls had given of that night, and they were to go through it step by step, as if they were in a play. She'd promised to go through with it, and there was no getting out of it now.

He watched her a moment, gauging her reaction, then satisfied with what he saw, he went on, "How did you arrange with Nan to meet that night? You said you were kept apart, but sent messages to each other. Is that what happened?"

"The chapel," she said. "We left messages in the chapel. Every morning and evening, there was an assembly in the chapel. That's where we left our notes." In her mind's eye, she saw the table in the narthex and on it the box the chaplain had set out for special prayer requests, requests that were anonymous and which he would offer to God in private. She and Nan left their notes beneath the box.

"Whose idea was it to go out that night?"

"It must have been Nan's."

"Why do you say that?"

She shifted restlessly. "Because I hadn't been feeling well for some days. I was feverish. My house mistress made up a special drink for me that night, fresh lemonade with a spoonful of brandy in it."

"I see. How did you leave the house without being seen?"

"I don't remember leaving the house."

He turned his head and gave her a long, measuring stare. Sighing, she said, "It wasn't difficult. Everyone was asleep. My dormitory was on the ground floor. There was a storeroom with a small window. I used to go in and out by that window."

"Why didn't you fall asleep? If one of the mistresses gave you something with brandy in it, and as you say, you were feverish, why didn't you fall asleep?"

"I didn't drink it," she said. "I poured it into the slop pail."

And that's exactly what she'd done. The memory came back to her as clear as a bell. She'd taken one sip and had poured it away. This wasn't a murky memory that she had suppressed for years and that had suddenly come back to her. It was something she had always remembered. She hadn't liked the taste of the brandy. That's why she had poured it away. It was from this point on that her memory differed from that of the senior girls. She had supposed that she'd crawled back to bed where she'd remained, delirious, till her fever had broken three days later.

"Where did you meet Nan?"

"At the chapel. It's where we always met."

"Take me to it."

When she set off along the drive, he halted her. "Surely you wouldn't have come this way, for everyone to see you? Isn't there another path, one that would conceal you from the house?"

He was right, of course. "This way," she said, and immediately turned aside and struck out along the back of the house, toward a stretch of trees and shrubbery.

The chapel was only a five-minute walk from the house, and was all that remained of the property of the first Baron Fleetwood who had lived in Tudor times.

Ross spent some time examining the chapel, trying doors, walking around it. "How did you get in?" he asked finally.

"What?"

"You told me this is where you and Nan met. Since you once rang the bell as a prank, you must have discovered a way to enter the chapel."

"Nan had a key."

He breathed deeply, impatiently. "And where did she keep the key, Tessa?"

She felt a strange reluctance to tell him. She didn't want to open that door. She didn't want to enter the chapel. It held too many memories.

If she went on like this, by the time they got to the lake, she would be a prime candidate for a lunatic asylum. She said with a newfound resolve, "Nan discovered where the chaplain kept a spare key. It may not be there now."

"And where was this?"

"In the chaplain's privy. It's at the back of the chapel or it used to be. None of the girls ever went in there. I believe it was on a hook above the door."

Ross left her with two of their companions. It was the first time she'd noticed that four of the men were no longer with them. Since no one seemed disturbed by this, she decided not to worry about it either.

He returned in a few minutes with the key, and was soon ushering her inside the chapel. Narthex was too grand a word for the cramped entry. It was no more than a narrow passageway with an arch leading into the chapel itself. Ross held up his lantern and paused. Over the backs of the pews, they had a clear view to the altar. On the right of the altar was a wooden Christening font, and on the left, a pulpit, both modern additions made by the last Baron Fleetwood.

She found that she was holding her breath, half expecting Nan to pop up from their hiding place. With slow halting steps, she approached the pulpit. Snatches of girlish conversation flitted through her head. Nan laughing when she, Tessa, complained that she couldn't come out at night anymore because she was falling behind in her studies. Nan was so clever, she didn't need to study. Everything came easily to her.

A different Nan. Now she was the one to complain. Miss High and Mighty Becky Fallon was a pain in the arse, Nan said. She'd been given another detention because Becky had reported her for eating a cream bun for all to see on the streets of Fleetwood. This, of course, showed a lack of delicacy and was against school rules. But Nan was going to fix Becky Fallon. She was no saint, oh, no, she was no saint.

It's a secret, said Nan. *You wouldn't believe it if I told you. You must come out! You must! It's only a sniffling cold, for heaven's sake.*

She felt a hand on her shoulder and jumped.

"I'm sorry if I startled you," said Ross. "But you were

staring so fixedly at the pulpit that I wondered if you had remembered something."

She moved away from him. "No," she said. "That's where Nan and I used to hide, crouched down in the pulpit. We discovered that the light from our lantern could not be seen from the outside if it was on the pulpit floor. That's all I was thinking."

"Why did you need a light?"

With a will of their own, her eyes flitted to the Christening font. *Our hallowed hiding place*, Nan called it. "We wrote stories," she said. "Sometimes we would take turns reading them to each other. We didn't always have a light."

"Where's the bell that you and Nan rang?"

When she pointed to the wall behind the altar, he went to examine it. "It's not much of a bell," he said, looking up through the tiny belfry.

"This isn't a cathedral, Ross. It's a chapel. And the belfry was added at a later date. The bell was rung only to summon us girls to morning and evening prayers."

He looked at the pulpit and the Christening font and observed idly, "Well, whoever made these additions has ruined the chapel."

She sat in the front pew and after a moment he joined her. "Now what?" she said.

He took her hand and looked up when he felt it trembling. For a moment, a fleeting moment, she thought there was a softness about him, but it was only a trick of the light, as his next words proved.

"We're going on with this, Tessa, come what may. We have no choice."

"I understand."

He was doing it for her sake. It was this thought that gave her the courage to go on. But her mind was already drifting to the lake, and the blood was beginning to move through her veins in slow, painful strokes.

"Think back to that night," he said. "It was June and close to the end of term. Many of the senior girls would be leaving. There was a ritual, wasn't there, where they went down to the lake to bathe?"

"It went on all week. They didn't go out all at once but a few at a time so that they wouldn't be missed by their teachers. It was supposed to be a great secret, but everyone knew about it."

"And you and Nan decided to play a trick on them?"

She exhaled a long, slow breath. She couldn't remember, but in this game they were playing, she was supposed to take her cue from him. "I didn't want to go, because I wasn't feeling well. All week Nan had been writing notes, trying to persuade me to change my mind." And that was the truth. "I suppose she succeeded." And that was speculation.

When he stood, indicating it was time to go, she clamped a hand under her breast to slow the furious pace of her heart. Slowly, she straightened and allowed him to lead her outside.

"You set off from here?" he asked.

"Yes." They'd always met in the chapel first. She had many memories of them setting out from this point, but that didn't mean they'd gone out together on that particular night.

"Show us the way."

"To the lake?"

"Where else?"

Something buzzed at the back of her mind, a memory that she groped for and couldn't quite reach. Ross was watching her, waiting for her to move. There was a well laid out path leading down to the lake. That wasn't the one she and Nan would have taken that night, supposing they'd gone out together.

Moving silently, she skirted the path, hesitated for a moment, then stepped with a sure foot into the undergrowth. It surprised her that she could remember the way so well. She didn't have to think about it, and when she did think, her steps faltered. But some things seemed to have been memorized by bone and muscle.

The way down was steep and wound down through a wilderness of trees, fallen branches, and thick shrubbery. Before long, she was breaking out in a sweat, and it wasn't only because her coat was too warm. She was anticipating the moment when she would come out on the lake.

Hurry, Tessa! Hurry! Nan's voice floated through her head. *We're late. If we don't hurry, we'll miss everything.*

Nan would be out in front, leading the way, not because she was always the leader, but because this was her adventure.

It didn't happen. It was all in her imagination. Ross was putting ideas into her head.

She hadn't realized she was running till she burst out of the trees and came to a sudden halt. After the dense shade of the woods, the lake seemed to shimmer with light, like a vast looking glass, reflecting the pale watery moon. But it wasn't a looking glass she ever wanted to look into.

She stood there rigidly, paralyzed with fear and doubt, wanting to run, unable to move a muscle. She shouldn't be here. Something was wrong. This wasn't how it happened.

"Tessa!"

She jerked away when Ross came up to her. Like her, he was breathing hard and fast. "I . . . I don't want to go on with this," she said hoarsely. "I shouldn't have come here. Please, Ross, let's leave this place."

There was no give, no gentleness in him. "You *must* go on with this, Tessa. You're beginning to remember things, aren't you?"

"No!" she cried out. "It's just a blur. Nothing makes sense."

"We're not finished yet. Perhaps this will help you remember."

He grasped her by the elbow and forced her to go on. They circled the lake until they were on the other side, looking back at the house. She knew why he had brought her to this point. This was where Becky had drowned. She looked up at the stars; she looked over the tops of the trees to the chapel. She looked everywhere but at the water.

"Look," he said, "look in the lake, Tessa."

He forced her head round and shook her when she closed her eyes. Opening her eyes, she looked down and moaned when she saw a huddled heap, no more than a dark outline, floating in the water.

"Becky," she whispered brokenly.

She sank to her knees and covered her face with her hands.

He wasn't finished with her yet. Kneeling down beside her, he grasped her by the shoulders. "Look, Tessa!" he said. "Look at the other side of the lake. Can you see them? Aren't those the girls you came to spy on?"

Tears blurred her vision, but she could not tear her eyes away. On the other side of the lake, she saw a light, a lantern, and silhouetted against the light, close to the water's edge, were four figures.

"Who are they, Tessa? Do you remember their names? No? Then let me remind you of them. Margaret, Johanna, Cassandra, and Becky. Do you remember now, Tessa?"

That cold, hateful voice was like a steel spike driving into her brain, giving her no quarter. "No," she whispered. "No."

"Margaret, Johanna, Cassandra, and Becky. Am I right, Tessa? They're in your dream, aren't they? Look at them."

She looked across the lake, but this time, she didn't see four indistinct figures. She saw four of the senior girls. But this wasn't right. There should have been only three girls. He was wrong about Becky. She shouldn't be there.

"Do you remember what happened?" he asked in the same relentless tone. "It's on record. They heard you splashing in the water. You wanted them to hear you, didn't you? You pretended to get into difficulty. Do you remember, Tessa?"

"Please, no. It wasn't me! I swear it wasn't me!"

He was immovable. "Then you called out. Do you remember what you called? That's on record too. Shall I tell you?"

The past and the present rushed together in her mind. His hands were powerful, digging into her shoulders, making movement impossible. She started to struggle, trying to pry herself loose. He was trying to drown her!

Oh, God, those powerful masculine hands were holding her under the water. She was going to drown!

In those few despairing moments, the past became the present, and she was that twelve-year-old girl again, crying out in helpless terror.

"Help me!" she screamed. "Someone please help me! I can't swim! Oh, God, I can't swim! You must help me! Please, please, why won't you believe me? Please! Please!" Over and over again, the words tore out of her throat till she was hoarse with shouting. At the end, the words faded to choked whimpers and sobs.

White-faced and shaken, Ross cupped her chin and made her look up at him. "It wasn't a prank," he said. "You meant every word."

"Of course I meant it," she sobbed out. "But they wouldn't listen. They turned their backs on me and walked away."

"What happened, Tessa?"

"It was Becky in the water," she cried. "Becky! She was kicking out, trying to get away from him. But he held her under! It was horrible, like a nightmare. I couldn't help her. I couldn't swim. And I was a coward, such a coward. And . . . and when it was over, and he came for me, I ran away and hid."

His breathing was hoarse and thick and made speech impossible for some time. At length, he said, "Who was he, Tessa?"

"I don't know. I didn't see his face, or if I did, I can't remember it. He was Becky's lover. They met in the greenhouse. That's where Nan took me that night. But everything went wrong."

"But you do remember everything that happened?"

"Oh, yes. Now I remember everything."

He was worried about her, so worried, in fact, that he did not take her back to the carriage but took her straight to Fleetwood House. The housekeeper answered the door in her nightclothes, and though she was at first suspicious, when she realized they were people of rank, she allowed them to enter. Ross told her only that his wife had taken a turn as they were passing the gates to the Hall, and as soon as she had recovered, they would be on their way.

Mrs. Doyle took one look at Tessa and became all sympathy. She led them the length of the west wing, the wing where Tessa's dormitory once was, and ushered them into what was evidently her own cozy parlor. The headmistress, she told them, was not expected back until the following day, and the girls who were home for the holidays, not until the beginning of the week. The house was almost deserted except for a few teachers and maids and the odd girl who had no home to go to, and they were all in the other wing.

She was a kindly, motherly woman who didn't fuss but seemed to know what was required without being asked. Going at once to the fire that had been banked for the night, she poked it into life, then added several lumps of coal. When Tessa was seated, she covered her knees with a shawl, and left to put the kettle on for a cup of tea. Ross had hardly time to draw a chair close to Tessa's before Mrs. Doyle returned with a bottle of brandy and two glasses.

Setting them down on the sideboard, she bobbed a curtsy and left.

Ross looked at Tessa. She had removed her coat and was sitting with her back hard against the chair. Her gown was dark and relieved by a white muslin kerchief that was tied at the throat. Her lips and face had no more color than her kerchief. Her eyes were closed and the hair on her brow was damp.

"I'm sorry I was so hard on you," he said.

Her eyes opened. "Are you?"

"Tessa—" He tried to take her in his arms but when she turned her head away, he let her go. "Everything I did was necessary."

"You were brutal, merciless. But I should have remembered that from France."

"You'll see things differently when you have a chance to think about them."

"I presume those were your men on the other side of the lake. I wondered where they'd got to."

A muscle in his cheek tensed. "I had to get you to remember. There's more at stake here than you realize."

A shudder ran over her. "Was it really necessary to put that bundle of clothes or whatever it was in the water to make me think it was Becky?"

"I wanted you to remember." He combed his fingers through his hair. "What else can I say except that I'm sorry it had to be like this?"

"Oh, yes, you're sorry," she said bitterly. "And now I suppose you're impatient for me to tell you all that I remember? It doesn't help, you know. I can't tell you who he was." Her voice cracked. "Don't you think I wish I knew, not only for Becky's sake but for Nan's too?"

"I'll get you that brandy," he said.

As he poured out the brandy, he cursed himself inwardly for having been so ruthless. At the same time, he didn't see what choice he'd had. Now at least they had their first real lead in a long while.

His mind teemed with questions he wanted to ask her. And she was right—he was impatient to hear the rest of her story. But when he saw how her hand trembled when he put the glass into it, he knew he had to give her time to come to herself.

"I want you to drink this glass of brandy," he said. "And I mean all of it. I'll fetch the housekeeper to sit with you while I see to the men. I might as well send them back to Fleetwood and have them send the carriage for us in the morning. You're exhausted and in no condition to travel. I think it best if we spend the night here. I'll ask the housekeeper to make up beds for us."

"No," she said, "not yet. Sit down, Ross. I want to tell you what happened that night. If I don't tell someone, I think I shall go mad."

When he was seated, she drew in a breath and began to speak. "I waited for Nan at the chapel. She was late, and I was feeling so unwell that I was ready to give up and go back to the house. She was very excited when she arrived. She'd stolen letters that someone had sent to

Becky, and Becky, she said, would be terrified out of her wits when she discovered that they were missing. If I'd been feeling better I would have questioned her about them, but I wasn't interested in the letters. All I wanted was to go back to my bed.

" 'It's only a sniffling cold,' Nan said, when I told her that I wanted my bed, and there was something she wanted to show me, something that would astonish me. So I let myself be persuaded.

"We didn't go down to the lake, though we passed close by. Through the trees, we could see the senior girls, but we didn't stop to watch. We went to the greenhouse. There were two people inside, Becky and a man. We could hear their voices, and they were quarreling. Nan went up close, and looked in through the window, then she came back to me. 'It's him' she said. 'Becky's lover.' And just as she said those words, the lamp inside the greenhouse went out.

"I can't remember exactly what happened next. Becky's voice was rising, then suddenly it was cut off. I don't know what I thought, but I knew I was terribly, terribly frightened. I picked up a stone and launched it at the greenhouse, but it bounced off a tree. Then Nan ran away."

When she paused, he didn't say anything. He didn't want to break her train of thought. All the questions he was impatient to ask her were better left till she had told him everything.

She stared at the fire as the memories came back to her. "I ran away, too, and hid in a clump of bushes. The door opened, and Becky ran out. He was right behind her. Becky didn't stop running, but he stopped for a moment and looked around, then went after her. I followed them."

She pressed a hand to her eyes, and her voice was no more than a shaken whisper. "I suppose Becky ran to the lake because she knew that's where her friends were and that's where she would get help. But they were on the other side of the lake. There was no one there to help her but me.

"You know the rest." She looked up at him. "They were in the water when I reached them. Becky was trying to fight him off. Then he held her under the water. I could see them in the moonlight, though not very clearly. Then I began to scream for help, but that only scared the senior girls away. When he came out of the water, I ran and hid myself. I don't know for how long. It seemed like hours. But I knew he was out there, looking for me, and I was terrified to move.

"I think he might have caught me if one of the senior girls hadn't come back to look for Becky."

"Cassandra Mortimer," he said softly.

"Yes, Cassandra Mortimer. I think I must have been in shock. All I could think was that she was too late. I heard him running away and came out and went back to the house. And that's all I know. I never saw his face. I wouldn't recognize him if I saw him again."

She turned her head and met his eyes. "I suppose you have a million questions you want to ask me."

Her words reassured him. She was pale and shaken, but she wasn't shattered by what he'd forced her to go through.

"They can wait till later," he said, and stood up. He put a hand on her shoulder. "You were a very brave girl. Now, drink the brandy and I'll get the housekeeper to sit with you."

"But where are you going?"

"To see to the men. This won't take long."

As soon as he had gone, Tessa set aside her glass, threw off the shawl that covered her knees, and got to her feet. It was so hot in that small parlor that she felt as though she were suffocating. Or perhaps it was the memory of that night that was making her feel so wretched.

She moved restlessly around the room, looking at everything, seeing nothing but the images that passed before her eyes. It didn't seem strange to her now that she'd locked away those awful memories in the darkest corner of her mind, never to bring them into the light.

She hadn't been brave, as Ross said. What she'd done was unforgivable.

She should have done more to save Becky. The water wasn't deep at that point. There was no danger of her drowning. She'd been so afraid of putting herself near those powerful hands that held Becky beneath the water. And so, like the coward she was, she'd just stood there at the edge of the lake while he murdered Becky.

She pressed a fist to her mouth to choke back a sob. Now she understood her most constant nightmare only too well. What Becky must have suffered in those last few moments had preyed on her mind. In her nightmare, she'd put herself in Becky's place.

It did no good to chastise herself now so many years later. She'd been a mere girl of twelve at the time and she hadn't been the only girl there that night. Nan must have been there too, hiding somewhere. And those other girls were older. They'd heard her calling for help and they'd walked away.

God help her, but that was her fault too. They'd recognized her voice and thought she was playing one of her tricks on them. If she'd been someone else, someone who wasn't always getting into mischief, they would have given the alarm and Becky might be alive today.

And Nan.

She sat on the edge of her chair, staring into the fire thinking of Nan. The last she had seen of Nan before the night of the opera was when she'd thrown the pebble at the greenhouse. Nan had been more frightened than even she was. But she hadn't known then that the man with Becky had murder on his mind.

And later, after her fever had broken, she was so weak, she'd been kept in the infirmary, isolated from the other girls. Someone had come to question her about the accident, and of course, she'd protested that the senior girls were mistaken. She hadn't been there. Two weeks were to pass before she was fully recovered. By that time, school term was over, and all the girls, including Nan, had gone home.

And the next term, her guardians had enrolled her in

another school. They had known of the accident, though not that she was implicated in it, and they'd been scandalized at such goings-on as midnight frolics in the lake.

Somewhere close by a clock chimed. She heard the rattle of carriage wheels on the drive, and though these sounds registered, she paid no attention to them. Her tortured thoughts had moved on to the night Nan had been murdered.

He would pay for it. As God was her witness, she would find him and make him pay for it. She might not have seen his face, but now that she remembered the events of that night, she had something to go on. She knew now what he'd been looking for when he'd torn Nan's house apart.

Now that she was thinking of bringing Nan's murderer to justice, she wasn't feeling quite so guilt-stricken or sorry for herself. Ross had put her through a harrowing experience, but if it helped unmask the man who had murdered Nan, it was well worth it. Perhaps this would help make amends for not doing more to save Becky.

Those other girls. I'm almost sure he killed them, Tessa.

Nan's words passed through her brain like an electric current. With a rush of horror, she made connections. Who else could Nan have meant but the girls who were there that night? Ross had even told her their names—Margaret, Johanna, Cassandra.

One thought gripped her mind. She had to find Ross and ask him about those girls. She dashed from the room and stumbled to a halt a few steps into the corridor. The lamp that had been burning when the housekeeper had shown them to her parlor had gone out.

"Ross?"

Her eyes flew wildly to every shape she could make out in that dark interior. Her nerves were shattered, she told herself. She'd been through a harrowing experience. It was this that was making her skin prickle and her fine hairs lift like a cat's fur.

But something was wrong. She'd heard the carriage leave some time ago. Ross should have returned by now. And Mrs. Doyle was supposed to come and sit with her.

"Mrs. Doyle?" The thin sound of her quavering plea vibrated the length of the corridor, then faded away. A shadow moved, but it might have been nothing but her imagination. Her hands were fisted so tightly that her fingers hurt.

Then it came to her, the faint and not unpleasant aroma of tobacco smoke. Her instincts were more alert than her brain. An instant before he came bearing down on her, she whisked herself into the room and shut the door with a snap. Her fingers had never worked faster as she turned the key in the lock. She hadn't taken a step back when something slammed into the door like a thunderbolt. Her scream lodged in her throat and came out a moan. One panel had split but the door held. She didn't have to think about what to do next. Snatching up her coat, she ran to the window.

As rational thought returned, her terror increased. Where was Ross and what had happened to him? Images too horrible to contemplate beat at the edges of her mind. Where, oh, God, was Ross?

When the door shattered under the next murderous onslaught, she opened the window and climbed over the sill.

Chapter Twenty-three

‏❧~❧~❧‎

She dashed for the cover of the trees, making for the less used track that led to the chapel, the one she'd taken earlier with Ross. Her overriding thought was to ring the chapel bell and raise the alarm. She wasn't thinking so much of rousing the teachers and maids who were at the school, but of the gatekeepers who had been on duty when they'd arrived. She remembered that there was another gate, with other gatekeepers. If she could only raise the alarm!

This path wasn't the quickest route to the chapel, but she had no choice. Its only virtue was that the trees and bushes hid it from the house. She had to get to the chapel without being seen, or before he could cut her off and prevent her from ringing the bell.

She pictured Ross, lying in a heap, bleeding and badly injured. More than that, her mind refused to accept. If she didn't get help soon, the murderous devil who was after her could take his time in finishing them both off.

He was stealthy, almost soundless, but her hearing had never been more acute. She was burningly aware of the instant he climbed over the windowsill and stepped onto the gravel drive. A burst of energy propelled her into the cover of the trees, and she flattened herself against the trunk of a towering oak and looked back. He was at the corner of the house, no more than a dark figure, silently assessing which way she'd taken. She didn't wait to see more, dared not allow herself that liberty. Time was passing and Ross could be bleeding to death. She had to move.

At first, she was cautious, flitting from tree to tree, picking her way around shrubs and fallen branches. A time or two, she paused to listen. There was nothing but the sound of her own ragged breathing. Fixing her eyes on the way ahead, she hastened her steps and tumbled headlong over an exposed root. She didn't cry out, but the sound of her fall, in her own mind, echoed like the report of a pistol shot. She was instantly on her feet, staring back the way she had come. A shadow moved, then melted into the deeper shade of the trees. Once again, the landscape was as silent and unmoving as a picture. But she knew, she *knew* he was stalking her.

From that point on, she ran like a hare. The strain and terror of the night's events was held at bay, submerged by a burning, mindless resolve to reach the chapel and ring the bell. When she moved, so did he. There was no attempt at concealment now on either part. But the advantage was still with her. She was well out ahead, and he could not know that she was heading for the chapel.

She burst upon the clearing where the chapel stood and veered to the right, running the length of the building to the chaplain's privy where the key was kept. When her fingers searched above the lintel and didn't immediately find the key, she let out a whimper of pure animal terror. She could hear him crashing through the underbrush. In another moment he would catch up to her.

Her fingers touched something cold and hard, grasped it, and plucked it from its hook. Quickly, silently, she slipped outside and flitted to the far side of the chapel, away from her pursuer. She had hardly turned the corner when he came charging out of the trees. He was on one side of the chapel, and she was on the other, and she had yet to unlock the door.

She clamped her hand over her mouth to muffle the sound of her breathing. He was less cautious, and because she could hear the harsh sound of air as it rushed in and out of his lungs, she knew that he was making for the privy. Without waiting to hear more, she made for the chapel door and quickly inserted the key in the lock. It grated as she turned it, and she winced. The door creaked when she pushed it open. At that moment he came round the side of the building and charged her.

She bolted through the door and raced down the center aisle toward the altar. His blow caught her in the back, and she went sprawling on her hands and knees. Her momentum carried her forward. In those few despairing moments, before she could recover her breath, she knew that she would never make it to the bell rope on the other side of the altar. She had lost.

She was terrified, but another emotion, stronger than her fear, was at work in her. She was coldly furious that it should end like this. He was a murderer. He had killed Becky and Nan. He may have killed all those other girls. It was possible he had killed Ross. He wasn't going to get away with it. If she had to fight him tooth and nail, he wasn't going to get away with it.

Galvanized by that thought, she sprang up and spun to face him. Behind him, moonlight streamed through the great circular window above the narthex, dappling the interior with ghostly shadows. She saw a man of medium height, but his features were in darkness. As she retreated, he advanced. She could tell that he was confident of victory. He was in no hurry to finish her off. He had trapped her and there was no way out except past him. She wasn't looking for a way out. She wanted to disable him, distract him so that she could ring the bell.

Thoughts that had been circling at the back of her mind ever since her memory had come back to her suddenly fused together, giving her the one chance she was looking for. If she was wrong . . . she pushed the thought away from her, not daring to complete it.

She had to make him think that she was beaten. He mustn't suspect that she wasn't finished yet. "If you let me go," she said, and the quaver in her voice wasn't all playacting, "I'll show you where the letters are hidden. They're here in the chapel."

He halted. "So, you admit that you know about the letters?"

She knew that voice! She'd heard it many times, but it was different now. It was cold and flat, with no expression, nothing that helped her place him. Who was he? Oh, God, who was he?

When he took a step toward her, she retreated, but she matched her steps to his, trying not to provoke him into pouncing on her. If he grabbed her, she would never get to the bell.

He went on, "I couldn't make up my mind about you. I was almost sure you had no part in this. I was astonished when you took my bait and led me to your accomplice, astonished and grateful, because until then I hadn't the least idea where to find her. Where are the letters?"

"Your bait?"

"My note."

"I don't remember . . ." Then she did remember, the first note that Nan had denied writing. "I didn't know what to make of that note," she said.

He laughed, and the sound made her cringe. "You weren't supposed to make anything of it. But you did exactly as I hoped you'd do. You arranged to meet your accomplice to show it to her. I'm not finding fault with you. As I said, I am grateful."

He'd been there at the Opera House. Watching her. And she had led him to Nan. He must have overheard their conversation. And then he'd killed Nan, just as he would kill her.

They were almost at the end of the pews. She reached a hand behind her, feeling for the altar. When she touched it, she began to edge her way around it. She had to keep him talking, keep him distracted. Only a few seconds more, and she would reach her goal.

"I wasn't Nan's accomplice," she said, "and I didn't find her. She found me. She needed money. That's why she came to me. But yes, she told me there were letters and where she'd hidden them." She was surprised how easily the words came to her and how convincingly she could lie. "If anything happened to her, I was to give them to the authorities. That's why we came down here, to get the letters."

"So, she told me the truth! The letters really are hidden in this chapel?"

"She told you?" She couldn't hide her surprise. The letters were a pretext to distract him. She had never seriously considered that Nan would hide them here. Then she remembered Nan's words at the Opera House. She'd mentioned their "hallowed hiding place." Perhaps they were hidden here after all.

"Oh, yes, she told me," he said, "but I wasn't inclined to believe her, not until I'd searched her house and could not find them. Why do you think I'm here?"

Her throat worked at the picture that formed in her mind. Nan had been strangled, Ross had told her. Suppressing that horrifying image, she said, "I presumed you had followed us down."

"No. I was here first. I decided that the letters should be my first order of business. Without them, the case against me is very shaky. I had not expected Sayle to be so quick off the mark. I was caught by surprise when you all turned up. As you can see, I haven't found the letters. It appears that Miss Roberts didn't tell me the whole truth. Are they still here?"

"Yes."

His voice lashed out at her, making her jump. "Don't lie to me! You've already been here once this evening. If the letters were here, you would have taken them."

With an agility of thought that was born of desperation, she cried out, "We did find them but my husband said that we should leave them where they were to show the magistrate when he gets here. He sent the men to the village to fetch him. Surely you must have seen them go?"

She was now in the small chancel with the altar between them. He would think that she was cowering away from him and that he could finish her off any time he wanted. She was completely hemmed in, with the altar in front of her and the font and pulpit on either side. Soon her back would be to the wall.

"Do you know what I do to little girls who lie to me?" he said.

She knew, and the thought made her courage crack. "You killed all the girls who were there that night," she whispered hoarsely.

"Just as long as we understand each other. Now, where are the letters? I'm warning you, my patience has quite run out."

She had to ask, though she was perfectly sure he would lie to her. "What have you done to my husband?"

"He'll live. And when I have my letters, I'll let you go to him. Word of honor."

Tears of rage welled in her eyes. He was playing with her as a cat plays with a mouse. He would never let her live. She knew too much, or so he thought, and the same applied to Ross.

"They are in the Christening font," she said. Her hand was reaching for the bell rope. "The pedestal is hollow. There's a panel near the bottom that pulls out."

"I think you should show me," he said.

He was coming for her, and as he made the turn, for the first time she saw that he held a pistol in his hand. There wasn't a moment to lose. She reached up and grasped the bell rope firmly in both hands, but before she could complete the movement, the night seemed to explode with sound. It was the report of a gunshot, and it came from outside.

Startled, her assailant swung round, looking toward the entrance.

Hope was singing in her heart. She was remembering when the groundsman had let off a shot to summon the searchers who were out looking for her.

She pulled on the rope, throwing her weight into the movement, then let it swing up, carrying her off her feet.

The bell began to peal.

Ross was leaning out of the open parlor window when the bell began to peal. It was he who had just fired his pistol in the air to give the alarm. Moments before, he'd found the housekeeper slumped unconscious on her kitchen floor. She had suffered the same fate as he, struck down from behind when least expecting it.

He hadn't taken the time to revive her, but had raced to the parlor where he'd left Tessa, only to find the room empty and the window open. He'd cursed himself then for the fool he was. He hadn't anticipated trouble and so he'd stupidly walked to where they'd left the coach and had sent all his men back to the village. When he'd returned to the house, the lantern above the portico had gone out, but even then, he hadn't become suspicious. Lanterns were always going out. He'd stepped unawares into the entrance hall and had been felled by a blow to the head.

He was still groggy, but his alarm for Tessa had gone a long way to clearing his mind. When he'd dashed into the parlor and found it empty, for a moment he'd been paralyzed by indecision. Now, as the chapel bell rang out, he knew exactly where to find her.

His pistol was spent and useless. Throwing it aside, he quickly climbed over the windowsill and began to run. Unlike Tessa, he took the straight route to the chapel. It was uphill and though he was still suffering the effects of the attack on him, each peal of the bell seemed to renew his energy. Suddenly the bell stopped ringing. His heart stopped with it, then gave a great lurch as he sprinted up the incline. Moments later he burst into the clearing.

The chapel door was open, but he was more cautious than he'd been earlier. He slipped inside and crouched down behind the back pew. He heard the sounds of a struggle, then Tessa's voice crying out in pain, and the sound of a slap, and Ross began to move. With a roar of rage, he launched himself at the figures who were struggling in front of the font.

Tessa saw him from the corner of her eye and heard her assailant's sharp intake of breath. "He has a gun," she cried out.

She was thrown violently aside as her attacker leveled his pistol at Ross. When the gun went off, she screamed.

Ross checked, then came on. Locked together, muscles straining, they went crashing into the pews in a brutal contest of strength.

From that moment on, she could not make out who was who. Fists flashed and fell; men grunted and lashed out with their feet. The sounds of their blows sickened her. She didn't know what to do, didn't know how to put an end to it. Weak with fear, she followed them as they lurched and fought their way down the aisle and into the narthex.

She heard the sound of a blow that made her flinch in horror. One man rose to his feet while the other gasped, crouched over. Her heart was in her mouth. Which one was Ross?

The man who was standing kicked out. If the kick had landed, it might have been fatal. But the man on the floor jerked back, and the kick missed its target. As the man on the floor gathered himself to spring, the other turned and ran out of the chapel.

She knew, then, that the man on the floor was Ross and she ran to help him. He was breathing heavily as he rose to his feet. As he moved toward the entrance, she cried out, "You're not going after him, not without help?"

He barely looked at her. "Stay here! This is between him and me! Do you understand? Don't interfere!"

Startled by the fury in his voice, she drew back, but when Ross charged violently out of the chapel, she went after him.

Outside, she could see men with lanterns on the drive, converging on the chapel from two sides. The thought that raced through her mind was that if they didn't stop Ross, it would be too late. But too late for what?

An obscure, unreasoning fear clamped her heart in a vise. For one moment more she hesitated, then screaming for help at the top of her lungs, she raced down the incline and plunged into the path that led to the lake. Ahead of her she could hear the crashing sounds of the chase. Behind her, men called out and came after her.

She went down that path at breakneck speed, leaping over obstacles, dodging branches and briers as though she had the eyes of a cat. When she burst out on the lake, she saw them at once. They were only a few yards away from her and they were in the lake, waist high in water.

One man was having the worst of it. He was doing no more than trying to fend off the blows of the other. Suddenly the stronger of the two grabbed him by the shoulders and pushed his head below the surface of the water. Tessa was on the point of throwing herself at them when she heard Ross's voice.

"You murderous swine," he gasped out. He dragged the other man up by the collar. "You murderous swine!" and he shoved his victim under the water again.

Tessa heard the thrashing sounds of the man Ross was holding down. Soon, he would let him up. When Ross continued to hold him under the water and the thrashing grew weaker, with a cry of horror she flung herself into the lake and leaped for Ross.

She clamped her hands around one of his arms and tried to pull him off. She was shouting and crying at the same time, an incoherent babble of sound that was born of terror. She couldn't budge him.

Light suddenly blazed around them as men came out of the trees. Now she could see Ross clearly, and the sight repelled her. His face was streaked with blood and sweat; his teeth were gritted, his lips pulled back; murder blazed from eyes that stared at her as if she were a stranger. Then friendly hands reached out to pull her away, and two of the men locked their arms around Ross and forcibly subdued him.

"It's all right, my lady. It's all right."

The man who set her down on the bank was one of the Sayle grooms. A moment later Ross flung himself down beside her. They didn't touch, didn't look at each other. He was hunched over, legs drawn up, head bowed, sucking air into his lungs. She was standing, eyes trained on the two men who were supporting the man whom Ross had tried to drown. He was alive, that much she could tell. Then one of the Sayle grooms held his lantern aloft and she had a clear view of her assailant's face.

It was Bertram Gibbon, Amanda Chalmers's cousin.

• • •

She awakened to the sound of birds chirping, and though the room was strange to her, she knew she was still at Fleetwood Hall. Turning her head on the pillow, she looked toward the window. Dawn had appeared on the horizon like a fiery chariot and the darkness was in full flight. She couldn't have been asleep for more than one or two hours.

There had been no chance to talk to her husband last night. In fact, everything that happened after those horrifying moments at the lake were little more than a blur. She understood that the Sayle coachmen had delayed to chat with the gatekeepers and had turned the coach around when they'd heard the report of Ross's gun and then the bell pealing. She remembered that Ross had left her in the care of one of the teachers while he and his men went off with the coach to take their prisoner to the roundhouse in the village of Fleetwood. But how she came to be in this room, wearing a nightgown she'd never seen before, was lost in a haze of fragmented memory. Maids weeping. A physician. Cups of hot, sweet tea. Mrs. Doyle more angry than hurt when she came to herself. Her wet clothes stripped off her. Ross's face, grim with fatigue, when he'd taken his leave of her with a promise to return in a few hours.

By rights, she should have slept all through the day and into the next night. But she'd awakened as though someone or something had shaken her awake. In the aftermath of last night, there was something she had overlooked, something that she now remembered.

She slipped from the bed and looked around for her clothes. Finding none, she opened the closet. Evidently, this was one of the teachers' rooms. The maids wore black; the teachers wore gray. In a few minutes she was dressed to go out.

In the corridor one of the grooms was dozing, seated in a chair that faced her door. He came awake at once, and she was quite happy to have his escort.

"There's something I must do at the chapel," she said.

The house was just beginning to stir when they

stepped outside. There was no need for a lantern. The edge of the sun was showing on the eastern horizon.

She left the groom in the narthex and entered the chapel. Memories skirted the edge of her mind, but she deliberately held them at bay, all except one. Nan had told her murderer that she'd hidden Becky's letters in the chapel at Fleetwood Hall, but she'd lied about the exact location.

She knelt in front of the Christening font. The loose panel wasn't quite as loose as she remembered it. This may have saved her last night after Bertram Gibbon had dragged her from the bell rope. He hadn't wanted to kill her until he had the letters. He couldn't find the loose panel and neither could she. But now that she could see what she was doing, she had no trouble finding it. There was a carved angel down the length of the pedestal, and the loose panel was carved with the angel's right foot.

She inserted one of her hairpins in the joint and pulled gently, then with more pressure when it resisted. When she applied a little more pressure still, the panel came away in her hands. Laying it aside, she thrust her arm into the opening. Her fingers closed around a sheaf of papers and she carefully withdrew them.

The rolled-up scrolls were stories she and Nan had once made up and read to each other by the light of their lantern. There was a paper tied up with a ribbon. She didn't open it. This was the pledge she and Nan had made of their undying friendship. Swallowing the painful lump in her throat, she set the papers on the floor. There remained a bundle of letters tied up with string. She sat down in the nearest pew and untied the string. Becky's name was on three of these letters, but there was one in Nan's handwriting. On the outside, it said simply, "To Whom It May Concern." Tessa spread it open.

The date was August eighteenth of the previous year, and it flitted through her mind that at that time she would have been in France with her grandfather. Ross Trevenan was his secretary, passing himself off as an American, always finding fault with her.

She pushed that thought away from her too, and began to read. Nan wrote:

Becky Fallon did not drown accidentally in the lake of Fleetwood Hall in June of 1795. She was deliberately drowned and I saw the man who murdered her. His name is Bertram Gibbon of Albany, London, and he killed her because she threatened to tell the world that she was going to have his baby and he refused to marry her. It's all in his letters, and they are his letters though he didn't sign his name to them. I found out about the letters and stole them just hours before he murdered Becky. I wanted to frighten her, to pay her back for carrying tales to the teachers. But everything went wrong.

I didn't come forward when the constables came to the school and started asking questions. I didn't know, then, the name of the man who had murdered Becky. And I was afraid because I shouldn't have been out that night. I thought I might be blamed for what happened, or that no one would believe me. I don't really know what I thought. I was too frightened to think clearly.

There was a girl at school, Tessa Lorimer, who was there that night also. She doesn't know as much as I know and had nothing to do with what follows, but she saw Bertram Gibbon drown Becky in the lake and can corroborate what I've told you. She tried to get help but the other girls who were there thought she was playing a trick on them. The last I heard, Tessa was living in France with her grandfather, and I thank God for it. No one knew I was there but Tessa. No one saw me, not even Gibbon.

I hid the letters I'd stolen from Becky in the chapel, in the pedestal of the Christening font. I never went near them again until years later. I would have left them there forever if I had not come face-to-face with Gibbon when I was working as a maid in a hostelry in Reading. He stayed for one night. He didn't know who I was, but I knew him. I'd seen him in the greenhouse with Becky that night, and I'd never forgotten his face.

The short of it is, I found out he was courting a great

heiress whose parents were very religious and who were withholding their consent to the match. Gibbon did everything in his power to persuade them that he was an upstanding young man and deeply religious. I believe he did marry the girl, but that was still to come when I conceived the idea of making him pay for my silence.

You see, I was in desperate straits. I know that's not a good enough excuse for what I did, but at the time, I couldn't see any other way out of my difficulties. And so, I went back to the chapel at Fleetwood to make sure the letters were still there. Then I wrote to him, threatening that if he did not pay me a large sum of money, I'd write to his future bride, telling her that I'd seen him drown Becky and had the letters to prove his involvement. And it worked. I thought I was very clever. I had him leave the money where I could get to it without being seen. He never saw me, never knew who I was.

I wasn't greedy, but when the money ran out and I couldn't find work, I wrote to him again. I never thought what the result might be. I'm almost sure he killed the other girls who were present that night, thinking that I was one of them. I would have stopped right there if I'd known about the girls, but I didn't know until quite recently, and by that time, I'd tried to extort money from him again. So now he knew about me.

I should have gone to the authorities right then with what I knew, but how could I? I'd known all these years he was a murderer and I'd never come forward. I knew I would be punished for what I'd done.

I'm afraid that he's going to find me and kill me. The last time I asked him for money, before I knew about those girls, he set a trap for me. Suffice it to say, I escaped, but now he knows my face. He must know I'm too afraid of the consequences to myself to call in the magistrates. So I'm writing to him again, not to ask for money, but to tell him that this letter exists, and if anything happens to me, it will be given to the authorities.

I beg your forgiveness. I never thought I would put anyone in danger but myself. I particularly beg the forgiveness of the families of the girls involved, Margaret

Hemmel, Johanna Vernon, and Cassandra Mortimer. I
know you must hate me for what I've done.
   I pray to God that in time you'll find it in your hearts
to forgive me.
   Helena Roberts

There was nothing in the letter that surprised Tessa,
no revelations that made her gasp in shock. Without
deliberately trying, she'd already worked most of it out.
Even the reference to Margaret Hemmel came as no surprise to her.

Now, as she knelt in front of the font, she allowed her
thoughts to wander back and forth in time, beginning
with the moment she had met her grandfather's
American secretary, and not long after, Julian, Sally, and
Desmond, and ending with the capture of Bertram
Gibbon.

Last night, when Ross had taken her through each step
of the little drama he had arranged for her, he'd known
far more than she had ever told him. At the time, she'd
been too overwrought to notice.

She looked down at Nan's letter and read the last para-
graph again. *Cassandra Mortimer.* It had to be Ross's
Cassie, of course. Nothing less could explain his murderous rage when he'd held Bertram Gibbon under the
water and tried to drown him.

She was cold, so terribly cold. Suddenly rising, she
replaced the wooden panel, gathered the letters and
papers together, and hurried from the chapel.

Chapter Twenty-four

❧⚬❧⚬❧

The champagne was chilled and ready to serve when Ross entered Desmond Turner's book room. The servant announced him, and as he stepped over the threshold, Julian jumped on him and pounded him on the back. Sally went on tiptoe and pressed a kiss to his cheek. As for Desmond, this was not the first time he and Ross had been together since Bertram Gibbon had been arrested for murder, and he'd had his chance to congratulate Ross when he'd helped him arrange Gibbon's transfer to a London prison.

Julian gave the toast. "To Tessa," he said, "without whom we could never have brought that swine to justice."

The toast cast a shadow over their gaiety. Ross had told Desmond and Desmond had told the others of the terrors Tessa had endured. Since their return from Fleet-wood she had refused to receive visitors.

"How is Tessa?" Sally asked.

Ross sipped his champagne. "Exhausted. She's been sleeping a good part of each day."

This was no lie. Tessa *was* suffering from exhaustion, but there was more to it than that. She'd been behaving strangely toward him, and he supposed he'd shocked her when he'd lost control and had held Bertram Gibbon under the water. He wouldn't have drowned him. He was certain in his own mind that he wouldn't have gone that far. But Tessa was in no mood to listen to him.

Suddenly conscious that everyone was watching him, he said, "When she's fit to travel, I thought I'd take her to Greenways. And when she's feeling better, you must all come down and we'll make a party of it."

At these words, everyone's spirits seemed to revive, and soon after they were asking Ross to tell them about his visit to Newgate where Bertram Gibbon was incarcerated.

"Did he agree to see you?" asked Julian.

"Oh, yes. He agreed to see me."

After a moment Sally said quietly, "Was it wise to visit him?"

"No, it wasn't wise." Ross smiled grimly. "In fact, it was nauseating."

In the same quiet tone, she went on, "What was he like?"

"If you can believe it, he was his usual urbane self, dressed to the hilt, shaved. I had never realized what a colossal ego he hides behind that supercilious expression. He's been disgraced. Death is staring him in the face, but he thinks nothing of it. No, that's not quite true. It's worse than that. He looks down on the rest of us, Sal. He lives by his own law and makes no apology for it."

He'd gone to see Gibbon for only one reason, and that was to look Cassie's murderer in the eye and tell him what he might expect when the noose around his neck tightened and he was left dangling from the gibbet. He'd wanted to see Bertram Gibbon cringe and beg for mercy.

Instead, Gibbon had been amused, and in his affected drawl said, "Scratch the surface and we're all tainted with the jungle, Sayle, as your own words have just proved. In fact, I think there's more of the savage in you than there is in me. I was never interested in making my victims suffer. But you—" He laughed. "You tried to drown me, and if it had not been for your wife, you might have succeeded. And now you want my sufferings to be prolonged. Well, at least I'll have the satisfaction of knowing that there's one person who has proved what I've always claimed: in the right context, no one is truly civilized."

"Don't tell me your victims didn't suffer," Ross bit out. "You tortured Nan Roberts. I saw what you did to her. You strangled her slowly."

"My dear Sayle, only to get her to tell me where she'd hidden that letter. Once she told me, I cut her sufferings short."

"Don't you regret anything that you've done?"

Gibbon's brows rose. "Guilt and remorse are for the faint of heart," he said. "I seek no forgiveness, divine or otherwise. Besides, Nan Roberts was a mercenary little bitch. I'm surprised you waste your sympathy on her. It was because of her that I had to eliminate those other girls, including your own wife."

At mention of Cassie, Ross froze. He was afraid that if he moved a muscle, it would be to spring at the other man and choke the life out of him before the guard could open the door and pull him off. Gibbon and Amanda Chalmers had both been guests at Cassie's birthday party. The knowledge sickened him.

When Ross did not rise to his bait, Gibbon tried a different tack. Though he knew they had evidence to convict him of only Nan Roberts's murder, he didn't bother to hide from Ross his part in the others. He could not help boasting about how clever he had been.

"I suspected you were looking for me," he said at one point.

"Why?" asked Ross.

"My dear Sayle, I'm not a fool. I was never sure whether Miss Lorimer was the girl who screamed for help that night. But when you brought her back from France, it seemed a strange coincidence to me that the husband of one of my victims would turn out to be Miss Lorimer's guardian."

By this time Gibbon was smoking a cheroot one of the guards had procured for him, and he blew a stream of smoke into the air. He smiled at Ross. "I suspected you were setting a trap for me. However, your wife was quite safe at that point. Once she led me to Nan Roberts, however, she had outlived her usefulness. So I kept my own appointment with Miss Roberts, then I waited for your wife to call. And I almost had her."

"Almost isn't good enough," said Ross. "We caught you, Gibbon, and now you'll stand trial for murder."

Gibbon made a dismissive gesture with one hand. "You simply had luck on your side. It was a most unfortunate coincidence that you turned up at Fleetwood Hall when you did."

Ross rapped on the door to alert the guard that he wished to leave. He looked back at the face he would have liked to smash to a pulp. "You're right," he said. "I am part savage. But you, you are lower than a savage. You are inhuman."

Those elegant brows rose, the only response Ross received.

Now, as he looked at his friends, the feeling that he'd bathed in a sewer gradually wore off. They were like a breath of wholesome, fresh air. He breathed deeply and began to speak.

There was a long silence after he'd finished telling them about his interview with Bertram Gibbon. Finally, Sally said, "There are still some points I'm not quite clear on."

"What are they?" asked Ross.

"Becky Fallon, for one. Where did he meet her, and why did he murder her? I mean, it seems so extreme. Why not simply refuse to marry her and leave it at that?"

Ross didn't tell her what Bertram Gibbon had told him, that Becky was no innocent schoolgirl, but a trollop who was any man's for the taking. "He met her when she was visiting relatives in Henley," he said. "As for why he murdered her, she threatened to sue him for breach of promise. He had to marry for money, and there was another girl on the horizon, an heiress he didn't wish to scare away."

"What about the letters? Why didn't he try to get the letters from Becky before he murdered her?"

"The letters he wrote to Becky were not incriminating," Ross said. "He hadn't even signed them. There was no way they could have been traced back to him. Nan Roberts had simply read too much into those. It was the fact that she was a witness to Becky's murder that set everything in motion. The letter he wanted when he went down to Fleetwood was the letter that Miss Roberts had written for the authorities."

"So that was why," Desmond said, "he began eliminating witnesses to an accident that had happened years before. Nan Roberts was the catalyst."

"He didn't know who was blackmailing him," said Ross, "so he decided to murder all of them."

Julian let out a long sigh. "I must be an idiot. I can't understand why he didn't kill them all right away. I mean, he knew he had been seen. He heard Tessa screaming for help."

"He didn't know that he'd been seen," Ross countered. "He had no idea that Nan and Tessa were outside the greenhouse. And at the lake, it was very dark. No one could have identified him. He thought he was in the clear, especially after the inquest. And the more time passed, the more confident he became that he'd got away with it."

Sally said, "But he didn't get away with it, thank God, nor with any of the other murders. He'll pay for what he did."

With an impatient oath, Ross rose and stalked to the window. Carriages passed in the street outside, but he wasn't aware of them. He was remembering Bertram Gibbon in his cell in Newgate, and his insufferable, superior air when he'd boasted about how clever he'd been.

When the door opened and Tessa pushed by the flustered manservant, they all froze as though they were conspirators caught in the act.

"Well," said Tessa, smiling brilliantly, "well, well, well! Isn't this cozy? This must be the victory celebration. I thought this was where I would find you all when no one called at Sayle House today. Now why didn't I receive an invitation? Ross, you should have told me."

She had left off her blacks and was dressed in a high-waisted dark blue pelisse with a matching bonnet. She looked the picture of charm and grace, a beautiful young woman with nothing more serious on her mind than paying a social call. But everyone there knew her well, and those stormy violet-blue eyes of hers told them that all was not as it seemed.

"Tessa," said Ross with a faint warning in his voice.

She stepped away from him as he came up to her. "Aren't I clever to have guessed where you all were? As soon as the thought occurred to me, I got dressed and had the carriage brought round. And here I am.

"Champagne," she exclaimed when she noticed the glasses in their hands. "Only the best, I see. Do the honors, Julian, and pour me a glass. No need to tell me what you're celebrating."

Julian said nothing as he handed her the glass. He was watching Sally's face, watching her shock change to dismay. As soon as Tessa took the glass from him, he went to stand by Sally.

Tessa said, "Now what shall we drink to? A toast to friendship?" She raised the glass to her lips, then lowered it without drinking. "No, not friendship," she said. "Friends are honest with each other. Friends don't use each other." She looked at each person in turn. "You know, you really should have told me I was the bait to entrap your murderer."

"No!" cried Sally. "It wasn't like that, Tessa. We were trying to protect you."

"Protect me? Is that how they persuaded you to be a part of this, Sally?"

The beautiful mask was beginning to crack as the pain of betrayal stabbed through her. For two days and nights, as she'd flitted in and out of sleep, she'd gone over things in her mind, and it had not been difficult to put everything in its proper place. She'd been so grateful for their friendship that she'd been blind to all the lies they'd told her. Now her eyes were wide open.

"You lied to me, Sally," she said. "And that is unforgivable. I thought you were my friend. I thought you came to Sayle House because you liked me. I hope you were well paid for all your time and trouble."

"That's enough, Tessa," thundered Ross.

Sally cried out, "I *am* your friend, Tessa. I liked you from the first."

"You were never a pupil at Miss Oliphant's! You befriended me to spy on me! You and Julian both! He was never courting you! It was all done to conceal your true motives and deceive me. You were always digging into my past, trying to get me to remember things. I gave you a name, Nan Roberts, and you straightway gave it to them. Nan told me Desmond had been asking questions about her. You have no idea how terrified that made her."

Ross grabbed Tessa by the elbow. His eyes were as turbulent as hers. "For God's sake, get a hold of yourself! Don't you understand anything? A vicious murderer has been caught! You would have been his next victim. Do you expect us to be sorry for it?"

She shook off his hand and flung back her head. Her breathing was quick and audible. Her voice shook. "I was never in any danger till you brought me to England. If I was a victim, it was of you and your friends. You can't deny that you used me as bait to entrap your murderer!"

He stared at her long and hard, then turning to the others, he said, "My wife is not herself. Would you excuse us for a moment while I try to talk some sense into her?"

"Tessa—"

Sally's appeal was silenced by Julian. "Not now, Sally! Come along. Show me the book that you found so entertaining."

Desmond hesitated, then followed them out of the room.

"A fine spectacle you've made of yourself," said Ross wearily. "Don't you know, can't you understand how devoted they are to you?"

Her lip curled. "As I remember," she said, "Desmond Turner was devoted to solving a crime that had long baffled him, the murder of Margaret Hemmel. As for you"—she had to swallow before she could continue—"can anyone doubt what drove you to such lengths? From the very beginning, you were in pursuit of your wife's murderer, and you let nothing stand in your way."

He stood there silently, his features hard and stern.

"I see you don't deny any of it," she cried out.

He moved toward her; she took a step back. Tears were stinging her eyes and that infuriated her. She was hanging on to her pride, and she refused to humiliate herself by crying in front of this man.

"I don't deny it," he said, "but there is more to it than you seem to realize. We didn't know that you were safe then. It was quite possible that the man we wanted would cross into France and deal with you too. Your grandfather was afraid of what would become of you when he was gone. So he entrusted you to my care, and I promised him that I would do everything in my power to protect you. And I've kept that promise."

Her chest felt as though it would explode. "Oh, I can't fault you there. You went beyond the call of duty. You married me, damn you!"

He came toward her again, one hand extended. When she flinched away, his temper began to heat. "May I remind you that the marriage was your idea?"

She shook her head furiously. "Oh, no, I only thought it was. You haven't made one move that didn't further your own ends. I thought we had a real marriage, but that was a lie too. I can't believe how blind I was. It was always Cassie with you, from beginning to end."

"Will you stop feeling sorry for yourself," he roared, "and try to put yourself in my place? My wife was murdered! Brutally! I loved her more than I loved my own life. She was expecting our child. When I found her body in the pool beneath . . ." His voice trembled, then cracked, and he abruptly turned away to stare out the window.

Tessa understood his pain. She could even feel sorry for him. But that didn't alleviate her own pain. It did, however, blunt her anger, and as her anger subsided, her shoulders drooped.

He swiveled to face her. "I'm not ashamed of what I've done. I'm not sorry that Cassie's murderer has been brought to justice. Why should I be?"

Cassie. Always Cassie. Bertram Gibbon had murdered five young women, and had almost murdered her too, but

Ross could think only of Cassie. What else had she expected?

Defeated, she said, "What I wished you had done was tell me the truth from the very beginning. I would have agreed to help you. I could have been one of you, sharing in this victory celebration that you were very careful not to invite me to." She shook her head when he began to speak, silencing him. "I know, I know. You thought you had compelling reasons for keeping the truth from me, but frankly, I don't want to hear them."

When she moved to the door, he said, "You're not going to leave without speaking to Sally? Tessa, you can't leave her like this."

She looked at him as though he were a stranger. "I don't care if I never speak to Sally again," she said indifferently, "or any of you."

He bit back the angry words. She wasn't herself. He hadn't explained things properly. She hadn't really thought things through. He'd talk to her tonight, after he made love to her. She wasn't receptive to anything he might have to say right now. It would be different when he held her in his arms.

He held the door for her. "I'll take you home," he said.

"Home?"

He frowned, not liking her abstracted expression. "To Sayle House."

"Thank you, no. Sayle House has never been my home. It never will be. It's Cassie's house, Cassie's and yours. I hope you'll both be very happy in it."

"Dammit, Tessa! Will you just leave it alone!"

"Oh, I intend to," she said. "Believe me, I intend to."

Sally watched them leave from an upstairs window. Julian was sprawled in a chair watching her.

"Desmond is with them," said Sally. "Tessa won't look at him. He's shaking hands with Ross." A moment later, "That's it then. They've gone, and she didn't even ask to speak to me, never gave me a chance to apologize." She sniffed into the handkerchief Julian had given her a short while before. "I don't suppose I shall ever see her again."

"Of course you'll see her again, Sal. This is only a misunderstanding. Tessa was . . . well . . . taken aback when she walked in here and found us all celebrating. Our mistake was in not telling her at once, after Gibbon was arrested, that we hadn't been completely open with her. Just you wait and see. Ross will talk her round."

"Do you really think so?" She took the chair beside his. "I just can't bear to think that I've hurt her."

He smiled into her troubled eyes. "Sal, just think how you would feel if it were not merely Tessa's feelings that were hurt, but Tessa herself. We all did our part in saving her from Bertram Gibbon. Surely you're not sorry about that?"

"Of course not! It's just that . . ." He plucked the handkerchief from her and dabbed at her cheeks as the tears welled over. "It's just that we deceived her abominably, Julian. You heard what she said. We told her so many lies."

"I didn't tell her any lies," he said, "or none that I recall."

She sucked in a breath. Pointing vaguely in the direction of Sayle House, she said indignantly, "How can you say such a thing when you came every day to Sayle House, just to protect Tessa, and pretended that you were courting me? If that's not a lie, I don't know what is."

He pocketed his handkerchief and sat back in his chair. His eyes were very clear. "It wasn't a lie, and I wasn't pretending. I *was* courting you."

"You—?"

He smiled. "Close your mouth, Sal, before you catch flies."

She closed her mouth.

"Well? Have you nothing to say?"

She opened her mouth. "If this is your idea of a joke, let me tell you, I am not amused."

He gave an exaggerated sigh. "Somehow I knew you wouldn't believe me." He smiled wryly. "Sal, I am deep in love with you, as deep in love as it's possible for a man to be. I'm asking you to be my wife. No, I'm not joking. Ask

Desmond if you don't believe me. Ask your father. I have his permission to pay my addresses to you."

"My father! Gave you permission!"

"Why do you think I went to your place for Christmas? I had to promise, of course, that I was all reformed. And I am reformed, Sal, and have been from the moment I met you. That's how I knew I loved you, you see."

She began to stammer. "B-but J-Julian, all you ever do is insult me."

He shrugged. "That's just our love play. Haven't you figured that out yet?"

"Love play! You called me a skinny, brown-faced Amazon!"

"But, Sal, you *are* a skinny, brown-faced Amazon."

She jumped to her feet. Her bosom was heaving. "And you, sir, are nothing but a frivolous, feckless, frippery, fatuous fop!"

In one lightning movement, he was on his feet and had captured her in his arms. Laughing down at her, he cried out, "Sal, you've been practicing! So you do think about me sometimes when I'm not here! Now I know you love me!"

Though she struggled madly, he crushed her to him in a long, relentless kiss. Suddenly the fight went out of her, and twining her arms around his neck, she kissed him back.

They broke apart when they heard the sound of footsteps pounding up the stairs.

"What the devil!" Julian released Sally and strode for the door just as Desmond burst into the room.

"It's Bertram Gibbon!" Desmond was breathing hard. "I've just heard the news."

"Don't say he has escaped!" exclaimed Julian.

"In a way. He poisoned himself. He's dead."

Amanda Chalmers received the report of her cousin's death with equanimity. She did not invite the constable who had brought her the news to remain for refreshments. He'd caught her at a bad moment, she explained. All the furniture was under Holland covers. Her boxes were packed. She was going down to her estate in Henley to escape the furor her cousin's arrest had stirred up. The constable was sympathetic. He understood how it was. People could be so cruel.

An hour later Amanda was in her chaise with the blinds drawn. Until they were clear of London, she did not want anyone to see her face. She did not want anyone she knew to witness her humiliating flight from town. Three nights ago she'd been fawned over at the theater by no less a personage than the Prince of Wales. Today, she was an outcast, shunned because it was she who had introduced Bertram to her influential friends. Every door was shut against her. No one would receive her ever again.

Other women might be crushed by these misfortunes, but not she. England wasn't the center of the universe. There were other countries, other societies where she could make a place for herself. She would change her name, of course, and her appearance. No, the world had not seen the last of Amanda Chalmers, not by a long shot.

She would miss Bertram. No one understood her half as well as he. There would be no one to applaud her successes, no one she could be herself with. She'd told him all this when she'd gone to see him in Newgate. He'd known she would come, though respectable women did not show their faces in such notorious places. To her, loyalty was everything, and when she gave her loyalty, right or wrong, she never turned back. Bertram understood.

She hadn't wanted to hear one word about the murders he'd committed. She'd heard enough to know that two stupid girls had provoked him beyond endurance. Someone should have told them that if they played with fire, they could expect to be burned. Bertram had not bored her with claims of innocence. He'd followed her lead. They'd talked about the old days, when they were children. They'd talked about everything but why he was there. And she had never admired him more. He was fearless, debonair, amusing, and that was just how she wanted to remember him.

As she was on the point of leaving, he told her not to come again. He wouldn't be there. She'd thought he meant he was to be transferred to another prison, but he'd shaken his head. When he'd kissed her good-bye, he'd whispered in her ear, "Remember me from time to time?"

She'd known, then, that Bertram had decided to cheat the hangman of his victim. She didn't know who had provided the poison, but she had heard that even in Newgate everything could be bought if the price was right, everything except freedom.

His last words to her had puzzled her exceedingly.

"Tell Sayle," he'd said, "that at the end I did not suffer," then he'd laughed at some private joke.

At the door, she'd turned back to look at him. He was watching her with that enigmatic smile she'd never quite been able to read. She would have said something, but the guard ushered her out, and the moment was lost.

Chapter Twenty-five

❦

Ross had not enjoyed his ride to Hyde Park. There should have been few riders about at that time, but word had got out that the elusive Lord Sayle could be found in the park at ten every morning, and he'd been practically mobbed by well-wishers. It was Tessa they really wanted to see, and they'd bombarded him with questions about her. She'd gone down to Greenways, he'd answered as patiently as he could, to recover from her ordeal. Yes, he was very glad that Bertram Gibbon had taken matters into his own hands and saved Lady Sayle from having to give evidence at his trial.

It wasn't only because of Tessa that he was glad Gibbon had taken matters into his own hands. Desmond, in his calm, sensible way, had pointed out that Gibbon had done them all a favor.

"I'm thinking of the parents of the victims," Desmond had said. "They'll have to know the truth of course, but there's no reason for the public to get their teeth into it. What would be the point? As far as the world will ever know, Bertram Gibbon was responsible for murdering only Becky Fallon and Nan Roberts."

Ross understood Desmond's point. He hadn't yet told

his grandmother and Larry that Cassie's death had not been an accident. He couldn't face that prospect just yet. They'd already come to terms with their grief for Cassie and this would only stir things up all over again.

He should be relishing his success. He *was* relishing his success. He wasn't sorry that he'd brought a monster to justice and the air would no longer be polluted by his presence.

He was sorry about Nan Roberts, bitterly sorry, but he couldn't help thinking that for a clever girl, Nan Roberts had played a very stupid game. Not that he had said so to Tessa. He was too much in her black books already. He'd had to tell her everything, how and why they'd tracked her down and how each of them had had a part to play in keeping her safe. She was unforgiving and could not accept his part in the chain of events that had led to Gibbon's arrest.

Their estrangement went deeper than that. On the journey to Greenways more than a week ago, she hadn't tried to hide her bitterness. She resented the fact that he'd been the driving force behind everything, and everything he'd done had been done for Cassie's sake. Even taking her down to Fleetwood to help her regain her memory was only to further his quest to find Cassie's murderer. Not once had he given a thought to her, Tessa. She didn't know if she could ever forgive him.

He'd given her what she wanted, a period of peace and quiet to sort things through. But he'd done it reluctantly. She was his wife. She belonged at his side. The past was over. They could make a good life together, if only she would be reasonable. All this he had patiently pointed out in the drawing room at Greenways. He might as well have saved his breath. She would write to him, she told him, when she had come to a decision about her future, and until that time, she'd be grateful if he would leave her in peace. So he'd given way and had returned to Sayle House feeling frustrated, misunderstood, and simmering with anger. But deep inside, he could feel the fear gnawing at him.

It had begun to snow, and he adjusted his cape more

closely around him. As he turned his horse into the grounds of Sayle House, his fear intensified. He gazed at the weathered, moss-covered bricks of his house and felt no sense of homecoming. There was no anticipation, no eagerness to enter its doors. Without Tessa, Sayle House was exactly what it appeared to be, a pile of moldering old bricks that ran off in every direction in a misbegotten maze—the result of too many enthusiasms of successive lords of Sayle. It reminded him of the chapel at Fleetwood Hall.

When he entered the house, a footman came forward to take his things. Ross paused to return the stares of his august ancestors who looked down from their portraits on the dark wood-paneled walls. All was gloom and doom. He wondered if any of them had ever cracked a smile. He thought of Tessa's clear, carrying laugh that he had once complained was too loud. He would give anything to hear it now.

Deciding that there was no pleasing him, he stomped into his library and drew up short. Someone was waiting for him, his brother-in-law, the Viscount Pelham. Larry seemed in no better humor than himself. He was standing stiffly at attention; not a glimmer of amusement lurked in his eyes; there was no charm in evidence, not a hint of a smile.

Ross frowned. This was all it needed to complete his joy. Muttering a curse, he crossed to his desk, seated himself, and gestured to Larry to take a chair.

"I see by your face," Ross began, "that this is not a social call, so we'll dispense with the usual courtesies. What is it this time? Are your debtors hounding you? Have you gamed away your estate?" Ross knew that his voice was both cold and sarcastic, and he made an effort to moderate it. "Larry, you've got to learn to stand on your own two feet. You can't always turn to me to bail you out of your scrapes. You weren't always like this. In fact—"

He was still speaking when Larry passed him a sheet of paper. "I remember a time when—" Ross suddenly stopped speaking. He had in his hand a bank draft made out to himself in the sum of five thousand pounds. Larry's signature was on the bottom of it.

"What the devil!" He scowled up at Larry.

"I believe," said Larry, and now he did smile, "that that sum cancels all my debts to you."

Ross tossed the paper aside. "Look, Larry," he said, "I know I've made mistakes with you, serious mistakes. I should have tried to be more of a friend to you, spent more time with you. I was preoccupied. I admit it. But, dammit, I'm not the villain you're making me out to be. The money means nothing to me. Can't you see that if I was hard on you, it was for your own good?" He knew he was being inconsistent, but he didn't *feel* inconsistent when he went on, "If you get into a scrape, I'm the one who should bail you out of it. We're family, for God's sake! I'm your trustee. Now, I don't know who loaned you this money—" A thought suddenly struck him and his voice turned deadly. "You won it gaming—is that it?"

Larry was looking at Ross with a good deal of embarrassment. "You don't have to tell me all that," he said. "I mean, about being my friend and family and being hard on me for my own good. Haven't I always turned to you when I was in trouble?"

"No," answered Ross. "Not for a long time. In fact, I was beginning to think you regarded me as your enemy."

Larry had the grace to blush. "Well, I may have rebelled a time or two, when you acted the tyrant. But— good grief!—you surely knew I didn't mean anything by it? Why, I look upon you as an elder brother and Sayle House as my second home. And I never thought you were a villain. If I kept secrets from you, it was because I wanted to surprise you." He picked up the discarded bank draft and offered it to Ross. "Go on, ask me again how I came by the money, and try if you can not to jump to false conclusions."

Ross looked at the bank draft, then looked up at Larry. The viscount's words, the eager look on his face, brought a memory sharply into focus. It was his grandmother's birthday, and Ross was no more than six or seven. He'd made a pendant for her from a polished pebble and a strip of leather and he'd anxiously watched her face as he'd put his gift into her hand. She exclaimed over it, and had kissed and hugged him. And for her pains, the following year, he'd made her a matching bracelet.

Ross relaxed against the back of his chair. "Larry," he said, "you astonish me. How did you come by this money?"

"At the Exchange," said Larry. "You yourself advised me how it could be done. Don't you remember—when you were explaining my affairs to me, and showed me how you had invested my fortune?"

"I didn't think you were paying attention," said Ross.

Larry shot him a look and grinned. "I had gaming debts, and you were playing the heavy-handed trustee. When I left you, I had only one thought in my head—I'll show him!"

Ross said, "I remember, but that was a long time ago."

"Two years," said Larry.

"And that's why you pawned the silver plate and so on, and sold the Titian?"

"I needed cash to invest, but I knew in time I would reclaim everything. Perhaps I made a mistake with the Titian. All right, I did make a mistake with the Titian. I got carried away. But everything worked out for the best. This is the money I owe you for buying it back. And, Ross, I've made a lot more than this."

Ross was having trouble reconciling himself to this new Larry. The boy wasn't a wastrel, he wasn't beyond redemption. He was simply a young man who was trying to prove himself. He gave a rueful shake of his head. "Why didn't you tell me that you were investing your money?"

Larry shrugged. "If I'd failed, I'd never have heard the end of it. And you were violently against gambling, and I suppose what I was doing was gambling. But I have a knack for it. I have a sixth sense when it comes to picking winning stocks. Oh, you need not think I'm addicted to it. Now that I've reached the goal I set for myself, I intend to be very particular where I invest my money."

Ross said, "You've done well, Larry! Now, perhaps,

318 / Elizabeth Thornton

you wouldn't mind giving me the benefit of your advice, you know, as your trustee?"

Larry's eyes shone and he laughed. "Of course."

To celebrate, Ross poured out two glasses of sherry. Handing one to Larry, he said, "To your next goal." Then after they had drunk to the toast, "What is your next goal, by the way?"

Larry sat up straighter. His expression became hard, verging on challenging. "I intend to marry Sophie Naseby," he said, "and no one is going to stop me."

Ross was still sipping his sherry when his grandmother poked her head around the door. "I saw Larry leave," she said. "Well, what do you think of the good news?" She crossed to the chair Larry had vacated only moments before and seated herself.

"What I think," said Ross, "is that I don't know what to think."

Ross absently picked up a pen and began to tap with it on the flat of his desk. "I've misjudged him," he said. "I suppose we all did."

"Not I," said the dowager. "I always knew Larry would turn out well."

"You did?" He looked at her in surprise.

"It's in his bones," she said complacently. "And I always knew the right girl would be the making of him. I'm sure I told you all this."

"Well, you did," said Ross, "but you'll forgive me for saying I found your logic unconvincing. I could never see what bones had to do with anything."

"Unconvinced, were you?" The dowager sniffed. "And who told you about Amanda Chalmers and Bertram Gibbon? Unpleasant, unwholesome characters—that's what I said—but you wouldn't listen."

Ross was smiling. "What I think," he said, "is that you have a sixth sense about people, just as Larry has a sixth sense about stocks, and from now on I'm going to listen to you both."

The dowager edged forward in her chair. "I'm glad to

hear it," she said, "because I want to talk to you about Tessa."

The smile left Ross's face. "What about Tessa?"

"I really must insist that you allow me to see her. Ten days have passed since she went down to Greenways. She must be wondering why all her friends have neglected her."

"No," said Ross. "I'm giving her what she wants, a period of peace and quiet to think about things. When she's ready to see her friends again, she'll send word to me."

The dowager sat back in her chair, her eyes anxiously searching her grandson's face. "What is it, Ross? Why do you look so bleak?"

Ross threw down his pen. He spoke with more feeling than he meant to. "You might as well know, Grandmother, Tessa may never come back to me."

"I see," she said faintly.

"I've written to her every day, and she hasn't answered any of my letters."

"That doesn't sound like Tessa. What have you done, Ross?"

He shook his head. "It's between Tessa and me, Grandmother."

"And Cassie too?"

He shot her a sharp look.

"Put it down to my sixth sense," she said. After a moment she rose, came around the desk, and planted a kiss on the top of his head. "Do you know what I think, Ross?" She smiled down at him. "I think it's you who needs to think things through." And on that parting shot, she left him.

Ross finished his sherry and looked at his watch. It was twelve o'clock, twelve more hours to go before he went to bed. Somehow, he had to fill those empty hours. He looked at the stack of correspondence on his desk, and couldn't find a spark of interest to begin on it. Restless, now, he wandered into the hall. He was preoccupied, reflecting on his grandmother's advice, and without conscious thought he ended up outside Cassie's rooms.

He tried the door and found it locked, and remembered the day he'd ordered the housekeeper to keep it locked at all times. He hadn't wanted Tessa to go through that door again. This was one part of his life he refused to share with her. He'd been brutal to her, he remembered, and had been torn by guilt and remorse, not only because of what he'd done to Tessa, but more especially because of what he'd done to Cassie. He'd allowed another woman to supplant her and the truth was more than he was willing to admit, even to himself.

Even now, when it came to the point, he could hardly allow the thought to form in his mind, and he wondered why it was so terrifying to admit the truth.

He loved Tessa. He loved her with his whole heart.

He stayed outside that locked door for a long time. When he turned away and walked along the corridor, there was a spring in his step. He was calling for his horse to be saddled before he reached the foot of the stairs. Then he went in search of his grandmother.

Chapter Twenty-six

*I*t was dark outside, and it had begun to snow again. Inside, Tessa was warm and cozy, curled up in a big armchair in front of the fire, going through her grandfather's letters. In the last ten days, since Ross had taken her down to Greenways, she'd gone over these letters many times and could almost recite them word for word.

Sighing, she stared into space. She could see her grandfather's face and hear his voice as if he were right beside her in his invalid-chair. She wasn't like Ross; she had no need of a roomful of mementos to remind her of someone she had loved and lost. Her memories were etched deeply in her heart. Perhaps, in time, they would fade, but they could never be completely erased.

Her hand went to the broach that was pinned to her bodice. She wasn't being entirely fair to Ross. She, too, had a memento that she treasured, the ruby broach her grandfather had given her for her birthday. *My English rose*, he'd called her. But the broach was as much Ross's gift as her grandfather's. He'd added to what her grandfather had given her, made it more than it was to begin with, made her more than she once was. The two most influential people in her life were there in her broach, and she could never look at it without thinking of them both.

"Grandpère," she whispered into the silence.

A moment later she looked down at his letters and smiled faintly. In hindsight, she now saw that there was far more to them than she had imagined when she had first received them. Her grandfather had seen this day coming, a day when she would cut herself off from all her friends because they had deceived her, and he had tried to soften the blow. He'd taken all the responsibility for what had happened on his own shoulders. And what he'd done, he wrote, was done with her best interests at heart, because he loved her. She mustn't blame Lord Sayle for his part in things. Everything had been done with her grandfather's full consent. It was for the best, and one day she would be grateful for what he'd done.

It was all in his letters to her. She'd thought at the time that he was referring to her being sent to England against her will. What a child she'd been then, headstrong and full of her own conceit, as though the world revolved around her. Looking back, she could see why her grandfather hadn't confided in her. She'd been unpredictable. He hadn't trusted her to do the right thing.

She wished she could go back and relive her last three months in Paris, when Ross Trevenan had become her grandfather's secretary. There would be no more temper tantrums, no more rebelling, no more wheedling when she didn't get her own way. If only she'd acted with more maturity, things might have turned out differently.

A gust of cold air rushed in through one of the open windows, making the candles sputter. Carefully laying her letters on a side table, she went to close the curtains. The snow had turned to sleet and bounced off the small windowpanes, making them rattle. The wind was rising. She loved this kind of weather, would have liked to don her warm woolen cloak and rush outside to become one with the elements. Not to think. Just to feel, to know she was alive.

She wondered if Cassie had ever had thoughts like these. Probably not. She knew that she and Cassie were very different. Yet, they had both loved the same man. There was something else that tied them. Had it not been for Cassie, she doubted if she would be alive today.

She'd gone over it in her mind endlessly, reliving that moment after Becky's murderer had come out of the water and was looking for her. She'd hidden in a clump of bushes and she'd known he was almost upon her. Then a girl's voice had cried out, calling for Becky, and Bertram Gibbon had quickly retreated. Only when his footsteps had died away had she dared come out of hiding. She knew now that she'd been in shock. Cassie was standing under one of the lanterns near the path, and she'd passed right by her without saying one word about Becky. Later, the memory of Cassie had become lost in a web of self-deception.

She shuddered, and turned back to the fire. Her grandfather was right. Now that she knew all the circumstances, she was glad that she'd done her part, however unwittingly, in bringing Bertram Gibbon to justice. They'd all done their parts, Sally, Julian, Desmond, and it was childish to hold grudges. Far more had been at stake than her feelings.

If she had anything to regret, it was Nan. If only she had trusted Ross more! If only she hadn't felt bound by that foolish childhood pledge! Nan and she had been their own worst enemies, and Bertram Gibbon had made the most of it. No, she wasn't sorry she'd done her part to bring Nan's murderer to justice. If she had to do it over, she would do it again.

Her eye fell on her writing table, on another set of letters that she'd been perusing earlier. These were from Ross, and though he'd scrupulously kept his distance from Greenways, as he'd promised, his letters were anything but scrupulous. It was unconsciously done, she supposed, but by giving her news of all their friends, he'd caught her in a vise. It was inconceivable that she wouldn't be present at Sally's marriage to Julian; inconceivable that she wouldn't be in the gallery of the House of Lords with Desmond and the dowager by her side when Ross gave his speech on the establishment of a national police force. For better or worse, she was bound to all these people by ties that could not be broken. And to Ross most of all.

It would have been so much easier if she had never fallen in love with him. He wasn't free to love her, and that's what hurt. It was nobody's fault. It was wrong to blame him for something he couldn't help. He would always love Cassie. What she had to decide was whether she could live with it.

The realization that she was wallowing in self-pity was the perfect antidote to her misery. Her tears dried and her eyes began to snap. She might love him, but she would be no man's doormat. He wasn't going to have everything his own way. On one thing she was immovable. She would never return to Sayle House.

Pens, ink pot, and paper were all laid out on the writing table. She'd had her period of seclusion to think things through. Now, she had a letter to write.

She had written no more than the date when she heard the clatter of a horse's hooves outside her window. Laying aside her pen, she went to the window and looked out. A stable boy was leading a horse away, but there was no sign of the rider. It was nearly midnight. Only a crisis could have brought a messenger to the house at this time of night and in this kind of weather.

Panic leaped to her throat and sent her tearing out of the room. Halfway down the stairs, she slowed to a halt. Ross was in the entrance hall. His blond hair was windblown and curling with melting snow. His long cape glistened with frost. A blast of cold air swept through the open door, ruffling his cape, sending droplets of moisture flying in all directions. One of the candles went out.

"Shut the blasted door!" he roared, and a footman hastened to obey him.

Her relief at seeing him safe and unharmed made her collapse against the handrail. Then another thought occurred to her, and she rushed down the last few steps. "Ross, what's wrong?" she cried out. "Why are you here?"

He was shrugging out of his cape. "Why shouldn't I be here?" he replied none too civilly. "This is my house."

"But . . . your grandmother, Sally, and the others? They're all well?"

He sent the footman away before he answered her. "They all send their love, if it's of any interest to you, which I doubt since you haven't bothered to write to any of them, no, nor to me either. I don't suppose you care that Sally has refused to set the date for her wedding until she hears from you? And Larry is engaged to Sophie Naseby. Well, I don't suppose you're interested in hearing about that either."

She was as angry as he. "You came down to Greenways in weather like this just to tell me that? Don't you know what could have happened to you? You could have frozen to death if you'd become lost in that snowstorm. And I was going to reply to all your letters. When you arrived, I had just begun to write to you."

His hands closed around her shoulders. "It was a damn silly idea to leave you here alone to stew about things, and I don't know why I let you talk me into it. You're not leaving me, Tessa, and that's final. That's what I came down to tell you, so you might as well throw your damn letter in the fire."

Tessa's heart began to pound, but it wasn't in panic. She felt the tremor in his hands as he held her, sensed the stark fear behind the bluster. She lifted her chin and looked directly into his eyes. "Give me one good reason why I should stay with you, Ross Trevenan, and it had better be the right reason."

"Because I love you, dammit," he roared, "and you love me."

She smiled a slow smile. "You're not as stupid as I thought you were," she said, and with a choked sob, she flung herself into his arms.

Tessa lay in the curve of her husband's arm and listened to the storm outside. She was pleasantly tired, but she wasn't sleepy. She wanted to savor this moment, when she felt at peace with herself and the world. Shifting her head slightly to look at Ross, she found that he wasn't asleep as she'd thought, but was watching her.

He brushed a thumb along her lips. "What are you thinking?" he asked softly.

"I was thinking," she said, "that my deepest, most secret fantasy has become a reality. You've finally fallen in love with me."

He shook his head. "I've loved you for a long time, almost from the moment I saw you." Her brows shot up, and he nodded. "You walked into your grandfather's study, and I felt as though someone had hit me on the chest with a mallet."

She gave a disbelieving laugh. "You had a funny way of showing it! You found fault with me at every turn. You know you did. I could never do anything right with you. Oh, I knew that you wanted me, that you came to care for me. But that was much later, after you brought me to England."

He rolled from the bed, donned his robe, and went to the fire. When he'd added several lumps of coal to the embers in the grate, he came and sat beside her, at the edge of the bed. Tessa hauled herself up with her back against the headboard.

"What is it, Ross? Why do you look at me like that?"

"You have to understand how it was with me," he said.

She watched the play of candlelight on his face and thought she had never seen him look more vulnerable. A lump formed in her throat. She knew he was going to tell her about Cassie.

He spoke quietly and gravely. "I blamed myself for what happened to Cassie. You have no idea what that kind of guilt can do, how it works on you. I knew I could never be at peace with myself until I had found her killer. I had let her down so badly, you see. You're right, I let nothing stand in my way, but I can't be sorry for it, Tessa. And I wasn't only thinking of Cassie. I wanted you to be free of the threat that was hanging over you. I wanted your future to be secure. I had failed once. I wasn't going to fail with you."

One of Tessa's hands was on the counterpane. He touched it, brushing his fingers lightly from her wrist to the tips of her fingers. His eyes were on her hand, not on her face. "Can you imagine how I felt when I saw you, met you, realized how much I wanted you? It felt like the ultimate betrayal of Cassie. I was disgusted with myself. So I fought your attraction tooth and nail. It was worse than that. I turned my self-hatred on you."

He laughed mirthlessly. "Of course, it didn't work. But the more ground I lost, and the more you invaded my heart, the harder I tried to convince myself that what I felt for you was nothing but lust. There's something else you should know." He looked up at her. "I loved Cassie, yes, but you made me feel things I never knew existed, sensations I'd never experienced before. I never knew it could be like this."

He was giving her own words back to her, the words he had so cruelly mimicked after he had kissed her in the gazebo in the gardens of her grandfather's house.

Tears stung her eyes.

He said hoarsely, "That's why I never wanted to talk about Cassie. I was afraid to face the truth about myself. I felt like a traitor. So I tried to lock you out of my heart, just as I locked you out of her rooms. I was afraid to let you open those locked doors. But now I know there can never be locked doors between us."

She linked her fingers with his, but she didn't say anything.

"I must say something about our marriage. I tried to tell myself I was doing it to protect you, that I was fulfilling the promise I had made to your grandfather, but that was a lie, another sop to my conscience. It suited me very well the way things worked out. I could have you without having to admit that I loved you.

"It would have been different if I hadn't been carrying all this guilt around, if I hadn't been obsessed with the thought that I was responsible for Cassie's death. If she had died naturally, I would have mourned her, but I would have gone on living. It was my own part in her death that made me believe I didn't deserve to be happy or to find love again. I'll always treasure my memories of Cassie, but they're not going to get in the way of what you and I can have together."

When he was silent for a long time, she said softly, "All this because you finally caught Bertram Gibbon?"

"That's part of it."

"And the other part?"

His eyes were hot and intense on hers. "I'm not going to lose you, Tessa. Whatever I have to do to keep you, I'm willing to do. I'm going to rent out Sayle House. I know how you hate it, and I would sell it if it were not entailed. But you'll never have to set foot in it again. I told my man of business to look for something we can lease until we find a house that suits us. Or we can build from scratch if you like. I don't care where we live, just as long as you are there."

He didn't wait for her to ask the question he saw in her eyes. "Cassie isn't in Sayle House. She never was. I know that now. She's here." He touched a hand to his heart. "But she's not trying to stop me loving you. She never did. Cassie wasn't like that. If you'd known her, I think you would have liked her. Don't hate her for my stupidity."

She was so moved, she had trouble finding her voice. "I don't hate her. What I hated was knowing, thinking, that you could never love me when I loved you so much. I don't even hate Sayle House. It's a beautiful house." Her voice dwindled to a shaken whisper. "I thought of you and your house in the same way, that you both belonged to Cassie and could never be mine."

He said hoarsely, "Tessa, can you ever forgive me for being such a damn fool?"

Tears of love welled in her eyes and she wrapped her arms around him. "I love you," she said simply. "There is nothing you could ever do that I wouldn't forgive."

His mouth was eager and warm on hers, with a lifetime's promise behind the kiss. The loving was slow and easy. There was pleasure in plenty, but they were beyond wanting pleasure. They filled themselves on love. All they had ever wanted, they found in each other's arms.

About the Author

ELIZABETH THORNTON holds a diploma in education and a degree in Classsics. Before writing women's fiction she was a school teacher and a lay minister in the Presbyterian Church. *The Bride's Bodyguard* is her ninth historical novel. Ms. Thornton has been nominated for and received numerous awards, among them the Romantic Times Trophy Award for Best New Historical Regency Author, and Best Historical Regency. She has been a finalist in the Romance Writers of America Rita Contest for Best Historical Romance of the year. Though she was born and educated in Scotland, she now lives in Canada with her husband. They have three sons and two granddaughters.

Ms. Thornton enjoys hearing from her readers. Her e-mail address is <thornton@pangea.ca> or visit her at her home page:

http://www.pangea.ca/~thornton

Watch for the next historical romance
from the nationally bestselling

ELIZABETH THORNTON

On sale in early 1998

*Read on for a sneak preview of her work in
progress, the spectacular tale of a fiery young
beauty who has lost her memory. . . .*

Jessica Hayward. She paused to savor the sound of her name, then went back to kneading the dough for the day's bread. She still found it hard to believe. She didn't feel like a stray anymore. She was a real person, Jessica Hayward, and she'd come home.

Not that Hawkshill Manor belonged to her. It had been sold to Lord Dundas to pay off unpaid taxes. It was no great matter. The house didn't feel like home. There was no sense of welcome. It was only a redbrick building, and "manor" was too grand a word for the six rooms on the ground floor and the equal number of bedrooms on the floor above. From the numerous outhouses, one could tell that Hawkshill had once been a working farm, but that was before it had fallen into decay. And a working farm it would become again if the Sisters of Charity had anything to do with it. It was a dream the mother superior had long cherished—to train the older boys in the orphanage for a trade, and everything had fallen out, so she'd said, as though it had been ordained.

Ordained. Jessica couldn't help smiling. All that meant was that when Father Howie had made inquiries on her behalf, he'd discovered that Hawks-hill had lain empty for three years and could be rented for a song. The landlord obviously had no interest in the place. He spent most of his time in London or at his estate in Hertfordshire. According to his attorney, there was every chance his lordship could be persuaded to waive the rent if he thought it was in a good cause. Lord Dundas was known to be a very generous man.

And so here they were on a scouting expedition, she and Sisters Dolores and Elvira, along with old Joseph, the burly former pugilist turned convent doorman who was now their watchdog. *Sweet*. That's what it was. The Reverend Mother and Father Howie wouldn't allow her to return to Hawkshill by herself, and when they'd seen that nothing could dissuade her, they'd found a way to satisfy her wishes as well as their own. There was one thing, however, on which she would not give way. She was no longer Sister Martha, no longer in the garb of a novice. Deep down, she'd always suspected she had no vocation, and after all the half-truths and evasions she'd told, she was convinced of it. She was plain Miss Jessica Hayward now, and dressed in the cast-off clothing of some anonymous benefactor's daughter, to suit her new station in life.

Her new station in life. She absently dipped one hand into the crock of flour by her elbow, rubbed her hands together, and began to divide the dough into three equal parts. She would not have been human if she hadn't been avidly curious to know all about herself and the life she'd once had. All that Father Howie had discovered was that she had no living relatives, no kin to go to. Whether she had friends or not remained to be seen.

She had one friend, Mr. Charles Wilde. Yesterday, he'd stopped her in Sheep Street and had seemed really pleased to see her. It had been an awkward moment for her. She didn't want anyone to know she'd lost her memory. Though she knew she was being irrational, she couldn't help what she was feeling. She was ashamed, fearful. She didn't want fingers pointing at her or people whispering behind her back, saying that she was odd. What she wanted more than anything was to be treated as an ordinary girl.

Oh yes, just an ordinary girl! If they ever got to know of her Voice, they would do to her what they'd done to Joan of Arc.

Time and enough to think of that later. For the present, it was her job to bake the bread. And when she'd finished with that, there were strawberry tarts to make. In fact, there was no end of work to keep her busy. The house looked well enough from the outside, but inside it was a shambles. The day before, after they arrived, they'd done no more that clean out the kitchen and one of the bedrooms. When Sisters Dolores and Elvira returned from Stratford, where they'd gone to fetch supplies, they were going to tackle the rest of the house, with Joseph doing most of the heavy work. Meanwhile, he was out searching for firewood and she had bread, scones, and pies to make.

She worked quickly now, patting the dough into three loaves and covering them with a damp cloth before setting them aside. There were no eggs to be had, so she used milk to brush the surface of the scones she'd just made, and grasping the long wooden panel at the side of the fireplace, she eased them into the brick oven. The heat from the fire was scorching hot, and when the scones were in place, she shut the door with a snap and swiftly stepped back. It took only a few moments to set out the ingredients for her strawberry tarts.

She straightened and stretched her spine. The table was too low for comfort, and if she were going to do most of the cooking, which seemed likely, one of the first things they would have to do was replace it or she would end up with a permanent backache. To ease her aching muscles, she took a few paces around the kitchen, then wandered into the breakfast room and into the front hall.

There was a long cracked pier glass between two doors, and though she always avoided looking at herself when the Sisters were there, she had to admit that nothing in the house fascinated her half as much as that looking glass. There were no mirrors in the convent that were bigger than a thumbnail. Until now, she'd never seen more than pieces of her face at one time.

The girl in the looking glass stared solemnly back at her. Jessica moved closer and traced the reflection of her eyes, her brows, her nose, her chin. She smiled, she frowned, she turned this way and that to get a better look at herself. Though she was by no means sure, she thought her best feature might be her hair. It was the color of honey and the curl could only be tamed when she did it in a long plait, as now. Her figure—she removed her apron and set it on a bench—she thought was too thin. The high-waisted spotted muslin hung on her loosely. She pinched it between her fingers to get a smoother fit. That was better. She wondered if that nice young man she'd met on Sheep Street thought she was pretty.

No sooner had the thought occurred to her than she gasped and jumped back. This was vanity! She shouldn't be thinking these thoughts! The mother superior was right. Idleness was an invention of the devil. She should get back to work.

She was reaching for her apron when she heard the clatter of a horse's hooves on the approach to the house. Her heart gave a leap. It might be that nice Mr. Wilde, coming to call, or a friend who had heard from him that she was back in Hawkshill. Nerves fluttered in the pit of her stomach. Breathing deeply, she opened the door and stepped onto the porch.

When she saw the horse and rider, she felt a shiver of alarm. The man on the horse looked as though he might have stolen it. The horse was a magnificent beast—black glossy coat, streaming mane, muscles that moved and rippled as it climbed the slope. Its rider was the opposite. He slouched in the saddle. His clothes were disheveled; his hair uncombed; his face unshaven. But it was his expression that alarmed her more than anything. His brows were down and his jaw was tensed. This was definitely not a friendly visit.

Her mind made a lightning connection. He must be one of those gypsies or tinkers—"those thieving rogues" as Sister Dolores called them—who had encamped in Hawkshill while it had lain empty. It was their mess she and the sisters were now forced to clean up. Joseph had warned her they might return and had prepared her for that eventuality. This called for a show of strength.

Swinging around, she darted into the hall and snatched up the old blunderbuss that lay, primed and ready, behind the door. Then she walked out of the house to face the intruder. A show of strength, that's all the blunderbuss was. She wasn't supposed to aim it at anyone. If worse came to worst, she was to fire it into the air and that would bring Joseph to her.

The stranger reined in a few yards away. He didn't dismount, but sat at his ease, eyes narrowed on her speculatively, as a panther might eye a rabbit that had suddenly turned on its hunter.

He spoke first. "I swore I wouldn't come here.

Curiosity got the better of me, that and an irre-
sistible urge to welcome my new tenants."

His meaning hardly registered. She was puzzling
over the sneer behind the words and the insolent
twist to his mouth. He was angry about something,
and she couldn't think what. She hadn't done anything. He was the one who was trespassing.

He leaned forward in the saddle and gave her the
same insolent smile. "Didn't my attorney tell you? I
own Hawkshill now."

"*You* own Hawkshill?" She could hardly credit it.
This was their landlord, this unkempt, disreputable
looking wild man? She shook her head.

"Oh, it's perfectly true. Ask my attorney if you
don't believe me. I, Lucas Wilde, am the owner of
Hawkshill."

Wilde? That was the name of the young man
she'd met in Sheep Street. They must be related.
"You are Lord Dundas?" she asked incredulously.

"Aye, a lord now, Miss Hayward, and rich enough
to buy and sell my neighbors ten times over." He
edged his horse forward. "But life is full of these
little ironies, don't you think?"

He might look like a gypsy but he spoke like a
gentleman. Lord Dundas. It must be true. Now she
understood the condition of the house. It was just
like its owner.

The conviction that he was telling the truth
hardly reassured her. From the look of him, she
would have said that he'd been drinking.

She'd dealt with drunkards before, when she and
the sisters had combed the stews of London for
abandoned children. But on those occasions, she'd
been dressed in her nun's habit. Even the most ram-
shackle dock worker showed respect for the Sisters
of Charity. She wasn't wearing her habit now.

She eyed him warily. He was their landlord and

she didn't want to get his back up. At the same time, she knew that drink made a man unpredictable.

As a subtle reminder that she wasn't as defenseless as he might think, she inched the gun into the crook of one arm.

His response was a low rumble of laughter. "Careful," he said, "you might hurt someone with that thing," and without taking his eyes off her, he slowly dismounted and tethered his horse to the hitching post.

She backed up a step, giving herself room to maneuver in case she had to get off a shot to summon Joseph. "The sisters aren't here," she said, "only our man, Joseph." The reference to Joseph was another subtle reminder that she wasn't as defenseless as he might think. "And I have no authority to act for the sisters."

He arched one brow. "Yes, I heard about the nuns, but I can hardly believe the story I was told. Why don't you explain it to me in your own words?"

"There's not much to tell. We're going to bring some of our boys from the orphanage here, to teach them how to run a farm, you know, so that they will have a chance of improving their lot when they leave here."

"Just you and the nuns?"

"Oh no. We'll hire people to help us."

He laughed harshly. "And you expect me to believe that?"

When he took another step toward her, it flashed through her mind that he was far more dangerous than she'd realized. Now that he was only a pace away, she saw things she hadn't noticed before. He was in the grip of some powerful emotion he could hardly control. He stood there, staring at her, jaw clenched, hands fisting and unfisting at his sides.

She heard the catch in her throat and was aware

that her pulse had leapt. If he wanted to, he could really hurt her. But she had the gun.

His voice was husky. "Why? Why did you come back?"

"I told you. For the children. We're going to teach them to be farmers."

"Was it for the title? The money? Did you think the past wouldn't make a difference? Answer me, Jess."

Whatever he knew of Jessica Hayward obviously wasn't to her credit. In fact, he looked as though he hated her. She didn't have time to think about that now. He was closing the gap between them, forcing her to retreat. Her next step took her into the hall.

She moistened her lips. "Lord Dundas—"

He acted as though she'd struck him. "Christ, if you call me that again—"

He was reaching for her, and she jerked up the gun, pointing it straight at his chest. He stopped dead in his tracks. "I know how to use this," she said, trying to control the wobble in her voice. "I'm warning you, don't come any closer."

The hard planes of his face gradually softened and he laughed low in his throat. "Now this is more like the Jess I know." He spread his arms wide and took another step toward her. "Go on then. Pull the trigger. You can't miss me from that distance. Aim for here." He touched his heart. "What's the matter, Jess? Have you lost your nerve?"

She aimed for the floor, shut her eyes, and squeezed the trigger. Nothing happened. It was a mistake that cost her dearly as she knew the moment she opened her eyes. His face was livid with color and his lips were pulled back, baring his teeth.

"Christ! You vicious little bitch! If you had remembered to cock that firing piece, you would have emasculated me."

Though she quailed before the thirteen stone of quivering masculine outrage that loomed over her, there was just enough of Sister Martha in her to be outraged as well. "Blasphemy," she coldly informed him, "is not tolerated in this house."

"The hell it isn't!"

With a suddenness that caught her off guard, he grabbed for the gun and with one yank wrested it from her hands. She had the presence of mind to give him a hard shove, then she took off like a hare. She heard another violent oath, then the thud of his boots as he came after her. Panting as though her lungs would burst, she flung into the kitchen and made straight for the paddle beside the brick oven. Without waiting to take aim, she swung it in an arc and caught him a glancing blow on the shoulder. He staggered and cursed, but still came on. There was no stopping this man! She swung the paddle again, missed, and sent the crock of flour she'd set out on the table tumbling to the floor. A fine brown powder floated up.

He gave one of his infuriating low laughs and lunged for her. She swung at him again. This time, her paddle collided with the pan of strawberry jam and sent it spinning. It hit the mantel with a resounding thud and exploded in a shower of gooey crimson rain. It rained on the ceiling, it rained on the floor. It rained on him, it rained on her.

Hands on hips, he threw back his head and hooted with laughter. "If you could only see yourself!"

She didn't care what she looked like, not when she was facing a madman. Her eyes were trained on him, watching his every move. Her hands were clenched around the paddle, holding it like a lance. When he came at her, she went for him, but he neatly sidestepped her. As she charged by, he grabbed her from behind, pinioning her arms to her sides, and he lifted her effortlessly off her feet. She bucked, she kicked, she twisted, she squirmed. She could not budge him. He was squeezing her so hard she thought she would suffocate. In a blind panic, she dropped the paddle. Almost at once, the pressure of his arms eased.

When her feet touched the floor, he slowly turned her to face him. "What in hell's name did you think I was going to do to you?" he demanded, giving her a rough shake.

She didn't have the breath to answer him. She was using the dregs of her strength to strain as far back as his hands would allow.

"Dammit, will you stop squirming?"

She stopped squirming.

His brows were a dark slash. His eyes moved slowly over her face. "You're frightened of me," he said, "really frightened."

She wheezed out, "You attacked me."

He gave a crooked half smile. "Jess, you were the one with the gun. You provoked me. You know you did."

He was using the tone of voice she, herself, sometimes used with the children in the orphanage, when she wanted to soothe their fears. He didn't seem like a dangerous lunatic now. In fact, that crooked half smile made him look almost harmless. With that thought, some of the tension drained out of her. She shrugged helplessly. "I thought you were mad."

"And I thought you were . . . sweet."

When he reached out with his hand, she jerked back. "Don't!"

His hand dropped away. Something came and went in his eyes: pain, regret—whatever it was, it made her feel less threatened.

"It's only a blob of jam," he said.

She brushed her face with her hand. "Jam?"

"Allow me." Again, his hand reached for her, but

this time she didn't flinch away. With the pad of his thumb, he removed the sticky substance from her chin. "Jam," he said, showing it to her. Then, with eyes holding hers, he spread the jam on his tongue and swallowed.

The muscles in her throat contracted involuntarily. She felt the swift rise and fall of her breasts. A strange expectancy gripped her. As his eyes continued to hold hers, her heart began to pound.

He let his breath out slowly. "It's still there, isn't it, Jess? You feel it, too. Is this why you came back? Is it, Jess? *Is it?* No, don't push me away. I won't hurt you. I just want to hold you."

She didn't resist when he drew her into the circle of his arms. Something stirred in her, something that went beyond memory. Her brow wrinkled as she searched his face. Here was someone who could tell her all she wanted to know about Jessica Hayward. Then his dark head descended and she froze as his mouth touched hers.

Before she could draw a breath to protest, every fiber of her being was electrified. The terror she had experienced only moments before at the hands of this man was forgotten, as were the rules she was sworn to uphold as a nun. Sister Martha might never have existed for all the impression she made on Jessica. The kitchen of Hawkshill Manor slipped quietly into oblivion. The only reality she was sure of was the rightness of being in his arms. Her mind might not recognize this man, but there was something in the deepest reaches of her psyche that was profoundly affected. In that moment, she could have sworn he was as familiar to her as the beat of her own heart.

She was captivated by the gentleness of the powerful arms that held her; she was enthralled by the reverence of his lips as they moved on hers. He kissed her again and again, each kiss sweeter than the last. Her lips softened beneath the pressure of his, and her hands moved of their own volition to slide over his shoulders and into his hair.

That small act of surrender changed everything. He tore his mouth from hers and covered her face with hard, random kisses, her throat, her breasts. His chest rose and fell rapidly. Air rushed in and out of his lungs.

"Jess," he whispered hoarsely, "Jess."

She cried out when he lowered her to the table, then she relaxed as he came down beside her. She wasn't afraid. Memories that were born and bred into every cell and sinew of her body had taken over.

He was staring down at her through the veil of his thick dark lashes.

"I trust you," she whispered, and the truth of it awed her.

He went perfectly still. "You trust me?"

She nodded.

With a savage oath, he pulled to his feet. A muscle clenched in his jaw and the violence was back in his eyes.

Shocked, she rose to her elbows. "What did I say?" she cried out.

He lowered his head till his face was within an inch of hers. "You have a poor memory," he said, snarling the words. "That's exactly what you said the last time. I lost Bella because of you, and for what? A toss in the hay that didn't amount to much."

His sneer became more pronounced when he straightened and began to adjust his clothing. "For God's sake tidy yourself. And get off that table before someone walks in here. Or is that what your scheming little mind is hoping will happen? If you think I can be browbeaten into marrying you, you can think again."

Jessica's scattered thoughts were beginning to come together, and the more they came together, the more appalled she was at her own conduct. She was the lunatic, not he! With a gasping cry, she scrambled off the table and stared at it in horror, wondering what on earth could have possessed her to go so far. Burning with shame, she turned to face him.

The contempt in his eyes goaded a temper that she had not known was there. "I didn't invite you here," she said. "You invited yourself. And as for browbeating you into marriage, I'd sooner take my vows."

His mouth curved in an unpleasant smile, then he turned on his heel and strode for the door. At the threshold, he turned back. "You still haven't answered my question. Why did you come back? And don't give me that faradiddle about the boys from the orphanage. That may do for the nuns, but it won't do for me."

She lifted her chin a notch and looked him squarely in the eyes. She wanted to shake him as much as he had shaken her. "I came back to find a murderer," she said.

All the color washed out of his face and his eyes flared. In a low, driven tone, he said, "I want you out of here. Oh, the nuns can stay, but you go. Get back to your nunnery, Jess. There's no place for you here. If you won't go willingly, I'll make you go. Do I make myself clear?"

He didn't wait for her answer, but slammed the door as he left.

DON'T MISS THESE FABULOUS
BANTAM WOMEN'S FICTION TITLES

On Sale in March

A THIN DARK LINE
the new hardcover from TAMI HOAG, New York Times
bestselling author of NIGHT SINS *and* GUILTY AS SIN

When murder erupts in a small town, Tami Hoag leads readers on a spine-chilling journey through the bayous of Louisiana and into the shadowy place where the boundary between law and justice, between love and murder is only A THIN DARK LINE.

_____ 09960-4 $22.95/$29.95

From the nationally bestselling ELIZABETH THORNTON,
author of DANGEROUS TO KISS

THE BRIDE'S BODYGUARD

Elizabeth Thornton's gifts for intoxicating passion and spellbinding suspense meet again in this story of a headstrong young heiress who finds herself married to a devastatingly attractive protector . . . and the key to a secret a murderer will kill to keep.   _____ 57425-6 $5.99/$7.99

PLACES BY THE SEA
from the highly acclaimed voice of JEAN STONE

In the bestselling tradition of Barbara Delinsky, this is the enthralling, emotionally charged tale of a woman who thought she led a charmed life . . . until she discovered the real meaning of friendship, betrayal, forgiveness, and love.   _____ 57424-8 $5.99/$7.99